Caught in the Crotchfire

The Trailer Park Princess Cozy Mystery

Book Three

Kim Hunt Harris

Kim Hunt Harris Books, LLC
Lubbock, TX

Kim Hunt Harris Books, LLC
3410 98th St Ste. 4-157
Lubbock, TX 79423
www.kimhuntharris.com

Publisher's Note: This is a work of fiction. Names, characters, places, and incidents are a product of the author's imagination. Locales and public names are sometimes used for atmospheric purposes. Any resemblance to actual people, living or dead, or to businesses, companies, events, institutions, or locales is completely coincidental.

Book Layout ©2013 BookDesignTemplates.com

Ordering Information:
Quantity sales. Special discounts are available on quantity purchases by corporations, associations, and others. For details, contact the "Special Sales Department" at the address above.

Caught in the Crotchfire/Kim Hunt Harris -- 1st ed.
ISBN 978-1533662842

DEDICATION

For years (and years!) I dreamed of the day when people would actually want to read my books. I can't put into words how much it thrills me to hear from a reader asking when they can get the next book in the Trailer Park Princess series. The phrase, "A dream come true" comes to mind, and is certainly fitting, but as with all clichés, it doesn't carry the full weight of what's in my heart. I am hesitant to encroach on anyone's privacy by naming names, but know that if you've contacted me via Facebook, Goodreads, or email and asked about the next book, I know your name, and I'm deeply grateful for you. This book is dedicated to you.

ACKNOWLEDGMENTS

My heartfelt gratitude for the people who helped me edit this book: Tisa Lovett White, Shirley Webb, Beni Hemmiline, Trina Meadows and McKenna Harris for editing. You not only made outstanding suggestions and raised excellent questions, you kept me from writing "To darned much!" Although that does bring to mind a fun hybrid Monty Python/Narnia theme, it would have been an embarrassing mistake. Whew, that was close!

Thanks to the women of Let's Read and Wine About It, the world's best book club. My life is richer since joining this group, and I hope this road goes on forever and our party never ends.

My thanks also to Chasen Harris, whose 12-year-old-boy sense of humor conceived the title. I thought it was funny, too, and I'm not a 12-year-old boy. I'm just very immature some-times.

And lastly, my never-ending gratitude to my two sounding boards, brainstorming partners, and biggest encouragers – Dar-ryl Harris and Kelly Hunt. When this book makes a boatload of money, I'm definitely taking you both to Europe with me.

Table of Contents

CHAPTER ONE

Smart Enuff

I looked carefully around the hotel room. I took in the flowers, candles, and the drapes pulled back to reveal the magnificent West Texas sunset.

A big ol' inviting bed.

Tony would be there any second. Actually, he was already supposed to be there. I checked my watch. Yes, he was late.

The realization made my stomach clench. Tony was punctual. Tony was earnest and diligent in everything he did.

Quite inappropriately, I snort-laughed. To be crass about it, I was very much hoping that Tony was on his way here to do me tonight. That's why I had set this whole thing up, why I'd shelled out hard-earned money on a swanky hotel room, flowers, and a fancy meal to be delivered . I was doing my best to seduce my own husband.

There was a knock at the door, and I leapt and ran across the room to open it.

Tony stood here, stone-faced. "What did you need?"

"Well, I just – I was – come in." I smiled my brightest smile and stepped back, waving a hand into the room.

He stepped into the center of the room and gave it a once-over. Then he turned back to me and waited for me to explain. He looked bored and annoyed.

My heart stuck in my throat and I couldn't get words out. I had planned to get Tony here, assuming he would take one look at the room and my sexy negligee, and get the general idea. I hadn't prepared for the need to explain myself.

I swallowed hard, and decided to go the "show, don't tell" route. I stepped close and put my hands on his solid chest. The moment I touched him, desire shot through me and I caught my breath, looking up into Tony's deep brown eyes in what I hoped was a very sexy way.

Still with the stone face.

"Tony, you know," I said, the awkwardness making me sound desperate. "You know we are man and wife. And God intended for man and wife to...... enjoy each other."

"What do you mean?"

Frustration and desire fought for the upper hand.

"Tony, don't you – don't you want to?"

"Want to what?"

I gestured toward the bed with a tilt of my head. "You know."

He looked at the bed and then back at me, his face a perfect blank. "Salem, it's just past 7:30. It's way too early for bed." Then he narrowed his eyes at me. "Good grief, Salem, do you go to bed at 7:30? That's not exactly an efficient use of your time.

Personally, I'm able to get a good deal of work done in the evenings. Probably as much as most people do in a full working day."

"No, I just thought, since we were here and there was a bed and everything..." I shrugged.

Another knock sounded at the door, and we looked over to see the bellboy pushing a cart full of food into the room. I had ordered steaks, salad and chocolate soufflé, but instead the cart was stacked artfully high with cheeseburgers. It was kind of like a big wedding cake. A giant silver bowl held a few thousand french fries.

"Here's all your food that you wanted to eat," the busboy said.

"No," I said, although I wanted to dive headfirst into that bowl of fries. "I ordered steaks. And salads."

"Nope. This is what it says on the order form." He held it up but didn't let me look at it.

"Salem, were you going to eat all this junk food?" Tony asked, his gaze shifting between me and the tray with disgust.

"Of course not," I stammered, guilty with just how much I did want to eat all that junk food.

"There are probably one hundred thousand units on that tray."

"I know." My voice sounded miserable to my own ears.

"Your next weigh-in is going to be a nightmare," Tony said, his mouth grim.

"I know," I said again.

"You'll probably gain back the thirteen pounds you lost, plus another twenty-five on top of that."

"No!" I gasped. I turned to the bellboy. "Get it out of here!"

But even as I was saying it, I grabbed a handful of fries and stuffed them in my mouth. They were hot and crispy and salty – pure heaven. I grabbed another handful and two burgers. "Take it out, now! Hurry!"

The bellboy smiled stupidly at me.

"Salem." Tony's voice was solemn with disapproval.

I was halfway through the tray by now, out of control, terrified and frantic. The food was disappearing so fast.

"Get it out of here!" I shouted through a mouthful of food. "I can't do this! I came here to seduce my husband."

"Seriously?" Tony and the bellhop said at exactly the same time and with the exact same tone of disbelief. "You?"

I looked at the mirror and saw myself with half-eaten fries hanging out of my mouth. Instead of the pretty negligee, I was wearing ancient sweatpants with bagged-out knees and a dingy t-shirt.

I froze, horrified at the sight. I met Tony's eyes in the mirror. One side of his mouth curled up in a sneer. Then as I watched, he opened his mouth and made a sound like a ringing phone.

"What?" I asked.

He made the ringing sound again.

I began to cry. This was *so* not the way I had planned it. The more I looked at the horrifying scene in the mirror, the more pockets and bulges of fat I noticed. They rolled along my arms and around my hips, making the t-shirt swell in mound after mound.

"This can't be happening," I said.

"It's not," the bellboy replied, a serious frown on his face.

Then I woke up.

My phone vibrated and rang on the nightstand. With a

groan, I flipped it open. "H'lo."

"They're coming! The robbers are coming and they're about to take everything I own!"

"G-Ma?" I sat up and scrubbed my face with my hand. "What's going on?"

"They keep driving by. They're casing the joint, that's what they're doing. Casing. The. *Joint*. Oh! They just pulled into the parking lot. I knew it!"

She sounded like she was on the edge of a stroke.

"G-Ma, calm down. It might not be the Bandits."

The High Point Bandits, as the people on the news had taken to calling them. Or the Knife Point Bandits, as everyone else said. The High Point neighborhood, where G-Ma's motel, The Executive Inn, was located on the Clovis Highway, had earned the perhaps unfair nickname years ago and was still called that any time a crime happened there. A string of armed robberies played right into its bad reputation.

"It's them!" G-Ma shouted. "I'm going to fight them off, but I think you should come over just in case. Bring your gun."

"G-Ma, please. I don't have a gun, that's Viv. What do you see?" I stood and reached for my jeans, unsure of what to do. The Executive Inn was a good five miles away. There wasn't anything I could do from my trailer, and I certainly wasn't going to get there in time to help her. Or, God help them, the people she'd decided to "fight off."

"I see a white four-door sedan, just like they said on the news, and I see four people in it, just like on the news."

I heard something that sounded awfully like a gun being cocked.

"G-Ma, please do *not* shoot anyone!" I shouted. I shoved my feet into my shoes.

"I have a right to stand my ground!" she roared.

The sound of wind whooshed over the line. She had opened the office door.

"You lowlife scum can just go back to hell where you came from!" G-Ma roared. "You're not getting — oh. Okay, sorry. Go ahead."

I heard the slam of a door and the wind sound stopped abruptly.

"It was just some people turning around."

I dropped onto the bed. "Seriously?"

"Yep. Just using the parking lot to turn around. Whew. That was a close one." I heard the rattle of the shade being lifted. "You know, I think that was Claudia Comer, from bingo night." She gave a light laugh. "Whew," she said again. Then she giggled. "You should have seen the way they peeled out of here."

I flung myself back onto the bed and covered my eyes, my heart still thudding painfully in my chest. This woman was going to be the death of me.

"I'll bet Claudia Comer is saying 'whew,' too, G-Ma," I said, fighting for calm. "I know you're nervous about all these robberies — "

"Of course I'm nervous! Those thugs are stealing from everyone around here! And I'm not going to let it happen to me."

"I understand you want to protect your property. But maybe you should just...you know, wait a second or two before you assume every white car is the Bandits. You're going to ruin your own business because people are going to be afraid to even slow down when they drive past the motel."

"Goes to show what you know. My business has, in fact, never been better."

"I can't imagine why. Listen — "

"Sorry, Salem, I have to go," G-Ma said. "I'll call you later."

She clicked off, and I snapped my phone shut.

I turned my head and looked at Stump, the precious doggie who shares my life and trailer in Trailertopia. "She's going to give me a heart attack," I said.

Stump jumped up and bounced her own considerable weight off my stomach. Then she launched off the bed with a thud and trotted down the hallway.

I stumbled behind her to let her out the front door. Early morning sunlight shot into the room. I drew the door almost closed, then leaned my arm against the wall and rested my forehead on it.

Between G-Ma and that awful dream, my mind was mush, and the day hadn't even really started.

As I slowly came more awake, I mentally cataloged all the ways that horrible dream was not real. I had not rented a hotel room. I had not tried to seduce Tony. I had not dived headfirst into a tray of burgers and fries. I had not instantly gained thirty pounds.

I reached a tentative hand down and patted at my stomach and thighs. Thank you, God. Still the same level of fatness as when I'd gone to bed.

I was starving. And if I didn't get a move on, I was going to be late for work.

As soon as Stump came in and I'd filled her breakfast bowl, I went back to the second bedroom of my trailer and knelt on the floor pillows I'd placed there for my prayer time. I lit the new three-wick candle I'd bought at Hobby Lobby (pear scented, which smelled delicious but also made me feel a little guilty because I was supposed to be focusing on the things of God and I wasn't sure if it was okay to like that scent so much when I was supposed to be praying. But then again, God *did* make pears, so...) and first focused on my breathing. I needed to take a break from G-Ma, the High Point Bandits, and that dream. I needed to spend time in prayer and let God fill me up and prepare me for the day.

I had had this routine for a while now, over a year. During that year I had come to count on the fact that I would be filled. I would be better prepared for the day ahead. Something in the devotional I read, or something that came to me during my prayer, would speak directly to whatever was weighing most on my heart at the moment. Sometimes it was an encouraging word, and of course I liked that. Sometimes it was more a word of what Les, my mentor, called "conviction" which was a nice way of saying that God showed me exactly what I was doing wrong and exactly what I needed to do to fix it. I didn't particularly like those days, but I did feel guided by them.

I wasn't sure what to expect today. Maybe that dream meant that I needed to give up on throwing myself at Tony and also quit throwing myself at cheeseburgers. Maybe God was going to tell me something to reinforce that.

Once I felt like I was prepared to handle whatever God was giving me today, I opened the devotional.

"God opposes the proud but gives grace to the humble." Humble yourselves, therefore, under the mighty hand of God so that at the proper time he may exalt you, casting all your anxie-

ties on him, because he cares for you. Be sober minded. I Peter 5b - 8a. (ESV)

Well, God should be pouring a ton of grace on me, then, because I felt very humble — if "humble" meant something kind of like humiliation.

I didn't particularly care about being exalted at the proper time, though. That brought to mind standing in front of adoring crowds while I gave a beauty queen parade wave. *So* not me. A *little* bit exalted, though — up from having Tony and the room service guy look at me with horrified disgust — I wouldn't mind that.

Be sober-minded. I had the sober. I had 378 days of sober, in fact. So...check. Sober-*minded*, perhaps not so much. Circumstances did have a worrying tendency to blindside me.

I read through the verses a second time, then a third. Each time the "casting all your anxieties bit resonated stronger and stronger.

I felt off-kilter because I'd had a bad dream. I'd had a bad dream because I was increasingly more worried that Tony was getting ready to reject me outright.

The realization made my stomach drop. I *was* worried that Tony was going to reject me outright.

And what could I do about that? Not a thing that I was aware of. So what did I do?

I cast my anxieties.

"I don't really know how this works," I said softly, bowing my head and closing my eyes. "But I want to cast my anxieties on you. I'm worried about Tony and me. I know he wants to do your will. And so do I, so...so...I'll just leave it to you two to work out between you."

It was one of those things that was so much easier said than done. Every time my mind went to worrying about me and Tony, I would have to do the same thing I did when I thought about drinking: I would have to think of something else.

Unfortunately, lately when I wanted to drink, I'd made my mind switch to thinking of Tony. So I would need to think of something else.

Food! was my immediate thought.

Something else that wasn't food, I thought. Although I didn't hold out a lot of hope.

I did feel a bit better, though. Not that everything was going to work out the way I wanted it to, (and how did I want it to? I still wasn't exactly sure, but the clench in my stomach could be a clue) but that God was aware of what was going on, and he was on top of it. That was a comfort.

Then I remembered there was something of a "Special Event" at work that day. The new cell phone store, Llano Wireless, that had gone into business beside Flo's Bow Wow Barbers (where I was gunning for the position of Head Groomer) was having their grand opening. The owners were two guys named Montana and Dakota from one of the small towns in the area, and they'd stopped by the grooming shop the day before to make sure we would be there.

"You don't want to miss it," Montana said. "There's going to be music, and a guy making balloon animals, and free Krunchy Kreems. Plus, the university radio station is doing a live broadcast, and we're giving away three phones and free service for a year."

He had had me at "free Krunchy Kreems," but when he said the part about giving away the phones, every head in the place had turned to me.

"You need to enter that," Flo had said, pointing at me. "You need a new phone."

"Salem," Tammy the Dog Bather had breathed, moving slowly toward me with hands held out. "You could have a decent phone." She had said this with the air of someone who'd just heard of a cure for their friend's life-threatening illness.

So okay, my phone was not fancy. It didn't have apps, it didn't keep a calendar for me or take pictures or suggest alternate routes to work when traffic was backed up. And I didn't care. I didn't *need* a smart phone. My phone made phone calls and told me the correct time, and for the life of me I couldn't understand why this bothered everyone around me so much more than it bothered me. Every time I pulled it out of my jeans pocket to call someone, a lone tear rolled down Tammy's cheek before she turned away.

"I don't need a smart phone," I had said. "I'm quite smart enough on my own, thank you very much." That might be stretching things, but so what?

"Oh, but you're going to want this one," Dakota said. "We call it the "Smart Enuff" phone." He held up the little fan sign they'd had made to hand out.

All the bells and whistles you want, it said. *None of the hassle you don't.*

"Smart Enuff phone," I repeated. I kind of liked that.

"Right. We did a study. Most cell phone companies pour money into creating these huge networks. That's how they advertise them, right? Show the maps with the points of their coverage and compare it to the other companies? But most people don't need that. They spend the majority of their time right here at home, or within a few hundred miles of it. So what's the point of paying for a huge network? None. No point at all."

"It's sad because it's true," I said. "I never get more than two hundred miles from home."

"And if you do travel somewhere," he went on as if I hadn't just revealed a super sad personal fact, "We have arrangements for all the major carriers. Each contract comes with a set number of days on wider networks, that you can use if and when you need them."

"Sounds great," I said. My resentment at the lack of respect for my minimalist attitude was being slowly edged out by the hope that I *could* actually have one of those phones. The truth was, a new phone was one of those things I had maturely decided wasn't needed. I'd worked hard the past few years at getting my life together, and things were on a definite — if somewhat shallow — uptick. I hadn't had a drink in over a year, which meant I also hadn't had a DUI, a hangover, been fired for showing up to work drunk, or had to beg my way out of getting the electricity turned off in over a year. One more visit to my probation officer, and one more payment on my fine, and I was free! No more peeing in a cup, and I would finally have some wiggle room in my budget.

Which meant, of course, that the toddler portion of my brain started screaming for new toys. And a fancy phone was one of the shiny things it kept getting caught on.

I was determined to get some money in the bank before I bought anything else, though. No new phone, no new car, no new clothes until I had some decent savings. Period. Who needed a smart phone anyway? Did I want to be one of those slack-jawed zombies walking down the street staring at their hand?

Did I want to be one of those poor saps who couldn't live five minutes without checking their Facebook status or their Instagram accounts?

Yes. Yes, I did. But I was being mature and I was going to Put. Money. In. The. *Bank*.

But if I could have a *free* phone...

So before I ended my prayer that morning, I said, "If you could see fit to let me win one of those phones, I'd really appreciate it. No pressure. Just...if there isn't someone more needy than me, of course. I'm just putting it out there that I would not be unhappy if I won. That's all."

As if on cue, my old phone rang. I ran to the bar where I'd left it charging and flipped it open, quite sure I knew who it would be.

"Hi G-Ma," I said. "Everything okay at the motel?"

"They're here!" G-Ma hissed into the phone. "It's the Bandits! They're trying to break down the back door!"

"Are you sure? Can you see anything?"

"No, they're in the back, by the alley. But they're making all kinds of racket. I don't care what they say, I'm going to call 9-1-1. Then I'm going to shoot — oh, wait. I think that's the trash truck."

I figured as much. I walked through my trailer to the bathroom so I could get ready for work while G-Ma worked through her fifth near-miss with the High Point Bandits. Multi-tasker extraordinaire, that's me. I didn't want to be late for work again because of one of G-Ma's dramas, but I also couldn't bring myself to hang up on her just in case it *was* the Bandits. There had been so many robberies in that part of town; G-Ma's strip motel was one of the few businesses that *hadn't* been hit yet.

"Yep, it's the trash truck. Good thing I looked before I shot."

"Good thing," I agreed, putting toothpaste on my brush. "What did you mean, you don't care what they say? You're supposed to call 9-1-1 if you think someone is breaking in."

"Apparently there's a limit. Last time the police were out here, they had a bad attitude about helping me out. A taxpaying senior citizen who could have been held at gunpoint."

"I don't think they can actually keep you from calling if you think it's an actual emergency, though. Can they?"

"Who knows? All I know is, they suggested I at least wait until I see a black mask before I place the call. Which will be too late, of course. They'd get there in time to clean up the bodies. But whatever."

So G-Ma was grounded from 9-1-1. That explained why her calls to me had increased so significantly.

It might be silly, but I kind of liked knowing that I was G-Ma's go-to for defense, after the police department, and her own pistol, of course. That one was always at the top of the list. I liked to think that it was a sign of growing respect that she had come to depend on me. More likely, it was that I was the closest family member to her, but still...I had, with the help of my best friend Viv, solved two murders within the past few months. I supposed the person who once changed your diapers had to respect that, even if both times were more accident than anything resembling detective ability.

"Well, feel free to call me if you think you're about to be robbed." I could at least be the middleman who helped keep her calm so she didn't shoot innocent bystanders.

At Flo's Bow Wow Barbers that morning, we took a break around 10:30 and went out to see the festivities. As promised, there were balloon animals, a mariachi band, and university radio station. The DJ took breaks between weird indie songs to extol the virtues of the Smart Enuff phone.

Viv drove up in her Cadillac and parked in the big middle of everything.

"You're not getting a new phone, are you?" I wasn't sure of Viv's age or her level of wealth, but I knew they were both significant. I guessed her age at 80-something, and her bank account at more-than-I-would-see-in-my-lifetime. Viv loved having all the latest toys and gadgets, and certainly would never go for a "Smart Enuff" phone. Viv had the newest "Smart Enough to Rule Humanity" phone and a shiny blinged-out case for it, too. She didn't know how to work it, but still.

"No, I came for the free Krunchy Kreems. I haven't had one since last time I drove to Amarillo."

"Shhh," I said. For some Lubbock people, "Amarillo" was a bad word. It was one of those weird neighboring town competitions that made little sense, but people seemed to get caught up in it. Plus, Amarillo had not one but *two* Krunchy Kreem franchises and Lubbock had not managed to score one. Some kind of weird Cain and Abel thing. I didn't want her to get anybody started on all the ways Lubbock was superior to Amarillo. Although it really kind of was.

"I also came to show you this." She handed me a postcard.

I looked at the front, with its full-color, high definition picture of a giant cockroach.

"Ugh!" I shouted, nearly dropping the thing. "Why?"

"Look at the back," Viv said.

I flipped it over. The card was addressed to Viv at the Belle Court Independent Living Centre, and the space saved for a note to the receiver simply said, "No sign yet. Staying on the move. Saw this and thought of you two hahahaha."

"Dale," I said with a sneer.

"Shhh!" Viv darted a look around us. "We swore to never speak of it!"

"I'm not speaking of it! But you're the one who brought me the postcard."

"I wasn't going to be the only one to enjoy that thing."

I handed it back to her.

She refused to take it. "I'm good, thanks. Almost ruined my appetite for donuts."

I dropped the postcard into a nearby trashcan and pointed to the donut line. After the dream I'd had that morning, I'd decided to forgo the little drops of fat sunshine dripping with golden sugar, but the length of the line reinforced my decision.

"Crud," Viv said. "I might have to play my doddering old lady bit and stumble to the front of the line."

"Don't do it," I said. "You really can't count on people being tolerant of a confused old lady, not when there are Krunchy Kreems involved."

"True. Hey, they're starting the contest, anyway. Did you enter?"

"Of course." I stepped around her, eager to hear my name called.

So eager, in fact, that when they actually *did* call my name, I jumped two feet in the air.

I won a phone! I raced up to stand on the sidewalk between Montana and his brother Dakota, ready to rip the thing from their hands.

I was so ready, in fact, that it took me a while to realize there were more than three names called. Montana had said they were going to give away three phones but there were...I count-ed...*twelve* people by the time they finished calling names.

Dang. I maybe had not won a phone after all.

"Let's have a round of applause for our semi-finalists." Montana lifted his hands high in the air and clapped, receiving a tep-id response from the crowd. Jealous, I thought with an inner smirk.

"Now, we have to do something to whittle this down to three people, because we only have three phones to give away. So we thought, what could we do? Our first thought was, dizzy bat! You guys know dizzy bat, right? You stand the bat up on the ground, put your forehead against it and circle the bat ten times, then try to run a straight line?"

The crowd cheered. They knew dizzy bat!

"So we thought we could have the contestants compete in a game of dizzy bat, with the top three taking the prize."

The crowd hooted and cheered.

Montana let them respond, then raised the microphone back to his mouth. "But that didn't seem quite right. Close, but not quite *it,* you know what I mean? What could we do?"

The crowd started shouting out ideas. When I heard "wet t-shirt contest" I decided I didn't need a phone after all, although I could probably win over the beer belly guy standing beside me.

"Plus, all this talk about Krunchy Kreems had us unable to get the idea of donuts out of our heads. So we figured, how about we combine the two things and make it fun?"

"Oh, dear lord in heaven, thank you," I prayed silently. A

Krunchy Kreem donut eating contest! I was about to win a new phone!

But it wasn't an eating contest. Even as my mouth watered and I began calculating how many hundreds of loops around Trailertopia I would need to walk to burn off the calories, I realized they were rolling out a cart not of real donuts but of...giant inflatable donuts. Colorful, with painted on icing and sprinkles. Giant, inner tube donuts.

Dakota passed them out one by one as Montana gave out instructions. We were to put the donut around our middle, then each stand behind a bat. Meanwhile, a group of twelve people were lined up at the other end of the parking lot, baseball bats held with the fat end against the ground. We were to do our ten spins around the bat, then run with the donut around our middle toward the stage about fifty yards away. The first three people to slap Montana's outstretched hand would win a phone.

I looked around at my competition. The guy with the beer belly was having trouble getting the tube around his shoulders. Two skinny girls already had their tubes on and had to hold them up. Rude. I decided I would need to accidentally bump into both of them during the race.

I hoped I could get my fake donut over my boobs. I had no hope of getting it over my hips, so my choices at this point were either to forfeit or cram the boobs through.

I kind of wanted to punch Dakota and Montana and any other state I could name. If they hadn't gotten my hopes up by calling my name, I might have declined this challenge, but I'd already started imagining that phone in my hand. Plus, I *had* prayed for it that very morning. If God had made them call my name and then I bailed when things got embarrassing, He might decide not to even try on my next request. And we both knew there *would be* a next request.

I sighed and stuck my arms through the tube. It went over my shoulders okay but, as feared, rested comfortably on my boobs like a bizarre scarf. I shoved with both hands.

"Want me to help?" Viv asked, coming toward me with hands helpfully positioned to push up on my boobs while I pushed down on the inner tube.

"No, I'm good, thanks." I kept shoving until it finally went over. I heard a click and realized Viv had her own phone out and was taking pictures.

At the look I gave her, she said, "Come on. How am I not going to take a picture of this?" She held the phone out to me and showed me the picture of me, looking none too thrilled, shoving the giant donut down over my chest.

"Do not post that on Facebook and tag me," I warned. "I mean it. I will tell the nurse you haven't been taking your meds," I said. Viv lived in fear of the power of the Belle Court nursing staff.

The twelve of us lined up behind our bats.

"Contestants ready? Counters ready?" Montana called out from the other end. "Your counters are going to count your turns around the bat and make sure you don't lift your forehead. Once you get to ten, they'll tell you to go, and then you run to me as fast as you can."

I gave him a hateful look, which he completely ignored, and lowered my head to the bat.

All this humiliation filled me with purpose, though. There was no way I was going through this and not coming out without a phone on the other side.

"On your mark! Get set! Go!"

I pressed my forehead into the bat and began a quick-shuffle step in a clockwise direction around my bat. Fortunately, this was not my first attempt at dizzy bat. Of course, all the other times I'd been drunk before I even got to the starting line, but I figured at least this time I had a decent chance of not hurling halfway through.

"One!" my counter shouted as I made my way around. "Two!"

I heard the shouts of the other counters and knew I was ahead of some, but just keeping even with others. I decided the best strategy would be to concentrate on keeping my footing and getting through it as balanced as I could.

"Ten!" my counter finally shouted, and I straightened to head toward the end of the parking lot. I immediately listed to the right and careened into one of the skinny girls. And I hadn't even meant to!

"Sorry," I said, purely for form's sake. I tried to get back on course but the best I could do was a wide, weaving path to the right. I leaned left, but my feet kept going right and I was about to run into a crowd of ruthlessly laughing spectators.

"Go!" Viv shouted. "You can do it!" Then she shoved me back into play.

I lurched back toward the middle of the lot, stumbling over a man who'd fallen and apparently abandoned hope then and there. I knew that, if I could stay upright, the dizziness would eventually pass and I'd be able to regulate more.

I glanced toward where Montana stood and realized with dismay that there were already three people ahead of me, and if the heavy breathing was any indication, beer belly guy was gaining on me. I tried to move my feet faster but the top half of me was leaning far ahead of the bottom half, and I wasn't sure how long I could keep up this weight distribution without eventually diving headfirst into asphalt. Was a "Smart Enuff" phone worth a head injury?

Yes. Yes it was. I lunged forward.

One of the three ahead of me took a dive and collapsed into a heap of raucous laughter, rolling around on her donut and hooting.

I plowed past her. I saw the beer belly from the corner of my eye, and it looked like he was marginally ahead of me but too far to the left of Montana to reach his hand once he got there.

My feet tangled together and I pitched forward. I scraped my hands hard against the asphalt parking lot. I shoved to right myself again. One skinny girl reached Montana and slapped his hand, jumping into the air with a whoop. She crashed promptly into the cart that had held the giant donuts and fell to the ground when it rolled away.

Ten yards away. I risked a glance at beer belly. He was looking at me, and I know we were both thinking the same thing.

There's the person who would steal my phone.

Then he *reached out and grabbed my donut.*

"Hey!" I screamed. "That's cheating! He's cheating!"

He yanked hard and I stumbled backwards, losing my footing. I pinwheeled my arms and landed on my butt.

Then came a high-pitched "Aaaiiiyeee!" sound from the crowd. A blue blur flew past me, and Viv slammed into beer belly, knocking him off track. He tripped over a curb stop and pitched forward onto the sidewalk with a "whuf!"

"Go, Salem, go!" Viv and everyone from Flo's screamed at me.

I lunged to right myself, but with the donut around my middle I couldn't do it. I collapsed back against the pavement.

"Get up, Salem!" Viv screamed. "Get up!"

I lunged forward , but again I fell back. Jeez-o-Peet, I was like a turtle stuck on its back. I flopped around, thinking that if I could just get on my knees I could find my way up.

But as soon as I rose, I overbalanced and fell forward. I rolled on my donut and ended up on my back again.

"Great idea!" Viv screamed. "Roll there!"

I looked at her.

She shooed me toward the finish line. "Go! Roll!"

I rolled. I pushed with one foot and momentum kept me going. I rolled as fast as I could toward Montana. All in all, it seemed easier than running. I didn't have to worry about falling.

As I approached Montana I stuck my hand up. "Slap my hand!" I shouted as asphalt and sky rotated around me.

He stared, horrified, at the crazy woman rolling toward him.

"Slap my hand!" I screamed, my donut bouncing off his foot as I reached him. "Come on, I got here, slap my hand!"

After another few second hesitation, he bent and slapped my hand, then straightened and stood, looking stunned. He looked from me to the beer belly guy and to Viv, opening and closing his mouth a few times. Probably he had not expected actual bloodshed.

He finally shrugged and said, "Okay." Then he lifted his hands and shouted into the microphone, "Ladies and gentlemen, we have our winners! Let's give all of our contestants a round of applause."

The crowd moved back into the parking lot and I accepted the congratulations of my friends, feeling like I'd just finished the final challenge of American Ninja Warriors.

Dakota toggled back and forth between my old phone and the new phone, using his thumbs to scroll through the screen and push buttons so fast it was like he was disarming an explosive device. "I can't believe you actually used this thing," he said with a laugh. "I mean, my grandma's phone is newer than this."

"Yes, well, it worked." I wanted to be grumpy at him, but he did just give me a free cell phone, and I did want a free cell phone, so I settled for shrugging and trying not to look embarrassed.

"Yeah, but for what? I mean, it doesn't even have a browser."

"It could make phone calls! That's what it was supposed to do. You know, some people don't like to be tethered to their mobile devices," I said, like any self-respecting old coot would do. "Some people like to see the wide world in front of them, be present in the moment. Pay attention to the road instead of causing accidents because they can't look away from their hand for thirty seconds."

"Well, now you have a phone that makes phone calls, surfs the web, downloads apps, and will give you directions if you get lost."

I couldn't help myself. Public humiliation or not, this was exciting. "I can finally get the Fat Fighters app!" I said. My Fat Fighters ring leader (that's what they'd taken to calling their meeting leaders) talked about that stupid app in every meeting. Other Fat Fighters members swore by it. My kinda-bff Trisha said she used it more than her cookbooks and her meeting materials.

"I'd be lost without it," she'd said in our last meeting.

"But now you're losing with it!" the ring leader said, they'd laughed together like a gag-inducing Fat Fighters commercial.

But the truth was, Trisha was losing weight faster than I was, but now that I had a smart phone I could maybe catch up.

"I'll download the app for you," Dakota said helpfully. He made a few swipes with his thumb.

Once it downloaded, he held the phone out for me. "Let me show you some of the features. See this? This is your home screen. It's just like the desktop of your computer. All your apps are in here. Want to check your calendar?" He tapped a little square with a calendar on it. "Right here. Now you have all your important dates at your fingertips. Need to calculate a tip in a restaurant? Right here. Listen to a podcast? Here. Log into Netflix and watch a movie? Here. Need directions? Right here." Tap tap tap.

None of these things held any interest for me. I had no life, so I didn't use a calendar. The only engagement I had to keep was my weekly probation officer visit, and not only was I unlikely to forget that – I was so paranoid about forgetting that I often woke in a cold sweat from a nightmare that I had missed it and was going back to jail – I only had one meeting left. So my calendar was wide open. Plus, I was too broke to go to restaurants where tipping was expected. And I never went anywhere, so I only got lost if I actually wanted to.

I reached my hands out. "I'm sure I can figure it out."

"Let me just show you one more thing. You know how iPhone has Siri? The search engine you ask your questions to, and she gives you the answers? Llano Wireless has that too, except it's called Windy."

"Wendy?" I asked.

"Windy, with an 'i'." He tapped an icon in the top left corner that looked like a wind cloud man with its cheeks puffed out. He smiled and then said into the phone. "Windy, where is the nearest place to get my oil changed?"

"Oil changed?" came a very West-Texas sounding voice. "There's a Jiffy Lube around the corner and about two blocks to the east, and Walmart does oil changes, too – that's half a mile north. Of course, if you want to be industrious and change your oil yourself, like men *used to do*, you can get five quarts of Baker State at Napa Valley Auto for $1.59 each. That's what my husband would do..."

Dakota grinned. "See?"

"What the heck?" I said, taking the phone from him.

"That's my aunt Windy. She lives out at Sundown."

"That's crazy."

"I know!" He grinned wider. "Check this out." He leaned toward the phone. "Windy, where can I get a new smart phone?"

"What is this nonsense?" Windy cackled back after a second. "You don't need a new smart phone. You already have the best one made. By those fabulous Channing brothers at Llano Wireless. You can trust them. I used to change their diapers!" More cackling.

"What the heck?" I said again, for lack of anything better.

"That's different," Dakota said. "She must have changed it overnight. Yesterday she was saying, 'I used to bust their bottoms.'"

"Mmm...I see."

"This is how we keep our costs low. My brother, my cousin and I do all the programming, we lease our towers locally from the big companies, and we keep our network low."

"I know, I heard all about it from Montana yesterday."

"See, most people never use 95 percent of the area they pay for. I mean, are you flying from New York to Los Angeles? I'm sure not."

"I'm trying to save up enough for a new bath mat," I said.

"Exactly. We spend the majority of our time within 500 miles of home. So why pay all that money to have service in Wyoming if you never go to Wyoming?"

"You don't have to keep selling me," I said. "I was sold when you said you'd give it to me for free."

"We just want to make sure you take full advantage of all the features. We want you to be so in love with this phone and find it so easy to use in every part of your life that it actually becomes like an extension of your own hand."

"That actually sounds...a little frightening."

"I know, right? Like a sci-fi movie, where the machines turn on the humans and we all become slaves to killer robots?" He laughed. "But don't worry. That probably won't happen."

Viv came up carrying a wide, flat box. "Look what I just won! Two dozen Krunchy Kreems!"

She opened the box and held it under my nose. The heavenly aroma of fried sugar wafted up.

Instantly, my stomach growled.

"Those are fresh from the bakery in Wichita Falls," Dakota said. "I drove there yesterday, spent the night in a hotel and got up at the crack of dawn to get them. I just got back into town around nine this morning."

Viv hooked a donut on her finger and took a bite. "You know there's a place in Amarillo, right?"

"Of course we do! No way in heck we're giving them our business!"

"You prefer to spend twice as much on gas, take twice the time and stay overnight in a hotel to giving Amarillo your business?"

"Absolutely!"

"Good man," Viv said.

The guy fiddled with the phone some more. "Okay, I transferred the number from your old phone, so you don't even have to worry about that. And I can transfer your contacts – oh, you don't have contacts." Then he squinted and looked at the screen of my flip phone. "Wait...three? You have three contacts?"

"I like to keep things simple," I said.

"Seems like you could just memorize those," he said with a shrug.

"One would think," I said.

"Okay, you're all set." He handed it to me.

As soon as the phone hit my palm, it buzzed and rang.

I gasped and jerked my hand back. The phone went flying.

Dakota and Viv both shrieked. We watched the phone arc through the air. Then Dakota did a dive – I kid you not, a full-out dive – onto his stomach and caught the phone right before it hit the pavement.

I bent to take the phone from Dakota's hand, while he gaped like a fish, the breath knocked clean out of him.

"Sorry. Hello?" I said into the phone.

"They're robbing me. They're robbing me right now. This is it."

My heartbeat kicked up a notch. "Are you sure, G-Ma?" I said. "What do you see?"

G-Ma typically sat on a stool *at* the counter or in a rocker recliner *behind* the counter, watching the TV *under* the counter.
That counter was basically her whole world. And her eyesight
wasn't what it used to be. So the robbers might be there, then
again it could be an actual paying customer.

"A white car, just like they're talking about, four doors, and
four people are getting out. This is it, Salem. I'm gonna stand
my ground. I don't care, I'm not about to let them just waltz in
here and take everything I've worked all these years for — "

I tilted the phone away and mouthed to Viv, "Call 9-1-1 and
send them to G-Ma's. She either about to be robbed or she's going to shoot someone."

I turned back to the phone. "G-Ma, be calm. Remember,
you've thought this before. It might be actual customers this
time."

I heard the cock of a gun.

"G-Ma?"

"Hang on." I heard a thunk and figured she had set the phone
on the counter. I could just *see* her lining up behind the counter,
aiming her gun at the front door.

I heard the creak of the motel door opening. Then a shriek.

"Oh! Sorry!" G-Ma said. "Come back, it's okay."

"Never mind," I said to Viv. "They'll probably get calls from
whoever that was just now anyway."

G-Ma came back on the line. "Well, heck. They ran off."

"They did?" I asked, managing to sound somewhat surprised.

"Crud. Oh well, if it had been the bandits, I woulda had
them."

"Better luck next time," I said.

"Thanks. Gotta go!"

I hung up and stared at my shiny new toy.

"I take it your grandmother didn't kill the bandits," Viv said as we walked slowly toward her car.

"Not yet. Give her time, though."

"We'd better catch them first," Viv said.

"We might as well," I said, flicking through apps on the app store. I already saw a few dozen I was sure I couldn't live without. "The police aren't doing it."

"That's what that old guy was ranting about on the news last night."

"What guy?"

"That old coot with the junk yard. Or is it a roofing business? Anyway, he owns a business over in High Point. You've seen him, he's on the news all the time. The one who looks like Redneck Santa?"

I nodded, but I had no idea what she was talking about, and my attention had become riveted on perfect golden circles of sunshine in Viv's hand.

"You want a donut?"

I wanted a donut. Any donut. But especially a Krunchy Kreem donut.

But I shook my head. "I had a dream this morning that I dove headfirst into a big pile of cheeseburgers right in front of Tony, and then he didn't want to kiss me."

"More for me." She chomped into another donut because she has the metabolism of a hyperactive three-year-old and about as much empathy.

I leaned against her car, still a little concerned about the dream and irrationally mad at Tony. "I think Tony is turned off by my weight gain," I said. "You see how he is — he's fit."

She made a sound of appreciation that bordered on inappropriate, which I chose to ignore.

"He's filled out since we were married, but he's not fat. I'm fat." I looked down in dismay. I had lost thirteen pounds at Fat Fighters, but there was still way too much acreage between the front of my body and the back of it. "For a while there, I thought we were getting our relationship on track. But I don't know. He doesn't seem to want any kind of physical contact other than a peck on the cheek and an occasional handhold."

"Maybe he's just taking his time."

"Maybe. But I'm going to stay away from the donuts until I get back into my old jeans, just in case."

"Sounds wise," she said as she chewed. "So, we need to do a stakeout tomorrow on Clovis Highway and catch these bandits."

"I can't tomorrow," I said. "Probation visit. My last one."

"Really?" She, my hand to God, licked her fingers and then hooked her finger around one more donut.

Times like these I wondered why Viv was my best friend.

"Really. Last one. Three years of peeing in a cup and paying fines. Over."

"You can still pee in the cup sometimes, if you miss it."

"I think I'm good, thanks."

Even though I was excited about the new phone, I couldn't stop thinking about Tony and that crummy dream. It hung like a cloud over what was otherwise turning out to be a decent day.

It wasn't just the dream, though. The dream was a sign of a problem that had been lurking around the edges of my consciousness for a while. My recent attempts to inspire Tony to...heightened passion, let's say, had been less than successful.

I'm using the phrase "less than successful" because I'm trying to avoid the more negative "a crushing failure."

Mine and Tony's marriage was...well, there were probably lots of words for it, but "different" covers it nicely. We'd been married over ten years, but we'd only spent the first nine or ten months together. Ours had been a shotgun wedding. I was eighteen and pregnant, and he was a scared kid who believed he needed to do "the right thing." When I was in a car accident somewhere along the sixth month and lost the baby, I had assumed he was relieved and happy to have a reason to get out of the forced marriage. When he shocked me by living up to every word he'd said in front of the priest that day, I handled it in my typical clumsy, hurtful fashion. I pushed him away. I treated him badly so he would see what a train wreck he had married and do the sensible thing, namely leave me high and dry. When he didn't, I pushed harder. When he *still* didn't, I left.

I filed for divorce, dove into a bottle of Bacardi Silver Label rum, and didn't crawl out again until almost a decade later. When I did, I discovered that Tony had never signed the papers and that the marriage I had assumed was long dead was still hanging by one very odd (to me, at least) thread: Tony had pledged "til death do us part," and he actually meant it.

I had asked him why he hadn't divorced me, and he said, "Because God kept telling me 'no'." What does one do with that kind of information? Before I became a Christian, I wouldn't have wasted five seconds on it. But since I *was* a Christian by that time, and I had made a commitment to do my best to follow God's will, at least as much as I could possibly understand it, I was left to accept the fact that I was, indeed, a married woman.

It wasn't as if we were now living like a regular married cou-

ple, though. I'd come to realize that Tony was just as freaked
out about the possibility of a life fully commingled as I was. He
lived in his nice brick house shaded by big trees, and I stayed in
my sad little trailer in Trailertopia. We'd agreed to take things
slowly, "be ourselves," and not rush into anything. And boy,
were we not rushing.

A few months ago, in a state of needy panic induced by sur-
viving a near-death experience, I'd made up my mind that I was
going to let Tony kiss me — a *real* kiss this time. The kind of
kiss that loving husbands and wives shared. I wanted him to kiss
me the way he used to, in those first months of our marriage
when we no longer had to worry about getting pregnant because
that train had already left the station.

In my naivete, I had assumed this was something he wanted
to do, and was simply waiting for a signal from me. You remember what people say about assuming? Turns out I just made an
ass of me.

And here I thought I had been confused before, when all my
neuroses had been centered on whether *I* could handle being
married to Tony. I had hurt him. Treated him very badly. Just
looking at him carried a ton of guilt, and I didn't deal well with
guilt. I was clinging to my sobriety one day at a time, sometimes
one second at a time, and I didn't know if I could work through
all the stuff with Tony at the same time.

Besides, I had spent years making myself hate him. He was
weak, ineffectual, too passive for someone strong-willed like me.
He hadn't wanted me enough to come after me. I needed someone stronger than that, someone determined.

But...how much strength did it take a young, hormonally active man to commit to a marriage so clearly destined for fiery

destruction — an unfathomable amount, that's how much. That's what Tony had.

Which made him *so* hot.

I had practically thrown myself at him that evening. And it wasn't as if he completely shot me down. He just didn't respond. What I'd planned as a passionate, spit-sloppy lip meld had quickly and much too easily become a chaste, dry peck. The kind you'd give the uncle who was your third favorite out of three.

So. He *didn't* want me. But why had he stayed married to me? Because God told him to. And where did that leave us? In a very polite platonic marriage?

But this was Tony, who had not been able get enough of me, once. Yes, he was ten years older now, but that was only ten years. He was still a man very much in his prime. A man who had been celibate for ten years of that prime. He should have been chomping at all kinds of bits, so to speak.

In the months since my failed attempt, Tony had been nothing but sweet and attentive. We danced around the awkwardness of the situation, neither of us willing to say out loud what we really wanted. We set up a weekly date night, which invariably ended with a quick peck on the cheek at the front door of my trailer. I joined his huge family for Sunday dinner. He almost always took my calls, even if he was busy. He told me I looked nice, whether I did or not.

So frustrating.

After work I decided to head over to G-Ma's and get some clarification on this 9-1-1 issue. G-Ma sometimes minimized situations that warranted a complete freakout, and vice versa. For instance, once when the motel was found to be in violation of the health code because the service she was using didn't wash the sheets right and they were all disgustingly stained, she bought new darker sheets that hid stains better.

On the way, I called Tony on my new phone. I couldn't help it. I needed to hear his voice and make sure he wasn't the cold, disdainful robot-man from my dream.

"Guess what?" I said as soon as he answered.

"What?"

"I'm calling you on the new phone I won today from that place that went into business beside Flo's Bow Wow Barbers."

"Seriously? That's fantastic!" He sounded genuinely pleased, and that made my tummy flutter.

"I know! A free phone and free service for a year. I don't know how to work any of it yet, but I can figure it out."

"Well, you called me, so you know how to do the most important thing. Bring it to dinner on Sunday and I'll have Ernie look at it for you. I'm sure he can help you."

Ernie was Tony's thin, brilliant, glasses-wearing nephew who was either going to be a brilliant doctor type who saved the world, or take out a mega-mall with a homemade incendiary device. He was quiet and kept to himself.

"I'm sure he can. Listen, are you busy later? I thought maybe you could come over and we could watch TV."

"Oh, sorry, I can't tonight. I need to monitor some new employees."

"No problem."

"We're still on for date night, though, right?"

"Of course." Thursday night. Three days away. He wasn't exactly dying to see me.

Oh wait. I was casting my anxieties. "Sounds good," I said. "See you then." I pushed the "end" icon, feeling a tiny thrill that it was an icon and not an actual button like on my dinosaur phone.

A car horn blared, and a white sedan roared past me, barely missing my front fender. I screamed and swerved, dropping the phone.

I was talking on the phone while I was driving and almost had a wreck!

My heart thudded in my chest and I pulled to the side of the street. My hands shook as I pulled slowly into the parking lot of a Just-a-Buck store and coasted to a stop, slamming the car into park.

From the passenger seat, Stump gave me an annoyed look and a "*hmmph*" noise, then rested her nose back between her front paws.

I put my hand to my chest, my heart pounding. I felt like an idiot for doing what I had complained just this morning about other people doing. I looked up and noticed in the rear-view mirror that a small crowd was gathered around the door of the Just-A-Buck. They were all staring in the opposite direction, where the sedan had just headed.

It was only then that I realized the near-miss hadn't been my fault. That car had come barreling out of this parking lot and swerved across traffic, directly into my path.

This crowd must have seen it and were outraged on my behalf. That went a long way towards making me feel better.

Except that must not be right, because they were all looking toward the car and a couple of them were now on their own cell phones, talking and gesturing excitedly.

Then it hit me. A white sedan. Clovis Highway. The High Point Bandits!

"Stay here," I said to Stump, hopping out of the car.

"Was that them?" I asked the first person I came to in the onlookers, a short skinny woman around G-Ma's age, wearing a purple velour track suit.

"Sure was," she said, her lips flattened. "Damned heathens."

"They almost plowed right into me," I said. "I was just driving down the street and they almost mowed me down." *I wasn't on my phone or anything,* I wanted to add.

"Well, they didn't *almost* rob me, they *for sure* robbed me." This from a middle-aged man with several thin strips of hair combed over his bald spot. He wore black slacks and a black and yellow Just-A-Buck polo shirt.

I looked around the small crowd. "Did anybody get a good look at them?"

"I did," one lanky guy with a beard said. "Four of them. All wearing black. Black clothes, black masks."

"They stormed in and started making a lot of racket," the woman in the track suit said. "Of all the hollering and carrying on. Animals, that's what they are. Heathen animals."

"I don't suppose anyone got a license plate, did they?"

There was some mumbling among the group, but it soon became apparent no one had. "Did they even have a license plate?" the lanky guy asked. He turned to me. "They drove right by you. Did you see?"

"I was too busy panicking that they almost t-boned me," I said. "I didn't see anything but spots, because my heart was pounding so hard."

"I hear that," the lady said.

At least three of the onlookers had reached 9-1-1 by this time, and the police were there within five minutes. I wondered for a minute if I should stick around and give a statement, but I decided that since I had Stump in the car and didn't have anything to add to what was by now general knowledge — a white four-door sedan with four people wearing black (and I wasn't sure if I'd actually seen that or just knew that from all the news reports) I decided to peel away and head to G-Ma's.

The parking lot to the Executive Inn, although not full by any means, was fuller than I'd seen it in years. Maybe ever. I pulled slowly through, past the filled-in swimming pool that was still surrounded by a short metal fence, still had the metal handrails for the steps that were no longer there. I looked from the motel to the small tamale factory in the center of the parking lot. It was here that a series of low-budget entrepreneurs had had their dreams dashed against the restaurant breakers until Mario rented the building from G-Ma and started a tamale delivery business that was doing so well, rumors sometimes circulated that he must be delivering more than tamales. This was only from people who had never tasted Mario's tamales, though.

The increased traffic wasn't due to Mario, though. He delivered all his wares through an army of nieces and nephews and cousins and grandkids. This traffic was all Executive Inn, so I supposed G-Ma was right. Business was better than ever. Who'da thunk?

"Guess who I passed on the way here?" I asked her as I lugged Stump through the door to the motel's office and G-Ma's apartment.

G-Ma glared at Stump, but didn't say anything.

I tucked Stump closer, making it clear that I didn't intend to let her down to run rampant all over G-Ma's 1984 vintage sculpted carpet. That appeared to mollify her.

"It wasn't Claudia Comer, was it? That *was* her this morning and now she's telling the whole town that I held her at gunpoint. Can you believe that? I've had three calls already. The whole bingo parlor is all up in arms about it. Like she was ever in any danger! Good Lord save me from melodramatic old hens!" She reached out from her rocker and slapped at a fly with the green plastic fly swatter she'd had for as long as I could remember.

Me too, I thought as I leaned over and hugged my own melodramatic old hen. "No, it was the robbers. They almost t-boned me as I was coming down Clovis Highway. They robbed the Just-a-Buck."

"No!" She hauled herself out of her chair and lifted the metal blind away from the window. "Those animals. They're going to keep going until people are afraid to come to this part of town."

I perched on the stool behind the counter where I'd spent a great part of my childhood. "Listen, I want you to think about something for me, okay? Just consider it."

Her drawn-on auburn eyebrows lowered and she frowned. "What?"

"Just keep an open mind, okay? I want you to think about keeping your gun unloaded."

"Oh yeah, of course," she said, her lips flat and her eyes flashing. "Right now when I'm more in danger than I've ever been, when I have more to lose than I've ever had, I'll just take away the one way I have to defend myself."

"G-Ma, just listen to me. You could still hold the gun. If the robbers came, they would see it in your hand and think you were armed. It would achieve the exact same effect, only without the risk of..." *You shooting an innocent bystander.* "Of something going wrong."

"I'll think about it." She crossed her arms over her bosom. "Okay, I thought about it. Nothing doing."

I sighed. "Well, as long as you keep an open mind."

"What I have is a mind that's sat here and listened to one business after another get taken down by these goons and the police not do one thing about it. They have no idea who's behind this and no idea how to stop them. I've had this motel for thirty years and I've been robbed more times than I can count."

So, she couldn't count to three. Because I happened to know that she'd been robbed three times. One time had been by a fifteen-year-old kid there on a dare who had been so terrified to begin with, and became more so when he saw her bring that big pistol out from behind the counter, that he'd actually started to cry. But sometimes it made G-Ma feel good to play the tough-as-nails heroine of her own dramatic life story.

"I defended myself through every one of them, and I'm not going to roll over for them now. This fat lady ain't singing yet. Did your mom call you?"

"Call me what?" For a moment, the question caught me off guard. "Oh, you mean, call me on the *phone*? No, why?" Mom never called me. If she happened to be in a family-calling kind of place (i.e. "I need money" or "I am getting married again") she called G-Ma and had her pass on any necessary messages to me. She avoided calling me because I "could be so judgmental."

"Does she need money, or is she getting married again?"

"Number B. Getting married again. This is the one, though, the big catch."

"Another one?"

"For real this time. She's swearing on her life."

"Does she want us there for the wedding this time?"

"I'm not sure. She said she was going to call you and talk about it."

Well, this *was* new. At least I had a new phone to take the call.

"Does that dog need to go poo? She looks kind of fretful to me."

I looked at Stump. She and G-Ma weren't exactly on the best of terms. For one thing, G-Ma knew her name and refused to say it. She never saw Stump that she didn't express concern that she was about to shoot out a geyser of poo, and I couldn't help but think that Stump picked up on these non-supportive vibes.

Stump yawned and let out a *humph* sound that had G-Ma on the edge of her seat.

"Is she —"

"Yeah, I better take her outside," I said, rising and tucking Stump against my hip. I was ready to go anyway. "Think about what I said," I reminded her on the way out, knowing it was a lost cause. "Please try not to shoot anyone."

"Not making any promises," she called after me as the door swung closed.

I did think Stump could use a walk around before we drove home, so I carried her around the back to the strip of grass between the motel and the empty lot behind it.

Except it wasn't empty now. A used car lot sat there, complete with plastic bunting slapping in the wind and one of those wind sock balloon guys lurching drunkenly. *Five Star Excellent Auto Sales* read the sign over the little portable building that sat toward the back of the lot.

Stump growled at the wind sock man, but needed to pee too badly to give it much energy.

I was quite sure that car lot hadn't been there the last time I visited G-Ma. She'd said that her business had never been better, so I supposed the robberies, worrisome as they were, weren't hurting the area very much.

CHAPTER TWO

A Wedding

I celebrated my big day by scrolling through the Fat Fighters app and finding a new recipe for a Chinese dish. I stopped by Greene's Grocers because Mandy Greene knew me from high school and would let me sneak Stump in while I shopped, as long as I didn't stay too long and the health inspectors weren't there.

I picked up chicken breasts, cabbage, and a can of water chestnuts – pretty sure I already had the rest of the ingredients. I was back home and busily chopping cabbage when the new phone dinged. It had such a nice little ding.

"Did Mother tell you? I finally did it, Salem. I found a good man."

"That's great, Mom. I'm happy for you." See? Does that sound "judgmental?"

"I am too!" she giggled. "I mean, after an entire lifetime of one loser after another. Finally."

"Mmmhmm." I refrained from pointing out that one of those losers had been my father. Because I mean...yeah. He hadn't stuck around, so there wasn't much in the way of a defense for him. Of course, I had only Mom's word for it that he knew he had a daughter, and Mom and the truth had an on-again, off-again relationship. Still, we'd stayed fairly close to home for the past thirty years, so I always thought he must at least suspect, even if he hadn't been told.

"He's a good man," Mom was saying. "Comes from a good family. A very good family, in fact. His mother was featured in *Amarillo Hearth and Home* last year."

"What is that, like a magazine or something?"

"Are you serious? Yes, it's a lifestyle magazine, a very prestigious one."

"Mmm," I said, in what I hoped sounded like an appropriately impressed tone.

"It's the best local magazine that all the lifestyle experts read and are featured in. They did a six-page spread on the house and yard. Gerry isn't in it, but he looks a lot like his dad. It's all online. You should look it up."

I could actually do that on my new phone, I thought happily as I fished celery that was only a little bit floppy from the fridge. While I was at it, I would look up "lifestyle expert," because that sounded like a made-up thing but I wasn't sure. Whatever it was, they probably wouldn't be featuring a six-page spread of Trailertopia anytime soon.

"I want you to meet Gerry. He's such a gentleman. I mean, he just waltzes into a place like Thunderman's and they all snap right to attention. I'm telling you, whatever he wants. They all act like their number one mission in life is to please him. I mean, seriously, I'll bet one word from him would get any of them fired on the spot."

I wasn't really sure if I was supposed to be impressed with that, so I just said, "Hmmm," again.

"The wedding is the day before Thanksgiving. Because we're just both so *thankful*."

"Mmm-hmmm," I said. "That sounds like a good plan." What was she, *fifteen*?

"Then we're going to the Dallas Cowboys game. Gerry has a suite at Cowboy Stadium. He's a big fan. Then we're on to Aruba!" She squealed.

"Gosh," I said. So, *Amarillo Hearth and Home*, "lifestyle expert," and "Aruba." "Sounds fantastic."

"So I need you and Mother there, at the wedding. I need some people for my side, you know? Do you think Tony could come, too? Maybe bring some of his people?"

"His people? Like...his family?"

"Yes. I mean, you know. I have you and Mother, and Gerry has this whole big slew of people. So I need some to balance it out a little more. Ask his mother. And he has what, seven or eight brothers and sisters? Surely some of them could come."

I made as noncommittal a sound as I possibly could. I was sure Tony would be happy to go with me. Or he'd go, whether he was happy to or not. But his mother — I doubted there was anyone Josephine Solis hated more than my mother. Mrs. Solis had forgiven me for "trapping" her son into a shotgun marriage when he was only seventeen (I'd helped prove Tony innocent of a murder charge last year, so she kind of had to). But she had no reason to forgive Mom and probably never would. She was certainly not going to agree to play an extra at Mom's umpteenth wedding. I wasn't even going to ask.

"Oh, I didn't realize what time it was. I have to go! Gerry is taking me out to for dinner, and I want to exfoliate first.

I hung up and tossed the celery into the skillet with the olive oil and garlic salt. I tapped my phone. "Windy, find *Amarillo Home and Hearth.*"

"Okay, sweetie, I'm huntin' for it now."

I looked at Stump, who eyed the phone with suspicion.

"Yep, it's going to take some getting used to," I told her.

"I think this is what you won't," Windy said, which confused me until I realized she meant, "what you want."

Even on the small screen of the phone, the website looked pretty. A pumpkin orange banner ran across the top of the screen, with golden oak leaves and pine cones wrapped in a green checked ribbon in one corner. I clicked through past issues until I saw "Cozy *and* Chic? Yes, It Can Be Done. And Neely Bates Can Do It."

I scrolled through the text, picking up bits and pieces.

"Neely's first passion is baking."

"I can be a bit particular about my cookies, but I find this pursuit of perfection very relaxing. It's hyper-focused, you know. Almost like a form of   meditation. I studied all the best small ovens available and had one specially made for our plane."

"Die-hard Aggies, the Bateses travel to every Texas A&M football game in their private plane."

"Gerald thought I was crazy, but it helps me relax while we're flying, and I promise you, nobody complains when they get one of my oatmeal   raisin cookies. That's what it's all about, for me. Those little moments of perfection."

"I'll bet," I said.

The article featured spreads from the Bates' dining room with a large silver vase full of pink hydrangeas from Neely's own garden.

"Life, to me, is be about enjoying the gifts that life gives us. Just those simple things, elevated to the perfect art they are. I mean, when you   notice the artistry in a simple pe- onie, it's almost heartbreaking. Every living thing belongs in the Louvre. But it's all out here, free to see   everywhere you look, if we just stop our busy rushing rushing rushing and open our eyes. Right over our back fence every night is a jaw- dropping spectacular show. It's called the sunset, and it's breathtaking. Have you ever really watched the sunset? Or the sparkle of diamonds on   a spiderweb, wet with the morning dew?"

"Oh, gag," I said to Stump. She grunted and rolled over a bit so I could rub her belly. "It's those simple things in life, I can see from the window of my mansion and private plane, right?" I leaned over and kissed Stump's soft wrinkled neck. She grunted and batted at my head with her paw. She wanted my attention, but wasn't crazy about me getting all up in her face.

I took the hint and rose back up, thumbing through the pho- tographs from the magazine, enlarging pictures as I went. One of Neely and Gerald Sr., laughing at some private joke, also showed a framed photograph of the entire family grinning from a ski slope somewhere, all brilliant white snow and white teeth. Another showed a backyard party with a few men who looked like they were straight from the Land's End catalog, standing around a large stone fire pit, with a line of Japanese lanterns strung in the background. A kid in a chunky white sweater and an all-American grin held a wire with a toasty marshmallow over the embers. The caption under the picture said, "No over-the-top screaming pizza parlor birthday parties for my family, thank you very much. We're backyard all the way. Birthdays should be about celebrating the existence of that person, not about how much you can spend or how many presents you get."

"Says the woman who probably has everything she's ever wanted," I mumbled to Stump. "She's probably one of those people who say, 'I'm hard to buy gifts for, because if I need something, I just go buy it myself. Hee hee hee.'"

Stump raised an eyebrow at my mocking tone.

I enlarged the picture and noted the picnic table in the background, with its festive red and turquoise tablecloth and coordinating bunting strung behind it. It was kind of blurry because the focus in the picture was on the kid and his freckled cheeks hot from the fire in the foreground, but I could see the red and turquoise theme carried over to labels on the water bottles and pinwheels stuck artfully into a tall vase at the other end of the table.

"Simple backyard party" to me meant an open bag of Fritos and a can of bean dip, but we all had our interpretations, I supposed.

I thought I might be getting an idea of what a "lifestyle expert" did, though. They found ways to trick out normal stuff until it became fancy and more expensive than it needed to be.

I shrank that picture and returned to the one on the ski slope to get another look at this family my mother was marrying into. I hadn't known, at first, what she meant when she said "good family. But I realized that I, like everyone else, knew it when we saw it. Here was a family who gathered together for birthdays and went on vacations together. They volunteered at soup kitchens and sat on charity committees, they paid their bills early and overtipped the waitress, their kids said "yes ma'am" and "no thank you." Their kids excelled in school and sports and donated their birthday presents to children's hospitals.

Good families lived in good houses and kept the lawn green and tidy and the kitchen floors spotless (with the help of the housekeeper, who *they insisted* was like family). Good families went to church together. Good mothers taught Sunday School, and good fathers led the Thanksgiving prayer.

I kept searching through the pictures, looking for something, then stopped when I realized what, exactly, I was looking for: some clue, somehow, as to how my mom had ended up here.

I tried to picture her fitting with the ski trip or laughing gaily around the backyard fire pit, and I could not. My mother was full-out raucous laughter, shouted four-letter words and flipping middle fingers. She was unpaid bills with never-ending excuses, empty promises, and idle threats. Mom was all of our belongings going into trash bags in the middle of the night, moving out before the landlord could catch us and yell about the overdue rent.

Frank came in and dropped into the recliner. Frank lived in the trailer next to me in Trailertopia. Hispanic with shaggy brown hair, he seemed to have no life outside of work, home (mostly mine) and the occasional visit to his family. He babysat Stump for me when I couldn't take her with me, and I repaid him with free dinners. We'd long ago stopped keeping track of the tally sheet. I assumed he would be there every night, and he assumed I would ask at any time for him to stay in the recliner with Stump so I didn't have to worry about her getting anxious and destroying things, as she was wont to do if I left her alone. Stump had major separation anxiety issues.

"Dinner will be ready in a bit," I told Frank.

He grunted, already concentrating on the wrestling match he'd turned on.

I set the phone aside and groaned, running a hand through my hair. I got up and stirred the stir fry, less enthusiastic for it than I'd been just a few minutes before. I was aware of an uncomfortable feeling growing inside me. I didn't like it.

"It's not jealousy," I told Stump.

She didn't move, just looked at me with her big brown eyes, one brow raised.

"It's not. I don't know what it is, but it's not jealousy."

It was surprise, I decided. That was all. I mean, Mom had been with a lot of guys, and a few of them were really decent. A couple of them had even been, if I was honest, too good for her — meaning they were dependable and would be faithful, if not exactly stellar providers or even good conversationalists. None of them would be considered anyone's most eligible bachelor, though.

I dished up the stir fry and filled two bowls, one for me and one for Frank, and set a bottle of soy sauce on the coffee table between us. The recipe had insisted on only one teaspoon for the entire dish, and that seemed suspiciously low to me.

Your ankles will thank you! The recipe had said.

I took a tentative bite. It was okay, but kind of bland. I looked at the soy sauce. I thought of my dream last night. I thought of my next Fat Fighters weigh-in. I sighed and took another bite.

Frank took one bite, then upended the bottle over his bowl and stirred. Frank had to wear a belt to keep his jeans up. The rat.

As soon as he was done, Frank announced that he had some things he needed to take care of and thanked me for dinner. I knew he didn't have anything else to do. The wrestling match was over and he was afraid I was going to offer him seconds. It was okay. I didn't have anywhere else to go, so I didn't need a dogsitter.

I turned off the TV and picked my phone back up. It was so shiny. I went back to the *Amarillo Hearth and Home* site and scrolled back through the pictures, trying to imagine my mom in any of them.

It still made no sense.

But it was surprise and not jealousy, I thought. Jealousy would be stupid. Besides, I *had* a man, and although his family hadn't been featured in any magazines, they certainly could be. Tony himself was certainly hot enough to be on a few magazine covers, and successful enough to be considered a great catch. What's more, we'd remained married for over ten years despite all the odds. The fact that we'd only seen each other a total of about one year out of the ten held no real relevance.

I called Tony. I would say "Hey, honey, how's your day?" All breezy-like, as if it was no big deal. As if we had the kind of relationship where we called each other honey all the time.

"Hey," I said. The "honey" just kind of died in my throat.

"Hi, Salem. What's up?"

"Nothing much. I just wanted to say hi. So...hi."

He laughed. "Hi."

"How are the new employees?" Tony owned a cleaning service business, and his clients were all other businesses and office buildings. He was a good boss, but there was still a fair amount of turnover, so new employee supervision was a common occurrence.

"They're catching on," he said.

Then silence, while he waited patiently for me to get to whatever I'd called for.

I stifled a sigh. "So, we're still on for Thursday, then?" *As we already discussed not two hours ago.*

"Absolutely. I wouldn't miss it."

He wouldn't, either. Tony was dependable. If he said he would do something, he would do it, if for no other reason than because he was a man of his word.

That wasn't nothing. Coming from a family where people threw words around like they were free, I knew the value of someone who kept his word.

"Excellent," I said. "I'm looking forward to it." For now, it would have to be enough that one of us viewed the appointment as something *not* akin to jury duty.

I hung up and called Les.

"Okay, tell me," I said, as soon as he'd said hello. "Is it lame, or super-lame, or just plain sad that I might possibly be jealous of my own mother's new-found happiness?"

"Might possibly?"

Les is my AA sponsor. He had seen me at my worst, heard *almost* all my horror stories, and somehow still took my calls. I'd been suffering through a three-day binge hangover in the county jail when I met Les. He had come to the jail and prayed for me, and my life had never been the same. He could take credit for basically every good thing that had happened in my life from that point on. But he didn't.

"I don't know." I stood and began to pace my narrow living room. Stump stayed on the sofa, smart enough to know there wasn't room enough for one of us to get in a decent pace, much less two. "I don't know how I feel, but it's not good. Not happy for her."

"Why not?"

"I don't know."

"Do you think this marriage might not be a good idea? Is the guy not a good candidate for marriage?"

"I have no idea. I don't really know anything about him because all she's told me is about his family. They have money. I mean, they're not bazillionaires, but they have enough that the dad flies his private plane to all the Aggie football games. Mom went on and on about their beautiful house on the golf course, their standing in the community, their fabulous friends. The guy could be a complete toad for all I know."

"Well, that's probably it, then. You're feeling uneasy because she could be getting in over her head, into a situation that isn't what it seems to her. That would make me uneasy."

He made it sound almost Gothic, like Mom was being conned into marrying into this family only to find out they kept their crazy aunt locked in the attic and the family plot was filled with the tombstones of Gerry's former wives.

I did a gut-check. "No, that's not it."

"I'm going to ask you a question and I want you to say the first thing that comes to mind, okay?"

"Okay."

"What are you afraid of?"

"That she's going to get everything she ever wanted." I froze.

"Good grief. That's awful. I'm a dreg. I'm an actual dreg of humanity."

"You're a child of God."

"Maybe, but that is awful, you have to admit."

"It's honest. Why would it be so bad if she got everything she ever wanted?"

"I don't know."

"Salem, you are on a good track, getting to the good stuff. Think of it like a splinter, festering under your skin. Let's dig it out and get it healed."

"That's disgusting."

"Why would it be so bad if she had everything she ever wanted?"

"She doesn't deserve it."

"Why not?"

"Because she was so — " One particularly painful memory sprang to mind, and I pushed it away. There was plenty else to deal with, we didn't need to go there. "She was so unhappy with *me*. With having me. With having to take care of me and all the inconveniences and hardships that came with being a single mom. And she made me feel like — like everything was my fault. Every time we had to move because the rent wasn't paid, she'd bring up how much it cost to feed me and clothe me. Every time she broke up with a boyfriend, she'd somehow work into the conversation that it was impossible to find a guy who was willing to take on a ready-made family."

"So, she wasn't happy being your mom, and it's hurtful to you that she finds happiness now that you're grown?"

I let that sit for a moment. "I don't know. That feels close."

Would I be happier for Mom, if she'd been happier with me?

That felt closer to the truth than the fear that she was in danger of being the next late Mrs. What's-his-name. Bates. But not quite...

Again, the thought popped into my head that I could tell Les about the *really* bad stuff, instead of just the bad stuff. Then he would be able to understand where I was coming from, and I wouldn't have to explain myself.

But I wasn't emotionally prepared for that level of heart-to-heart, not at the moment. Besides, Les knew enough of the dysfunction of my childhood, all Mom's boyfriends and husbands. He had probably figured out the rest.

"She did so much to make sure I *wasn't* happy," I finally settled on. "I mean, I'm still dealing with all the crud she left me with. I'm probably *always* going to be dealing with the hangups and neuroses. It just...it seems unfair that she basically gives me a big pile of neurotic crud to work through and then goes on her merry way."

I did another gut check. It didn't feel good, but it felt like the truth.

"Do you think you'd be happier for her if your own life was more under control? You had all your own crud, as you say, worked out?"

I sighed. "Hopefully. I hold out faint hope that when I eventually get my act together, I'll be a nicer person. So yeah. Maybe."

Les laughed. "Well, there's that possibility. You know, of course, that most of us don't ever get all our crud worked out, right?"

"But we still try."

"We still try. The question now, Salem, is what are you going to do with this new-found realization? When is this wedding?"

"Two months, she said. They want to have it around Thanksgiving. Because she's so thankful. Gag. And because he has a suite at Cowboy Stadium and they can go to the game and then to Aruba for their honeymoon. Also gag."

"So that gives you two months to work through your crud and be happy for her."

"Not going to happen."

"Then you're going to have to decide how you're going to handle it. Want to go over your options?"

"Is staying drunk for the whole thing one of the options?" I was mostly joking. "Or maybe just slightly buzzed?"

"Of course, as long as you consider the entire picture associated with that choice. Losing all the progress you've made in your recovery so far. Another rock bottom. Another round of relationships down the toilet. Another season of not being able to look at yourself in the mirror. Self-loathing, disappointment."

"You make it very enticing."

"Still just being honest. What's another option?"

"I suck it up and paste a smile on my face until it's over."

"That's a possibility. Hang on a second."

I heard a muffled sound, as if he'd put his hand over the phone, and I heard him talking to someone, probably his wife, Bonnie. I sat back on the sofa and Stump slid over and put her chin on my leg. I scratched her ears and felt a moment of gratitude that no matter how screwed up I was, I was doing a fairly decent job with Stump. She seemed to be doing okay, and my neuroses weren't rubbing off on her.

"Okay," he said when he came back on. "There's another option you haven't mentioned."

"What's that?"

"You could talk to your mom. Clear the air."

"Also not gonna happen."

"You should at least consider it. Chances are, Salem, she wants to have a good relationship with you, and would welcome the chance to have an honest conversation."

"You don't know my mom."

"I don't. But I know mothers. Most of them want to do the right thing. Most *people* want to do the right thing. They just need someone to tell them what that thing is."

"Believe me, I tried having conversations about these very things, the entire time I was growing up."

"How'd that go?"

"You know. We fought." This was far from the first time Les had heard my grievances over my childhood. "Every time I brought up how I would like for things to be different, she got offended and acted like I was criticizing her and never satisfied with any of her hard work. It was all about how difficult *her* life was, and she didn't have any sympathy left over for how our life was affecting me."

"Well, time has passed for her, too. She's older now, probably a bit wiser. And now, if she's in a good relationship and happy with her life, she'll feel less pressure and be more open to hearing what you have to say."

"Maybe," I said, to appease him.

"Don't agree just to appease me. Really think about it. You have two months. You could invite her to stay with you and maybe you two could reestablish a relationship. I'll bet she would welcome the chance for that."

"Maybe," I said again, every bit as doubtful as before.

"Why don't you ask her to just come for a few days. Visit you, and you just love on her. Put everything else on the back burner and just love her. Don't worry about having any big heart-to-heart breakthroughs or anything. Be around her. Get comfortable around each other again."

Mom and I had never spent more than two hours together without getting into a fight about something. But he was right — she was older now, and happy. I was somewhat calmer. Plus, I would be neither drunk nor hungover, so I should find it easier to control my own mouth.

"After that, maybe what you should do next will be a little more clear to you. But even if it's not, love never fails, Salem. God's word never fails. If you set out to love your mom, it won't return empty."

It should not have surprised me the next morning when the Bible verse from my devotional was the exact one Les had quoted to me the day before. But it did, a little.

Love bears all things, believes all things, hopes all things, endures all things. Love never fails. 1 Corinthians 13:7 (ESV)

I rolled my eyes — prayerfully, of course — and said, "So, what you're telling me is, every time I think something is pointless, you're going to come at me with this verse?"

No answer from God, but I assumed he was nodding smugly. I sat back on the floor pillows and stared at the triple flames of the candle.

God and I had been round and round about my mom. I knew I needed to forgive her. And I had. With Les' help, I had made the decision to forgive all her bad choices because I had made my own bad choices, and I knew what it was like to need forgiveness.

Maybe I had done it wrong. My forgiveness didn't seem to stick. I hadn't done it with love. Because love never failed. Or so I'd been told.

My phone dinged, putting prayer time to an early end. I ran back to the kitchen and picked it up, seeing that the call was (surprise!) from G-Ma.

"Everything okay, G-Ma?"

"I just want you to know that if I don't make it out of this, I'm leaving the motel to you!" She shouted. "You be nice to the new girls, they'll make you some good money."

"G-Ma, what's going on? What's happening?"

"They're here! The bandits. They're here and they're coming this way now! It'll all be over in just a few minutes. I'm not going down without a fight, Salem."

"Hang on, G-Ma, just hang on. Maybe it's not them."

"It's them! I can hear them shouting in the next room. They're probably going room to room, roughing up all the guests as they go. Animals! Oh wait." She went silent for a moment. "Oh, I think that was just the TV in the next room." She huffed out a breath. "Well, good. They turned it off."

"Just the TV?" I dropped onto the sofa, wondering when my heart was going to catch and stop kicking into stroke territory every time G-Ma called.

We said goodbye and I hung up, lugging Stump onto my lap to cuddle while I waited for my heart rate to slow down enough that I could walk again.

I briefly wondered if I could work that "love never fails" thing into catching the High Point Bandits. Because I would *love* to put an end to these calls from G-Ma.

She immediately called back.

"Is it them this time?" I said when I answered.

"No, it's your mom. I forgot to tell you, she wants us to go to a fancy getting-to-know-you brunch at her fancy new mother-in-law's house."

"Good grief. When?"

"Saturday."

"But I work on Saturdays. I work every Saturday. Dog groomers always work on Saturday. It's the law." It wasn't actually a law.

"You're going to need to ask off. We'll drive up early Saturday morning. We're supposed to be there by eleven."

I frowned. It really was a big deal to ask for a Saturday off at Flo's. Saturday was our busiest day, and having one groomer out meant a harder day for everyone else. Plus, with me working on commission, that meant my biggest money day of the week was going to be a goose egg. And for what? One of Mom's soon-to-be failed relationships? There was no point.

Love never fails.

I leaned my head against the back of the sofa and put my hand over my eyes, groaning.

"I know," G-Ma said. "We have to go and let her play high-falutin' with her new friends. All those Amarillo people who think their you-know-what don't stink. I hope I don't vomit."

"Please don't vomit," I said, because I couldn't put it past her that she would do it on purpose.

"Not making any guarantees. I'll see you Saturday morning around nine."

I twisted and lay down on the sofa, then looked at the ceiling. "You could send me a couple of things that are a bit easier to love," I said.

As if on cue, Stump stepped on my stomach and plopped her chin down between my boobs, giving me a sympathetic look.

I scratched her ears, unable to keep from smiling. "Okay, point taken."

My appointment with my probation officer was at ten, and I had planned to lie on the sofa and play with my new phone until time to get ready, but Viv texted me and said, "Come to my place a little before nine. I have something to show you." So I hauled myself up with a groan and got ready for the day.

Viv's apartment at Belle Court was always spotless because maid service was one of the many extras Viv paid for, but it looked even nicer today. Fresh flowers bloomed from a vase on the coffee table, candles glowed on a side table, and soft music played on her sound system.

Viv hurried into the room wearing a smart tan suit with dark red Louboutins. "Oh good! You're here! I was afraid you were going to miss it."

"Are you having a party or something?" I asked, a little dismayed at my jeans and t-shirt, and the portly dog tucked under my elbow. "I thought you were going to show me something about the robberies."

"Oh, we're going to be looking at pictures, alright. Do I look okay? I'm going for wealthy matron, but still kind of hot."

I gave her the once-over and pretended to give this serious consideration. Then I gave her a thumbs-up. "You're good."

"Okay, good. Sit down. Wait. Maybe at the dining table?"

"What are we going to be looking at?"

"Salem, I am buying a car!" She grinned a manic grin and

waved her fists in the air. "From home! The Cadillac guy is coming over and bringing his catalogs, and I'm going to order it sitting on my own sofa. Or dining room chair, I haven't decided yet."

I knew enough about Viv from our AA conversations to know that she'd spent plenty of time living paycheck to paycheck just like I had. Then a couple of her later husbands — who eventually became her *late* husbands — had introduced her to the world of money. For the most part, she seemed to have acclimated just fine. But occasionally something came along to make her go mad with the power of it all. This appeared to be one of those times.

I had to admit, though, this was pretty cool.

"Aren't you uptown," I said, plopping onto the sofa. "Oh, wait. Stump and I are going to ruin your entire scene. Do you want us to put on maid's uniforms or something?"

"Don't be silly. Every rich person worth their salt has eccentric friends. Now, don't laugh when I play hard to get, okay?"

"Oh, I won't."

"He's going to talk me into the top of the line model with all the bells and whistles. Just because I can afford it doesn't mean I want to be ripped off. Back me up when I get snobby."

"Understood. I'll be the voice of reason and restraint."

"You know that little old man with the white hair who lives down the hall?"

"Ummm...probably. Which one?"

"The little one. Cute. Looks like Mister Rogers' grandfather. Wears bow ties."

"Oh, yeah, him." I wasn't entirely sure who Mister Rogers was but I put together the "little guy with white hair" and "bow ties" and was fairly sure I knew who she was talking about.

"His nephew owns the Cadillac dealership! He sells to quite a few people up here."

"Really?" I couldn't imagine that there was a big pool of drivers to choose from. But what did I know?

Her doorbell dinged and she did this preteen girl squeal thing.

"Okay, sit down and look bored," she said. She hurried to the door, then stopped, took a deep breath and smoothed her jacket, then stepped to the door. "Mr. Bernard! Come in!" It was more of an order than a welcome.

I glared at him when he came in. Stump snorted and looked away.

Viv and Mr. Bernard sat at the table, and Viv brought us all a cup of coffee in her fancy coffee service. They made small talk wherein Mr. Bernard was condescending about everyone at Belle Court, and most particularly to his uncle (who was leaving him the Cadillac dealership, it turns out) in what he probably thought was a humorous way. Wasn't it so cute how "active" all these old people were?! How they loved their cars they rarely drove and their water aerobics and bus trips to the casinos in New Mexico! So cute!

After the requisite small talk, Bernard brought out the catalogs. "What do you have in mind? Coupe, sedan, SUV?"

Viv shrugged and crossed her arms over her lap. "To tell you the truth, I'm not even sure I need a new car. I mean, mine is barely over a year old. Has practically no miles on it. And you know us old farts. We barely get above twenty just driving to the grocery store and church. It hasn't even needed a car wash for six months."

This was patently untrue. I had personally sat in that car as

Viv barreled down rutted back roads, through mesquite thickets, and across at least one cotton field. But I kept my mouth shut and my expression one of contempt for this man and his obnoxious tie showing up here with the effrontery to assume Viv wanted to buy a new car.

"Well, that is not a problem, Ms. Viv," he assured her. "You're not committing to a thing today. We're just looking at some pictures. If you don't see anything you like, we don't need to go any further. While I'm here, of course, I would like to get the keys to your car and take it in for an oil change, because according to my records it's almost due. I can take care of that for you — it'll take no more than an hour. I can drive it up to the dealership, get the guys to run it through, and have it back in no time."

"Oh, I'm sure it doesn't need it. I've barely driven it since the last oil change."

Another lie.

"Well, we like to keep the oil changed even if it's not driven, every three months or three thousand miles, whichever comes first. Around here all the dust in the air gets in that air filter even if it's just sitting."

She shrugged again as if it made no difference to her.

"So, do you even want to look at the catalogs?" Bernard asked. "I don't mind leaving them here, if you just want to flip through them. I know you're busy. My uncle tells me you're involved in almost everything they offer here."

"Well, that's true." She sighed and looked at the stack of glossy books in his hand. "Well, I guess there's no harm in looking."

"That's the spirit," he said as he handed her the first one.

"Okay, these are the coupes. Three models to choose from, with a range of colors and options."

Viv flipped through the pages with the expression of someone thumbing through a textbook on communicable skin diseases. "These aren't as powerful as my car. And start at ten grand more."

"Have you thought about an SUV?" Bernard asked. "Take a look at this one — it's one of our most popular models. Four cameras, so you can see everything when you're backing up. No more worries of plowing into someone not paying attention."

I could have told him he'd lost that sale at "one of our most popular models." Viv had no interest in doing what everyone else did.

"SUVs are obnoxious," Viv said.

He nodded, unperturbed. "No problem, they're fun to drive but not without their obstacles. Big, you know. Difficult to park."

"Oh, I could park it just fine. To me, they're just an expensive sign to show how wealthy and important you are. Attention-seeking."

"Well, that just leaves the sedans, and right now we're only offering this one. The LR8. Big V-8 engine, all the bells and whistles. Comes in eight colors, with four choices on the interior color. I have several of these on the lot and could get you one today, or we could order one custom and it would take about two weeks." He opened the book and began to talk through the various points.

"What's that?" Viv asked, pointing to the one catalog left in his hand.

"Oh, I didn't even mean to bring that. That's the racing

model. I just picked this one up when I got the rest, but we don't need to worry — "

"*Racing* model?"

My heart stopped. A *racing model Cadillac?* If Viv had a kryptonite, surely this would be it.

Viv snatched the book out of his hand. *"Command attention on and off the track,"* she read. *"These special models will be available at select dealers only."* She narrowed her eyes at Bernard. "Are you a select dealer?"

"Well, actually, yes we are. We're representing everything between Dallas and Phoenix. But Ms. Viv. This is really a high performance vehicle. People drive it at driving school programs. It's not meant for — "

"On and off the track, it says. What, are you saying it would be illegal to drive this in Lubbock?"

He laughed. "Well, no, not illegal. Just...overkill."

Viv's middle name.

"Oooh!" she said. "Crystal White Frost limited edition. Only 99 made. Matte finish available in both the Carbon Fiber and Luxury Packages. What does that mean?"

He blinked and stammered. "Well, there are two different packages available — "

"What if I want both?"

He blinked again. "Well...you can't have both. Unless you get two cars."

Viv looked back at the catalog as if she might seriously consider that option.

It was clearly time for me to step in with my reason and restraint. I stood and went to look over Viv's shoulder.

"Seriously?" I said with as much disdain as I could muster,

considering the thing was breathtakingly beautiful. "Crystal *what*? I mean, it's *white*. Not even a shiny white. Crystal Frost, puh-leeze. Talk about obnoxious."

"So, can you get me one of these or not?"

Bernard took a deep breath. "I think so. Last I heard there were a couple left. I'll have to call — "

"Then call, man, call!" She stood and pulled her phone from her pocket. "You can use my phone."

He declined the offer, fishing in his trouser pocket for his own phone.

"Viv, can I speak to you in the kitchen please?" I said through my teeth.

"Yeah, in a second. I want to find out if I can get this car."

"Viv, just for a moment, please. In the kitchen, *please*."

"Salem, hang on. This is important."

"This is not important, Viv. You have a car, you don't have to act like this is the last one in the world — "

"Holy cow, Salem, listen to this." She lifted the catalog and read as if she were reading from a religious text. *"Track, analyze and share. The available Performance Data Recorder lets drivers record their driving experience by capturing real-time video, audio and performance metrics. The front-view camera captures each curve and straightaway, and when parked, lets you watch and analyze your driving performance. Or you can save the footage on the SD card to watch or share your performance later."* She lowered the book and looked at Bernard. "What's an SD card?"

"Ms. Viv, no offense but I think this might be a bit out of your depth..."

The room went silent. I felt my own eyes go wide.

"I'm sure you could handle it just fine, Viv," I said hurriedly. I turned to Bernard. "Viv is actually quite a proficient driver," I said, thinking that "drives a lot" could count as proficient, if "drives well" didn't quite apply. "But Viv, these are bells and whistles you just don't need." I looked over her shoulder again at the screen shot of the software for driver performance tracking. Actually, it might be a good thing for Viv to get driving feedback from an unbiased source. The screams of her passengers didn't appear to faze her. "You're not actually going to be racing anyone."

"What if the Hombres really do come back, huh? What about that?"

I wasn't sure how to respond to that. The Hombres were a very scary motorcycle gang that — we'd been told — were mad at us for killing their prize cockfighting rooster, and had a price on our heads. But the more time passed, the more I suspected that was a story that Bobby Sloan cooked up to punish us for showing him up again.

Bobby was a homicide detective with the Lubbock PD, and I'd had a crush on him through a major portion of my formative years. He was even hotter now than he'd been then. I didn't *want* to still have a crush on him, but I kind of did owing to his extreme hotness. Said hotness was offset by his even more extreme annoying-ness, though. Bobby didn't like it that Viv and I had solved not one but two murders before he did. That's why I was *fairly* sure he was making up the story about the Hombres.

I still fought the urge to scream and wet my pants every time I saw a motorcycle, though.

"If the Hombres were after us — and it's doubtful that they ever were — we've managed to evade them just fine in the car you have," I pointed out. "This is one of those big decisions that requires some time to contemplate. You don't want to rush into anything."

She whirled in her chair. "Did you *hear* what I. Just. *Said!* Limited edition. Less than one hundred made! They could be selling the last one *right now.*" She looked again at the catalog. *"Straight from the road to the track. Aggressive acceleration."* She spun again in her seat. "Salem! Aggressive acceleration! We need this!"

If Viv was able to accelerate any more aggressively than she already did, she was going to become airborne, with me in the passenger seat.

I took her bony wrist in my hand, tugging her to a stand. "In the kitchen. Now."

I kept a tight grip on her wrist in the kitchen. "So much for playing hard to get!" I hissed at her. "Look at you! You're like a kid crazed on too much sugar. You do not need a high performance vehicle."

"But I do, Salem. I do!"

"How much is that thing?"

"Oh, I don't know," she said, as if this were a minor consideration.

"You could probably get two regular cars for the price of that one."

"Oh, is that what this is about? You're thinking I should buy us both a car?"

I blinked and drew back, dropping her wrist. *"What?* Of course not."

In all our time together, I had never asked her to buy me anything. She could easily have done so, and there had been

times when it would have been very much needed and appreciat-
ed. But her money was hers, and even though I'd indulged in the
occasional fantasy when she'd show up at my door with a set of
keys to a new car and a "Happy Best Friends Day" card, I knew
she didn't owe me anything of the sort. "Viv, you're the one who
told me to help you stay strong."

"Yes, but that was before the Crystal Frost *racing model*. Salem, come on! Don't pretend this wouldn't be an awesome tool
for the agency."

"Oh, we're an agency now?"

"Hello? Where have you been? We're working an active case
at this moment."

"We heard a story on the news and we've asked a few questions. We have no actual client."

She gasped and narrowed her eyes at me. "It's like you've
completely forgotten your own grandmother. And Mario! Think
of Mario. He's out there, poor man, working his fingers to the
bone and trying to provide a legacy for his family. A sitting duck
on that highway, just waiting for those men to come and take
everything he's worked all these years for — "

"Jeez-O-Peet," I said. "Get a grip on yourself. I don't think
you can stretch this excuse any thinner."

She gave me a hateful look, then frowned, dropping her gaze.
She gave a deep sigh. "I guess you're right. If I missed out on
the limited edition color, it wouldn't be that big a deal. And we
don't really need the super high performance model." She
looked at me, a touch chagrined, and put her hand on my shoulder. "Salem, thank you. I lost my head there for a minute, but
you performed your duties, just as I asked you to."

She headed back into the dining room. "Mr. Bernard, I appreciate your time and attention. I'm going to need a few days to think. I will definitely be getting back to you." Then she turned to me. "Now, I hate to be rude but my physical therapist is supposed to be here in ten minutes and I need to get ready for him."

"No problem, Ms. Viv. Just to let you know, there *is* one more of those special editions in Fort worth, and I could get it by tomorrow morning if you want it."

Viv froze, gave me the side-eye, then turned back to him. "Well, I'll still need a couple of days to consider. That's a lot of money to just be throwing around on a whim." Which I supposed was a safe assumption even though she had no idea how much money it actually was.

As she walked us to the door, she stopped at a side table and picked up a pen, talking the entire time about how grateful she was to both of us. She scribbled something on the brochure and handed it to Bernard. "You can take this one back, and I'll keep the coupe book to look through a little closer. That's more my style, and probably what I'll go with, if I go with anything." She patted the catalog now in Bernard's hands. "You hang on to that one, now, and give it a good look through. There is some very interesting information in there and I'm not sure you've even read it all."

He gave a confused nod and allowed himself to be shooed out with me.

As we rode the elevator down I nodded toward the book. "You know she left you a note in there, right?"

"What?" He flipped open the book and scanned the pages. "Wait — " He lifted it to peer closer. "Wait five minutes and then come back up. I want that car!"

"Told you," I said.

"What do you know," he said with a laugh and a shake of his head. "These crazy old coots. They cannot resist their Cadillacs."

"So, this will be your last monthly appointment with me," Maggie said. She hiked up her pants and sat with one foot curled under her in her big office chair, as she always did when I visited. She reached across and rubbed at the base of Stump's ears. "Are you excited about that?"

I nodded, smiling. "Yes." Then I frowned. "Actually, no. I thought I would be excited. I feel like I should be excited. But mostly what I feel is nervous."

She nodded and spread her hands. "Perfectly normal. A lot of people say the same thing."

"I seriously don't know if I can handle it. I mean, knowing there's somebody watching over me to keep me on the straight and narrow — that's a pretty big motivator."

"Are you still going to meetings?"

"Every week."

"Go every day for the next few weeks. Then every other day."

I nodded, although I knew that wasn't going to happen. I tried not to look at Stump because sometimes I felt like she could tell when I was feeding someone a line. I looked quickly out the window, as if I'd seen something.

Maggie did this deep breathing thing she did sometimes that made me think she had just decided *not* to say what she was thinking. Which was fine by me, but made me kind of curious, still.

"You are finished with your visits to me, Salem. But you're not finished with needing a support system. I would encourage you to honor all the hard work you've done so far by maintaining that support system and leaning on it all you can in the coming weeks. You might, of course, even think about being the support for someone else. That helps, believe it or not."

"Oh, I believe it," I said. "I just have a hard time finding anyone who needs help more than I do." I laughed.

She laughed, too, but as is always the case with Maggie, I didn't think she was really feeling my humor. "You haven't looked very hard, then."

"I guess that's true." I needed to talk to someone, I decided, about how nervous I was, and Maggie was not that person. I knew who was, though.

I stood and held out my hand, clumsily tucking Stump up against my hip with the other arm. Stump grunted. "Well, Maggie, it's been fun, but I hope I never see you again unless we happen to run into each other at Target."

She laughed again in that humorless way. "Salem, I can say exactly the same thing."

On the elevator, I pulled my new phone out and started to flick through the icons to find Les' phone number. I saw that cloud symbol, though, and looked around the elevator, although I knew perfectly well I was the only one on it. "Windy," I said, feeling like a fool. "Call Les."

"Okay, sweetie," Windy said. Her little cloud waves floated.

Les didn't answer, but after four rings his voice mail picked up.

"This is Les. Leave a message. If it's an emergency, please call this number and somebody will find me." Then he rattled off the number for Exodus Ministries, where he spent the bulk of his time working with people fresh out of prison.

"Les, it's me. I just got out of Maggie's office. For the last time! Ever! Ever in my life. I'm kind of freaking out, actually. I thought I would be happy but that call from my mother has me freaked out. Call me back." I started to click the "End Call" button, then put the phone back to my ear. "Oh, and it's not an emergency. Just call me back when you have..."

I stopped, because I had come out of the elevator, out the front door and into the parking lot. Where Les stood beside his ice cream truck, holding a big bunch of balloons and a little bundle of flowers. His wife Bonnie stood beside him, holding a homemade sign that said, "Congratulations on your Graduation, Salem!"

I burst into tears.

"Oh no!" Bonnie said, tossing the sign onto the top of my car and coming to me for a big hug. "We didn't mean to make you cry!"

"Then you shouldn't have sucker punched me like that!" I wailed, hugging her neck and then Les'. "This is so sweet. But kind of pathetic, too. Congratulations, you're off probation! Woohoo! I mean, it's not like I graduated from Harvard or something."

"Hush," Les said. He took Stump from me, then opened my car door and deposited her in the driver's seat, rolling the window down so she could raise up on her front legs and hang out with us. Then he tied the balloons around my wrist like a six-year-old having a birthday party at Chuck E. Cheese. "We all have our lessons to learn and it's a smart person who learns them where they are. You can tackle Harvard next semester."

"This is a big deal, Salem, and you have earned the right to celebrate it."

I dried my tears and told them about the final visit to Maggie's office. "Seriously, I never want to see her again. I mean, she's nice enough, but seeing her again will mean failure. Plus, she never gets my jokes. I don't know how to relate to anyone who doesn't get my jokes."

"It's okay to think in terms of 'never again,' but I want you to focus on the right now for just a little bit, okay? How's your head right now?"

"Freaked out," I said.

He nodded. "Okay, what do you need to do when you're freaked out?"

"Talk about it. Take care of myself. Face one day at a time."

"Good girl. Are you getting enough sleep?"

I waggled my head back and forth. "I kept waking up last night thinking about seeing my mom again. About another round of marriage and break-up drama. And I'm supposed to *see* her Saturday. Like, be face to frigging' face. G-Ma and I are driving up to Amarillo to have brunch with her fancy-schmancy new friends. I thought I had a few weeks to prepare myself, but it's starting already."

"Are they really fancy-schmancy?"

I shrugged. "They have brunch."

"I see. Is that what's bothering you most? Do you feel intimidated by that?"

I leaned against my car door and rubbed Stump's fat back through the window. "I don't know, part of it, maybe. But mostly it's just Mom. You know, we've talked about it enough. Remember that night when you had the bonfire at your place, and we had that ceremony where we wrote what we wanted to let go of, and then burnt it in the fire? That's what I wrote about —

my mom. Or not about her, exactly, but my resentment of all that. My wishing things could have been different, and anger with her that they weren't."

I remembered that night very clearly, along with the fantastic feeling of freedom and release when the paper curled and turned black, then disappeared into the flames. I had felt *free*. Tons lighter. Like a whole new world was opening up before me. I'd cried buckets that night, utterly convinced that I was free from all that forever.

That feeling had lasted until the next time I talked to my mom.

"I hate how bitter I feel, how bitter I sound. It's not supposed to be like this."

"Let's just drop the 'supposed to' for now and deal with what is. How long has it been since you've seen her?"

I thought for a moment. "Two years, I guess."

"So you haven't been around her since you were sober?"

I shook my head. "Nope. I mean, she knows. I told her I was going to AA and I'd quit, but..." She didn't know what a big deal my sobriety was to me, the transformation that I had been trying to live. She didn't know I was a Christian. I had tried to tell her, but when the moment came I went with a less-definitive (i.e. more chicken) "I'm going to church now." She'd warned me about being taken for a ride by sham preachers who only wanted my money or to control me and add them to their harem.

No need to worry about any of that. I had no money to be scammed out of, and I'd only actually spoken to the preacher to say, "good morning" and "amen" when he was passing out communion wafers.

"What time are you leaving on Saturday morning?" Les

asked.

"We're supposed to be there by eleven. So we'll need to leave G-Ma's by nine."

"Okay, I'll be at your place by eight-thirty, and we'll pray before you go. It could be, Salem, that God is bringing her back into your life because He knows you're ready to tackle this."

I shrugged. "He has more faith in me than I do."

Les nodded. "Oh yeah. He always does." He hugged me again.

I opened the car door and sat down, wondering how I was going to make it back to Trailertopia with all these balloons.

Les helped me arrange them. "Now, rest your arm on the window here and let the balloons fly free. They're tied on good, they won't go anywhere."

"You know what's awesome? I paid my last fine payment today, too. So that means I can start saving for a newer car. I mean, I like this car and everything, but I'll be glad to get something a little newer and put some money in the bank."

Les gave me a proud smile. "You're moving on up."

"I just need this one to last about six more months, and that will give me time to save for a decent down payment on a new car."

"Good girl. I'll see you tomorrow morning." He patted the top of the car.

I took a deep breath and sniffed, touched again that he and Bonnie had known what a big deal this was and had been there to celebrate with me. I said a quick thank you prayer for Les, and turned the key.

The car rumbled and made a high-pitched whining noise. Then the engine caught, and it roared loudly to life. Much more loudly than normal. Like, waaay too loud. I reached for the ignition to shut it off, but before I could, something exploded and knocked so hard that the hood jumped. Then I smelled burning.

CHAPTER THREE

Moral Crimes

It was, sadly, not the first time Les had towed me home with his ice cream truck. At least he refrained from playing "Pop Goes The Weasel" as we drove. "Seriously?" I groused to God as Les dragged me out of the parking lot and down the street. "A few months? You couldn't help me out for a *few more months* while I saved up some money for a down payment? Why is it that every single plan I make and work towards *fails*?"

Love never fails.

If having this verse pop immediately to mind was meant to bring me comfort, *it* failed. It's entirely possible, in fact, that I went a bit mad with the stress of it all. I decided as we crawled through traffic and I nodded, grinning maniacally, at the people who pointed and laughed at my broken down car and soaring balloon bouquet as we passed, that if God wanted me to love my way through this, fine. A-O-freaking-K! I would love my brains out, and we would see how things turned out.

When Les unhooked the tow rope on the car in front of my trailer, I laughed and offered to paint "Ice Cream and Full-Service Towing" on the side of his van. I hugged him after he looked under the hood and proclaimed the car "totally fried, not worth more than scrap metal now." When we called the junk yard and they towed the car away, I held up the check for $200 they gave me and said with a big smile, "Toward the down payment on my new car!"

Les and Bonnie gave each other a worried look. I grinned on, my teeth starting to dry out, and proclaimed how much I *loved* calling each of my co-workers so I could ask someone to give me a ride to work. It would give me a great chance to get to know them better.

God met this with having everyone else be busy except for Doreen, a new bather who was also Flo's cousin. Doreen was very sweet, but a walking bundle of anxiety. She hated driving in traffic so much that she drove to work an hour and a half early so she could avoid it. Seriously. To avoid the "traffic" in *Lubbock.* She waited in the parking lot for an hour and half. This was her knitting time.

So at dark-thirty Friday morning, I sat with a plastered-on smile and did my best to love Doreen, knitting away in the driver's seat and talking nonstop about her Snow Babies collection just loudly enough to keep me from drifting off. Actually, it wasn't hard to love Doreen, but I hated mornings in much greater measure. And I wasn't that fond of Snow Babies, whatever the heck they were.

It was as if one of us — me or God, I wasn't sure which — had thrown down the gauntlet. God was sure love wouldn't fail.

I was determined to show Him that no matter how much *I* loved, failure was gonna rear its ugly head and then He'd need to come up with some kind of amendment or something.

The first thing I did when the shop was open was to arrange with Flo to take Saturday off. I expected a bigger fuss than I got, but Flo said I had been working hard and I deserved a day off. That was a small miracle in itself, and I took it as a sign from God that I really had to go to Amarillo even though I almost had a decent excuse not to.

To make up for this, he sent Butterscotch Reynolds, a 100-pound Labradoodle with hair so thick you literally couldn't get a comb through it; Butterscotch had recently taken to crashing through the neighbor's fence and rolling with glorious abandon all over the neighbor dog's poo.

He sent McTavish, a foaming-at-the-mouth Scottish Terrier who had made the rounds through every grooming shop in town at least once, and been asked not to come back by most of them.

He sent Phoebe Harris, a cute little silver Poodle who might have been a good dog if she didn't scream high-pitched, ear-bleeding screams every time anyone touched her. Or almost touched her. Or looked in her general direction.

I smiled. I gritted my teeth. I refused to harbor ill-will toward any of these dogs or their owners.

At two o'clock, God called my bluff.

My phone ding-donged.

"They're here! The Handits! They're coming down Clovis Highway right now and I'm not going to take it lying down."

I smiled. I loved G-Ma. I loved the bandits.

"G-Ma, take a breath. Now tell me, what exactly do you see?"

"A white four-door sedan. Driving down the highway in

broad daylight. Oh, these jokers are bold, aren't they? Wait until they see what happens when they meet someone who's not
afraid to *stand up to them!*" I heard the whoosh of the door
opening as she shouted this last bit.

"G-Ma," I said as lovingly as I could. "Don't pull the trigger
until you see the whites of their eyes."

"You Godless heathen can just — "

She stopped abruptly. The door slammed again and the
whooshing sound cut off.

"G-Ma?" I asked, concerned at the deadly silence.

"It was the cops," she whispered. "I almost pointed a gun at
the cops."

"I'm sure it will be fine," I said, dodging McTavish's snapping white teeth.

"We'll see. Oh, I almost forgot. We're staying in Amarillo for
the weekend."

I went still. My blood ran cold. "What?"

"Your mom wants to have a girls' weekend with us and her
new sisters-in-law. So we're going down tomorrow morning and
coming back Sunday night. We're getting pedicures. That's the
one on your feet, right?"

I murmured something, I wasn't sure what. The blood was
rushing through my ears too loudly for me to be sure.

A girls weekend? With G-Ma and Mom? And the *sisters-in-
law?*

I'm not sure I even said goodbye. The next memory I had was
of staring at my phone, trying to decide between Viv and Les.

"Windy, call Les," I finally said.

When he picked up, I said, "I give. I can't love this."

"What's going on?"

I briefly considered that Les was to me what I was to G-Ma. Which was fine, but since the converse must also be true — I was to Les what G-Ma was to me — I took a deep breath and asked myself if I might be overreacting.

No. No, I was not.

"Mom wants me and G-Ma to spend the weekend with her and her new family in Amarillo. A girls' weekend. With frigging pedicures! I seriously don't think I'm ready for that. It's enough to contemplate a few hours. But an entire weekend? And I have to take my shoes off? And they drink. I saw some pictures of one of their parties and there was wine and some other mixed drinks. I'm sure there will be alcohol. I can hold out for a couple of hours. But not for an entire weekend of enforced together-ness."

"Then you won't stay for the weekend."

"I won't?"

"You'll go up for the brunch, you'll be supportive of your mother, and then you'll come back."

"That's not going to go over very well." I could already feel the drama. I would be deliberately trying to sabotage Mom's re-lationships. I would be selfish and childish. She would think of some passive-aggressive way to get back at me.

"You'll tell your mother you're very happy to go to the brunch, but unavailable to spend the entire weekend on this short notice."

"How will that even work, though? I'm driving up with G-Ma and I have no way to get back."

"We can find a way."

I felt really bad then, because if he had to, Les was not above driving the ice cream truck all the way to Amarillo to pick me up.

"I'm sure I can find a way back home. Maybe I can bring G-Ma's car back and then Mom can bring her home Sunday. Or I can meet her halfway or something."

"See, when you put your mind to it, you find a way."

"Are you sure this is the loving thing to do?" I asked. It felt kind of chicken-booty-ish.

"Absolutely. You're on the list for loving, too, Salem. You're not being difficult, and you're not being selfish. You're taking care of yourself. That's love, and you don't want to fail yourself or you can't be there for anyone else."

I hung up and put a bow around McTavish's neck, narrowly missing one last snap of his brilliant white teeth. I thought about what Les had said. Les was the most selfless person I knew, and if he thought it was okay for me to bow out of the girls' weekend thing, it should really be okay.

I couldn't help but think I needed a way to spin it, though. After considering a few things, I called G-Ma back.

"Who are you getting to watch the motel while you're gone this weekend?"

"Rosa. Why?"

Rosa was Mario's sister, and she worked the desk while G-Ma was at bingo and her weekly hair appointment. Rosa was dependable and sweet but had begun to show some alarming narcoleptic tendencies.

"Oh..." I let that hang there for a few seconds, so the doubt could build. "I'm sure she'll be fine."

G-Ma didn't respond.

"Does she also shoot? I mean, you know...in case the Bandits show up?"

"She said she would, if the Bandits came."

"Then she probably would. I mean, she's probably braver than she seems."

Rosa was short and round, with red cheeks and a smile that never faded. And she could be quite fierce with things like roaches or mold on the motel shower curtains. So it was possible...

"I'm not going," G-Ma said. "I can't be waltzing out of town like I don't have a care in the world, not now that my very livelihood is threatened."

"Oh, don't say that," I said, sweeping up McTavish's hair while I held the phone to my ear with my shoulder. "You know how Mom will be if you don't come. She'll say you're being selfish and childish. That you're trying to ruin her happiness."

"She'll find some passive-aggressive way to get back at me."

"Exactly." I paused for a second, but not too long. "You know what we could do?"

"What?"

"Wait, let me think this through...what if we get Rosa to work the front desk just for the day. You and I will drive up to Amarillo. I'll drive your car back home. I can be back by mid-afternoon. I'll relieve Rosa and stay the night at the motel. Watch over things."

"Hmm..."

A year ago, this would have been a non-starter. Then again, a year ago I was newly sober and about as undependable as a person could get. Since then, I had been sober and faced down not one but *two* cold-blooded murderers and — perhaps most frightening of all — a dognapper. My street cred had gone up considerably in G-Ma's estimation.

I jumped into the breach left by her silence. "Mom could bring you back Sunday afternoon. Or we could meet halfway."

"There's that truck stop at Tulia."

"Exactly. Then, in a couple of weeks or so, Mom can come down here, and we can do another girls' weekend here."

"Well..."

I decided that sounded enough like yes. "It's settled, then," I said. "This will work out better. You can enjoy your time with Mom, knowing the motel is in good hands, and I won't have to mess with getting a sitter for Stump."

I dropped the broom and clamped my hand over my mouth. I should not have brought up Stump!

"You're not bringing that dog to my motel," G-Ma said. "No. We're not allowed to have animals in there anyway." Like she wasn't the one who made that rule.

"Oh, I didn't mean not mess with finding a sitter," I said. "I just meant, she can stay with Frank and I'll rest easy knowing I'm still close enough in case an emergency comes up."

She made a few more noises of protest, but I lovingly mowed down all of them by repeating things like, "You're exactly right, this is going to be a lot better," and "Exactly, that's why this is such a good idea. I'm glad you thought of it."

Love might never fail, but sheer bullheadedness also had its day from time to time.

I went home that evening (courtesy of Doreen, who also promised to bring me her next-to-latest Snow Baby catalog so I could see what I was missing) expecting a few more calls from G-Ma. There would be the requisite false alarm calls about the Bandits, of course, but I knew she wouldn't get through the evening without at least three reassurances that we had a good plan for the weekend and everything was going to be fine. What I did not expect was an *actual* problem the first time my phone ding-donged.

"Well, we're not going."

"G-Ma, what's wrong?"

"My car. It's cratered. I went to the post office this afternoon and it blew a gasket or something right in the middle of Buddy Holly Avenue."

"You're kidding!"

"No, I am not. And you're not going to guess who was Johnny-on-the-spot to call the tow truck and drive me back home."

I couldn't imagine. "Who?"

"Your friend. That — that — "

I knew of only one person who could cause this level of sputtering in G-Ma. "Viv?"

"Exactly! I wouldn't be one bit surprised if she had something to do with it."

"I would. She knows less about cars than I do. And why would she do that, anyway?" The two of them had never been within spitting distance of each other without Viv goading G-Ma into a hissing, cursing fit.

"Oh, you should have seen her, like an Empress in that gaudy new Cadillac of hers. Acting all helpful and concerned." She made a *humph* noise.

I almost felt bad for Viv. She would hate the idea that G-Ma was trash-talking her and she missed it — especially the "gaudy new Cadillac" remark. I would have to remember to tell her.

My phone made a beeping sound, and I pulled it away to look at it. What was this?

Incoming call from Viv.

"G-Ma, hang on. I have another call."

"Your other call can wait! I've just been left stranded on the other side of town and now here I am, high and dry. What if the Bandits show up now, huh? What then?"

I took a deep breath and did not say, "What? Were you planning to mow them down with your Lincoln? If they survived the shooting?" Instead, I said, "Let me just reject the call, then, and I'll be right back."

I seriously meant to reject the call, but I accidentally hit "accept" instead. Or maybe it was a Freudian finger-swipe, I don't know.

"You'll never guess where I've been," Viv said, before I could finish saying hello.

"You rescued G-Ma from Buddy Holly Avenue and drove her back to the motel."

"She already called you? I wanted to tell you! You should have seen her! I thought she was going to flare her neck out and start spitting poison at me."

"She called your new car gaudy."

"She did?! Seriously? Oh, I wish I could have heard that!"

"I knew you'd want to know."

"Yes, thanks. Take notes of anything else she says. I showed her how to use the zoned climate control and the 37-point seat adjustment. Did she say anything about that?"

"We didn't get that far. We were just talking about how the trip to Amarillo is off now and — "

"Oh, that's why I called! I am going to Amarillo to have my car worked — I mean, looked at, by a, um, software specialist from um, Germany. He's only in Texas this one day and I am taking the car up there so he can check the programming — "

"You're having trouble with the car already?"

"*No.*" Her tone was resentful, as if it was stupid to even think it. "It's just one of those normal bugs that happen when you introduce cutting edge technology. And it's nothing, really, just an occasional dinging sound that needs to be reprogrammed. But they'll have to send the car back to Detroit unless I can get it to Amarillo tomorrow, while this guy's in town."

"The guy from Germany?"

"Something like that, yeah. He has a layover in Amarillo tomorrow at three. So anyway, I can drive you up there and bring you home."

Driving up and back with Viv sounded so much more fun than driving up with G-Ma and driving her car back alone. Plus, maybe G-Ma really would flare up and spit poison, and I hated to miss a chance at that.

"Excellent!" I said. "Les and Bonnie are coming to my trailer at eight-thirty so we can pray before we go. Can you be there then?" I didn't say, but I thought it wouldn't hurt to ask Les to throw in an extra prayer for safe travels, since Viv was driving.

I called G-Ma back. "Sorry about this. It's this crazy new phone, I can't figure out how to work it."

She humphed again. "I'll call your mother and tell her we can't make it. She's going to pitch a fit, of course, but it can't be helped."

"It can be helped," I crowed. "Viv is going to drive us. She's going to Amarillo anyway."

"The hell she is!" G-Ma barked. "I'm not going — "

"Ooops, G-Ma, hang on," I said, pulling the phone away from my ear. I bounced it against my leg a couple of times, then blew lightly into the speaker. "G-Ma, are you there?"

"Of course I'm here, where would I be with no car and no way to get — "

"G-Ma? Can you hear me?" I bit my tongue to keep from laughing.

"I can hear you fine. It's you who can't hear me! If you'd have a regular phone like normal people — "

"Okay, well, I guess I'll see you tomorrow morning around nine o'clock. Bye!"

By the next morning I was beginning to feel kind of bad for how I'd treated G-Ma. Her passionate hatred for Viv might be amusing to me (and to Viv) but she deserved my respect, if nothing else than for all the time she'd provided a safe haven for me away from Mom and her many male "interests." So while Les was praying for compassion, family renewal, open hearts and safe travels, I was praying repentance for manipulating G-Ma and finding pleasure in her displeasure.

I might as well put that prayer on a loop, I thought as Viv and I pulled up and G-Ma scowled through the blinds at us, her chin jutted out.

She started in as soon as we got there. Rosa wasn't there yet, but she'd called and said she was on her way.

"They're gonna rob me blind. I know it. As soon as I step out that door, they're gonna come in here and take everything I got."

"You don't keep cash in the office, do you?" I asked. I knew she regularly made Friday afternoon deposits, so there probably wasn't much to steal anyway.

G-Ma threw a suspicious glance toward Viv. "Of course not.

I'm no fool."

Viv rolled her eyes. "Honey, whatever you have in this room, I don't need."

I stepped between them to avert a certain old-lady cat fight. "It's just one afternoon, and Mario will keep an eye on the place, won't he?""

"He said he would." She rolled crimson lips together. "But he's busy with his own stuff and keeping his eyes on all those kids."

"How about I go over there and talk to him, make sure he understands the need for vigilance," I offered. "You finish getting ready."

"Yeah, we'll go talk to him. Looks like it's going to be a while before you're ready to go anyway," Viv snarked over her shoulder.

Mario did, indeed, have his hands full with cooking and dispatching orders in rapid-fire Spanish to the army of nieces and nephews who carted the soft-sided tamale carriers all over town, spreading joy like a Tex-Mex goodwill army. One after another, he sent them out the door with a carrier full of tamales and an ear full of instructions. One by one, they smiled and nodded and left for their routes.

He dusted his hands and then grabbed a warm foil-wrapped package to hand to me. "You eat?"

It was clearly too early to eat tamales, but I didn't want to be rude, so while I talked I peeled back the foil. "G-Ma is worried about the robberies," I said.

He nodded vigorously. "*Sí, sí*, the Bandits." Then he pounded on the metal door to his right, which rang impressively. "New door." He moved faster than his short legs should have allowed over to the drive-thru window and ran a hand around the edge. "New window." He pointed across the room at the walk-up window. "New window." Then at the back door. "New door. New — new —" He snapped his fingers together a couple of times, looking for the word. "New alarm system." Then he spread his hands wide and smiled. "No Bandits!" He swiped his hands back and forth. "No Bandits here."

I smiled back. "Excellent. It looks like you're well protected."

He nodded. "*Si.*"

"Would you mind just kind of keeping an eye on the motel office? Call the police if you see anything suspicious?"

He looked confused.

"You know, if a car pulls up and four guys with black masks get out? Call the police?"

He smiled. "Si, yes, I'll call the police." Then he held up a finger and gave me a wink. "For the Bandits. But not for the *chicas.*" He nodded.

"The *chicas?*"

"*Si.* The *chicas.*" Again with the wink.

"What *chicas?*"

He grinned. "The *chicas.*" He held up a hand and rubbed his thumb against his first two fingers in the universal symbol for money. "Virgie's finally making some money. I won't report her. She needs the money." Then he laughed. "Now she make so much, she crooked the bank."

Viv frowned. "What are you even saying, she crooked the bank?"

"She put so much money in," Mario said with a grin, sliding his hands forward as if laying something on a shelf. "The bank, it goes crooked." He leaned to the left from his waist, as if demonstrating a tall building going "crooked."

"Really," I said. I looked over at the motel parking lot. As I watched, a pickup pulled into the lot and a fat man with filthy jeans and an oily ball cap got out, followed by a woman wearing very short shorts and very high heels. At nine o'clock in the morning.

"What the heck?" I said.

"Is that — "

"*Sí*," Mario said with a bright nod. "It is."

I marched out the door and across the parking lot, Viv right behind me.

I pounded on the door the fat man and hooker had just gone into.

A scrambling noise, followed by silence.

I pounded again. "Hey!" I shouted. "Open up!"

"Don't tell them to open up!" Viv hissed at my elbow. "What if that fat man is already naked? We don't need to see that!"

"What do you want?"

"I'm Virgie's granddaughter. She needs to talk to you."

"Ummm, I'm a little busy at the moment."

"Just for a second," I said. "It won't take long."

The door opened a crack. "What?"

"How much are you paying for this room?" I asked, because the first question that came to mind (what are you doing in there?) seemed suddenly very stupid.

"What's it to you? We settle up with Virgie at the end of the night. She hasn't been shortchanged yet, and she's not gonna be." She looked at me, then at Viv. "Now, if you don't mind, I have work to do."

"*Work!?*" I shrieked. "This is my grandmother's motel!"

"I got that," the woman said.

"You can't — can't *work* at my grandmother's motel."

"You wanna watch?" Then she laughed. "Actually, you can, but it's extra."

"Ewww!" Viv said.

The door slammed.

I pulled my phone out of my pocket. "Windy, call Bobby Sloan with the Lubbock PD."

"You're calling the cops?"

"Of course I am. There is an actual crime in progress right now."

"Eww," Viv said again. "Stop."

"Sloan," Bobby said when he answered the phone.

"Bobby, there is a prostitute working at my G-Ma's motel right now."

"Well, I'll be," he said flatly.

"Are you going to do something?"

As I spoke, another pickup pulled up, this one small, and a man about as thin as the last one had been fat got out, and opened the door for a woman wearing skinny jeans and a tank top. They went into the room two doors down from us.

"Bobby, this place is crawling with — with *chicas*," I whispered into the phone.

"Is this the place out on Clovis Highway?"

"Yes," I said. "You remember it. You've been here before." Once when I was fourteen, I'd been staying with G-Ma, and Bobby had come in to get a room for him and some girl from Idalou. I had cried for a solid week and scratched 'Salem Sloan' and 'Mr. and Mrs. Bobby Sloan' out of the margins of all my school papers.

A couple came out of the room next to us and walked toward an old boat of a car parked near Viv's new Caddy.

I gaped, then gave Viv a look, like, "Can you *believe* this?!"

Before the motel room door could close all the way, I stuck my foot in and held the door.

"Get a forensics team out here ASAP," I ordered Bobby. "I'm going to preserve the evidence."

The room was as old and depressing as all of the rooms, made more so by the rumpled sheets on the bed. I did not want to think about what was on those sheets. While we waited for the cops, I called G-Ma.

"Where are you?" she said. "We're going to be late."

"G-Ma, I think there is a prostitution ring using your motel as its base of operations."

"There most certainly is not."

"I think so. There was a couple here just a minute ago."

"Them? They come in all the time. They're just a couple in love, cheating on their spouses."

"Just?" I said. "How is that okay?"

"Who am I to judge?" G-Ma said with a sniff. "Who are any of us?"

"G-Ma, the point is, I seriously think they're prostitutes. I called Bobby Sloan — "

"You called the cops!? Are you serious!?"

"Yes, I did. You need to know — "

"I don't need to know anything! I don't need to know the personal lives of all my customers! All I need to know is whether or not they can pay their bill, and these girls pay their bills."

I looked at Viv. "Oh my gosh. I think she knows already."

"You did notice that not one of these girls has checked in at the front desk."

I had not noticed that, but Viv was right. As I watched out the window, another vehicle pulled up, straight to the room. The girl already had a key.

"She can't be in on it," I said. "Can she?" I put the phone back up to my ear. "You can't possibly be on on this, G-Ma. That makes you, like, a madam or something."

"It makes me nothing of the sort. All I am and all I have ever been is a business owner." Then she gasped. "Oh my god! It's the pigs!"

Two patrol cars pulled up.

I hung up the phone. "Calling Bobby might have been the wrong decision," I said.

Things went quickly downhill from there. Motel doors were flung open, there was lots of girl screeching and men bellowing. One man cried. G-Ma got stompy and said something to Viv, who said something back, and before I knew it they were both in handcuffs. A white van pulled up, and while I was trying to explain which ones were the prostitutes and which ones weren't, I ended up in handcuffs, too.

"I'm not a hooker!" I shouted at the cop.

"Me either," said the hooker sitting beside me in the van.

"But seriously," I said. "I am a — a *granddaughter.*"

"Me too," the hooker said. "Let me out of here, I gotta grandma."

I shut up then, intent on making sure Bobby Sloan paid for this.

We were booked and fingerprinted, then put into a holding cell.

"I want to speak to Bobby Sloan," I said to the officer who shut the door behind us.

Bobby took his sweet time getting there. It was as if he had another job to do.

He looked delighted to see me, though. Behind bars.

"Salem. Oh, and look! It's Viv, too. " He laughed and clapped, looking back over his shoulder as if to give whoever was back there an ovation. "I heard you two were picked up for soliciting." He stopped as if to take in the scene.

"You know we don't belong here," I said hotly. "I'm the one who called it in."

"You what?" The girl who sat beside me in the van now raised up from where she'd been leaning against a wall. "You *what?*"

"I didn't call it in," I said. I turned to Bobby and hissed through clenched teeth. "Get me out of here."

Viv took one look at the girl who was now breathing steam in very near proximity to my neck and decided to launch her own form of defense.

"Mommy, are we still going to the circus?" she asked in a creepy imitation of a little girl voice.

G-Ma sat on a metal bench, her legs crossed, one foot tapping the air furiously. She set her laser-beam glare on a rotating schedule between me, Viv and Bobby, then back to me. She seemed to bear no animosity for the girls who were conducting illegal activity on her premises.

"Seriously, Bobby, you have to get us out of here. Do you have any idea how much trouble I'll be in if I'm arrested again? I'm off probation in two weeks. Two weeks!"

"But, you already were arrested. That's why you're in here.

Back up, Felicia," he said to the girl who, I noticed, had an alarmingly well-developed upper body.

Felicia didn't even consider backing up. She looked down her nose at me with a sneer and sniffed. "You. *What?*"

"Bobby, you know this is wrong. Even a jerk like you knows that this is too far for a joke."

Bobby leaned forward. "I'm sorry, a what like me?"

"I mean, you know, it's funny and all, but this could get serious real quick. This has serious consequences. I'm just now getting out of trouble for my *actual* misdeeds. I don't want to get back in over something I didn't even do." I had to latch onto my self-control real quick, because my voice shot up and I realized I was going to cry if I didn't shut up. I could not cry in front of Bobby and I could not cry in front of these women. Only Felicia looked dangerous at the moment, but I imagined they could all become like sharks with blood in the water if I showed any weakness.

"Please," I begged. So much for not showing weakness.

Viv stepped close to the bar. "Listen to me, Officer." Her voice was clipped and her eyes flashed. "I will have your badge before this is through." Like a scene straight out of a weekly cop drama.

I was beginning to learn Viv's looks, though. She was pretending to be mad, but she was actually loving every minute of this. She could afford to. At her age, she could become an internet sensation overnight for being arrested for prostitution. She could afford bail and a good lawyer, and she could spin it all into a good joke by the time she was through. She'd probably end up on The Ellen Degeneres Show or something.

Me, I would end up with fines I couldn't pay, another couple years of weekly probation visits, and go on peeing in a cup every couple of weeks.

And I had been so close to freedom!

Bobby looked at Viv with exaggerated concern. "Careful, ma'am. Don't go having any heart attacks or anything."

That might have been a cruel thing to say, except Viv *did* fake a heart attack one time to trick Bobby into giving us information. I think he was still a little annoyed that we'd gotten the best of him on that murder case. And on the next one. That solving both cases had been complete accidents really didn't seem to be stroking his ego any.

"Oh, believe me, I feel one coming on. And it's going to be a doozy. Six figures, at least." Then she looked around the room and remembered she was supposed to be a bit delicate in the head. She gave a simpering laugh. "Let's play hopscotch."

"Harley!" Bobby called over his shoulder. "I think we need to call psych eval back here!"

I stepped between them. "Okay, look, you two. Let's not make this any bigger than it needs to be. Bobby, you've had your fun. You know we don't belong in here."

"I don't belong in here, either." Felicia crossed her arms and glared at me. Like I could do anything about it!

My insides quaked. I looked at Bobby. "Maybe Felicia doesn't need to be in here either. And you know Viv and G-Ma for sure don't need to be in here. Look at G-Ma, Bobby. She's about to blow a gasket. She hasn't done anything. She didn't know what those girls were doing." God, please tell me she did not know what those girls were doing. Please?

Out of reflex, I looked up at Felicia, hoping she didn't dispute me.

Felicia didn't say anything. I risked a glance over at G-Ma, who might as well have had a stormy black cloud over her dyed-crimson hair. The other girls who'd been brought in with us looked mostly bored. While I watched, one stretched out and said, "Wake me up when it's time to go."

Bobby crossed his arms over his chest and put one hand to his chin. "Now, tell me again what happened. Start from the beginning."

Felicia blinked and waited.

I swallowed. "I — um, well I'm sure I don't know. We were just getting ready to pick up G-Ma to go to Amarillo, and all of a sudden there were cops everywhere and we were being arrested." Something occurred to me, something that I had seen from a weekly cop drama. "Hey, aren't you supposed to have some kind of — some kind of cause to arrest us? Like, you have to hear an actual offer of sex for money or something. I think there's a rule, right?" I turned to the girls. "There's a rule?"

"There's a rule," the one lying on the bench said, her eyes still closed.

I tried to remember if anything I'd said, anything any of us had said, could be misconstrued as an offer of sex for money. All I could remember, though, was outrage and Viv and G-Ma at each other's throats and general pandemonium.

I chewed my lip and studied Bobby. "You know what, Bobby? I don't think they really had a right to arrest us. I think this is a false arrest." Was that a thing? I wish I had Windy here to ask her.

"You think?" Felicia asked. She gave Bobby the side-eye.

"You think?" Bobby asked. His brows drew down in exaggerated concern. "Gosh. That's really bad. Let me go talk to the guys and see what they have to say." He strolled to the end of the hallway, then turned around and came back, his key already out. "Looks like you're right. You're free to go."

He opened the gate while I glared at him, outraged. The woman on the bench groaned and said, "Man. I can't never catch fifteen minutes to get some rest." She hauled herself up with effort and stumbled after the others.

Viv fell into line with the working girls and G-Ma and I brought up the rear. I was so freaked out that I didn't even know what to say. He really had brought us in on absolutely nothing but my phone call. Could this be legal? Should I really call a lawyer?

The three women and Viv were discussing how they were going to get back to the motel so they could pick up their vehicles. Viv said she'd call a cab for the three of them.

"G-Ma and I can come in another one," I said.

"Not so fast," Bobby said, his hand on my shoulder. "You and your *G-Ma* need to just cool it here for a few minutes."

Bobby showed us into his office, then closed the door and sat down behind his desk. "So, was that fun?"

"What is wrong with you?" I hissed. "Is this your idea of a joke?"

"This is my idea of a warning." He looked hard at G-Ma. "We've been hearing rumors about your place, but we haven't had a chance to set up an operation yet. But what you just saw this morning — that's how it will go down. Quick and painful. Except it won't end with you going home with your granddaughter next time."

G-Ma looked mad enough to spit blood. "You have no right — "

"If I did what I have a right to do, you'd be in jail right now. It wouldn't take much to set up a sting and get you roped in good and tight. You're not a foolish woman. You've run that place for a long time and never got into trouble before. You don't want to go blowing it all now."

"I don't want to lose it all to the Bandits now, either, but who's going to stop that from happening? You're sure as heck not doing anything about it!"

His lips flattened and he gave a short nod. "Believe me, we're working on it."

"That's all we've been hearing for weeks. *Working on it.* How hard is it — "

"How about we focus on the matter directly in front of us for the time being? You — " He pointed at G-Ma. "You need to watch yourself. Run a clean business. These Bandits are going to be caught and things are going to be back to normal. You don't want to be left with a rough trade you can't get rid of."

I sat looking back and forth between them, trying to keep my jaw from dropping. Suddenly, I was struck by the memory of watching black and white TV with G-Ma at the motel. That old western, Gunsmoke, was one of her favorites.

My G-Ma was Miss Kitty, the madam. She even had the poofy red hair.

And Bobby probably would not have minded being compared to Marshall Dillon. He knew he was hot, and he had his share of authoritarian swagger. I would gladly have sucker punched him in the gut for locking us in that cell, if I didn't know that (1) it would probably hurt my fist more than his rock hard abs, and (2) he would put me back in the cell, for real this time.

I was also weirdly grateful to Bobby. Maybe he *had* protected

G-Ma from a real arrest. He probably could have found a way to do it without rounding me and Viv up, too, but still.

He let us go with one more finger-pointing at G-Ma, then had a patrolman drive us back to the motel.

G-Ma was silent on the ride back, her mouth chewing over something that wasn't there. I occupied myself by looking at my phone and trying not to think about how mad Mom was going to be at us for being late to her Very Important Brunch.

CHAPTER FOUR

Road Trippin'

Viv was all smiles when we got out of the patrol car. "You two ready?"

I turned to G-Ma, expecting her to come up with a few more procrastinations, but she just frowned and moved, head down, toward Viv's Crystal Frost Cadillac.

Dora waved from the motel window, and G-Ma lifted one hand slightly in reply, then yanked open the back door. "Let's get going," she said.

As I suspected, Viv was pumped up from the morning's adventures. "I'll tell you one thing, the Lubbock jail could use a fresh coat of paint! That was a disgrace. Not to over-share, but I've seen the inside of jails in Cleveland, New York City, Oklahoma City, Los Angeles, and Las Vegas. You'll never believe which one was the nicest. Go on, guess."

Yep, she was prepping for Ellen. "Which one?" I said.

"Cleveland!" She slapped her thigh and laughed. "Can you believe it? Vegas was the worst, of course, but Lubbock wasn't much better. The vomit smell wasn't quite as strong, but I could still smell it. Need new paint and some disinfectant in that place."

G-Ma was on the phone in the back seat, alerting Mom to our delay. I checked my phone. Exactly one hour behind schedule. Not bad, considering everything that had transpired.

"Did you tell her what happened?" I asked.

"Of course not. She's around her fancy new friends. What's that dinging noise?" G-Ma grumped from the backseat.

"Yep, I remember when they put ATMs in the jails," Viv said as if she hadn't heard, swinging the Caddy off the Loop and onto the Interstate.

She had to have heard, though. Now that G-Ma brought it up, I could hear an occasional ding, too.

Viv sailed down the ramp and onto the Interstate. "Gosh, ATMs. I remember the first time I used one of those, too. Felt like something from a space movie, you know? Money, right out of the machine. Crazy."

Ding.

"What *is* that?" G-Ma shouted.

Viv shook her head. "Hmmm...what? Did you say something?"

"I said, what is that dinging sound?"

"Dinging sound? What dinging sound?"

Ding. *Ding ding.* Ding.

"That dinging sound," G-Ma said. "Oh, I'm sorry. You probably have some hearing loss at your age. There's a dinging sound — "

"My hearing is just fine, thank you!" Viv snapped. "I hear the dinging sound. You are probably unaware of some of the technological innovations of the last decade or so." She tapped the steering wheel with a satisfied look. "That, my friend, is state of the art technology right there."

"But for what?" I asked. I had suspicions of something quietly going horribly wrong under the hood, and the ding was probably supposed to alert us to this malfunction. But we didn't know what it was and we'd only find out when we were in the middle of the desolate prairie between Lubbock and Amarillo and the Caddy burst into flames.

"For the optimum driving experience, of course." Viv gave me a look that said she questioned my intelligence.

Ding.

It wasn't as if there was any set rhythm to the dings. Or, I noticed as we hurtled down I-27, a set volume. If I strained, I could hear a series of short, soft beeps. Then a louder one. Then nothing. Then three long beeps.

"It sounds like some sort of Morse code," G-Ma said. "State of the art, my —"

"It's not Morse code!" Viv narrowed her eyes and said into the rear view mirror. "It's — it's actually a new technology, a kind of — of subliminal technique to induce a feeling of calmness and clarity for the driver."

"A what?" G-Ma's mouth hung open in disbelief.

"It's a subliminal signal that aids in driver focus. It's called a clarity enhancer. It induces a feeling of calm and focus."

"It induces a feeling of annoyance," G-Ma said.

"It's frigging soothing!" Viv said. "It *is!*"

I looked closely at her. Her knuckles were white on the steering wheel and her chin jutted out.

Things became suddenly clear to me. She didn't know what the noise was, either, and that's why she was taking the car to Amarillo. She'd made up that calibration tale because she didn't want to admit there was something wrong with her new toy, not after I'd tried to talk her out of the impulse buy.

A nice person would have had her back.

"Is that right?" I asked, cocking my head and pretending to contemplate the idea. "That's really interesting."

"It is," Viv insisted. "I mean, these Cadillac people have thought of everything. They've — "

Ding ding ding ding ding! Frantic this time.

"That sounded dire," I said. "Does that mean your mind was wandering off and the machine was roping it back in."

Viv laughed — through clenched teeth — and hissed, "Silly. How would I know how subliminal programming works? I just know that it *works.*"

A loud ding this time, and higher pitched. More of a beep.

I leaned over to study the dash, looking for warning lights. Nothing was glaringly wrong, but then, if they were relying on the ding to get the message across, there wouldn't be.

"I don't feel soothed *or* focused," I said.

"It's not for you. It's for the driver. It's calibrated to every driver's...you know. Brain waves."

I gave her the side-eye. I could see that the temperature gage was normal, though, and that made me feel better.

I straightened back up. "I should stay away from that side of the car. It might get my brain waves mixed up with yours and send us into the ditch or something."

"I don't see what good it does to have the driver be focused if it makes the passengers want to shoot somebody," G-Ma groused.

"Are you kidding? That's when a driver needs to concentrate most!" Viv shot back.

Frantic dings.

Viv's eyes bulged and she shifted in her seat, gripping the wheel. She barked a high-pitched laugh. "I mean, the driver has to be able to focus through every distraction. It's — "

Ding-ding-ding. Dong.

"It's paramount to safety."

"So, the dings help the driver concentrate through the distraction of the passengers, who are driven crazy by the dings?" I asked.

She narrowed her eyes at me.

"Just trying to get it clear in my mind." I pointed to the complex control panel on the sleek dashboard. "What about all these fancy buttons? What else can she do?"

This turned Viv's mood. She got all excited about the "driver assist" this and the "4G" that.

"Are you recording this?" I asked. "Your driving performance?"

Viv's smile faltered. "Nah." She leaned back and flapped a hand. "I didn't want to mess with it."

"Couldn't figure out how to work it, huh?"

She frowned in the general direction of the rear view mirror. "It's a very sophisticated system. It's not like you can just sit down and get it all down in an hour."

She spied a button. "Oh! You know what I'm anxious to try out?"

"Aggressive acceleration?" I guessed.

"Got it in one."

I tugged at my seatbelt to make sure it was secure, and recalled from the glossy brochure how many airbags were on the passenger side of the car.

But instead of speeding up, Viv slowed down.

"What are you doing?" I asked.

She checked the rear view mirror again. "Waiting. There's one of those new Camaroes coming up behind us. Lime green, good lord. Probably some kid barely old enough to shave," she said.

I knew the truth, though. The only reason she didn't have a lime green Camaro was that it hadn't occurred to her to buy one. If the salesman had shown up at Belle Court with a brochure for a lime green Camaro, G-Ma would be squeezing her grumpy butt in the back seat of it on the way to Amarillo at that very second.

Viv slowed even more, giving the Camaro a chance to catch up.

"We're already late," G-Ma said from the back seat. "We don't have time for games."

The car dinged again.

"Besides, are you sure this thing is even going to make it there? I'm not sure I feel quite confident — "

Maybe it was the fact that the Camaro was now even with us, and maybe it was meant to shut G-Ma up, but Viv punched the gas.

G-Ma slammed back against the seat, but her poofy hair

cushioned the impact.

I tried to look over at the Camaro, but the g-forces held me pinned to the seat. I swiveled my head to the left.

"Slow doooowwwwn," G-Ma howled from the back seat. "You're going to kill us all, you crazy bat."

Viv hunkered over the steering wheel, cackling like a mad old lady. Which, of course, she clearly was. She leaned forward enough that I could see not one but two guys barely old enough to shave, and another one in the back seat. They were all laughing at Viv.

Between the two front seats, a young, beautiful girl with thick brown hair and flawless skin leaned forward, looked at Viv, and burst out laughing.

I sneered at her. Little punk. She had no idea who she was messing with.

The girl looked at me, then at G-Ma clinging to life in the back seat. She put her hand over her mouth, still laughing, and pointed at us.

"Punch it," I said.

"No!" G-Ma said. "Stop it! Let me out! I'll walk home!"

Viv was in her own world anyway. She did something on the dash and then slammed her foot down again. We sprang ahead.

The boy tried to keep up, but couldn't. I spun around to watch them get farther and farther behind us, both cars flying past the road markers. I didn't even want to know how fast we were going.

On the other side of the highway, a patrolman passed and swung toward the grassy median.

Viv and I looked at each other, wide-eyed. I thought I had heard somewhere that, if you were going above a certain speed, you could actually get arrested instead of just a speeding ticket. Viv was probably there.

I checked over my shoulder again.

"There are two of us," Viv said. "He can't catch us both." She punched the gas again.

"Stop!" G-Ma screamed. "I'm going to tell him you are holding me against my will!"

But Viv was carried away with her victory, laughing at the thought of that young punk getting a speeding ticket while she got away.

Her euphoria carried her as far as over the next hill, five miles away, where another patrolman waited for us.

"You can outrun the cop, but you can't outrun that radio," G-Ma said spitefully from the back seat.

"I don't even care," Viv said. "That was worth it." She began to pull to the side of the road before the patrolman even had his lights on.

She was less philosophical when she found out how much the ticket was going to cost her, and the patrolman started asking questions that hinted that she might be too old to be driving.

"How long has it been since you've had your eyes examined?" he asked. "How about your balance? Have you been having any trouble keeping your balance lately?"

I could have told him that Viv was healthier and stronger than he or I would ever be, she was just a really bad driver. Instead, I suggested that maybe I should drive for the rest of the journey.

Viv gave me a look, but agreed because that seemed the quickest way to get back on the road, and if she put up a fight he might suggest a compulsory retest for her driver's license.

G-Ma was somewhat pacified by the thought of me driving, too, although she was clearly not having the best day of her life here. She sat in the back seat with her blood orange lips clamped tight, her dark shades on and her arms crossed. She didn't utter another word for the rest of the trip.

Unfortunately, without the roar of the engine and G-Ma's screams of terror to drown it out, the dinging sound rose back to the fore.

Which was a shame, because the Cadillac driving experience was, indeed, an experience. Smooth as silk, effortless handling. I felt like I was driving on a cloud. The first thing I did was set the cruise control at the speed limit, because it would have been much too easy to go rocketing along just as Viv had done.

"This handles like a dream," I said. I briefly wondered if there was any way I could afford a nice used Cadillac to replace my car. But anything I could afford would have to be twenty years old and had maybe been through a fire.

I tried to figure out how I could work the "love never fails" angle to get a car like this. But no matter how I came at it...no. No, there was no legit way I could use "love never fails" to manipulate God into giving me a new Cadillac. Sigh.

But the dinging. I tried to tune it out, but it was at the perfect pitch to cut right through everything. Viv turned on the satellite radio and found a pop radio station, turning it up.

"What are you doing?" G-Ma said from the back seat. "Salem needs to hear that dinging so she can stay focused."

"Oh yeah," Viv said with a scowl.

So we listened to the dinging.

Every once in a while, Viv would sigh, as if in contentment, and look out the window. "Isn't this nice? So relaxing."

Her left eye had developed a twitch.

So it was that we found the neighborhood for Mom's brunch. G-Ma puffed up and smoldering in the back seat, Viv with a rictus smile and an eye twitch, and me depressed. It was going to be even harder to drive whatever I could afford after driving this.

We turned down a shady tree-lined road across from the golf course and wound through the narrow curvy streets. The houses were big, the yards were green and impressively landscaped, and the streets were squeaky clean. It was a far cry from the rent houses I'd grown up in around Idalou, Texas.

"Not as nice as Lubbock's golf course," G-Ma said with a sniff. "Look at that. Brown spots all over the green."

I couldn't see any brown spots, but whatever.

"And who the heck is driving these little hatchback things? Hopefully it's the hired help. In Lubbock, they make the hired help park around back." She grumbled some more, then gasped. "Would you look at that?" She leaned forward and squinted. "Good Lord. I can see the Walmart sign from here." She cackled. "Can you believe that? I'll bet those snotty old millionaires around here about crapped their britches when they built a Walmart within viewing distance of their mansions."

I chuckled along and nodded as if this was, indeed, the very height of irony, but I was thinking a few other things. One, that G-Ma's own view included a parking lot that was mostly potholes, a four-lane highway that was mostly abandoned, and a grocery store that advertised (in a sadly unironic way) "cold dranks." And two, it really was no wonder my mother had turned out the way she had.

Said mother was digging through something in the backseat

of her own car as we drove by. "There she is," G-Ma said as I pulled to the curb.

I wasn't crazy about the way my heart hammered. She was my mother. Seeing her shouldn't make me nervous.

But it did.

I covered it up by smoothing my shirt a thousand times and looking around the neighborhood. Yep, we were out of our league.

"Mother," Mom said, walking toward G-Ma with her arms outstretched. My mom was a cute, petite thing, her hips still as narrow as a teenage boy's, silver bracelets dangling from her slender wrists, her hair cut in a cute bob and frosted a tasteful, muted blonde.

"You must take after your dad," Viv said.

I let that pass, because I'd often thought the same thing. I'd never seen the man, though, so I couldn't say for sure.

I'd never heard her call G-Ma "mother" before, but I guessed in the scheme of things, it wasn't a big deal. I smiled and raised my arms for her next hug.

She turned to me with a blank smile on her face. Her eyes widened in comprehension — she hadn't recognized me.

It had been about two years since I'd seen her. In that time I'd quit drinking, and the moment I'd quit drinking I'd started eating. Quite a lot, actually. Even with the thirteen pound loss I'd chalked up, I was still far enough on the plus side that I was unrecognizable.

"What hap – " She stopped herself before the "What happened to you?!" could complete itself. "You've...changed," she said.

"Tell me about it," I said. "It's been a while."

"Yes, well..." She gave a flat, worried-looking smile and flapped her arms as if to say, *Nothing I can do about it now.*

I introduced Viv.

Mom greeted her like she'd been taking lessons from the *Texas Lady's Complete Guide to Over-the-Top Etiquette.* "Aren't you such a doll to bring them all the way up here! A living doll! I don't know how I can ever thank you!" She hugged Viv.

Viv's eyes met mine over Mom's shoulder and I shrugged. I kid you not, the woman used to get drunk at my high school football games and never used less than three swear words in a sentence. If you looked up "crass" in the dictionary, you would see her face. She would rather have eaten dirt than thank anyone for anything. But here she was, playing the gracious socialite.

Viv backed away and said, "Yes, well, no big deal. I was coming anyway. Speaking of which, I have to get to the Cadillac place so they can, uh — "

"Calibrate your software?" I reminded her.

"Yes. That. I'll be back in a couple of hours."

As she drove off, G-Ma said, "I am not riding back with that woman. I'll walk home first."

Mom gave her a pained smile. "Of course you're not, Mother. We're having a girls weekend and then I'm driving you back tomorrow afternoon. Now, let's go in so you can meet everybody."

G-Ma lifted her chin and squared her shoulders, hitching her forty-pound white leather handbag onto her shoulder.

Mom kept casting worried glances at me behind G-Ma's back, but no matter how hard she looked, I remained fat.

As Mom introduced me and G-Ma to the gaggle of women who awaited us inside, I smiled a stiff smile and wished I had insisted that Viv stay for a while. She had grown up poor ("we were so broke we couldn't even pay attention!" she liked to say) but she'd had no trouble acclimating to Easy Street. She wore $800 shoes and carried $1200 handbags like I carried the $20 one I got on sale at Target. Viv was handy to have around when you needed someone to be brave around scary society women.

And they were scary. They smiled huge smiles and drew out their vowels and acted like they hadn't seen each other in months. They kissed each other's cheeks and complimented each other's shoes, new cars, successful children and grandchildren. At least four of them had the exact same hairstyle and frost job that Mom had. They reminded me of older versions of the cheerleaders in high school — girls so terrifyingly perfect that I had little choice but to get drunk and make fun of them.

With getting drunk no longer an option, and Viv not handy to make snide remarks to, I had to make do with Mom and her imitation-is-the-sincerest-form-of-sucking-up hairstyle, and G-Ma, whose resentment at the well-to-do-ness around us was glaringly obvious. Between the two of them, I decided the best I could do was hold tight to love-never-fails and try to make it through. I would smile and nod and give only yes or no answers.

"Now Cappy, I know what you're waiting for," said one of the frosted women. It was Neely Bates, I remembered from the article I'd read. The woman herself. She lifted a tray of glasses onto the bar. "You've held out until almost one o'clock. That's a record for you."

The crowd laughed and Cappy (apparently, from the saucy way she cocked her hip and stood with one elbow out) tilted her chin before she took a glass off the tray.

"What on earth makes you think this is my first drink of the day? You might notice that Brenda and I have taken care of the biggest part of the mimosas already."

The drinks themselves were beautiful. Golden champagne with a ripe, juicy raspberry lying in the bottom of each glass. Bubbles fizzed charmingly to the top. Neely placed another tray of mimosas — short a few glasses, in fact — beside the first one. So many tall, fluted glasses.

That would work, I thought, my mouth watering as I stared at them. I could have one of those, two of those, maybe, and this awful party would get a whole heck of a lot better. I could relax. I could go with the flow. I could even make a joke or two and contribute something to the event, instead of being the girl with the pained smile frozen to her face.

Instead, I followed the rest of the women out onto the terraced backyard, where the summer heat cooperated by being filtered through the huge trees and the fountain burbled refreshingly in the background. We settled into black wrought iron chairs with fat cushions in red and gold stripes. When a girl came around with a tray bearing drinks, it took everything I had to pick up an iced tea.

I pretended to listen to the conversations around me, and laughed when others laughed. But what I was really doing, I realized after a few minutes, was studying this group of women whose husbands were bankers and CEOs, and who probably appeared in the newspaper for every gala event. I was trying to figure out how, exactly, my mother had infiltrated. It just didn't make sense.

"So, Salem. That's an interesting name," said one of the four frosted women. This one had red glasses, I noted frantically, terrified I would say something to betray the fact that they all looked the same to me. "Is there a story behind it?"

"I'm named for — "

"Oh, honey, don't go telling them that story," Mom interrupted. She twisted in her seat with an embarrassed/pleased coquettish smile and said, "They don't want to hear silly old conception stories."

"Conception stories!" one of the women guffawed. A few more laughed.

Mom turned to Neely and said, "Suffice it to say, her father and I lived in Oregon for a while, when he was in grad school."

The women giggled as they were expected to do.

My own jaw dropped, though. One time I'd asked my mom where she got my name, and her drinking buddy Susan had hooted and said, "You were named for your mother's first love — menthol cigarettes!"

For a second my heart thrilled at this new information. I had been conceived in some far-flung (from Lubbock), exotic (to someone from Lubbock) locale to my young mother and her husband the grad student!?!

But of course it was a lie. She'd made up this slightly embarrassing "fact" to cover a more embarrassing one — she used to smoke — and be the kind of person who named her kid after cigarettes.

My first clue should have been the "honey." She never called me that before. Ever.

I cast a glance at G-Ma to see if she was taking it all in, but she had her chin stuck out and appeared to be mentally calculating the value of the swimming pool and hot tub beside us.

"Do you work, Salem?" someone asked.

For a second, I could only stare. I assumed she was asking if I was sponging off the government. But then I realized that she came from a world where women didn't necessarily have to work. It was a choice.

"I'm a dog groomer," I said without thinking. I instantly regretted it. If you're looking for ways to impress people, well...let's just say that telling people you're a dog groomer is iffy at best.

"You're still doing that? I thought that was just until you..." Mom trailed off. I think she'd been about to say something like "finish your doctorate" or "get that 501c3 charity off the ground" or something equally preposterous. "I thought that was just temporary," she finished lamely.

"It is. It's just until I retire."

A few more dutiful laughs.

"Surely Tony will want you to quit work, though. I mean, you don't need to." She turned to Neely. "Her husband is a very successful businessman. Building services. About forty employees."

So Mom had learned to Google. And she had heard — probably from G-Ma — that Tony and I weren't as divorced as I'd told her we were. I wondered how many times she'd practiced saying "building services" so she didn't slip and say "cleaning services."

Mom was right about it being successful, though, and I got a glimpse of one of the reasons she'd wanted us to get there early. I was undoubtedly supposed to play up the successful husband and play down the dog grooming.

"I'm a successful business owner, too," G-Ma piped up. Heads swiveled in her direction. We'd all kind of forgotten she was there since she hadn't done more than grunt a couple of times since we arrived.

What she said next could have been just a thing she let slip, unmindful, or it could have been something specifically designed to throw a wrench in Mom's little we're-perfect-too tableau. I'll never know for sure, but my money was on the latter.

"And I'm not a madam, no matter what the Lubbock police say."

The group went completely silent. In the background, the fountain splashed. Mom's mouth fell open.

I looked around contentedly, relieved that G-Ma's slip had pushed mine far to the background.

"She gets...confused," Mom said weakly.

"I do not," G-Ma insisted. "I ought to know if I'm operating a brothel or not."

"You ought to," I offered.

"Those girls never told me a thing. I mean, if I was a madam, I'd be getting a cut, wouldn't I? And I haven't made a dime off all that nonsense."

"Well, I mean, aside from the increased traffic."

"Yes, but...they never gave me a cut of their profits." Her scowl deepened, and I realized this could be what bothered her most.

"Umm, Virgie, what are you talking about?" Cappy asked, leaning forward, eyes bright.

"It's just a little misunderstanding this morning," I said. "No big deal. There were some rumors going around about the motel —"

"Rumors!" G-Ma cried. "Were those rumors of handcuffs on your wrists? Am I going to be paying my lawyer with rumors?"

The table erupted at once.

"Handcuffs?"

"Were you arrested?"

"Lawyer? Mother, what on earth — "

"You're a *madam?*"

I couldn't help but notice that this had been said with much more admiration than my career had seemed to elicit.

"I am not a madam, and she — " She pointed a knobby finger at me. "She is *not* a prostitute."

When the din finally died down, I turned to Mom — who, by the way, had given up on the "honey" business and was glaring at me with murder in her eyes.

My heart thudded, and I had to remind myself that we were in a crowd of witnesses, and I was now quite a bit bigger than she was. Actual physical harm was unlikely. I'd grown up knowing what that look meant: Run. Run now, and run fast. So it was kind of hard to keep my own wits about me.

"It was really all just a misunderstanding," I said. "There has been a gang of armed robbers running around, robbing businesses."

"I heard about that," one of the regular-haired women said. "My sister lives in Lubbock and says it's terrifying. These animals are hitting every business on that side of town."

"They sure are," G-Ma said. "They'll hit mine next, I know they will."

"That's why I'm going back tonight instead of staying here. So I can keep an eye on the motel," I explained.

"That doesn't explain the handcuffs and the arrests," Cappy said, her eyes entirely too bright with excitement.

"Well, it's just that, the entire side of town is going a little crazy and people are getting spooked by all kinds of nonsense.

Seriously. It's crazy. Someone called in a complaint — " which was the actual truth — "So the police came. But we weren't arrested."

"But you were handcuffed?"

I ignored that question because it was kind of hard to reconcile the handcuffs part with the not being arrested part. "We had to discuss things with the police, of course. You can't just ask them to wait until Monday on something like that, right?" I laughed and shook my head, searching my brain frantically for something to steer the conversation. "I'm telling you, Lubbock is crazy. We don't even have a Krunchy Kreem yet."

That did it. The group launched into all the ways Amarillo was superior to Lubbock, and the tension eased as individual conversations sprang up among the group. Then the food was brought out, and I focused on mentally calculating the units value of all the food.

After a few minutes I darted a glance back at Mom.

Her smile was stiff, and I could practically see the wheels spinning behind her eyes. I checked my phone. Only one hour and fifteen minutes to go.

Viv, bless her heart, showed up fifteen minutes early. I said quick goodbyes all around and kissed Mom on the cheek, assuring her I couldn't wait for our girls weekend the next week.

"How did it go?" Viv asked as we pulled onto Georgia.

"Could not have gone worse," I said cheerfully. "And your errand? I don't hear any dinging."

"They fixed it. But now..."

"Why are we going so slow?" Car were whizzing by us.

"We're going the speed limit," Viv said with a frown. "We're going above the speed limit, actually."

"The other cars are passing us like we're standing still."

"I know!" Viv wailed. She hated for cars to pass her — took it as a personal affront. "But the speed limit is forty and I'm already going forty-five."

I leaned over and looked at the dash. It said forty-five alright.

"You should at least keep up with the traffic," I said when we were almost rear-ended by a pickup.

"I can't! I can't get two speeding tickets in one day. They'll take my license for sure."

I started to offer to drive again, but I certainly couldn't afford a ticket. I leaned back in my seat and decided to enjoy riding with Viv and not feeling like I was taking my life into my own hands.

"You know what I realized, right before you came? I realized I was looking for some clue as to how my mom ended up in that group."

"Did you meet the guy?"

"No, it was women only. But from everything I heard about him, he seems fairly normal. A little irresponsible, maybe. This will be his fifth marriage."

"That's not irresponsible, necessarily," said the five-times-married Viv. "You don't really know the story."

"I'm not judging, I'm just saying that was the only thing..." I stopped because I couldn't think of anything safe to say next.

I took out my phone and pulled up the Windy app. "I wonder how well this thing works up here," I said. "They told me the network wasn't very big."

"Search for something. Search male strip clubs."

"Windy, find us some male strip clubs," I said into the microphone.

Windy hesitated and then beeped. "Are you looking for a den of iniquity where men take off their clothes and women act loose and immoral?"

"Exactly," Viv crowed.

"I'm sorry, that location is not found." Windy sniffed sanctimoniously.

"How about Krunchy Kreems, then?" I asked. I had not had the champagne, and I had limited myself to one tiny spoonful of chicken salad because it looked like it was more mayonnaise than chicken. It had been delicious, but thoughts of my next weigh-in at Fat Fighters had me determined to steer clear of it. Doing so had used up my entire store of self-control. Weigh-in or no, it seemed too much to ask for me to be so close to fresh Krunchy Kreems and not get at least one tiny donut.

"Two locations near you," Windy said helpfully. "Turn left at the next exit, then go down three blocks."

"You're very helpful, Windy," Viv said.

"Thank you. Items often searched with Krunchy Kreems include Fat Fighters. The nearest Fat Fighters location is one block west of the Krunchy Kreems."

"Never mind," I said with a sigh. Windy had gone and ruined it for me. "Let's just go home."

I leaned back in the seat and closed my eyes. The sight of the mimosas lined up on the counter kept popping into my head. Those berries looked so fresh and juicy. Luxury. Fun. Decadence.

I tried to think of something else. But those glasses kept popping up. The truth was, that lunch would have been a lot more fun if I'd had a couple of those tall fluted glasses. No matter what anyone said about being powerless over alcohol and it being a liar, the truth was, that lunch would have been better. Yes, I would have thrown away a solid year of sobriety. Yes, I would have had to fight my way back out of a huge hole. Who knew how far down I would dig myself this time? Maybe too far to ever get out.

But today would definitely have been better.

"Does it ever freak you out," I asked, my eyes still closed, "To think you're *never* going to drink again? Ever?"

"Of course," Viv said. "Sometimes.

"I mean, *never*? Never, *ever* again can I have a drink?" For some reason I couldn't fathom, the concept was more frightening to me now than it was a year ago, when I first got sober. It was as if I'd gotten a tiny taste of the long view, and it was longer than I thought.

"That's why they tell you to focus on one day at a time."

"Because if we think about it, we'll realize that we'll never, ever be relaxed or have fun or get to feel like a normal person again, with a normal life." Suddenly the one-day-at-a-time mantra seemed more like brainwashing than a way to handle life.

"Tell me who's normal," Viv said.

I had to think about that one. Of course, Tony was the first person who came to mind.

But was he? I mean, who stayed married to someone for ten years and didn't even talk to them? Didn't even try?

Had Tony ever sat back in his seat, freaked completely out not at the thought of never drinking again, but of never *dating* again? He couldn't possibly have known that I would one day sober up and become, prospectively, real marriage material. So he had faced the very real possibility that he would reach the end of his life, and his entire sexual experience had been a six-month period during his seventeenth and eighteenth years. And he'd accepted that. He'd been okay with that.

That was just not right.

"Do you think Tony has...issues?" I asked Viv.

"Oh, heck yeah," she said without a second of hesitation.

This irritated me more than it probably should have. "What do you mean?"

"Healthy, handsome young man like that? I mean, he's hot. Women have to be throwing themselves at him right and left? And he stayed married to you?"

"Hey!" I said.

"I'm not saying he shouldn't be married to you, but you weren't married to him, right? I mean, you weren't living like you were married to him. You hadn't talked to him in years. So, no nookie for the guy for a decade, and he could have. He could have signed the divorce papers and been done with it. But no. That's not normal."

"So what do you think it is? Do you think he's got some emotional issues, seriously? Or...you don't think he's gay, do you?"

"You'd have a better idea of that than I would. Did he seem gay to you?"

"Definitely not." But that kiss. So...chaste. He hadn't been like that when we were married. He had just turned eighteen then, and I was already pregnant, which took some of the worry out of it. He would have been perfectly fine having sex three times a day. "It's just...he doesn't seem all that interested in me."

"Well, I'm sure it's weird. Maybe he's thinking about all the men you said you were with while you two were separated."

I leaned back again. "Maybe." I didn't like to think about that, but there wasn't a lot I could do about it at this point. I *had* been with a lot of guys. I'd thought we were divorced. I thought I was free to do whatever I wanted. I kind of resented Tony for not making it more clear to me that we were still married, but at the same time I knew that wasn't reasonable. He'd sent me a lot of letters. I'd thrown them straight into the trash, figuring if he wanted to talk to me he could be a man and come talk to me.

Tony wasn't like that, though. He would not force himself on me. He wouldn't even come close to forcing himself on me. He would wait on me to make the first move.

I had to be the leader, I realized. Me. I had to be the leader, and I had to be sober.

This was doomed.

CHAPTER FIVE

Trapped

The two-hour drive back to Lubbock took three and a half hours. I kept looking at the speedometer and it said eighty-five. But every car on that highway passed us. Three separate times Viv had to swerve to the shoulder to avoid being rear-ended.

"There's something wrong with your speedometer," I said.

"There is not," Viv snapped. "It's just that people drive crazy these days."

"Whatever. I was supposed to be home by now. I have to pick up Stump and then go back to the motel to spend the night."

"I'll swing by there and take you back."

"Okay, but you'll have to circle the block until Rosa leaves, then bring Stump back. G-Ma will probably grill Rosa when she gets back. I want Rosa to have plausible deniability."

So we swung, slowly, so slowly, by Trailertopia and picked Stump up from Frank. I was so tired from our epic journey that

I didn't try to make conversation. This was fine, because all Frank cared about was whether or not I would be making dinner. Upon learning that I was not, he headed cheerfully out to the barbecue rib joint down the street.

"Now, just let me out and drive off," I told Viv as we neared the motel. A car horn blared behind us and I braced for impact, but they swerved around us, honking again and screaming out the window at Viv.

"Viv," I said as I opened the car door. "Seriously, you should call that salesman guy and tell him they did something to the speedometer in Amarillo. They can probably fix it in no time."

"It's not broken!" Viv snapped. She looked exhausted. "You know how crazy people are. They're all crazy, driving around like their hair is on fire."

"Okay. Just drive around the corner and wait, and I'll call you as soon as Rosa leaves."

That took all of ten seconds, probably because I was almost two hours later getting back than I was supposed to be. Rosa didn't complain, though — she just grabbed her purse as soon as she saw me and headed out the door. "No robbers, no customers." She gave a bright smile and a wave and was gone.

I stood in the office doorway, pretending to survey the empty parking lot. I waited until Rosa's car drove out of sight, then pulled my phone from my pocket. "Okay, it's safe now. Bring Stump."

She was there within twenty seconds.

"That didn't take long," I said as I reached in and pulled Stump out. I had expected to wait half an hour or so for her to make the block.

"I pulled into that used car lot next door." She patted the

dashboard. "Gave those other cars something to aspire to."

"You want to hang out for a while?"

"Are you kidding? You might be able to fool your grand-mother about Stump, but she'll be able to tell as soon as she opens the door that *I've* been here, and she'll be in a tizzy."

That was, sadly, true. G-Ma would be able to detect a hint of Shalimar lingering in the air, even if it were one part in a billion. And she *would* be in a tizzy.

"See you tomorrow, then, and we'll go car shopping?"

"It's a date. I hope you get some rest."

"Oh, this place is blown, now," I said, shifting Stump to my other hip. Rosa said there were no customers all day. Now that the prostitution gravy train has ended, Stump and I will watch some TV and go to bed without talking to anyone."

It happened pretty much that way. The only person who showed up was an old man who wanted a free room. No way I was going to incur G-Ma's wrath with that, but I did take some pity on the guy and gave him ten bucks. I pointed him in the direction of the shelter, which he knew very well, and he left looking reasonably happy.

I wasn't quite as relaxed as G-Ma, who greeted middle-of-the-night guests in her fuzzy pink bathrobe and thought nothing of it, but I wasn't going to spend the night in my jeans, either. When Stump yawned for the third time and glared at me, I went to the bathroom and changed into sweatpants and a T-shirt, locked the door, and turned over the "Ring Bell For Service" sign in the window.

"Okay, let's hit the hay," I said.

Stump had far less compunction than I did about sleeping in G-Ma's bed. I turned back the flowery bedspread and she jumped in (it took three tries), burrowed under the covers, and sniffed a wide circle, then emerged, tossing the sheet with her nose.

"Scoot," I said, sliding in beside her. "This is weird, huh?

I'd spent many a night in the motel, but I'd had my own twin bed in what was now a storeroom. There was no place to sleep but G-Ma's bed, but it still felt weird. The room hadn't changed one bit during my lifetime. She had the same bedspread, the same curtain, the same ceramic woman's head on the same embroidered runner on her dresser. That woman used to creep me out.

Stump did not care. She flopped and scratched around until she had a nice little swirl of covers around her head, with just her little black nose sticking out and one eye barely visible. I snuggled in beside her, and she was snoring within thirty seconds.

I left the closet light on and the door cracked, because I didn't want to wake up in the middle of the night and freak out about where I was. I was fairly sure I wouldn't be able to sleep at all, until I woke up to Stump's growling.

I freaked out, even with the closet light on. I was still mostly asleep when I leapt out of bed, careened around the room and knocked G-Ma's woman-head off the dresser, catching it before it hit the floor.

"What? What? What?" was all I was capable of saying.

Stump rose and growled again, the hairs on her back rising.

It was probably just a customer, I told myself as my heart thudded and I my knees went weak. Stump wasn't used to people coming to our door in the middle of the night. I picked her up and hugged her to me, hurrying to the front door.

There was no one there. Stump growled again. Then she barked.

I jerked so hard I almost dropped her. "Stop it!" I said. Okay, whined.

I took a deep breath. One of us needed to get a grip.

"Stop," I said calmly. "Everything is fine."

She relaxed, then tensed again and barked so hard she made herself choke. My heart hammered. What a couple of hardcore chicks we were.

I checked the lock on the door, then remembered the back door and went to check it. It was locked, too. I listened hard for whatever it was that was setting Stump off.

Nothing. Occasional traffic on the street.

I was just about convinced that nothing was wrong when she stiffened, pointed her nose toward the parking lot, and howled.

Oh, good Lord! The horror of that sound. Like being in the eye of a tornado or something.

I reached for my phone. I had dialed 9-1 when I remembered what G-Ma said about being grounded. Did that count for me, too? And what would I say when I got them on the phone? My dog is howling and I'm scared? I'm sure they wouldn't care for that. Plus, I had been — however falsely and unfairly — arrested for prostitution at this very motel about fifteen hours ago.

"Hush," I said to Stump, but it was more of a plea than an order. She didn't hush. She shoved at my stomach and lunged toward the door, raising an unholy cry.

I tiptoed to the window and peered out again, craning to see the sidewalk close to the door. What if someone was hunkered down right there out of sight, just waiting for me to open the door so he could pounce?

I deleted the numbers. I stared at the phone. Tony?

I had his number pulled up and was about to hit the send button, but couldn't bring myself to do it. What if nothing was wrong? Probably, nothing *was* wrong. I couldn't see anything out of the ordinary. If there was a bad guy hiding out of sight, he was either very small or a contortionist. Stump was probably just freaked out because we were away from home.

If I called Tony, he might think I had dragged him down there just to get his attention. Plus, if I wanted to focus on making myself appealing to Tony, probably a seedy motel trapped in 1984 wasn't the best setting for it.

Stump subsided into a low growl and I began to relax a little. Maybe she'd just had a bad dream.

She jerked stiff, then began a baying howl that had me in tears of terror.

I punched in Bobby's number.

"Sloan," he answered.

"Look, I know it's probably nothing but it might be something and you are the police and it's your job to help me."

Bobby sighed. "Salem. What's going on?"

"I'm at G-Ma's motel by myself and Stump keeps barking and growling like she hears something or — or *senses* something."

"She probably senses a leftover cheeseburger in the wastebasket of the next room."

I gripped the phone between my shoulder and ear, then covered Stump's ears. "This is not the time for fat-shaming my dog, Bobby. I really am kind of freaked out. Can you just drive by here and check it out real quick? Please?"

"Your grandma is gone?"

"Yes, she's in Amarillo with my mom."

"And she took her gun with her?"

"Yes," I said. I kind of wish I had it with me, although I was almost as afraid of accidentally shooting Stump as I was of any bad guys.

"You do know we have patrolmen all over part of town, right? If you call 9-1-1 — "

"We're grounded," I said. "G-Ma's raised too many false alarms."

"You can't get grounded from 9-1-1, Salem. Not even you and your grandma."

Maybe I should call them. It was late, they probably weren't too busy —

Stump leapt out of my arms and set up a furious bark at the door.

"Holy crap," Bobby said. "Is that your little fat dog?"

"Please, Bobby," I said. "She's hearing or seeing *something*. If it's the robbers you will never forgive yourself..."

"Give it a rest, Salem, I'm half a block away."

"You are?"

"Just stay inside and I'll look around."

Within ten seconds, I saw his car slide into the parking lot and bang his undercarriage on the giant pothole outside Room 3. I winced. Hopefully he wouldn't blame me for that.

He drove slowly around the parking lot, over to Mario's restaurant, past the metal fence that used to encircle the swimming pool, and then back toward the office. He pulled up before the front door and shut off his lights.

I opened the door, assuming that if a bad guy *was* hunkered down there, Bobby would have shot him by now.

"Nothing?" I asked.

"Nothing," he said. He grinned, taking in the bare parking lot. "Business looks slow."

"Don't let G-Ma see you smiling about that. But yes, it looks like you've scared the trade away for a while."

He bent and scratched at Stump's ears. "What are you doing causing trouble, huh?"

Stump moaned and arched against his hand. I probably would have done the same thing if I wasn't a married woman. But I was, so... I just watched and sighed inwardly.

"I'll walk around and take a look, but I don't think you have anything to worry about. I didn't see — "

Stump gave a high-pitched yelp and took off across the parking lot.

"Stump!" I shouted, running after her in my bare feet.

Bobby's footsteps pounded the asphalt behind me. "Good Lord, I had no idea she could run that fast," he shouted.

"Me either," I huffed.

She hadn't run that fast, in fact, since I'd had her. Then again, her exercise was mostly just sniffing around my postage stamp yard at Trailertopia, and the short trek from our front deck to the car. Running was never a necessity.

She was hauling butt now, though. She disappeared around the back of Mario's restaurant. Bobby passed me. He had longer legs and boots on his feet.

We rounded the back of the restaurant. The back door stood wide open. Stump was nowhere to be seen.

Bobby whipped around and motioned for me to stay back.

"But Stump!" I hissed. I moved around him to go after her.

Bobby grabbed my arm and hauled me back. "No, Salem! You

don't know who's in there."

"Exactly!" The thought of Stump alone in there with some bad guy had me frantic. "We can't just leave her in there."

A crash came from inside. I gasped and lunged toward the door.

Bobby gripped my arm again. "I'm going to call for backup. We'll wait until — "

"That will take too long." I stepped around him again. "Stump!" I whispered frantically. I patted my legs. "Come here, baby! Stump!"

Bobby made a sound in his throat that I was pretty sure meant he wanted to throttle me. He handed me his phone, then pulled his gun and a flashlight from his belt.

"Call 9-1-1 and tell them to get a patrol car out here. I'll see if I can see anything."

With trembling hands, I fumbled with the phone while Bobby slid along the wall toward the open door.

Just like TV cops, he poked his head around the doorway with his gun and flashlight drawn. He swept the room quickly, then entered.

My hands were shaking so hard, I kept pulling up icons that weren't the phone. I listened intently for another crash, the yelp of a dog that had just been kicked, or — and my knees went weak at the thought — the sound of a gunshot.

I finally got the phone pulled up and struggled for half a second to remember the number for 9-1-1. I dialed it and put the phone to my ear, struggling to think of the words I would say once I got the dispatcher on the line.

Nothing. Nothing from the phone, and nothing from the restaurant. The world went silent around me as I waited an eternity.

I pulled the phone away from my face. I had forgotten to hit send.

I reached to do that when:

"Oh, dear God," came Bobby's voice from inside.

My heart stopped. "What?" I shrieked, running inside. "Stump!"

Bobby flipped on the overhead light as I came in.

I blinked against the bright light, expecting to see carnage everywhere I looked. Instead I saw Mario's kitchen, same as it ever was, and Bobby, tucking his gun and flashlight back into his belt. Stump stood over a pile of garbage spilled onto the floor, licking her lips. She'd turned over a trash can.

I stood, breathing heavily and trying to keep from fainting. "What? What happened?"

In answer, Stump let out a belch.

Bobby jabbed a finger in her direction. "That! What in the world is wrong with your dog?"

In another second, I realized what he was talking about. The most unholy smell emanated from Stump's belch, instantly filling the room with stench.

I darted glances around, my mind still focused on bad guys with guns.

"It's clear," Bobby said. "Whoever closed up must have left the back door unlocked, and your dog smelled day old tamales at a hundred yards."

I dropped to the floor beside Stump and hugged her, tucking Bobby's phone into my pocket. I regretted the hug instantly; the squeeze made Stump belch again. I was weak with relief and needed to breathe clear air.

Bobby stomped around the kitchen, clearly lacking the perspective to see what a joyous occasion this really was. Oh well. His loss.

I stood and began to pick up the trash. "I know she wasn't just after the tamales, Bobby. She woke up from a dead sleep. She heard something, and not just the siren call of stale Tex-Mex."

Bobby mumbled something and kept on checking out the empty building. He walked outside to check out the door. When he came back in, it was with a completely different demeanor. "The back door's been jimmied."

"I knew it!" I bent to scratch Stump's ears. "Good girl. You scared the bad guys away."

Bobby went into the storeroom and pounded on the back wall beside the back door, testing something out.

"Is there a broom and mop bucket in there?" I'd picked up all the big trash, but there was a mixture of corn meal, coffee grounds and something I didn't want to determine left behind.

"Yep," Bobby called back. "Still water in the bucket, in fact."

That didn't sound very hygienic. I picked up Stump and carried her with me toward the storeroom to get the mop. "You're a proper hero, Stump my girl."

Bobby's phone rang and made me jump again. I pulled it from my pocket and fumbled with it, trying to hold Stump with one arm and get the phone right side up with the other.

My toe knocked up hard against something beside the door. "What the — " I yelped. I couldn't see what it was with my hands full, but I'd hit it hard enough that it slid aside.

"Your phone is buzzing," I said to Bobby, hopping around on one foot.

Bobby turned toward me to take the phone, then his eyes went wide. "No!"

The bad guys must be right behind me! I spun, the phone flying out of my hand.

The room was empty, save for a big metal door swinging shut.

Bobby's phone plopped into the mop bucket.

One by one, realizations slammed into me.

The door was locked from the outside.

My phone was back in the motel office.

Bobby's phone was in the mop bucket.

No one knew we were there.

The restaurant was closed on Sundays.

I was trapped with Bobby Sloan.

I needed to pee.

I grabbed the knob and turned with everything I had. The door rattled, but didn't give.

"Here." Bobby edged me aside and fiddled with the knob. He bent over and peered at it.

He muttered a bad word. "That's a good lock."

"Mario just replaced all the locks, inside and out."

"Because of the robberies." He bent and fished his phone out of the mop bucket, fixing me with a look.

"I'm really sorry," I said. "You screamed and I thought the bad guys were behind me."

"I didn't *scream*," he said, indignant, shaking the phone so nasty mop water flew around the room. "I just said no and then you threw my phone in the mop bucket and locked us in this room."

"I panicked, okay? I'm sorry. I'll buy you a new one." I wiped droplets of mop water off my arm and wondered if he would accept a Llano Wireless "Smart Enuff" phone. Not likely.

"That's issued by the department. They'll replace it, but they won't be thrilled about it."

I hadn't been thrilled at the thought of it coming out of my pocket, either. I told myself I really was paying, via my tax dollars. So it was okay. Except for the trapped in the room part.

Bobby's gaze traveled around the edge of the door, and he ran a hand along the hinges.

"You have your radio or something, right?"

Bobby remained silent, staring. Then he turned and stared in a different direction. He didn't say anything, and that made me nervous.

He *didn't* have a radio or something. The room was small, one very strong metal door and three cinder block walls. No escape.

"Well, I know one thing. I'm not going to panic," I said, feeling the panic build exponentially with every breath I took. "We might be trapped in here, but it's not like we're going to die. I mean, what's the worst that could happen?"

"We could suffocate, the place could catch fire, Mario could have a family emergency and decide to close down for a week, we could starve to death — "

"Shut up," I said.

"Already? I didn't even get to tornadoes." He looked around. "Although with these walls, we'd probably make it out of a tornado."

"Come on, tornado," I said sarcastically.

Bobby shoved a shoulder into the metal door. It didn't budge.

I sat on a box that held five gallon buckets of cooking oil.

"We won't starve. We're in a room full of food."

"All of it in cans. Unless you want to drink that oil you're sitting on."

I looked around in growing dismay. He was right. There were giant industrial size cans of tomatoes, beans, oil, spices. None of them were accessible without a can opener.

Because I didn't think I'd be much help in the escape phase of this adventure, I put my energies into the area of survival. Surely there was something here two people could subsist on.

Styrofoam cups. Corn husks. Were those edible? Stump would undoubtedly try, if we were in here long enough. Corn meal. Salt, pepper and cumin. What the heck, Mario? Not a single bag of Doritos?

"Help me find a screwdriver," Bobby said.

Under the circumstances, I decided to forego the lecture on using the magic word. I set Stump down and slid aside cans and boxes, looking for anything resembling a tool of any kind. Nothing on the upper shelves. I bent and searched the lower shelves.

"There's a box of order books. This looks like menus from the old Italian place. Here's a pen. Can you use that?"

"For what? To write a note and slip it under the door?"

"You know, if you were MacGyver you would build a communication device out of two bean cans, a couple of paper clips and a good wad of spit, and get us out of here." I knelt and slide aside a few more boxes — all containing heavy duty aluminum foil. If worse came to worst, maybe we could make a tool out of aluminum foil.

"Yeah, well, if you hadn't thrown my phone into a bucket of water, I could call someone and do the same thing. No spit required."

"I was making a joke, and I didn't throw it. I dropped it when you screamed." I sat clumsily on the concrete floor. Stump immediately jumped into my lap and curled up, resting her broad nose on my thigh and watching Bobby. "No need to begin the blame game."

"That's what the losers always say."

"Are you calling me a loser?" I smiled to let him know I really *was* only joking, that it was okay to give me a hard time. It was my fault, after all, that we were in this mess. Despite the fact that I had dropped the phone because he scared me, I felt seriously guilty about it.

He looked at me for a moment in that silent way of his. It was funny. Tony was silent a lot, too, but usually with Tony I had no idea what he was thinking. With Bobby, I at least had a fairly good idea the words "pain in the neck" were in there somewhere.

"How about we concentrate on how we're getting out of here?"

"Great idea. Think positive." Something positive occurred to me on the whole 'loser' front, and I said, "Besides, it's highly unlikely we would be in here long enough to starve. I could do with a few days of fasting, personally. I could go to my next Fat Fighters meeting and finally beat Trisha."

"Who?" Bobby asked, his brow furrowed as he bent and rummaged under a shelf. "Oh yeah, on TV. She's lost weight, right?"

I frowned, deciding that Bobby and I were now even.

"Yeah, well, I will too if we're stuck in here for a few days. So there." I hadn't actually meant to say that last part out loud.

"So there what?" He dropped to the floor beside me, his

hands across his upturned knees. He reached over and scratched Stump's ear, which she pretended not to love.

"Nothing. I just... I've lost weight too."

"You have? Good for you."

"You have, question mark?" I said. "Question mark?"

"What?"

"Why the question mark?"

"Why the...what?"

"You said, 'you have?' with a question mark. Like, 'you *have*?'" I might have hit the 'have' with more emphasis than was strictly necessary.

"Okay."

"Because it's hard to believe, right? I mean, I still look like the same old fat Salem. Not an ounce of difference."

"Oh." He opened his mouth, then closed it again. "Yeah, ummm....sorry, but no, I hadn't actually noticed."

"Oh, don't be *sorry*. Why would you be sorry? Just because I'm working my butt off, trying to literally *work my butt off,* and it's clearly not working. I don't know why it's not working. It's working for Trisha. It works for everyone else at Fat Fighters. Why not me?" I shrugged and pulled my face. "Who knows? I didn't eat the donuts. I took one pathetic spoonful of chicken salad. I didn't drink the champagne."

That got his attention. "Champagne?"

"I didn't *drink it,"* I said, furious that that seemed to be the only thing he cared about. Anyone cared about. "I didn't drink the frigging champagne. I wanted to. I could have used a drink at the moment. Just one drink. I didn't even want the donut. Well, okay, I wanted the donut. But only because I couldn't have the champagne. And now I can't have either one. Good grief."

Bobby clearly had no idea how to react to anything I said, so he just sat and stared.

We sat in silence for a long moment. I told myself to keep quiet. I was stressed, frustrated, and guilty. Nothing that came out of my mouth just then was going to be good. I needed to exercise some self-control in the area of just keeping quiet.

"It's just that," I said, because I had used my entire supply of self-control on champagne and Krunchy Kreems, leaving nothing left to control my mouth. "Sometimes I have a really hard time remembering why drinking was so bad. I mean, really? Was it *so* bad? At least I was skinny then."

"Salem, give me a break. You act like you're as big as a house or something."

"I *feel* like I'm as big as a house."

"Come on."

"Seriously. Okay, I know I'm not as big as I could be. But...ugh!" I looked down at where my waist used to be. "I am so uncomfortable in my own skin. I feel like my real body is buried underneath this — this foreign — *crap*!" I spread my thumb and forefinger to cover the roll of fat over the waistband of my jeans. "Look at this! What is this? Who left this here? This isn't mine."

At the look Stump was giving me, I said, "Not you, baby. Mommy loves you." I kissed the top of her head.

"Everybody gains a few pounds as they age, Salem. It's no big — "

"Age!?" I shrieked. *"Age?"*

Stump raised her head and gave Bobby the stink-eye.

"Not age," Bobby said.

And then, because I was already teetering on the precipice of hysteria, and because Bobby's face had taken on a decidedly *backpedaling furiously* kind of look, I burst out laughing.

After a few seconds, Bobby laughed, too. But he looked mostly confused.

"You looked so scared," I said, pointing at him as I tried to catch my breath.

"*Yeah*, I was scared," he said, without a second of hesitation. "We're talking a woman's weight and age. I'd rather face down a meth junkie with a loaded semi-automatic."

I punched him in the shoulder, but I was laughing too hard for it to cause much damage.

I laughed until I fell over and Stump tumbled, grumping out of my lap. I braced myself against the hard concrete floor, then wiped tears from my eyes and tried to right myself.

"I'm sorry," I finally said, when I could breathe normally again. "I'm in kind of a weird place at the moment."

He looked around the room. "Yeah, me too."

"No, I mean..." What did I mean? "I'm just...having a hard time adjusting to this new persona. I'm used to being the hot young thing. I need some time to acclimate to matronly."

Bobby snorted. "You're still a hot young thing, Salem."

"Oh, please. You're only saying that because you're constitutionally incapable of being alone with a female and not flirting with her."

"Am I?" He looked at me then, his eyes suddenly so intense on mine that I was unable, once again, to breathe.

My eyes locked to his. I could have made a joke. I could have rolled my eyes and punched him again. I could have blown the moment off.

Instead, I sat frozen, pinned by his gaze, unable — or unwilling — to break the spell. Part of me was afraid he was joking, making fun of me. But another part — a much stronger part, at the moment — wanted this to be real so I could, somehow know — *See? I'm not a total gargoyle now! Some people are still attracted to me.*

We sat, side by side and completely silent. His gaze flicked to my lips, back up to meet my mine, back down to my lips.

I kept waiting for the punch line. It didn't come.

"Who says you're not hot?" he asked, his voice low.

I swallowed, unable to find my voice. "Well, I mean...no one's actually *said* it. Out loud."

He stayed silent, his eyes intent on mine.

"It's just...you know. Tony. My husband." I threw the word out there to throw a wet blanket over the whole hot-as-fire scene that had suddenly sprung up around us.

It didn't work. Bobby raised one eyebrow slightly, as if he couldn't believe this to be true. "No?"

I swallowed. "He doesn't seem...well. He doesn't seem to think I'm particularly irresistible."

"Well, he's a fool then."

I knew I should defend Tony. Or make a joke. *Yeah, well, he stayed married to me, so he can't be too bright, haha.* I needed to do that. Tony deserved for me to do that. He didn't deserve for his wife to be sitting here, seriously contemplating kissing this handsome specimen of a man. Again.

We'd kissed before, Bobby and I, after I'd been released from the hospital when Tony's aunt had tried to have me murdered. And lots and lots of times in rich teenage fantasy life. I'd spent a major portion of my childhood quite certain I would someday be Mrs. Bobby Sloan.

But at that moment, my need for affirmation was a tiny bit

greater than my need to defend Tony. I didn't protest. I just sat, silent, breath held. A voice in my head wondered, *Why not? Tony's not going to kiss you. He doesn't want you. He's staying married to you out of some fundamentalist sense of obligation, but he doesn't really want you. If he did...*

If he did, he would look hungrily at my lips the way Bobby did now. And Tony did not look at me like that, ever. He had not looked at me that way since we were eighteen and living like a real married couple.

And I was here, and I had not drunk the champagne and I had not eaten the donut, and I was trapped and trying not to freak out, and the promise of Bobby's lips on mine his arms around me...it felt like something good and thrilling and...not boring. It felt like living. Actual *living* instead of just trying to hang on and run out the clock until bedtime, so I could sleep and dread the thought of white-knuckling through another day of sobriety.

This moment felt like the old Salem. The Salem who lived in the moment and didn't worry about what anything "meant" or if it was "smart." The Salem who did what felt like the right thing to do at the time and didn't think beyond that.

I missed that Salem, I realized. I missed not giving a rat's butt about consequences. The old Salem might have overdue bills, but she also had fun. She went out if she felt like going out. She ate Fritos if she felt like eating frigging Fritos. She didn't second guess everything. She didn't think about whether or not someone was attracted to her, because she was too busy deciding if *she* was attracted. If she was, well then. Giddyup.

And she was attracted to Bobby.

I stifled a groan and struggled to stand, moving to the other side of the room. It was no good. I wasn't going to make out with Bobby, even if he was looking at me like the last slice of chocolate cake. I couldn't do it to Tony. Again.

"Cut it out," I said. "We're stuck in here together and it's not going to be good for either of us if you keep looking at me like that. No way it would end well."

He raised an eyebrow. "No? In my plan it ends *very* well."

"You know what I mean."

He stood and crossed the narrow space between us with a couple of slow steps, his eyes still on mine. He really was quite dreamy. I was growing increasingly uncomfortable, but not because I feared him. He wouldn't force himself on me. I simply had no confidence in my own level of self-control. And there was this part of Bobby's neck, right at the spot where his shirt collar parted, that my lips very much wanted to touch.

I put a hand out. "Stop."

He froze and his eyes went wide.

Ha, hadn't expected that, I thought. I was sure he didn't get turned down very often. Poor thing.

I opened my mouth to say something to soften the blow to his ego.

He spoke first. Loudly. "Hey! That's sheet rock!"

"That's...what?"

He'd stepped around me and was reaching through the shelves to tap on the wall behind them. "Sheetrock! I thought all these were cinder block, but this is — " He drew back and looked around again. "What's on the other side of this wall?"

I couldn't keep up. I just stood with my mouth open.

"The restrooms, right? Yeah, restrooms. And then around to the dining room. So we could..." He began to pull cans off the shelf. Then he turned to me. "Come on. Help me get this shelf cleared off." He pulled at the back of the shelf. "Ha! Not bolted in. Good!"

He moved more cans from the shelf and placed them on the floor at the other side of the room. Not knowing what else to do, I followed suit. Stump stood between us looking as confused as I felt.

Once we'd gotten the heavy stuff cleared off, Bobby tugged on one end of the shelves. With a heavy scrape, he managed to swivel them around so one end protruded into the middle of the room. He stopped and looked at me. "Come over to this side. I'm going to kick this wall out and we'll have to squeeze through the struts."

I didn't like the sound of that. "Mario's going to be furious that we've wrecked his place." I slid around the end of the shelf and patted my leg for Stump to follow.

"He'll be happy to find out we stopped the bandits." Bobby leaned back and kicked the heel of his boot hard against the wall. A dent appeared in the sheet rock. He kicked it again. Another dent, deeper this time. He kicked again. And again. Soon, sweat stood out on his forehead and he was breathing heavily.

Stump whined and looked at me. I shrugged and whispered "Shhhh," into her ear.

Finally, his boot broke through the wall. Bobby grabbed an edge and tugged it back. A bigger chunk broke off.

This part I could help with. I set Stump down and knelt to pull at another piece further down the wall. It was chalky and harder than I expected it to be, but I felt triumphant when a piece broke off in my hand. Once we'd made a big enough hole, Bobby stuck his head through and surveyed what was inside the walls.

I sat back, looking at the size of the hole. Would I really fit between the struts? I cringed at the thought of getting wedged in there like Winnie the Pooh in that hole in the tree.

Bobby tugged at the wall and peered down the wall. "Good. It looks like the pipes are down there. So I can kick through here and not run up against a sink or toilet. Stand back."

He grabbed onto the struts and kicked hard against the other side of the wall. This one was much easier, I supposed because the wall was coming out the same side it had been nailed to. I picked Stump back up and huddled against the other shelf, watching as Bobby's muscles bunched and flexed against his shirt.

With a crash, the wall came apart and we saw through to the small room on the other side. Bobby kicked aside the crumbled sheet rock and held out a hand to me. "Hand me your dog, and then you can come through."

I handed Stump through, feeling sorry for her. She looked confused and annoyed. *I feel you, honey,* I thought.

I stepped up to the wall, then stopped. "Why don't you go around and see if you can open the door from the other side?"

"The shelves are blocking that door now," he said. "Come on, just come through here."

"I can fit through there fine," I said, although the space between the shelf and the opposite wall didn't look any bigger than the space between the struts. I just didn't want to squeeze through anything with Bobby watching.

He sighed and turned, leaving Stump in the middle of the rubble.

After he'd gone, I turned sideways and shoved myself between the struts. It wasn't as bad as I'd feared, but I was still glad to leave no witnesses.

"Never mind," I called out to Bobby as I stumbled through the broken sheet rock and picked Stump up. "I'm through."

We went back to the motel office. Bobby called the police and I called Mario, apologizing for waking him at three in the morning. Stump went to G-Ma's bed and whined until I picked her up and put her into the covers. She turned around a few times, plopped down with a snort, and promptly fell asleep.

I knew how she felt. After the cops and Mario showed up, and I explained to Mario what had happened, the exhaustion of the day and the night suddenly collapsed on me. I really didn't want to be around when Bobby showed Mario what we'd done to his storeroom and restroom.

"Do you mind if I stay here with Stump?" I asked Bobby. "If she's alone she freaks out and makes this horrible keening, wailing sound. She destroys stuff, and I don't — "

"No problem," Bobby said. "Get some rest."

After they'd left, I stumbled to the bed and collapsed beside Stump. I'd never been so grateful for anything as I was to know I didn't have to work the next day.

CHAPTER SIX

But Who Shot JR?

Stump and I hung out at the motel all day on Sunday, watching church on TV in our sweats from G-Ma's green velvet rocking recliner. Not a single soul came to the office, and I was starting to feel a little guilty that I had been the one to put an end to G-Ma's cash flow. It needed to end, of course, but if I had it to do over again, I would prefer to be uninvolved.

As I would have preferred to be uninvolved with Mario's now necessary renovations. He didn't seem to hold a grudge, though. He waved cheerfully to me as he drove up, listened as Bobby explained everything, and nodded as if he had walls kicked in all the time.

Rosa came over so I could go home and shower in my own bathroom. I told her to call me if G-Ma wasn't home by six, so I could come back.

Stump was so glad to be home, and I was super relieved when Rosa called and said G-Ma had made it back just fine.

"Why didn't she call?" I asked Rosa.

"I don't know, hon," she said. "I told her you were coming back if she didn't make it home by six, so she asked me to call you."

I hung up and made a face at Stump. "Yep, she's mad at me."

Oh, well.

Monday was a new day, though, and after spending all day Sunday doing practically nothing, I felt plenty rested up to face the day of work and then car shopping with Viv in the afternoon. I was especially glad when I saw that Bear and Charlie Clancy-Pigg were coming in to be groomed that day. There were a lot of dogs that I felt a personal affection for at Flo's, and Bear and Charlie were two of my favorites. Bear had come first, a red Pomeranian that Charlotte Clancy-Pigg had had when she was still just Charlotte Clancy, before she got married and saddled her normal name to her husband's not-quite-so-normal one. After a year of marriage, she and her husband got a little Chow-Chow puppy they named Charlie. Bear was bigger than Charlie at first, but of course Charlie outgrew him within the first couple of months. Neither of the dogs ever seemed to pick up on that fact, though. Bear was the boss, and Charlie only too happy to play the goofy beta dog. If the shop wasn't too busy, we'd let them out to play in the floor. Charlie would flop over on his back while Bear jumped in the middle of his chest, growling and worrying the fur there like he was about to gut the big guy.

I hoped I would have time to play with them without Stump witnessing it. Stump had a jealous streak as wide and black as her snout. If she got jealous, she inevitably peed on something of mine within the next twelve hours. She had to refresh her mark on her territory, I supposed.

I was talking to Doreen about my car situation when Charlotte came in with the boys.

"I'll bet you can find something decent on Craigslist," Doreen said. "My boyfriend's brother found a ten-year-old Buick Skylark for only two thousand dollars."

I thought of the money I had saved up. It was supposed to be for emergencies, not for a car. But when your car craters and you need it to get to work every day, didn't that constitute an emergency? I hated the idea of forking over everything I'd saved for a car that might very well also crater within the next month itself. Then I would have another emergency and no emergency fund.

"I'm going to look around at the used car lots and see if I can find something with reasonable payments," I said. "Surely I can negotiate something." Although who was I kidding? I was rubbish at negotiating anything.

"Salem, are you looking for a good used car?" Charlotte said as she handed Bear over the counter to Flo. "My brother-in-law just opened a used car lot on Clovis Highway," she said. "He could probably find you a good deal."

"Is that the one right next to the Executive Inn?" I asked.

Charlotte laughed. "Yeah, that's the one. The Executive Inn, right?" She rolled her eyes. "I hate to think the kind of executives who stay at that dive."

"Yeah, that's my grandmother's place," I said, smiling to ease the awkwardness. I was of the same opinion as Charlotte. G-Ma had changed the name from Traveler's Motel to Executive Inn, in the hopes of attracting a better clientele, but clearly more was needed.

"Oh, sorry," she said.

"Don't be sorry, I agree completely. It's a dive. She's had it for thirty years and it's been a dive the entire time. I think when she bought it she thought she really could attract an executive crowd, but within a couple of years she was just trying to keep the doors open and make a living."

"Your brother-in-law is brave to open a business out there," Doreen said. "All those robberies. You couldn't pay me to go over there now."

"You don't know the Pigg family. They're so devoted to that side of town, it's like their own little fiefdom. If it was possible to be passionately nationalistic about a of couple square miles, that family is. Anyway, Salem, go by there and tell Five I sent you and he needs to make you a good deal."

"Ummm...Five?" Surely I'd heard that wrong.

Charlotte nodded. "That's what he goes by, the youngest Pigg son. The fifth, obviously, and all the sons' names start with the letter R. I don't even remember what his real name is, to tell the truth. Early on, people started calling him number five because they were five little stair step boys."

That was interesting, but all I really cared about was whether this Five guy would give me a real deal.

"What kind of cars do they have there?" I asked.

She shrugged. "They're not the latest model or anything, but you can count on them being decent and reliable. Plus they offer something like a two-year warranty at no extra cost."

That was encouraging. If I could put half my emergency fund toward a down payment, then negotiate a payment less than my probation payment had been, I could still manage to put a little bit into the bank. Not as much as I had planned, but still, some. Some would be good.

"You oughta have enough money to pay cash for a decent used car," Flo said over the Airedale she was scissoring. "Don't tell me you spent all that reward money already."

"Oh, yeah," Charlotte said. "I forgot you got that twenty grand when they caught that guy who killed C.J. Hardin."

I shook my head quickly. I did not want to go into what had happened to that money. "Actually, no. There were three of us, so I didn't get the whole thing. And, besides, taxes and stuff. You know. It does go pretty quick and I want to keep as much in the bank as I can."

"Well, I won't tell Five that you came into some money, or else he'll be less motivated to make you a deal."

"Thanks," I said. "I appreciate that."

I thought of that conversation when Viv drove me out to Clovis Highway after work so I could see if there was anything remotely affordable for me.

As we neared the motel she asked, "You want to pop in and check on your grandmother?"

"No, I think she's mad at me for having her arrested for being a madam and ruining her cash flow. Is it a good idea, do you think, for us to drive up there in this car, though? It might give them an idea that I have more to spend than I do."

"No, this is good," Viv said. "It'll confuse them, and confusion is always a good battle tactic. They'll wonder why we're here and not at a real car dealer's."

I had to admit she was probably right, even as my pride wanted to bristle at her choice of words. Just because it was all I could afford didn't make it "not real." I would be paying with real money, I knew that for sure.

"The name makes a lot of sense now," I said as Viv neared the Five Star lot. "Can't imagine why he didn't want to put the name Pigg on his business."

"Is this one of those Pigg guys?"

"Yeah, you know them?"

"I don't know them, but you know their daddy. You see him on the news all the time. City Councilman? Always talking about the short end of the stick this part of town gets? Looks like a redneck Santa Claus?"

"Oh yeah," I said, remembering she'd talked about him the other day. I still had no idea who she was talking about, though. I wasn't much for civic affairs.

We drove under the streamers of brightly colored triangle pennants and parked in the center of the lot. I got out and looked around, already nervous that I was going to be taken for a ride. I picked up Stump and tucked her under my arm.

"Promise you'll back me up while I negotiate," I said to Viv. Although she'd negotiated her own car deal like a total sucker. But she was bound to be less emotionally involved in my car than she was in her own.

"Don't worry, you'll be driving out of here with a good car you can afford," she assured me, sounding like a salesman herself.

Redneck Santa himself walked out of the little portable building that was the dealership office and waved toward us. His long white beard and hair were tinged with yellow, and his hair was tied back in a loose pony tail at the back. He wore jeans and boots and a red button down shirt with a black belt that I couldn't help but feel was designed to capitalize on his Santa image.

I immediately felt my hackles rise. He wasn't going to fool me with that act. I'd wake up in the morning with a crappy car and no green at all on my Christmas tree.

"How are you ladies doing this fine day?" he boomed as he got closer to us.

"I can't spend much," I said.

Viv gave me a look.

"Might as well get it out of the way," I said.

"Nothing wrong with setting clear expectations," he said with a laugh. "Don't worry, we've got something for all budgets. Well, maybe not your budget," he said with another laugh, leaning with a meaningful eye toward Viv. "Can I ask, is that the new Cadillac LR8 racing model?"

"It is!" Viv crowed. "You want to see?"

They fell into a cackling conversation about the wonders and awes of the Cadillac, and within fifteen seconds the Mr. Pigg was sitting beside Viv on the front seat while she pushed different buttons and they oohed and ahhed.

"It beeps sometimes for no reason," I said, annoyed that he was so quick to overlook a paying customer, even one who couldn't spend much.

"Oh, I got that fixed," Viv said.

"And sometimes it goes way slower than it says it's going."

"Got that fixed, too. I had Bernard come over yesterday, and he took care of it right away. See this?" She pushed a little button on the dash. "It's the metro button. So when you drive in other countries you can switch to their numbers. Like, in Mexico I'd be going, like, Mexican miles an hour." She smiled like this made complete sense.

"Metric," I said. "Not metro. Metric. So we were going seventy kilometers an hour on Saturday, not miles."

"Exactly," she said, beaming. "Very metropolitan, huh? That's why they call it the metro button, probably."

I blinked, then turned to the Mr. Pigg. "I talked to Charlotte Clancy-Pigg, and she said her brother-in-law owned this place."

"Yeah, my boy Five owns it, but he's out just now. We can take care of you, though." He turned back to Viv. "Did you get the Performance Data Recorder?"

"Oh yeah. Take a look at this."

"I'll just look around," I said. Unnecessarily, since they weren't listening.

While Viv and the Redneck Santa were all agog over the Caddy, I wandered through the lot under the huge "Buy Here Pay Here" signs to the sound of plastic bunting snapping in the wind overhead. I immediately ruled out anything that was less than seven years old. I made myself focus on cars that I knew had been budget cars even when they were new, and ruled out anything too sporty. I selected three to choose from — a white hatchback, a small white four-door, and a small red two-door.

I shifted Stump and held her up to the hatchback. "What do you think, Stump? Can you see yourself driving around town in one of these?"

Stump seemed unimpressed. But then, nothing much impressed Stump except fast food in paper bags.

I walked back and forth between the three cars, trying to psych myself up. Eventually, I got annoyed with the anxiety and decided to get it over with.

"Okay," I said when I got back to Viv and the Papa Pigg. "I have three contenders." I pointed to them one by one. "First thing we need to determine is whether any of them will fit within my budget."

"Right you are!" he said. "So what's your budget?"

I told him how much I could put down and how much I could spend every month.

I was met with total silence. Then Viv said, "Seriously?"

"Seriously!" I snapped. "I need a car, and I need it to be dependable. I don't need it to be fancy or have all kinds of bells and whistles. And I just got out of debt, and I'm not crazy about getting back in. So I'm sticking to my budget. Now, do you have anything in that range?" I put my hand on my hip and narrowed my eyes at the Mr. Pigg.

"Well, I might have. Not those three, though. They're all going to be a bit above what you said you could pay. I have a couple around back..." He headed that way, and my stomach sank. They must be really bad if he was keeping them behind the building.

"Now this one just came in, and we haven't even cleaned it up yet. Keep that in mind — a clean car, no matter how old or banged up, looks a lot better than a dirty car."

My stomach sank further at the "banged up" part, but as we rounded the back of the building I felt a little better. It was a hatchback that had probably at one time been black, but was faded to a flat dark charcoal. It had a black louvered thing over the back window, and I could imagine that, sitting in the showroom a decade or so ago, it had been a pretty sharp sports car.

I walked around it and eyed it critically. It would help if I had any idea what I was looking for, but I really didn't. I kicked the tires and peered through the window. Nothing shouted "unreliable piece of junk."

"Now, like I said, we'll clean it up and tighten up anything loose, give it a good going over. Replace the floor mats, stuff like that. So don't judge it by all the cosmetic stuff."

"What's up with the hood?" I asked. A lighter gray spread across the hood like a stain. If it had been fabric, I would have thought it had had bleach spilled on it.

"That? Oh, that's just fading from the sun. The hood is made from a different material than the rest of the car, so the paint sits on it a little differently. That's just part of having an older car, you know. Little wear and tear. Now, take a seat there and start her up. See what you think."

I climbed into the driver's seat and swung Stump over to the passenger side. She gave me an anxious look but didn't move. I took the key from Mr. Pigg and slid it into the ignition, giving it a crank.

Nothing.

"Go ahead, crank her up," he said.

"I'm cranking," I said. I leaned over and peered at the ignition. It looked like the key was all the way forward, but I tried turning it again.

Nothing. The key wouldn't go any farther and the engine didn't make a peep.

I straightened and looked at Papa Pigg. "Is the battery dead?"

Just then, the engine coughed, then roared to life, then coughed again and backfired loudly. Then it died again.

Viv screamed and ducked. Stump shot into my lap and whined.

I swung my legs back out of the car. "Okay, how about we look at what's behind door number two?"

"Sorry about that," he said with an embarrassed laugh. "Obviously, Five still has some work to do on that one. We'll be giving it a good once over and fixing whatever is wrong with that."

"I can give you a number for a wrecking yard," I offered. "They'll tow it and give you a few bucks for the scrap metal."

"I have one more, like I said. It's around the other side, actually. I figured this one would be more to your liking. But this other one is good, too. You'll just need to keep an open mind about it."

Viv and I gave each other a look.

"You know the old line about a used car being owned by a little old lady who only drove it on Sundays? Well, in this case, that turns out to be true. We just got this from an estate sale last week. Little old lady who lived at Belle Court — "

"Earline Whatley?" Viv asked.

"Why yes, that is her. Did you know her?"

Viv nodded. "Yep. We played Bunco together."

"Her grandson brought this in last week. I'm telling you, it's like taking a step back in time."

We rounded the corner and I saw with a sickening feeling exactly what he was talking about.

Parked beside the building was a low-slung tan and and white car that stretched the length of the little portable building.

Viv whistled through her teeth. "Is that a 1975 Monte Carlo?"

"Seventy-four," Mr. Pigg said. "In mint condition."

Viv ran her hand over the vinyl roof. "Landau edition," she breathed. "Oh my. I wanted one of these so bad back then. This is what Sue Ellen Ewing drove on Dallas. Remember that show?" she asked the Papa Pigg.

"Of course I do. We had a pool going to bet on who shot J.R. I lost twenty dollars on that and have never forgotten it."

They laughed, clearly transported back to a time when this — this car that was half the length of my trailer — was not ancient. Since I hadn't been born yet in 1974, I had a different perspective. To me, this was only one step removed from Fred Flintstone's car powered by his own fat feet.

I circled the car in a daze while they went on and on about how this had been the IT car, back in the day. I opened the passenger door and stuck my head inside. It was clean, I had to give them that. The upholstery looked brand new.

In fact, everything about it looked brand new. Old but new. It was weird.

"Can you pop the hood?" I asked.

"Oh yeah, you need to see this."

He reached under the dash and pulled a lever, and the hood popped up.

He waddled around the front and fiddled under the hood, then lifted it.

"Would you look at that?" he asked. "I mean, look at it. How in the world did they keep it so clean? I mean, in this area? Dirt gets all over everything, right? They must have had a hermetically sealed garage!"

As before, I had no idea what I was looking for, but it did look clean and new. The hoses were all shiny and black, and the engine itself didn't have a speck of dust on it. Papa Pigg was right — it was highly unusual to see anything without dust in West Texas.

"Now sit down here and crank this baby up. You're not going

to believe it."

I was less than enthusiastic, given the results of my last cranking, but I set Stump onto the bench seat and sat down.

Stump had apparently never seen a bench seat before. She curled up beside my thigh and let her breath out with a big snuffle. By the time I got the key into the ignition and turned it, she was snoring.

The engine turned over easily. As it did, I gave Viv a panicked look. It actually felt like the car lifted slightly off the ground.

"Feel that power?" she asked with glee. "Now this is what a car is supposed to feel like."

I *could* feel the power through the steering wheel. It was as if I was sitting in the cockpit of a fighter jet or something. I pressed gently on the gas.

Vrrooooom.

Stump startled awake and looked at me. She seemed impressed.

Viv hurried around to the passenger side and climbed in. "Salem, you have to buy this car. Did you hear that? Man, we'd be chasing bad guys all over town in this thing!"

"Viv, this thing is half a block long. I don't even know if it will fit in my driveway."

"Of course it will. It's probably the same age as your trailer anyway."

That was depressingly true.

"And look at it. It's as if it's been in a museum or something." She ran her hand over the dashboard. "Oh, I wanted one of these so *bad* back in the seventies!"

An uncomfortable thought niggled at the edge of my mind.

Viv was one of the wealthiest people I knew. I mean, most everyone I knew was living paycheck to paycheck like I was, but still. I knew just living at Belle Court wasn't cheap, and she lived in the nicest place there. That guy from the Cadillac dealer had treated her like their best customer, and for good reason. I'd known her a couple of years and she was on her third brand new car. She wore thousand dollar shoes and carried three thousand dollar handbags. I counted her as one of my best friends, and I loved hanging out with her. But sometimes I had to admit, I was envious of her ability to throw money around.

And now *I* could have something *she* wanted.

Such a stupid reason to buy a car.

"I'll bet it drinks a ridiculous amount of gas," I said, trying to talk myself out of it.

"So what? Gas is cheaper right now than it's been in five years. I heard it on the radio this morning. And it's just going to go down. It won't go up again for the next eighteen months. By that time, you'll have saved enough to trade up."

"Let's take it down the street a ways so you can get the feel for how it handles," Papa Pigg said.

That was a good idea, but I was not sure about driving this thing down the street. I mean, it was huge. Would it even fit in one lane?

"Let's take it around the Loop!" Viv said.

"We're not taking it around the Loop," I snapped. "Good lord. This thing is seriously enormous. I'm nervous about driving it."

"Don't worry, you'll get used to that," he said. "You just need to spend some time behind the wheel. No time like the present."

With a great deal of unease, I buckled my seatbelt and

reached for the gear shift on the steering column. I'd never used one of those, either — in every car I'd ever driven, the gear shift had been to the right of the driver's seat.

I pulled down on the shifter, and nothing happened.

"Pull it toward you first," Viv said. "Good lord, how old are you?"

"I'm twelve years younger than this car," I said calmly.

"Oh."

That shut her up. I sometimes got the feeling that Viv operated under the impression that she and I were about the same age — not that I was as old as she was, but that she was as young as I was. Moments like this had to be a bit disorienting for her.

I pulled the shifter toward me, then down to D. The car felt like a powerful wild animal beneath me. I slowly took my foot off the brake.

The car leapt forward like a racehorse leaving the starting gate.

I panicked and slammed my foot back on the brake.

Viv and Stump both glared at me.

"Sorry," I said. "I wasn't expecting it to take off like that. I didn't even touch the gas."

"Just one of those things you have to get used to," he said calmly. "Don't worry about it. Just ease off the brake and then let the car do its job."

I eased off the brake, swinging the car around the side of the building. I checked the side mirror obsessively, unsure of how much clearance I needed to make it around without hitting the building.

In front of me, the hood stretched out like an acre of tan desert.

Slowly we moved through the car lot toward the street. I almost had a stroke as we passed Viv's Cadillac. It didn't seem possible that I could squeeze the Monte Carlo in the lane between her car and the cars for sale without scraping something, but I did it.

At the street, I watched for traffic from the west before I pulled out.

"Good Lord, girl," Viv said. "Any time today would be good."

"I want to wait until nobody's coming," I said. "I don't know how much room I need to get this thing onto the street."

"You drive like *my* grandma," Viv said.

"Shut up," I answered calmly. When all visible traffic was cleared, I eased up on the brake.

"Hang on!" Viv shouted, looking to the west. "I think someone just crossed the New Mexico state line. Better wait on them."

I thought about flipping her off, but I was afraid to take my hand off the wheel. I made a mental note to do it later.

We headed east on the Clovis Highway, and although I was nervous, I had to admit the monstrous thing handled beautifully. The ride was smooth as silk, the steering effortless. A signal light a block ahead of me turned red, and I panicked again and threw on the brakes. Again, Viv and Stump glared at me, but I let off and slowly coasted to a stop at the light. Maybe I could get the hang of driving it.

Meanwhile, Viv was busy checking out all the buttons and knobs. "I'm not a bit surprised that Earline Whatley's car would be in this shape, to tell you the truth. The woman was obsessive about everything. She got one of those motorized scooters and the handyman who takes care of that stuff said she was in there every week, wanting something adjusted or replaced. She hired her own cleaning lady to come clean her apartment, wasn't satisfied with what the staff did."

As she prattled on, I asked myself if I really wanted a forty-year-old car, even one in good shape. I tried to imagine parking it beside my trailer, or at Flo's. Driving it to Walmart. What would it be like, to be the laughingstock of *Walmart*?

But the fact remained, it fit in my budget. And as I got used to driving it, and if I ignored the age factor, it did feel *kind of* luxurious.

I had another minor heart event when I considered turning around in the Taco John's parking lot, then panicked and pulled back onto the street. At the next block, I turned and circled the empty high school parking lot to get headed back toward the car lot.

"Okay," I said, hunched over the wheel and driving like a turtle. "I'm going back in there to try and get five hundred off the down payment."

Viv nodded. "But keep in mind, this is a classic. It's worth putting in a few extra bucks."

I would have given her the side-eye if I wasn't afraid of taking my eyes off the road for a second. I managed to get the car inside the lot without hitting anything again. I killed the motor and sat for a few seconds, letting my heart rate go down.

Inside, the Papa Pigg was talking to a woman and a younger man. The woman had to be Mama Pigg. She had that short-haired, hard-working, no-nonsense West Texas woman look. She looked like the kind of woman capable of raising five sons.

"How was it?" Papa Pigg asked. "You in love with it?"

"Yes!" Viv said.

This time I didn't settle for the side-eye. I gave her a full-on *shut your mouth* frown.

"I mean, we'll need to do a bit of negotiating first, of course," Viv said.

"Of course. Five here can handle that for you."

Five was maybe a few years younger than I was. He gave his father an uncomfortable look, then motioned with his head for me to come to the counter. Viv struck up a conversation with the Pigg parents and left me to handle this bit on my own. The fink. I glared at her, but they were off on their own conversation about taking the Cadillac to Amarillo for "adjustments."

"Amarillo?" Papa Pigg said. "That place is the worst. Think they're such a happening place just because they have their own Krunchy Kreems."

I turned back to Five, who shuffled through some papers behind the counter and cleared his throat. "Okay, well. Let's see. The list price on that one is..." He searched through his papers.

"To be honest, I'm really not sure that's the car for me," I said.

He looked up, his shoulders dropping in what looked like relief. He nodded. "I mean, it is pretty ancient, right?"

I blinked. "Yes, well..."

"I don't blame you," he said. "We have cars that are twenty years newer than that one. And, I mean, they're still really old. You want to look at them?" His eye twitched.

Was he trying to wink at me? "Umm, no. I already looked."

He frowned. "Well, then." He went silent. Then shrugged as if to say, "What can you do?"

Wait. What was happening here? Did I have to talk him into

selling me the car?

"I already looked," I said again. "I think the Monte Carlo is *almost* what I can afford. I'll just need you to come down on the down payment by five hundred dollars. And the monthly payment will have to come down by — " I looked at the ceiling as if I was thinking hard. I said the first thing that came to mind. "Gosh, at least forty percent."

"Sold!" Five shot his hand out.

In a daze, I took it. It had all happened so fast, and I'd been prepared for much more of a struggle. Any struggle at all, in fact.

"Okay." Five stood and reached for a folder. "Here are the sales forms. Just fill these out and write me a check, for..." He looked a little confused, like he couldn't remember what we'd just talked about.

I told him how much the down payment would be with the five hundred knocked off, and he nodded. "Yep, write out a check for that much, and I'll get your keys." His eye twitched again. If he was trying to wink, it was weird.

The forms were ridiculously simple. I filled in my name and contact information. There were blanks for my down payment amount and the monthly payment amount and I filled that in with what I guessed was about forty percent under what the elder Pigg had quoted me. I signed at the bottom, wrote out my check, and joined the grownups' conversation, which had, of course, turned to the robberies.

Mrs. Pigg was shaking her head. "It's a shame. Just a shame. So many people have been put through the wringer by this thing. I guess we just need to be thankful it's not been worse than it has. I mean, nobody's been hurt."

"That's right. And I'll tell you what." Papa Pigg pointed his finger at Viv. "It's making this little community even stronger than it was before. That's the way hard times affect people. We're banding together, watching each other's backs. We look out for each other. One of these days these robberies will be over, those High Point Bandits or whatever they call themselves will fade into the background, and we'll still be standing, stronger than ever."

"Maybe," I said. "I'm not sure how much longer my grand-mother can handle the strain. If they don't catch these guys soon, she's going to end up shooting someone just for the sake of having someone to shoot."

"Is Virgie McDonald your grandmother?" both Piggs asked at once, which made me a little nervous.

I nodded.

"Well," Mrs. Pigg said with a laugh. "She doesn't need to worry about those Bandits. They're not going to bother her."

"No? They broke into Mario's tamale restaurant two nights ago. That's awfully close."

"Oh, I know, but..." She laughed again and waved a hand like it was simply out of the question. "They wouldn't bother with someone like her."

"She's quite certain she's next on the list."

"I suppose you do never know," Mama Pigg allowed. "Our son's insurance office was robbed, what, about two weeks ago?" She turned to Papa, who nodded. "An insurance office. I mean, seriously. How much cash could be there? People don't bring cash to an insurance office. Still, he lost what he did have there, and they did some damage. Stole some things — computers and stuff."

"Everybody's taking a turn," Five said from behind me.

I jumped. I'd kind of forgotten he was there. He was a bit creepy, to be honest, even if he had an easygoing smile on his face.

"Hopefully the police will catch them soon," Mr. Pigg said. "Although I'm not holding out a lot of hope. If this was happening on the other side of town, they'd be all over it and these criminals would be locked up already. But we're not quite the priority over here on the other side of the tracks. We have to help ourselves."

Viv nodded like she was one of them. "Indeed, we do. Salem and I are going to do a stakeout tonight, in fact, to see what we can turn up."

"We are? This is the first I've heard of it."

"No, we talked about it, remember? I said we should catch them before the police, and you said we might as well."

"That hardly translates to a stakeout tonight."

"How else are we going to catch them?" she asked, as if this was completely obvious.

"Well, you two stay safe out there, if you do go out," Mr. Pigg said. "Nobody's been hurt yet, but we certainly wouldn't want you two to be the first."

CHAPTER SEVEN

Stakeout

I had about five more heart events on the way home. I was driving too slow, but every time I tried to go the speed limit I felt like I was driving a runaway train, and I panicked and threw on the brakes. That made people pass me, which terrified me even more. I was quite sure I was taking up more than one lane, and I was sure each time that they were going to scrape the side of my car, but I would be the one to get the ticket, because I was probably supposed to be carrying some kind of regulation WIDE LOAD sign. Every time I saw someone coming along side me, my heart hammered and I said, "Hang on, Stump." After the third time, she started to ignore me.

So I was wired when I got home, but weirdly proud of myself for making the trek and getting that cruise ship parked in my space. Plus, I'd negotiated a decent deal. I wondered if Mr. and

Mrs. Pigg were going to be mad at Five when they realized he'd completely rolled over on my terms, but I figured I'd let him be the one to deal with that.

As for me, I felt like celebrating. I went over and knocked on Frank's door, planning to let him know he had to fend for himself for dinner and also have him come admire my new car. But he wasn't home.

Let down, I went back to my deck and sat on one of my cheap plastic chairs and stared at the car. If a person looked at my old trailer and my old car, they might wonder for a second if they'd been transported back to the mid-70s. Of all the times to travel to.

I wanted to celebrate with someone, though. I pulled my phone out of my pocket and said, "Windy, call Tony."

When he answered, I said, "Guess what I got?"

"What's that?"

"A new car! Well, it's a very old car, actually. But, you know. New to me."

He was very happy for me. He couldn't wait to see it. Thursday, when he picked me up for our date night.

"You could come over now," I said. "If you're not too busy, I mean. Viv and I are going out in a few hours to do a stakeout for the Knife Point — I mean High Point Bandits, but right now I'm just hanging out."

"Is Viv there?"

"No, it's just me right now."

"I'm sorry, Salem, I have some things I have to take care of for work and can't get away for a few hours. But I'll be by Thursday to pick you up, and I'll be happy to see it then."

I hung up, a bit bummed out and feeling rejected by Tony.

Again.

I was still feeling a bit of a rejection hangover as Viv and I drove around the High Point neighborhood that night. She'd asked if we could take my car, but I refused. I was going to keep my trips in that thing to the bare minimum until I got used to driving it.

So we were doing stakeout in the Caddy, and I was telling Viv, again, how freaked out I was that Tony didn't seem to want to be around me. Viv drove through the potholed parking lot of the bingo parlor and swung the car around to go back the way we'd come. Street lights arced through the car window and Stump snuffled as the light washed over her eyes. She stirred, then stood and slowly stretched her neck, planting her heavy feet on my thigh to brace herself.

"I asked him to come over to see the new car, and first he asked if you were there, too, and when I said it was just me, he said he had other stuff he had to do. It's like he doesn't want to be alone with me."

"Maybe he's just respecting your boundaries," Viv suggested.

"That's what I think," I said. The thing was, I'd never really had boundaries before. I had no idea what they looked like or how they operated. "It's just...he's respecting my boundaries *so hard*. And are boundaries supposed to be so — so restricted, for married couples?"

"Honey, there is no manual for you two." Viv slowed and looked through the darkened windows of a law office, the last office in a row of red brick storefronts with white awnings.

"You see something?" I shifted Stump back into the seat beside me and leaned to look closer.

"Maybe." She swung the Caddy into the space beside the

building and then into the alley.

"What are we going to do if we see something?" I asked.

"Who knows," Viv said casually, easing the Cadillac down the alley between that building and a row of houses. "We'll probably scream and I'll drive over something and put a dent in my new car. Maybe a little loss of bladder control thrown in for good measure."

"As long as we have a plan," I said.

She eased up behind the back door of the law office. There was a metal door over a square of concrete for a step, and a glass block of windows that was dark.

"Have there been any robberies at offices?" I asked. "I thought it was mostly retail."

"No offices yet, but you never know."

She killed the motor. "Do you hear anything?"

I hit the button to roll the window down, but since she'd killed the motor, nothing happened. "Turn the key on so I can open the window."

She turned the key. The windshield wipers swooped across, making me jump. Viv cussed. "Hang on." She fiddled with different knobs and levers. "Okay, I think that got it. Try it again."

I hit the down button for the window. The horn honked.

Viv cussed again. "This crazy thing."

"There is seriously something wrong with this car," I said.

"If there is anyone in there, they know we're here. Just go up to the back door and see if you can hear anything."

"Seriously? You just said they know we're here. What if they're aiming a gun at me right now?"

"Let me remind you that in the entire history of the High Point robberies, there has been no violence or bloodshed."

I gave her a look. Then I opened the door and leaned out.

Nothing. Nothing but faint traffic noises from Clovis Highway. Then, a low rumble. Growing louder. And louder.

I turned to look at Stump. She snorted, then curled into a tighter ball on the seat and settled back to the low rumble snore.

"There, you hear that?" Viv said.

"Over Stump's snores?"

"Seriously, I heard something. Go up and listen at the door."

"You go up and listen at the door."

"I'm the getaway driver. If there is someone there, we'll need to get out of here quick. The door is closer to your side. Just hop up there and listen."

I rolled my eyes, but by this time I was quite sure there was no one there. The building was dark, the alley was silent. Our was the only car near the place. I was so sure that I had only minor qualms about slipping quietly from the car and closing the door softly behind me so as not to wake Stump. I tiptoed up to the square of concrete that sat outside the metal back door. I put my ear to the crack between the door and the jamb, and listened as hard as I could.

Nothing. Not a peep. No bad guys discussing their nefarious plans. Not even any crickets chirping. Of course, if there was someone in there and they'd been alerted by Viv's car horn, they could have a pistol pointed directly at my head at this very moment. The nerves on my scalp and back snapped to attention, and I tried to listen for the telltale sound of a pistol being cocked.

"Nothing?" Viv asked from directly beside my left ear.

"Gah!" I lurched and cried out, tripping over my own feet and stumbling off the concrete block and into the grass and weeds beside it. "Viv! You scared the crap out of me!"

"Calm down. I don't think anyone is here."

"It's a good thing," I said grumpily. "You're being loud enough to wake the dead."

"Me? You're the one who just screamed."

I tiptoed back to see if I could discern any shapes moving beyond the glass brick window, but couldn't make out anything.

"Just as well," Viv said, heading back around to the driver's side. "If we caught the bad guys here, the lawyer would probably file some kind of suit against us."

"Why would they do that?"

"When you have money, people always want to sue you."

"Thank goodness I don't have to worry about that." I reached for the door handle. It was locked.

"I didn't lock it," Viv said.

"Well, this side is locked." I tugged lightly at the handle.

"Hang on, I'll open it from my side." Then, the unmistakable sound of a door not being opened followed.

Our eyes met over the roof of the car. Surely she hadn't...but of course she had.

I bent and looked at the ignition. In the dark, the ruby studded key chain didn't shine quite so brightly, but it was still there.

"You locked the keys in the car!"

"I did not!" She jiggled the handle.

I looked at Stump, sleeping obliviously through everything.

"You locked Stump in your car."

"I'll bet she did it," Viv said.

"How?"

"She probably stepped on a button or something."

"That only happens in sitcoms. Besides, look at her. She hasn't moved a hair." Suddenly, an uncomfortable thought occurred to me. "Viv, if she wakes up and sees she's alone, she's going to come unhinged."

Viv's eyes grew wide. She'd seen one of Stump's separation anxiety meltdowns. When Stump got freaked out that I'd left her alone, she started this high-pitched keening that carried for miles. More than once, residents of Trailertopia had called animal control and one time even Child Protective Services on me. This was why I always took her with me, or had Frank keep her if I couldn't.

"Don't you have some kind of hi-tech service that you can call and get it unlocked?" I asked.

"Uh-huh. I can do it right from my phone."

Neither of us said a word. Viv's phone glittered prettily on the dashboard, under the alley's one weak yellow light.

"You ought to teach that dog to do tricks, like unlock car doors," Viv suggested.

"I'd be happy to teach her to sleep on her side of the bed," I said. "Let's just table for now the idea of teaching her to use your smart phone to dial 9-1-1."

As we watched, the phone trilled shrilly and lit up, little musical notes dancing brightly across the screen.

"No, no," I whispered. "Shhh!"

The phone, of course, did not shhh. Stump stirred, then lifted her square head. She glared in the general direction of the annoying noise, then to the side. Where I should be sitting.

After staring at the empty seat for a moment, she struggled sluggishly to her feet, looking left and right at the empty car.

Her eyes met mine through the window.

I smiled, trying to project calm. I'm afraid it held a tinge of desperation, though, because I did, indeed, feel desperate.

She ran to the window and put her front paws on the arm rest. I could hear her whining through the window.

"It's okay, sweetie. I'm right here. See? Right here."

Stump scratched furiously at the window.

"Is she going to do that screaming banshee thing?" Viv asked.

"Probably." I kept smiling through clenched teeth and put a hand to the window, like a visitor to an inmate in a prison movie. "What about a spare key?" I asked, bending to feel around the edge of the bumper.

"What is this, the 80s? No one does that anymore."

Stump scratched desperately at the window. "Oh no. She's going to leave scratch marks all over your new window." Stump's meltdowns had, before I caught on to her "special needs," cost me a sofa cushion, a comforter, two pairs of shoes, and all my house plants.

Her whines turned to yips. Yips were the precursor to the ululating howls of anguish.

"Oh no!" I said, looking frantically around. "Should I break the window or something?"

"Calm down!" Viv ordered. "You two are making me crazy!"

But then, the howling started. Low at first, but still managing to carry through the closed window. Then higher. And louder.

Viv and I looked uneasily around the alley. In the yard on the other side of the fence behind Viv, a light went on.

"Shhh, it's okay," I said through the window. "I'm right here. Everything is okay."

Of course, there was no hearing me now. The Stump's howls crescendoed into an ear-splitting tsunami of sound and drowned out everything else.

Another porch light went on, then another.

In the distance, I thought I could hear voices.

Viv had her hands over her ears. "Good lord," she shouted. "It's like one of those things they do to torture war prisoners into giving up state secrets!"

I could definitely hear shouts now, coming from the houses behind the fence. As I watched, another porch light flashed on at the next street over. A couple more dogs joined in the howling pandemonium.

I looked up to see the small light of a flashlight bouncing down the alley toward us.

"Somebody's coming!" I shrieked.

"So what?" Viv shouted back irritably. "We're not doing anything but creating some really awful noise pollution."

"Hey!" shouted a very large and menacing sounding voice. "What's going on out here?"

More shouts from the other side of us. Also menacing sounding.

"It's okay," Viv said, walking toward the flashlight. "We just locked — "

The gunshot went off like a cannon and Viv screamed. She dropped to the ground and for a heart-stopping moment I thought she was hit.

"Viv!" I ran toward her, my arms up for the gunman to see. "Viv! Are you okay?"

Viv was up and crab walking as fast as anyone has ever crab walked before, toward the other end of the alley. "Time to get the heck out of here," she said as she rounded the car.

The guy with the flashlight was getting closer. I turned toward him and held up my arms. "Don't shoot!" I shouted. "I'm not armed!"

I don't know if he heard me or not, because Stump was still going full force. Another shot went off and I dove behind the Cadillac. Then I heard another shot, sounding like it came from the opposite direction, and heard glass break.

Suddenly, the air was alive with gun shots, screaming and yelling, and what sounded like glass bottles hitting the wall near me.

Stump! If bullets were flying, she could be hit!

I cowered down beside the car, one hand against the door, terrified. "Get down, Stump, get down!" I yelled over and over. As if she could hear me. As if it would make any difference.

I yanked at the handle a few more times, but it did no good, then I dropped to the ground and scrambled to the bottom front corner of the door, where the floorboard would be. I put my lips to the crack.

"Stump! Come here, baby!" I yelled, hoping the sound would carry through the din. "Come here. Down here." I knocked on the car fender frantically. I was pretty sure I heard her hit the floorboard and then a snuffling sound as she sniffed around the edge of the door. I closed my eyes tight and felt tears leak as I imagined a stray bullet hitting her poor body.

After another fifteen seconds or so of pandemonium, the night quietened enough that we could hear sirens.

The guy with the flashlight came running by. "Where'd they go?" he shouted.

I opened my mouth to answer, but having none, shut it again

and looked around. Where'd who go?

Another guy ran by, and then another from the other direction, all of them excited and gesturing.

"I think I winged him," one of the guys said.

"Yeah! Clipped that sucker!" another shouted. "Teach them to mess with this neighborhood!"

People were coming out from all over the block now, gathering in clumps of two and three. I dusted myself off and looked through the window at Stump. She was sitting, frozen, staring hard at the edge of the door where my voice had come from. She wasn't bleeding, though.

I sagged against the Caddy in relief.

Two patrol cars screeched up around the same time, then two more a few seconds later. There was lots of shouting and more pandemonium while the cops tried to figure out who was who and what had happened. I was too freaked out to even respond. I just stood staring at Stump through the window, who sat staring at the door, apparently as shell-shocked as I was.

It took me a while to come out of my inner freak-out, but when I did, Viv was talking to two cops and a man wearing a Harley Davidson t-shirt and a white baseball cap.

"I don't know, four or five," the guy was saying. "They took off down that way."

Bobby pulled up. He got out of the car, spoke to a couple of cops, then saw Viv.

He immediately started to look around. For me, I assumed. I waggled my fingers at him.

He walked over. "I'm not even going to ask."

"We have a stake in this community, Bobby. We need to look out for each other."

"*'Cause the Lubbock PD is sure not doing it.*" His voice was mocking, like he was quoting someone else — someone annoying. "Believe me, I've heard all about it. Councilman Pigg was in my office for two solid hours last week."

"I didn't say that. We're just saying, if everybody is looking for these guys, they have to be found, right?"

"Or we could just have enough innocent bystanders who get caught in the crossfire that people forget about the robberies for a while."

"Yes, well..." Since I had recently been fearful of that very thing, I didn't have a good retort.

"So, what happened here? I'm hearing there were five or six guys, maybe more, and someone screaming in agony. That was before the shooting started."

"I have no idea," I flat-out lied, because it was beginning to dawn on me that Stump's cries had set off the entire melee and the Bandits were actually nowhere near here, just a bunch of trigger-happy neighborhood watch soldiers. I certainly wasn't going to tell Bobby that. "Can you get Viv's car unlocked? She locked the keys in it and I need to let Stump out. All this noise probably startled her." It was the only explanation for her silence. I didn't want to take any chances on her 'screaming in agony' to start back up again, though. She might set off another round of gunfire.

"So, you're here doing your community service duty, and you get yourself locked out of your car?"

I sighed. "What else would we be doing here, Bobby? Oh, I know. *We're* the Bandits. We're here because we're robbing places."

He shook his head and and grinned that sexy lopsided grin of his. "I don't suspect you two for a second. These robberies have been way too successful for that."

I stuck my tongue out at him. The fact that he was right was no reason to say it out loud.

Viv charmed one of the younger cops into contacting her fancy car service and got the door unlocked remotely. I snatched Stump up and squeezed her. We drove back to Trailertopia in silence, me clutching Stump so close in my lap that she started to grumble and push at me.

It was just past ten o'clock, but after everything that had happened, I felt like I'd been through the wringer, and Viv looked as bad as I felt. As I reached to open the door, she stopped me. "There were no Bandits, were there?"

I shook my head. "I don't think so. I think that was all us."

Viv looked at Stump. "You set off a riot out there, girl."

I dragged myself into the living room and collapsed on the sofa. Stump bounced off me and went to find her food bowl. Viv sat beside me, silent.

Frank held his usual spot in my recliner, watching TV, but he dragged his attention away enough to take in me and Viv, looking a bit shell shocked.

"Yallright?" he asked.

I took a deep breath. "I'm never taking Stump with us on an investigation again. I don't care if I have to leave her here and she shreds everything I own. Never again."

"She almost got us killed," Viv said.

"She almost got killed, too! She could have been caught in the crossfire."

I felt like the world's worst parent. What was I thinking, having Stump in the midst of all that? Seriously, never again.

Ever.

CHAPTER EIGHT

Concerned Citizenry

If Viv was traumatized by the excitement of the night before, she was over it by noon the next day. She called me at work.

"I heard a story on the news about all the leads the police are getting. They say they're following up on all of them, but I'll bet they're not."

"Of course they are," I said, sweeping up dog hair with one hand and holding the phone to my ear with the other.

"Not like we would, though. I'll bet we would do a more thorough investigation."

"Maybe."

"They won't give me their leads."

"The police won't?"

"No."

"How do you know?"

"Because I asked. I wanted to follow up on the ones they've

interviewed, and they won't give them to me. I'm telling you, there is no professional courtesy in this town."

The first time Viv and I got involved in a criminal investigation — quite by accident — Viv became immediately carried away. Turns out, she was bored out of her mind and terrified of her brain atrophying while she died a slow death at Belle Court. Viv is a woman with a lot of energy, and I can understand how she would have trouble reconciling herself to old age. Plus, there was sobriety to think about. You have to believe there's a decent life to be won, to be worked toward, or sometimes it's hard to see how all the struggle is worth it. I can imagine a life of bingo nights and quarterly bus trips to the casinos in New Mexico wouldn't do it for Viv. She needed the excitement of a new case to keep herself occupied. She'd decided early on that we were PI partners, which worked out just fine for me because it meant I got to ride around in nice cars and sometimes she bought me dinner.

Unlike Viv, though, I was under no delusion that we were "professional" anything. We were something more along the lines of nosy busybodies who'd gotten lucky a couple of times.

Rather than point that out, I sighed and said, "That's a shame. But what can you do?"

"You can call your friend."

"Which friend?"

"Patrice Watson. She said on the news last night that they were getting a lot of calls at the station, a lot of tips. They were passing them on to the police. I don't think there's anything wrong with them passing those tips on to us, too. Right?"

"I can ask," I said, feeling kind of guilty because Viv knew what Patrice Watson said on the news and I didn't. Patrice and I had been best friends for years, back when she went by Trisha. I always *meant* to watch the news, like respectable adults did. I just kept forgetting.

"I'll call her," I said. "I'll be done in about forty-five minutes. Come by the trailer and pick me up."

"You don't want to take your car?"

"I'm not used to parking it yet. I had to park at Walmart this morning, by the trucks and RVs, and walk to work from there. The thing is so huge."

"You just need practice. And there's no time like the present. We'll take your car and I'll talk you through the finer points of large car handling."

"Viv, I'm really not up for the stress of it."

"Salem, this is for your own good. Now, I won't take no for an answer. You can't go through the rest of your life afraid to park your own car."

"I can too."

"No. You can't. We're taking your car, and that's that. I'll pay for the gas."

"Your car is in the shop again, isn't it?"

"It's not in the shop. Well, it is, but just for some regularly scheduled maintenance."

I had an idea. "Viv, do you want to drive my car? That way we can — "

"Fantastic idea. You can learn by watching. Okay, come get me, and we'll do some detecting. Beat the police at their own game."

And there it was. The other reason Viv was so into this High Point Bandit thing. We'd solved two murders before the police did, and it would be such a feather in her cap to do so again with the robberies, since half the town was mad at the police for not solving the case.

As for me, I wanted to believe I did it because I enjoyed helping people. But yeah. I liked being able to tell Bobby I'd figured out who the bad guys were before he did. Especially after he'd had me falsely arrested for prostitution.

I pushed the "End Call" button and said, "Windy, call Tri-Patrice." That's the hybrid name I'd come up for Trisha, not to be cute, but because that's what came out of my mouth every time I said her name. Although she'd been back in my life for over a year now, my brain wasn't catching quickly to calling her something new.

"Look at you with that fancy new phone," Tammy said with a grin. "You're uptown now."

"As uptown as I can be with a personal assistant named Windy with an "i"."

Tri-Patrice was prepping for the evening news, but she didn't have any problem sending me the same list she'd sent the police. "You can't get email on your phone, can you?"

"Oh! I can, actually. I think I can." I held it out and tapped the screen. There was an icon for my email box. "Yes, I can." Yay me.

"On its way," Tri-Patrice said. "Let me know if you turn up anything newsworthy. And by newsworthy, I don't mean just weird people saying weird things. We're fully stocked on that."

I used the force dryer to blow the loose dog hair off me, then loaded Stump into the car and set off for Belle Court, the swanky "Independent Living" place where Viv lived. One of my pipe dreams, up there with winning the lottery or maybe a Grammy for Best Vocal Performance in the Shower, was someday living at Belle Court. I didn't even mind that I'd have to be old to get in, because it would also mean I was loaded — or "high falutin'" as G-Ma called it. The place was nice. Viv had a three-room suite with a little kitchen she never used and a walk-in whirlpool tub. There was a private spa on the fourth floor, for residents of that building only, and a hot masseuse named Ramone.

Fortunately, they allowed pets, so nobody put up a fuss when I carted Stump in. Betty, the pink-haired woman who usually sat in one of the wingbacked chairs by the fireplace in the reception area, waved me over and scratched at Stump's ears.

"When I was in my early twenties, I had a little Chihuahua named Pepe. He was the sweetest thing! I used to go to the drive-in movies with him, and I'd order popcorn and a root beer float and share it while we watched. I swear, he'd climb up on my shoulder, and curl himself around my neck," she said in her shaky voice, one blue-veined, knobbly hand lifting to gesture around the back of her neck. "He'd sit there and watch the movie. Every once in a while I'd give him a piece of popcorn." She lifted her hand again, the automatic offering to a dog who was no longer there. "And he'd eat it right in my ear!" She laughed and slapped her knee softly. "He was a gentleman, though. But if I waited too long — you know, if I got too engrossed in the movie and forgot to give him a piece, after a few minutes he'd let out this soft little, *brf!*" She made the kind of soft sound that Stump would make, in that same situation. Although Stump would probably be a bit more aggressive. She was no gentleman.

"I used to say that Pepe was my first husband. He went everywhere with me, he slept in my bed. He even killed spiders for me. He would eat them!"

"Oh my," I said, trying to look shocked. I'd heard all of this at least once a week for the past year. Every time I came to Belle Court. But I didn't mind. I could easily imagine myself in a few decades, telling the same stories about Stump over and over. I hoped some nice person would be willing to listen to the same thing dozens of times and still smile for me.

"Oh, that dog. I don't think he ever forgave me when I really did get married."

"Dogs can be jealous," I said.

"Oh, he was. So jealous. He pooped in my husband's shoes. Every day."

"Oh no!"

"He did! My husband threatened to take him out on a back road and toss him out the window, but he knew that if Pepe came up missing, he'd lose me, too." She laughed, her watery blue eyes twinkling.

Viv came out then and managed to hide her eye roll before Betty saw her. Viv didn't have quite the patience with oft-repeated stories that I did.

"Hi Betty. Hope you're feeling better."

"You know, I think I am. The doctor put me on some new medicine and I think it's doing the trick. Thank goodness! Last week I just vomited and vomited until I was sure — "

"Gotta go." Viv was halfway out the door by the end of the first "vomited." It wasn't that she was uncaring about Betty's illness. She just had a phobia about digestive issues in general. The fastest way to get her to move, I'd discovered, was to threaten to heave up lunch if she didn't.

"See you later," Betty called happily after us. I gave her another smile and waved as I followed Viv out.

I could usually tell what kind of detective show Viv had been watching that morning by the way she dressed and acted. Today it must have been one of the newer shows with the hard-as-nails-but-still-sexy female detectives. Viv wore a black suit with a gold satin button-down sleeveless shirt and strappy black heels. Thankfully, it was too warm for her Columbo trench coat.

"We have to swing by Trailertopia to drop off Stump with Frank," I said.

When we got there, Frank was nowhere to be found. He was not in my recliner, at any rate, which was where he always was when he wasn't in his own trailer. I knocked on his door several times and even tapped on some windows, but he didn't answer.

I stood looking from Viv to Stump. I'd promised myself less than twenty-four hours before that I would not involve her in any more of our detective work.

"It's broad daylight," Viv said. "It's not like anyone is going to start shooting in broad daylight."

"A lot of the robberies have happened in broad daylight," I said.

"But there were no shootings with them. And it's not like what happened last night could happen again. We're in your car, and won't get locked out. You keep her close, and she won't start that horrible howling thing and set off a riot."

I still wasn't sure, though. If I left her at home alone, she would definitely destroy something. She always did.

I could stay home. Let Viv go detecting on her own.

I sighed, trying to decide. I checked the window to see if Frank's truck was in his driveway. Nothing.

"Okay, here's the deal. I keep her with me. If anything slightly odd comes up, we're out of there. Instantly. Got it?"

Viv saluted me. "Yes sir!"

"And you're driving. So if shooting starts, I can cover her with my own body."

"That's your call, but yes, I'm driving."

"And paying for the gas?"

"And paying for the gas. Now, let's get going!"

I picked Stump up. "Parenting is full of hard choices."

Back at the Monte Carlo, Viv wiggled her skinny butt behind the wheel. "Okay, I made a list of all the places that have been robbed in the last month. We can take them after we get through with the leads Patrice Watson gave you."

"Sounds like a plan to me."

We went straight to the first name on Tri-Patrice's list: Nita Malone at Gino's Italian Kitchen. We took a seat out on the patio and I set Stump on the concrete beside my chair. She glared at me because she was supposed to always sit in my lap, but I figured we were pushing our luck enough just having a dog at a restaurant.

Nita Malone was a short roundish woman with apple cheeks and a constant smile. She made a nervous face when Viv told her we were there to follow up on her call to the station about the bandits, but agreed to speak to us. She sat on the edge of her seat at the iron patio table.

Viv pulled a little notebook and gold pen out of her handbag. "As I'm sure you've heard, the police are getting a lot of leads coming in." She cocked her head and squinted. "Maybe a few too many for them to handle by themselves, in fact. That's where we come in. We dedicate ourselves to one case at a time, so we have the time to follow up on every lead, no matter how far-fetched it might seem, and run it all the way down."

I nodded. I had to hand it to Viv. She'd managed to hint that the police were using us for their overflow work, without saying anything of the kind.

"Now, I just want you to tell me everything you know, anything suspicious you might have seen or heard, anything at all. We're just talking here. This isn't like a formal statement or anything, where you have to go on record. This is just us girls sitting around talking."

The woman nodded, but still looked nervous. "Okay, yes. Okay."

We all sat there, looking at each other, nodding like bobble-heads, when she jumped. "Oh! You mean — now? Just — just spit it out?"

"Just spit it out," Viv said, her face grave. "Just let it come."

"Okay, well." She took a deep breath. "So, there's this guy who comes in every Thursday night. For half-price baked spaghetti night."

"Yes." Viv nodded encouragement.

I took out my phone like I was entering notes on the notepad. Thursdays, half-price spaghetti at Gino's.

"I mean, he never misses. He comes in every week, he has the spaghetti and unsweet tea. And he leaves a three dollar tip. Every week for — oh — two-and-a-half years? Three years. Every week."

"And, he missed this week?"

"Oh, no." She shook her head. "He still came. But this week, he left a *five* dollar tip."

Viv and I sat in silence, taking that in.

"He has more money to spend. I mean, that's almost double.

Almost."

I nodded. "It *is* almost double."

"The police said to be on the lookout for someone who looks like they've recently come into some money. And at first I didn't think anything about it, but you know, later I got to thinking..." She spread her hands and shrugged. "I mean, it might be nothing. But then again..."

"No, you're right, you're right." Viv nodded. "This is the kind of thing that might seem insignificant. Until you look a little closer and see there's more to it than just this one thing. Do you have a name for this guy?"

She shook her head. "Oh, no, he always pays cash."

"He's been coming here for two or three years and you've never asked his name?"

"He's real quiet. Keeps to himself, you know." She jerked upright, looking wide-eyed between me and Viv. "Oh my gosh. That's what they always say, don't they? *They were quiet and kept to themselves.* That's what they always say about the bad guy after he gets caught." She put her fingers to her mouth and gave a nervous laugh. "Oh, my goodness."

"Do you have any way we could follow up with this guy? Any idea where he lives? What kind of car does he drive?"

"I don't know where he lives, but he drives a white Ford F-150."

Viv and I exchanged a look. That narrowed it down to roughly 60,000 men in the county.

"That's helpful. Anything else?"

She shook her head. "No, not that I can think of."

Viv frowned and tapped her pen on her pad. "Have you ever noticed what direction he drives in, when he leaves? Maybe we could just head that direction and see what we see."

That sounded like a waste of gas to me, but she was paying, so...

"We could just come back Tuesday and see him for ourselves. Pick up the tail there." Because half-priced spaghetti.

Viv nodded and flipped her notebook shut. "Excellent idea. That's just a few days. We'll do that." She stood and shook the woman's hand, then handed her another card for good measure. "Please, if you think of anything, anything at all, don't hesitate to call. Day or night."

Back at the car, she tossed her purse into the seat and said, "Well, that was a waste of time."

"Really? It could be something."

"It wasn't. A two-dollar increase in tip is not a smoking gun."

"It was a clear break from his pattern."

"He was out of one dollar bills and gave her a five instead. It's nothing. Plus, he's a loner. He's been here every week for three years and they have no idea what his name is, even. Our guys come in a four-pack."

"Still, I think it's worth pursuing —"

Viv spun on me. "Good grief. Is this about the half-priced spaghetti?"

"A little."

"Fine. We'll come back next week for the half-priced spaghetti. But if she has any more *leads* —" She made air quotes. "You'll be the one to write them down."

"Okay," I agreed, happy.

Our next stop was the laundromat a couple of blocks from Gino's. The sheet Tri-Patrice sent me had a written note beside her name: "Called four times. Angry."

The woman was folding laundry with a plastic folding thing. She had a tiny stud in the side of her nose. "Oh yeah, I know who did it. The cops aren't giving me the time of day, but I'm telling you. This woman? She's behind it. I guarantee." She slapped a t-shirt onto the plastic, made three quick motions and bam! Neatly folded shirt.

"Who is this woman?" Viv poised her gold pen over her notebook.

"Her name is Erlinda Roman, and she lives down there on Twelfth. Red brick house with lion statues out by the driveway."

"And why do you think she's got anything to do with this? The police said we're looking for four males."

"Well, they have masks on, right? And black jackets? It could be women."

"I suppose," Viv said.

"And she's real butch. I mean, she wears makeup and stuff, and curls her hair? But she's really aggressive. Like, bossy. Has to run the show." She held up her pinky finger. "Her husband? He's like this." She swirled her other index finger around her pinky. "Wrapped around her finger."

Viv nodded and jotted down something that was most likely along the lines of "whack job."

"Okay, what else? Has something happened lately that makes you suspicious?"

The woman gave a satisfied nod. "Sure did. The other day they drive up in a new car. Brand new. Well, not brand new, but nearly new. Very nice. Flashy, even."

"Uh-huh." Viv blinked.

"And here two weeks ago, my kid was selling popcorn for Boy

Scouts and she says she doesn't have money for popcorn. I mean, come on. She's got money for a new car, but not for popcorn?" She drew her brows down and gave a head shake. "That don't even make sense, does it?"

"No," I said. I shifted Stump to my other hip. "What kind of popcorn was it? That chocolate caramel kind?"

"Yeah, he had all kinds. You want some? I have his order form in the office."

"Maybe," I said. I was afraid to ask how much and end up a suspect on her list.

"Anyway," Viv said. "One day she says she can't afford popcorn, and the next thing you know, she's buying a new car?"

"Exactly." The woman gave a sharp nod, as if this sealed the case.

"Okay, let's talk this through." Viv stood and folded one arm against her middle, the other hand to her chin. She paced slowly before the windows. "Let's say she *is* one of the four. Who are the other three?"

"Well, her husband, for one. I mean, seriously. That guy does whatever she tells him to do. One time we were at a barbecue and I swear, every other thing out of her mouth was, "Roman, bring me this, Roman, get me that. She calls him that, too — by his last name. Weird, right?"

I nodded for form's sake.

"So that's two," Viv prompted.

"Yeah, okay, and they have a son. He's, oh, about sixteen, I guess. Seventeen. And pretty tall. So I think if he was all dressed in black, he'd look like any other guy." She nodded as if this sealed the deal.

Viv paced a little more. "Okay, so by my count, thats — that's three. And we need four."

Viv and I looked at each other. She looked tired, actually. We were working this angle a little too hard.

"Yeah, I don't really know about that."

"Do they have any family here?"

She shrugged. "Not that I know of."

"Friends?"

"No, nobody likes them." She gave a smug smile. "Well, nobody likes her. Her husband's okay, when he can get a word in edgewise. But not her."

"So we're still at three. And all the reports have said there were four."

"Yeah, well, I guess that's what the detectives are for, right? Find the details."

"You're right there," Viv said. She clicked her pen and began to shut her notebook, then said, "Oh, one more thing."

So she *had* watched Columbo lately.

"Is she new around here, Erlinda? Recently moved to town?"

"Erlinda? Heck no. She's been living here since second grade."

"Oh, you went to school together?"

"Yeah. Since second grade. In fact, I beat her here by one day. I was the new girl for one lousy day before Erlinda moved in and took that." *Flip flip flip* with the board, and the stack grew another color. "Then, in *tenth* grade, the hussy stole my boyfriend. I guess she's just always been one for taking whatever she can get her greedy hands on."

"Sounds like it," Viv said. "Okay, you've given us some very good information to go on. Please don't hesitate to contact us if you think of anything else that might be helpful."

Back at the car, Viv tossed her purse into the seat and dropped behind the wheel with a groan. "Good Lord. This whole street is nothing but whackos."

"Man, she was intense. Ready to send her neighbor up the river over stealing her tenth-grade boyfriend."

"Yes, well, that and getting a new car. That tends to make people a little crazy sometimes." She leaned into the rear view mirror and checked her lipstick. "Speaking of your G-Ma, how is her whorehouse — I mean, motel business going?"

"I don't know," I said. "She's been suspiciously silent."

"That's good, though, right? No more calls about the bandits headed for her door."

"I suppose. I think she's mad at me because I helped cut off her gravy train."

Viv applied a new coat of lipstick and clamped her lips on a tissue before tossing it back into her bag. "That sounds about as reasonable as I would expect from her."

"Maybe instead of interviewing Trisha's leads, we should interview one of the people who's been robbed. That dry cleaners down the street is one, I think." I didn't want to talk about G-Ma. I didn't see how I could have done anything different than what I'd done, but I still felt guilty for her loss of income. G-Ma hadn't exactly had it easy in life. She worked hard, and she'd been excited that she was finally making a steady income. And I hated for her to be mad at me.

Viv perked up at the thought of interviewing Bandit victims. "We'll go back to some of the call-in leads if none of these pan out."

Bobby Sloan was already at the dry cleaners.

"Oh look," he said, with obvious dissatisfaction. "It's the *detectives.*" He put his fingers up to make air quotes.

"You know who else does that all the time?" I said, squinting. "Dale. Remember Dale? You know, I knew when I met him that he reminded me of somebody. I guess it was you."

"Yeah," Viv said. "They both know everything. They do have that in common."

"Yeah," I agreed. "The knowing everything and the air quotes."

"What happened to that guy, anyway?" Bobby asked. "How come he's not hanging around with you two anymore?"

Viv and I looked at each other. Uh-oh.

"You're the one who knows everything. You tell us," Viv said, because she's a lot better at thinking on her feet than I am.

"I know you better hope you don't pass a street cop," Bobby said, with a nod toward my windshield. "Your inspection sticker is about half a year past due."

I gasped and whirled around. He was right!

"Crap!" I said. I turned back to Bobby. "How much is that fine?"

He shrugged. "Couple hundred bucks, last I remember." He grinned. "I'm sure there's a beat cop nearby. They're patrolling this area pretty hard these days. I can call one over and ask."

"No, no, that's okay."

"Salem, maybe you ought to concentrate on taking care of your own business and leaving the police work to the police."

"Yeah, 'cause they're doing such a bang-up job," Viv said.

"Umm, Viv." I put a hand on her arm. "Let's not antagonize him." I had no idea if he really would call a cop, but I didn't want to find out.

I pulled out my phone. "Windy, where's the nearest place to get an inspection sticker?"

Windy's little windstreams waved a few seconds, then she said, "Okay, honey, it looks there's one just right over yonder, about fifty yards to the west. Estacado Auto Repair. And if that doesn't work, there's another place a few blocks further north, and another one back toward town."

Bobby was staring at my phone. "What the heck?"

"I know," I said. "I won it. It's 100 percent local."

"She sounds like my aunt," he said.

"I know, right?" I turned and gave him my best I'm-sorry-officer smile. "I seriously didn't realize about the inspection sticker."

"I gathered that from the way you freaked out when I told you. You need to get that taken care of."

"I swear I will. As soon as we interview this guy, I'll drive it straight over to Estocado Auto Repair and get it inspected. I promise." I held up my hand in what I could only hope approximated a Girl Scout salute. "It's just right over yonder."

"See that you do." He gave me and Viv and nod, then moved toward his car.

"That's it?" Viv said, not bothering to hide her disappointment. "You're not even going to warn us about staying out of danger? About steering clear of the criminal element?"

I didn't want to admit it, but it was kind of anticlimactic to see Bobby and not blow off some of his dire warnings.

"Not at all." He grinned broadly and opened his arms wide. "Conduct all the interviews you want. Knock yourself out."

"Aren't you even a little bit concerned for our safety?"

"Not really. These guys? They aren't actually hurting anybody, not physically anyway. So far they haven't shown a single weapon. We only have their word for it that they even *have* weapons."

"What about the lecture about staying out of your way? Columbo gets that one at least once an episode."

"You're not in my way," Bobby said, still looking altogether too blase about the whole thing. "At least, not any more than anybody else is. Clete Pigg has his own citizens task force watching the *police*, for the love of Pete, so they can make sure we're actually doing our jobs. For once, you two aren't the biggest pains in my butt. Like I said, have at it. Get what you can out of the guy. Maybe it'll help."

He didn't look very hopeful, though.

I followed Viv into the dry cleaners, my lips clamped. Crap crap crap. Would that car even pass inspection? Yes, it drove like a dream, but there was no telling what impending doom a close look would turn up.

A tall, thin kid of about fifteen stood behind the counter. He looked like the kind of kid who would be handsome, once he grew into his nose. "Can I help you," he said, not like a question, but like one who had been instructed to say the words.

"We are investigating the recent robberies in this area," Viv said.

The kid's bland expression slid to me, as if to ask, "Seriously?"

I shrugged.

"We understand this establishment has been targeted by the robbers. Is that correct?"

"Yeah."

"Were you here at the time?"

His chin lifted, indicating upward. "Upstairs."

"Who was here?"

"My dad. He was the only one in the front. My mom was in the back, but by the time she got up here, they were gone."

"Where's your dad now? Is he here?"

"Next door."

I stepped back and looked at what was next door. A donut shop?! I had been so busy dealing with Bobby and the horrifying out-of-date inspection sticker that I had not noticed there were donuts nearby.

"He'll be right back. He just went to make sure the ovens were off."

"You guys own that, too?"

"Yep." His mouth went flat and his eyes bulged a bit, like, *Yep, the American Freaking Dream, right here.*

A few minutes later a man came in, just as thin as his son, a bit stooped, but with the same formidable nose.

Viv explained to him what we were doing.

He eyed me and Stump. I shifted her a bit and tightened my arms around her, indicating that I had no intention of putting her down to run loose on his fifty-year-old linoleum.

"I just talked to the cops," he said, with a nod toward the door.

"Detective Sloan?" Viv asked. "Yeah, he's a buddy of ours, actually. You know, the police department and private eyes like us, we work together a lot more that people think. We have to, you know." She laughed. "I mean, it takes a village, right?"

"No, the Bandits are taking the village. So hopefully one of you can figure out who this is and get them locked up where they belong."

"Absolutely. So now. Can you tell me exactly what happened?"

"Exactly? Well, they exactly ran in here, almost knocked the door off the hinges, yelling like banshees, and shouted for me to give them everything in the register. So I did. Then they left."

"You say they. How many were there?"

"Four," he said with a little side-eye of his own. Everyone knew there were four.

"You're sure there were four?" Viv asked.

He waited a beat. "Quite sure, yes." *I can count to four*, his eyes said.

"Okay, you said..." She moved back toward the door, and I shifted Stump to the other hip and stepped out of her way. Viv opened the door. "You said they almost knocked the door off the hinges. This door?"

He looked around the tiny area. There was no other door to be seen. "Yes, that door."

"So they came in and they — " She stepped outside and took the door handle from the outside, then made a big show of yanking it open. "Almost knocked the door off the hinges. Is that right?"

She was going full Columbo now. It must have been a full morning of Columbo and CSI Fashion Week or something.

I, on the other hand, was feeling Stump. She was solid and practically square, so carrying her was something like carrying a warm furry cinder block.

"That's right."

"And there were four of them?" She held up four fingers.

He nodded.

"And where were they standing, exactly?"

Again, the guy looked at the area. Between the front door and the counter, there was a space maybe five feet deep and ten feet wide. If they had more than three customers in line, someone would have to wait outside.

He spread his hands and waved them back and forth vaguely. "They were here. That's the only — just here." He looked at me with an expression that said, "Is she for real?"

"All right here? All four of them?"

He nodded again, frowning. "Look, there's not a lot to say. Four guys, they came in, they made a lot of noise, they took my money."

"Now, about that," Viv said. "They made a lot of noise. What did they say, exactly?"

"No words at first, just you know." He opened his mouth wide. "Just Ahhhh! You know. Shouting. Like, the kind of noise football players make in a huddle."

"Football players in a huddle," Viv said, her hand to her chin, nodding gravely. "Football players in a huddle. So what you're saying is, these guys were a team."

"Well, not a team, exactly. They were just — "

"No, you know what, Mr. — I'm sorry, what was your name?"

"Mr. Indah."

"Mr. Indah," Viv said. "I think you might have subconsciously hit upon something there. These guys function — " She held her hands out and laced her fingers together. "They function as a team. They have a relationship."

Mr. Indah drew his head back. "A what?

Viv shook her head and gave a light laugh, pacing back and

forth in the tiny space on her brown suede ankle boots. "I'm not implying anything romantic. I'm just saying, they have some kind of history together. They fit together like cogs in a wheel." She laced her knuckles together again, turning her hands to mimic cogs working together. "It's possible," she said, her finger up to emphasize her point. "It's possible they have been training together for weeks, months, perfecting their movements, developing a kind of — a kind of shorthand, a language of their own, even."

Enough theorizing, I decided, as Stump slid a bit and looked up at me, annoyed. "So, how much did they take?" I asked.

"The police asked me to keep that information secret," he said. "But it wasn't a lot. Too much, but not a lot."

"And you own the donut shop, too? Did they get that also?"

"No," he said, with obvious relief. "Thank goodness. There's usually more cash over there, and especially on a Saturday morning."

"I wonder why they didn't rob that while they were here?" I said.

"I don't know, but I'd prefer they not come back."

"Of course," I said. "I'm really sorry that this happened."

"You and me both. It's been a nightmare. Every time my wife hears a noise, she thinks it's them, come back for what little we have left."

"Well, tell your wife she can rest easy. We have a 100 percent success rate, and we don't intend to change that any time soon."

"I'll tell her," he said, with the same frown. I figured Mr. Indah was about done with us.

"Thank you for your time," Viv said, pulling one of our business cards from her Michael Kors bag. "Please call us any time, day or night, if you think of something else. Anything at all. Oh!" she said, as if she'd just remembered. "Did you see what kind of car they were driving?"

"A white four-door Camry."

We all looked kind of glum at that. Every other car in town was a white Camry.

Even Viv couldn't put a spin on that one. "Pretty lame," she offered.

He nodded. "Yeah, for violent thugs, it is."

"Oh, that's another question," I said. "Bobby Sloan just said that so far, the robberies have not been violent. No weapons, even. Did you see a weapon?"

He shook his head. "No. They just ran in, made a bunch of noise, slammed their hands against the counter, and — "

"Slammed their hands against the counter?" Viv said, her eyes narrowed. "You didn't tell me that."

"Well, they did. A couple of them did, I mean, not all four of them. They were yelling and making a bunch of noise, like — like shock and awe, you know."

"I would advise you, Mr. Indah, not to withhold information from us. It is in your interest to provide every bit of detail you know."

"I did provide you with —"

"We're on your side here, Mr. Indah." Viv lowered her head and looked at him with disapproving eyes.

He looked abashed for a second, then lowered his own brows as, apparently, he realized he didn't owe this crazy old coot one thing.

"So, no weapons," I said, bringing the conversation back around. "Did they threaten to use a weapon? Like, act like they had a gun and just didn't show it?"

He shook his head. "No, not a word about a gun or anything. They were just so — so big and black and loud. And it was so surprising. They caught me off guard."

"The element of surprise," Viv said with a sage nod of her curly white head. "Even in the animal kingdom, it's a powerful tool."

Seriously, now that was enough. I shifted Stump again and stuck my hand out. "Mr. Indah, we appreciate your time. We will be getting back with you if we hear anything that might help." I gestured to Viv with my head. "Okay, I think we're done here."

"Yep." Viv snapped her notebook shut, not having written a single word.

I followed her out the door, then stopped and turned back to him. "Say, do you know the people who own Estacado Auto?"

He nodded. "Yeah, a little."

"Do you know how...flexible they are, in terms of giving inspection stickers?"

He looked out at the gold boat, then back at me with sympathy. "I've heard they can be very accommodating," he said with a knowing look.

"Really?" Yay! "I mean, that could be very good for me."

"What I've heard is, they give you exactly what you ask for. If you go in and say you need an inspection, they'll give you an inspection. If you say you want an inspection sticker, then that's what you get. Ask for Marty."

"Really?!" I said again, indecently thrilled. "That's exactly what I need. An inspection sticker."

I ran back out to the car. "Viv! Guess what?"

"Did he think of another clue he didn't tell me?"

"No, and by the way, Good Lord, what was that?"

"What was what? That, my friend, was working a case." She pushed her Kate Spade sunglasses higher on her nose and opened a tube of lipstick.

"You were even freaking me out a little bit."

"That is called keeping them on their toes, my friend."

"Okay, (a), stop calling me "my friend." And (b), you do get that he's not a suspect, right? He's a victim."

"Is he? Everyone is a suspect until they guilty party is caught and convicted."

"So how'd he do it? Dress up in black and scare himself into giving up the money? To himself?"

"How do we even know he was even robbed? I mean, it was just him. Nobody else saw the robbers. We have only his word for it. He could be conniving some insurance fraud — "

"I seriously think we're going down rabbit holes here." I put the key in the ignition and turned it. The car roared to life and seemed to levitate.

"Hey, wait a minute. Why am I driving? You're supposed to be driving now."

"It's time to throw you in and let you sink or swim, Grass-hopper."

"You're freaked out about the inspection sticker, aren't you?"

"I just got a ticket, remember? Five days ago? If I get another one they'll definitely make it compulsory for me to retest. So you're driving until we're legal again, sweetheart."

"Okay, well...it's not that far. One block so I can get a sticker for this monster. Then it's your turn again."

I turned in my seat and looked as far back down Clovis

Highway as I could, then turned and looked the other way. So far as I could tell, there were no cops.

I looked "down yonder" to the entrance of Estacado Auto, hyper-aware of all the times I'd heard "increased patrols" over the past few weeks. Surely I could get two hundred yards down the road without being pulled over.

I sat frozen at the edge of the parking lot.

"What?"

"I'm looking for cops. I don't know how a ticket will affect my probation."

"We've been driving all afternoon on an out-of-date sticker. What are the odds you'll be caught in the next forty-five seconds?"

"The odds are astronomically in favor of me getting caught in the next forty-five seconds! Think about it. Every time I drove the car and didn't get a ticket, I increased those odds. It has to catch up to me at some point, right? Plus, we were blissfully unaware before. Now that I know, it's like I have a giant radioactive awareness cloud over my head that says "Catch me! Catch me!"

"You are riding this freak out a little too hard," Viv said. "Ease up on the spurs a bit."

"Tell me about it." I looked both ways again. I stepped on the gas, but didn't take my other foot off the brake. The car lurched but didn't go anywhere. My feet seemed to be aware that as long as I didn't move onto the road, I hadn't broken any laws.

"Wait," Viv said. She leaned to look past me, then craned her neck the other way. "Okay, go now! Go now!"

I screamed and floored the accelerator. The car fishtailed onto the road, throwing gravel behind us. I was certain I was about to be t-boned by a semi.

"What?!" I shouted at Viv as we tore down the road.

"I just wanted you to get moving. But you can slow down now. Slow down!"

I swooped the car into Estacado's parking lot, spraying more gravel when I came to a screeching halt in front of the building. The car rocked back, and I killed the engine. My heart was pounding so hard I saw spots. Stump was scrambling for balance in the seat, and once she'd gotten stable she glared up at me.

"Blame her," I said, jerking a thumb at Viv. "You scared the poo out of me," I said.

"Well then, we're even." She took a deep breath and fluffed at her hair.

I looked up then at the automotive to see three men staring, slack-jawed, at us.

"Stay in the car," I told Stump.

I picked up my purse and went into the building. "I'm looking for Marty," I said.

The three remained frozen, staring at me. Then slowly, two of them lifted their fingers to point at the third.

"Marty, I need an inspection *sticker*," I said. I gave him a wide-eyed look that I hoped conveyed my meaning. "A *sticker*."

He stared a few more seconds, then said, "Well, we know your brakes work, at any rate."

"Yeah, uh, sorry about that. I was in a hurry because I just realized my sticker was past due and I didn't want to take the chance of getting a ticket for that."

The four of us stood in silence for a moment. I hoped the other non-pertinent facts of the moment — that doing approximately twice the speed limit and nearly running the Monster Carlo through the front windows of Estacado Auto Repair, thereby killing three people were *also* ways of catching negative attention from the authorities — would remain unsaid.

Finally, Marty cleared his throat. "Well, we're required to see your insurance card."

I went back out to the car. Viv was standing beside it, looking a bit dazed but none the worse for wear. I pulled the insurance card out of the glove box and handed it to him, then petted Stump to reassure her after our Lubbock Motor Speedway performance.

She was over it, though. She curled up in the sunshine and went to sleep. Resilient, that girl is.

Back in the office, the other two men were gone, presumably out to the bays where cars waited on lifts.

"I have to call this in and make sure it's current," he said.

I looked at Viv. I'd never heard of this before.

He went behind the counter and into an office and closed the door.

I set my keys on the counter and hesitated. I looked back at Viv.

"Do they do that? Have they ever done that with you? I thought if you just handed them the card they took it."

She shrugged. "Is it legit?"

"Yeah," I said, defensively. "Pretty sure."

The problem was, I wasn't always great about taking care of the petty details of life, like paying bills on time. I was getting better. But I'd screwed up enough times in my life that I was only maybe eighty percent confident that I was on top of everything at any given moment.

I leaned my head against the door. Nothing.

I turned back to Viv and jumped when I saw one of the two guys standing there, watching me.

"Oh!" I put my hand to my chest. "Sorry. I was just — he said he had to call it in and make sure it was current. Is that what you usually do?"

He shrugged. "I guess so. I can go ahead and get started, though."

I turned back to the door, wondering how much a ticket for no sticker and no insurance would cost. Hundreds and hundreds, no doubt. And maybe more hundreds.

I stepped up to the door and leaned my ear against it.

The door opened and I almost fell inside. "Oh!" I said again. "Sorry. Any problems?"

"None at all. You're right as rain."

"Okay, well, that's good. I recently switched companies and..." I looked at the counter. "Where are my keys?"

"The guy took them." Viv nodded toward the parking lot. Which was now empty.

"He took my car?"

Marty laughed. "Calm down. He's not stealing it. He's just testing the brakes and the — "

"He took my Stump!?"

I ran out to the parking lot and looked both directions. Half a block further "down yonder" I could see the Monster Carlo driving away.

"Oh no!" I said, imagining the unholy noise Stump was going to make when she saw a strange man driving away with her. I hoped she didn't tear a hole in the seat.

"See?!" I shouted to Viv. "I knew I shouldn't have brought

her. Never again!"

"Would you relax? Look, he's just driving down the street. She's fine."

I saw brake lights. The car came to a screeching halt in the middle of the road. Then he pulled over and made a wide u-turn.

They were about fifty yards away when I heard Stump's ear-splitting cries.

The guy sped up as he got closer.

"What...?" Marty said.

"My dog," I said, trying to sound like it was no big deal. "She has separation anxiety issues."

He was silent for a moment. "That's one dog?"

"I know, right?" Viv said. "She caused a riot the other night."

The guy jumped out of my car, looking haunted. "I don't know what's the matter with your dog — "

"Nothing. It's okay, she just likes to stay close to me."

Stump's horrifying racket shot up an octave when she saw me. I ran around to the passenger door and lifted her. "Shhh, you're okay."

"I didn't touch her," the guy said. "She was just asleep on the seat, then she woke up and saw me, and started screaming. I swear."

"Oh, I believe you," I assured him. "She's — " I tucked her tight to my side so one ear was covered, and covered the other ear with my hand. She reduced the noise to an occasional yip. "She is a bit...tightly wound.

"Real tight," Viv said. She reached over and scratched Stump's head, though, so neither of us took offense.

The four of us stood there silently for a few seconds, and the guy shuddered. "You're sure she's okay?"

"Oh, she's fine. See?"

Stump chose that moment to yawn hugely. When her mouth opened, the guy took a step back, his hands raised in defense. Then he realized she was yawning and relaxed a bit. She finished the routine with a little yip, though, and he jumped.

I gave him a sympathetic smile. "I'm sorry she scared you."

Marty laughed. "Tough guy like him? He can't get scared that easily."

"Oh, I was scared alright," the guy said, nodding. "You should have heard her." He turned to me. "You might want to just hold her while I finish the inspection, though. Just to be on the safe side."

"Yeah, about that," I said. "See, I said I wanted an inspection sticker. Just the sticker."

The guy nodded. "Yeah, I know. So you can hold her while I drive around the block and check the brakes and turn signals and stuff."

I took a deep breath and smiled again, although this time it felt distinctly less good-natured. "See, the thing is, I'm almost positive it will pass. Almost positive. But if it doesn't...what happens then?"

"Well, you don't get your sticker. You fix whatever's wrong and bring it back. And there's no charge if it doesn't pass, of course."

"But then I have to drive home without a current sticker."

"Well, we can take a look at whatever we find — if we find anything. It might be that it's something easy to fix. We can take care of it right away and then you'll be good to go."

"Yes, but what if it's not easy to fix?"

Marty and the guy both kind of sighed. I could tell I was getting on their nerves. I was kind of getting on my own nerves.

"I'm sorry," I said. "I just — I heard that you were sometimes a little flexible on the regulations. You know." I raised my eyebrows. "You know, just a little. Flexible?"

"Flexible?" the guy asked. "Flexible how?"

I frowned. This was so much more awkward than I was prepared for. "Nothing major. I just heard that Estacado Auto will give you exactly what you ask for. If you ask for an inspection, you get an inspection. If you ask for an inspection sticker, you get the sticker."

Marty laughed. "Is that right?"

The guy gave Marty a look, and something passed silently between them. He frowned heavily, then backed up, his hands held in the air. "I don't want no part of this." He looked from me to Marty. "You hear me? No part. I tried to do a clean inspection, by the book. I'm not issuing no sticker for no car I didn't do a full inspection on. You got me?" He pointed at Marty. "No part."

Marty laughed. "Xavier, don't worry about it, man. You haven't done anything wrong."

"Yeah, well, I'm not going to, either." He frowned at all of us, then turned, one hand raised in farewell. "Not gonna happen."

"It's okay. Don't get yourself upset."

But Xavier was back in the garage by now, having washed his hands of us.

"Jeez Louise," Viv said. "Stump's not the only one who's tightly wound."

"I'm sorry," I said. "I didn't mean to upset him."

"Aw, he's okay," Marty said with a wave toward the garage. "He's just got out of the pen, and he's a little snakebit. Not anxious to go back anytime soon."

The pen. *Penitentiary.* Well, that explained a few things.

Marty took my keys. "How about I take a look at your car? I bet it'll pass." He winked at me.

While we waited, I walked over to the garage and found Xavier, who was busily wiping down hand tools.

"Listen," I said. "I'm really sorry about all that. I didn't realize it was that big a deal. I was just worried about getting a ticket, and I wasn't sure I could pay for a ticket."

He gave me a look. "You're worried about *you* getting a *ticket?* But you're okay asking me to do something that'll get me in a lot more trouble than a ticket?"

"I honestly didn't — I'm sorry. I didn't realize it was that big a deal." I repeated. My excuse sounded lame, and I knew it.

He laid one wrench into a box and picked up another, glared at me, and said nothing.

"Yes, well, I'm sorry." I tucked Stump closer to me and turned away.

The car didn't pass inspection. The left turn signal was out.

"I can fix it, but not today," Marty said. "They don't make parts for this model anymore. Have to get them made special from this outfit out of state."

"What do I do?" I looked around in desperation. I now had a car I couldn't legally drive.

"Okay, here's what we can do. I'll give you this receipt that shows you tried to get it legal. If you get pulled over, just show them this. They hardly ever give tickets when they know you're trying to do something about it."

"Hardly ever." That was little comfort.

"Hardly ever," Marty echoed.

"I can't believe I let you talk me into buying this car," I said to Viv. "One day and I'm already about to get a ticket."

"You just bought this car?" Marty said. "Well, this ought to be covered by the dealer, then. Take it back to them and get them to fix the turn signal and give you the sticker. That ought to be covered by your warranty. I thought you'd maybe inherited it from your grandmother or...great-grandmother or something."

"When is your car going to be fixed?" I asked Viv.

"It's not broken. It's just getting some routine — "

"When will it be available for you to drive again?"

She sulked. "Tomorrow. Maybe. Probably Thursday or Friday, though."

I sighed. "Well, we have to get home somehow. I guess I'll take my chances with this — this thing. Maybe I can make it down the highway without anyone looking too closely and still get the sticker this evening."

My heart hammered the entire length of Clovis Highway. The Monster Carlo wasn't exactly inconspicuous as it was. It was well after seven o'clock, but the light was still good and I felt like my windshield had a flashing neon sign that said, "Ticket me!" on it. We passed two cop cars, and I died a little bit both times.

Five Star Automotive was on the left side of the road. I drove past, turned right, then right again two more times, until I was able to park on the street at the side of the place.

It was already closed. "Seriously?!" I was done in. "I don't think I can drive that thing one more minute. Let's call a cab."

"What about your G-Ma? Maybe she can loan us her car."

"It's broken down, too, remember?"

"It must be fixed now," she said. "It was sitting at her office when we drove past."

"It was? I didn't even notice."

We walked over to the Executive Inn and I opened the office door.

"Don't be bringing that dog into my office," G-Ma said from her rocking chair.

I bit back a sigh and stood in the doorway. "Hi, G-Ma. How are you?"

"Fine," she said, in a way that meant she was clearly not fine and clearly still mad. "What do you need?"

I decided to forgo any pretense that I was here to check on her welfare only. "I need a ride home. We both do." I gestured toward Viv with a tilt of my head. "I bought a new car next door but it's — it needs a few details updated before I can drive it home."

"Then you ought to keep your trade-in until it's ready for you."

I explained about buying the car the day before and how we'd come to be driving it today.

"What about her car?" G-Ma did the same head tilt thing at Viv that I had done.

"It's in the shop," I said, at the same time Viv said, "It's having routine maintenance done."

"There's something wrong with it," I said, loudly. I knew there was no quicker way to get G-Ma into a happy and generous mood. Viv would just have to suck it up. "We're stranded over here and we need your help to get home."

G-Ma smiled. "Is that right?"

I risked a glance at Viv. She was glaring at me with thin lips.

"Just go with it," I said through clenched teeth.

Viv gave me another look, then reached into her handbag. "I can pay for your gas money." She held up a hundred dollar bill.

G-Ma grabbed her purse from under the counter and said, "I don't need your money. Let's get going."

She put up a cardboard sign that said, "Back directly," gave me strict instructions to keep Stump securely in my lap so she didn't poo on the car seat (in G-Ma's mind, dogs were nothing but spewing fountains of poo covered in fur) and drove cheerfully back toward Belle Court.

Once we got there, Viv said, "Virgie, I insist on paying you for the gas. You've done us a big favor and I appreciate it."

"I don't need your money," G-Ma said. She sounded less convincing this time, though.

Viv sighed. "I know you don't. But it's the right thing to do. Please. Allow me to do the right thing."

G-Ma was silent.

Viv got out of the car, opened G-Ma's door, and handed her the money. When G-Ma reached for it, Viv grabbed her hand, leaned close, and whispered something into G-Ma's ear.

G-Ma sat back, still silent.

"What?" I asked.

"I told her thank you for the ride. I'll see you tomorrow, Salem."

G-Ma was silent as we drove out of Belle Court. I wanted to ask what Viv had said, but something about the look on G-Ma's face kept me silent.

I noticed we weren't heading toward Trailertopia, but back down Clovis Highway.

"Where are we going?" I asked.

"Back to the motel. You can just use my car until you get yours taken care of."

"Seriously? You're letting me borrow the Lincoln?"

This was a full-blown miracle. I could have had it certified by the Vatican, if they knew how much G-Ma loved that Lincoln and how little she trusted anyone else with it.

"Yeah, just be careful with it. You know. Go the speed limit." She frowned like she was already regretting the decision. "You have to get to work tomorrow and everything. So this will be easier than me carting you all over town."

I didn't know what to say, so I kept my mouth shut to avoid saying anything to change her mind. The Lincoln was still a bit big for my tastes, but certainly smaller than the Monster Carlo. Driving it to work tomorrow would be a lot less stressful.

G-Ma pulled up to the motel and looked at me and Stump. "Wait here," she said.

As she went in, I texted Viv. "What in the world did you say to G-Ma?"

A few seconds later, she answered. "That you loved her and put up with her craziness and helped her every time you could, and that she ought not blame you for doing something to protect her."

I felt a sudden burning in my nose and swallowed a lump in my throat. "Thanks," I texted back.

A few seconds later, my phone dinged again. "I might have called her an old fool, I don't remember."

G-Ma came out with three thick towels and laid them all out on the passenger seat. Then she motioned for me to lay Stump there.

I did as I was told and gave her a hug. "Thank you, G-Ma.

This is very generous of you."

"Yes, well. Get out of here. I don't want you driving it after dark."

CHAPTER NINE

Again with the Dumpsters

Wednesday morning, I woke up so nervous about driving G-Ma's car that I actually wished I had the Monster Carlo back. If I dinged that thing, it wouldn't even be noticeable, much less set off the family drama to end all family dramas. I went to the tiny second bedroom of my trailer and lit my candles, intending to devote my morning devotional time to praying for the Blood of Jesus to protect G-Ma's Lincoln, and therefore my own life.

I always read the daily Bible verse first because in my experience there was almost always something in the verse to address whatever my freakout of the day was about.

Today, though, it let me down.

Judge not, and you will not be judged; condemn not, and you will not be condemned; forgive, and you will be forgiven. Luke 6:37 (ESV)

I frowned. What did that mean? Did that mean I was going to need forgiveness soon?

My panic ratcheted up a notch. Was God trying to tell me something?

I said a quick, "Dear Heavenly Father," and launched immediately to the point. "What? What are you telling me here? If I forgive G-Ma, she'll forgive me? For what? I mean, on both sides, what are we forgiving each other for?"

I waited for a divine revelation. I had nothing to forgive G-Ma for. Yes, she was difficult to deal with from time to time. Who wasn't? I wouldn't have taken her disrespect of Stump from anyone else, but still. G-Ma had been my rock all my life. She had given me the only stability I'd known in my life. She gave me sanctuary from Mom and all her men.

Mom.

I sat back on my heels, annoyed. I'd come in here looking for peace about the morning drive and God was springing the heavy stuff on me? That was hardly fair. It wasn't even seven o'clock in the freaking morning yet.

Tony.

Okay, I *knew* I had nothing to forgive Tony for. Tony was nothing but good. He had lots to forgive me for. Tons. Things that were 100 percent my fault and that I had no decent excuse for. Things that had hurt him.

My mind spun, and I didn't get it. I tried to bring G-Ma and the Lincoln back into the picture, figure out what all this had to do with each other. But it didn't make sense.

Mom.

Tony.

Mom.

Tony.

Finally I sighed and stood, blowing out the candle. "You're going to have to be clearer than that, God," I said. "All I'm asking is that you get me through the day without something happening to G-Ma's car." I didn't want to deal with Mom or with all the stuff I'd done to hurt Tony. That was too much this early in the morning. Or ever, taken together. Those were two separate issues, and it was asking too much for me to deal with them both at the same time.

So instead of ending my morning prayer time comforted and at peace, I was mad at God. And not very happy with Mom, G-Ma, or Tony, unreasonable at that was.

Stump greeted me at her food bowl, sticking her nose in it and sniffing around elaborately to let me know there was not a scrap of anything to be found there.

"Sorry," I told her. "We're driving G-Ma's car and I'm not filling your tank until we're safely at the shop. Just in case."

I kept the three towels in place and made Stump ride in the passenger seat all the way, so I could concentrate on safe driving. I honked at two people who looked suspiciously like they might be thinking of drifting into my lane. They both looked at me like I was crazy.

At Flo's Bow Wow Barbers, I called Five Star Automotive and talked to Mrs. Pigg, explaining that I'd left the car on the street and what I needed done. She promised to look into it and call me back.

She called back a few minutes later. "Five will get the car re-paired and inspected, but it's going to take a few days because he has to order a part from out of state."

"How many days?"

"It's supposed to be here by Monday. He can put it in and give you the sticker the same day."

I wanted to be mad and complain, but I remembered the scripture that morning. I didn't want my unforgivingness to Five Star Automotive to come back and bite me.

"That's fine," I said. "I can manage for a few days."

"I'm really sorry. We'll get it quicker if we can, of course."

I hung up and went back to work on my dogs, my mind swirl-ing with everything I had to contemplate. I *had* been asking for God's guidance on mine and Tony's relationship. I had, in fact, been thinking about it a lot, wondering where we were headed, how we could possibly get past everything that lay between us or if, in fact, we should even try.

That had nothing to do with Mom, though. Well, everything he had to forgive me for had to do with Mom, because it was mostly Mom's fault that I had been such a dumpster fire myself, when Tony and I were married for real.

Maybe I needed to get Tony to forgive Mom for screwing me up so much. Maybe that was what God was saying.

I doubted it, though. In my experience, God worked pretty much one-on-one with His people. Plus I was uncomfortable blaming Mom for choices I'd made, even though I could see very clearly how choices she'd made had gone into making me inca-pable of accepting that a guy like Tony could be for real. Her choices had done that for me.

So forgiving her, again? What more could I do? I'd made the

decision to do just that, months ago, and I was where I was. I had spent two solid hours with her last weekend. I had smiled and done my best — such as it was — to play the happy family for her friends. I was spending the entire upcoming weekend with her and would do my level best to let love never fail all weekend long. That was as much as I was prepared to do at the moment.

I kept thinking about it until I got myself worked into an irritably tizzy, at which point Viv called.

"My car is fixed! I mean, it's back from its routine maintenance. Let's go interview some more people."

I was only too happy to agree. "Let me check with Frank first and make sure he's able to watch Stump."

"You know, you could put her in the bathroom. Take up the rugs and stuff. She couldn't do much."

"Yes, she could. She's chewed through three baby gates. The doors on my bathroom are thin plywood. She'll claw through them and then I'll have an open air bathroom. If Frank can't watch her, I'll have to skip it."

Fortunately, Frank answered and was perfectly willing to spend yet another night in my recliner, curled up with Stump and the remote control.

I drove the Lincoln back to Trailertopia and tapped on Frank's door to let him know it was time for him to come over to doggie-sit. He settled into the recliner with Stump, a bag of Doritos and the remote control.

I started a load of laundry, then headed back into the living room, tucking my phone into my pocket. "She doesn't get any of those," I said, pointing from the chips to Stump.

Frank gave me a halfhearted salute and Stump gave me a

dirty look. He patted her and said, "Sorry, girl, but we gotta keep you safe. No junk food, and no getting caught in the crotchfire for you."

I blinked slowly, then said, "Exactly. Listen, could you do me a huge favor? I don't know how late we're going to be back, and I'm afraid I'll forget. I just started a load of work clothes in the washing machine. Can you toss them into the dryer for me, please?"

Frank gave me another salute and said, "You betcha, boss."

I had very little hope he would remember. But it was worth a shot.

When Viv pulled up, she already had an idea of who she wanted to interview.

"Did you see that hot guy's picture at the car lot Monday? Back on that shelf behind the counter? Let's find him," she said as we drove out of Trailertopia.

"Hot guy? No." Five Pigg wasn't ugly, but he certainly wasn't hot. "Was it one of the other Pigg brothers?"

"Probably. He was wearing a black t-shirt with suspenders, and had this wicked bright grin. Try to find him on Facebook. Maybe we can get an idea of where he'd be hanging out on a Wednesday night."

"I told you I know one of the son's wives, right? I think his name is Randy. Something with an R. Oh, wait." I remembered that Charlotte said they all started with R. "Anyway, I think she said he's a firefighter. If this guy was wearing suspenders, it might have been him. Maybe we could go by the fire station and talk to him."

"Oooh, excellent idea. God don't make no ugly firemen."

I entered "Pigg" into the Facebook search bar and flicked

through the entries. There were several names, most of them female. I chose one that looked about the same age as the Pigg brothers would be.

"Destiny Pigg," I said. "Okay, this has got to be true love, to take that name. I'd at least hyphenate, like Charlotte did."

"Salem Grimy-Pigg," Viv laughed. "Yeah, that would be way better."

"It's Grimes, not Grimy," I said, but I had to laugh with her. Destiny Pigg was cute, with chin-length blonde hair and a button nose. Her profile picture was of her and the Grimes brother and their three sons, each one blond and blue-eyed like her. I scrolled through her pictures.

"Oh, this is the football coach. Apparently he married the girls' basketball coach. Oh, and she's the cheerleading coach, too. I thought she looked like a cheerleader."

"Is he the hot one?" Viv asked, leaning over to look at my screen. The car veered into the right lane and someone honked.

"Viv, eyes on the road," I said, reaching to grab the wheel and keep us on course. "He certainly looks hot to me." I held the phone so she could see it without taking her eyes too far off the road.

"Ummm, maybe. I think that might be one of the other brothers, though."

"Okay, this one is Randy. Randy is married to Destiny, and they both coach at the high school where we turned the car around Monday. Make a note so we can keep them straight."

I tapped a few more things.

"This must be another brother — yep. Robby Pigg. Good grief, he looks almost exactly like Randy Pigg. They aren't twins, are they?"

"I don't know. I wouldn't mind being the peanut butter on that sandwich, though, let me tell you."

"That's disgusting," I said mildly. I scrolled down and found Valerie Pigg, then clicked on her page.

Valerie was gorgeous but in a different way from Destiny. She had dark hair, brown eyes, full red lips, and a supermodel figure. Her profile picture was of her and Randy standing on a mountainside with a forest of aspens in blazing fall splendor behind them. They both wore All-American smiles and puffy down vests over white long-sleeved t-shirts. Gag. There was another picture of Randy in a suit and tie, either giving or accepting an award, I couldn't tell which. "I'll bet this is the insurance agent." I held the phone back up for her to see. "Is this him?"

"I don't think so. This one didn't look so straight-laced."

"Here he is. Ricky Pigg. Jeez-o-Peet. He's maybe even better looking than the other two."

"Not possible," Viv said, leaning over again.

"Good grief, Viv, you're going to get us killed. Pull over, and I'll drive while you pant over pictures of hot Pigg men."

"Deal." She pulled into a Dollar General parking lot and slid out.

No slouch at Facebook investigations herself, Viv found Ricky Pigg's wife, a short and cute Hispanic girl with a wide red smile. "This is the insurance salesman," Viv said. "They're all on here except the firefighter."

"Then Charlotte must be married to the firefighter."

Viv was silent for a while as she thumbed through the pages. "My my my..." She said softly. "It appears the Pigg brothers are fond of deep sea fishing in hot climates that require them to remove their shirts."

"Don't drool on my phone," I said.

"I'm not making any promises. Come to mama, you hot young things."

"Seriously, that's a brand new phone," I said. "Don't defile it."

"Okay, here we go. Roger Pigg is thirty-two — my favorite number — and married to Charlotte Clancy-Pigg,and he works at Station Thirty-Seven on Buena Vista."

"We're on our way," I said, hitting the lever to activate the turn signal. Instead, the horn honked.

"Oh, I forgot to tell you. Hit the up button on the radio station to turn on the left blinker."

"What? Why?"

"Because, it's some — " She waved a hand. "You know, like a keyboard shortcut or something."

"What if I want to turn right?"

"Then hit the radio down button, of course." She looked at me like I was wasting her time with my silly questions.

"Of course."

Since Viv and I had been friends and started solving crimes together, she'd decided we needed to get legit and she had some business cards made. When I pulled up at the fire station and we walked toward the open garage door, I hoped fervently that she didn't pull one of those cards out. They were eye-catching all right. There was a pair of handcuffs tossed haphazardly across the front of the card, and the words "Discreet Investigations" written in blood-red lipstick. It could just as easily been an advertisement for a kinky escapade as it was a private eye agency. The general response to this card was a confused look and a half 'is-this-a-joke?' smile.

But of course, Viv was rummaging in her oversize tote for a card as we neared the door. She'd also, I noticed, unbuttoned the top button of her blouse.

As she'd said, God didn't make no ugly firemen. Within seconds, all I could see were black t-shirts over stunning pectoral muscles. I tried to look away, but everywhere I turned there was another drool-worthy chest. And the faces. It was as if beefcake poster looks were one of the prereqs for applying to the fire department.

I finally had to settle for looking at the ground while Viv talked.

"We're looking for Robby Pigg," she said.

"Roger," I corrected, examining a crack in the concrete.

"Yes, Roger Pigg. Is he on duty today?"

He was indeed. One of the guys called to him and he came walking out, drying his hands on a towel.

Charlotte was so lucky. Heck, that *towel* was lucky.

Viv held out one of those awful cards and introduced herself. "This is my partner, Salem Grimes."

I nodded and grunted something unintelligible.

"We're investigating the rash of robberies on this side of town, trying to interview everyone who might have seen or heard anything. We spoke to Mr. and Mrs. Pigg on Monday, and they mentioned that you had been robbed?"

"No, that was my brother. Ricky."

"Oh, I see," Viv said. She was good. I almost believed this was a real misunderstanding on her part, and I knew better.

As she talked, Viv cocked her head and leaned closer to him, giving him a view, should he want one, of cleavage. It was rather sad cleavage, but still. She laughed and flirted and kept asking questions while I stood there like Boo Radley, my tongue too big for my mouth. When my phone rang, I almost jumped out of my skin.

It was Frank. "So, when your washing machine gets through washing, is all of the water supposed to be out of it?"

"Do you mean, like does it drain out?"

"Right. Does it drain out?"

"Well...yes." Of course.

"Oh, well then." He sounded relieved. "I think your machine is broken. I wasn't really sure, but yep. Sounds like it's broken."

I groaned. Of course it was. I had, after all, managed to keep half my emergency fund, which would maybe almost cover a new machine.

"Okay," I said with a sigh. "I'll be home in a little while."

I hung up and tugged at Viv's sleeve. "I need to go home," I said.

"Now? They were just telling me about a meeting tonight at the community center. To discuss the robberies. We definitely need to go and gather more intel." She smiled up at another fireman who stood with his arms folded across his chest. She put a hand up to the rounded bicep that strained against his t-shirt sleeve. "Will you be there? At the community center meeting?"

He nodded with an amused smile. "I should be."

She nodded. "You definitely should be." She stroked the curve of his bicep with one bony, liver-spotted finger before pulling her hand away.

"Viv, seriously, it sounds like an emergency."

"Everything okay?" Roger Pigg asked, his body immediately stiffening.

"Yeah, no, I mean, it's not that kind of emergency. It's a — a laundry room emergency."

"Oh." He gave me a sympathetic grimace. "Sorry about that."

Viv wasn't thrilled with me when we got back into the car and drove away. "Seriously, you had to pull me away from all that testosterone for *laundry*?"

"I'm sorry, but I have to take care of this or I won't have anything to wear to work tomorrow. Besides, those guys were *too* hot. I couldn't look at them. It was like looking directly at the sun."

"I could look at them all day." Viv shook her head and sighed.

"You heard what that one guy said. He will be at the meeting tonight, and I'm sure a few of the others will, too."

"That's right. Shoot. I knew I should have had my legs waxed this morning."

Back at Trailertopia, I pulled heavy, sopping wet clothes out of the washing machine and dumped them into a laundry basket. I wasn't sure what to do about the water. I tried to let it spin again, without the clothes, to see if that would help somehow, but the machine wouldn't even turn on. I finally got a plastic pitcher from the kitchen and drained the machine as much as I could, one pitcher at a time. Then I wrung out my sopping clothes over the bathtub and hung them up to dry. By this time I was also sopping wet and grumpy to boot.

I changed into dry clothes and came back into the living room.

"You're wearing that?"

"Viv, I really don't feel like going," I said. "I'm tired and I need to figure out how I'm going to get my washing machine fixed."

My phone dinged. I picked it up and saw a text from Tony.

"Community meeting on Clovis Highway in a little while. Is your grandmother going? I can take notes for her if she's not able to."

"Hang on," I told Viv. "Let me get changed."

After way too much consideration, I called G-Ma and asked if she wanted to go to the community center meeting with us. "They're going to be talking about the Bandits, of course, and what the citizens can do to protect themselves."

"Oh, I'm protecting myself, all right," G-Ma said. "Little as I have to protect. I'm not going to sit here like a goose and wait for them to come cook me. Little as I have to be cooked."

"You should come to the meeting tonight with me and Viv. You might even have a chance to speak, I don't know. But it would be good, wouldn't it, to hear what others are doing and to, you know...band together?"

"Is she going?"

"She? You mean Viv? Well, yeah." I had just said that, hadn't I?

"She's not driving my car."

I sighed. "Of course not. In fact, I'm bringing your car back tonight anyway, with my sincere gratitude."

"Is your car fixed, then?"

"Almost. Viv got hers back, so I won't need mine for the next few days. You can have yours back."

"I can't go to the meeting, though. It'll be over too late. I don't have anybody here to watch the motel. I could miss out on the few customers I have left.

"Tony and I will take notes for you," I promised.

I hung up, kind of relieved that she wasn't going. Getting between her and Viv was tiresome.

I took the Lincoln back to the Executive Inn and brought her towels in. "I'm sorry I didn't wash them," I said. "I was going to, but my machine broke."

G-Ma took the towels with one hand, staring out the window at Viv pulling up in her Cadillac. "Would you just look at her? Prancing around like she owns the durned world."

"You're an independent business owner, and you drive a fancy Lincoln with all its own bells and whistles," I said. "It's not like you're doing so bad yourself."

She frowned and let the shade drop. "I guess that's true enough. I hope I don't have to sell it all."

"Why would you do that?"

"My business is going in the tank. I had steady income for a few months, but now it's back at next to nothing." She lifted the shade again and looked over at Mario's tamale factory. "If it weren't for Mario, I'd have no steady income at all." She moved back to her recliner and dropped into it. "The best luck I've had the past few years is renting to other businesses."

I started to say that the prostitutes could hardly be called business owners, then decided it would be better to just concede the point. "You know what you could do? In Amarillo, some of the old motels have been converted to little shopping centers. They don't even do a major renovation, they just take all the furniture out and rent out the rooms as small shops. Hair salons, nail salons, candle stores. It's really cute."

G-Ma sneered. "Amarillo. Another one that thinks it's hot stuff. With its *Route 66*. Like we don't have highways in Lubbock."

I leaned down and kissed her cheek. "Well, think about it.

You're resilient and have a head for business. You'll end up on top."

There was already a crowd at the community center. I looked around for Tony and spotted him getting out of his pickup. He wore a black v-neck sweater that looked quite yummy against his tan skin.

I waved to him, and he lifted his hand when he saw me.

I looked down and smoothed my own blouse over the stomach that was still bigger than I wanted it to be. It fit better than it had last year, but still...I couldn't help but wonder if people would look at me and Tony together and wonder why he was with me.

I sucked in as I crossed the lot. Tony held the door open for us and I was so focused on trying to look skinnier that I didn't notice until I was almost to him that he wasn't alone.

"Hi, Salem," Tony's sister Margaret said, from behind and to the side of him.

"Oh! Hi," I said. "Good to see you. Are you here with... with Tony? I mean, of course you are. You came together?"

"Yes, it looks like they have a good turnout tonight. That's really good."

I nodded too hard. "Great. Absolutely fantastic."

As Tony led the way toward empty seats, I wondered for a moment if I'd even be able to sit beside him.

Tony and Margaret chatted and Margaret called out to people she knew here and there, with a wave and a friendly laugh, while I tried to keep from feeling like a middle-school drama queen because I hadn't gotten to sit beside my boyfriend.

An older guy took the short stage and brought the meeting to order. He introduced himself as the recently retired principal of the local middle school. "Wow," he said with a big smile. "We usually have a crowd about twenty-five percent this big at our quarterly meetings. We ought to get robbed all the time!"

The crowd laughed, some looking a little guilty, as they were no doubt intended to.

"Seriously, it is so great to see all of you out here, ready to do what needs to be done to keep our community safe. We're all concerned about the rising crime and we all want to do something about it. Neighborhoods like ours are a treasure. We have families that have lived for generations in this neighborhood. My family is one of them. My great-grandmother moved here when Lubbock was about twenty-five thousand people. My father grew up here, went to college at Texas Tech, and met my mother there. I grew up here. I raised my own kids here. Not just in this town, but in this neighborhood. For people like us, this neighborhood is our home. We don't want to leave. These crimes aren't just happening to other people — they're happening to *us*. And it's good to see that we are doing what we need to, to take care of us."

The crowd applauded.

"Now, the man who's about to come up here needs to introduction, but I'm going to introduce him anyway."

Laughter.

"I think everything I just said about my family could be said about Clete Pigg and his family. That man loves High Point more than — well, more than is probably healthy, if you ask me."

More laughter.

"Seriously. He not only grew up here and married a local girl, he opened a business and had a son. Then he opened another business and had another son. Then he opened couple more businesses and had a couple more sons."

"And they're all hot," Viv stage whispered.

The group around us laughed louder than the rest of the crowd.

I elbowed her, but of course she paid no heed.

"All together I think he's got a couple dozen sons — "

"Five, but it seems like a couple dozen," Papa Pigg shouted from his seat.

"Five sons. Every single one of them devoted to this neighborhood. One of them is a fireman, one's a businessman, ones the best football coach in the state — "

The crowd erupted in cheers.

The principal held his hand out to quiet the crowd. "What I'm saying is, nobody is more invested in this neighborhood than Clete Pigg. You've all heard about the High Point Small Business Development Initiative he started here. *He* did that. He had the idea, he drummed up the funds, he put together a consortium of small business leaders in our community. And now anybody who lives in High Point and wants to open a business in High Point — they can go to this committee and apply for a grant to get started. If they qualify, they can get the start-up capital, they can be mentored by an experienced business owner, and they can get all kinds of support to make their businesses successful. Now, they're not huge grants. It's not for opening a factory or anything like that. But to start a small business, you could do that. Something like that — a few thousand dollars? Something like that could make the difference in a person being able to achieve their dreams. The business would stay here. The money would stay here. The success will be here, in High Point.

Clete Pigg did that.

"He even — and a lot of you know this already — he even lead an effort to get Lubbock's first Krunchy Kreem franchise right here in High Point. *Right here!* Before those on the south side of town. We were going to be the first!"

This brought almost as much cheering as the football comment had.

"Now, that didn't work out, because that's the way it goes, sometimes, heartbreaking as it is."

"South side still doesn't have one," Clete Pigg shouted from his chair. "We still have time!"

"That's the spirit, Clete," the principal said. "Stay in the fight. Fight for those donuts!"

After the laughter died down, the principal said, "What I'm trying to say is, what you're looking at are the people who are walking the walk in this neighborhood. They've invested their very lives in this area and they're not going to let a small-time-hood crime wave scare them away. We've been through it. Maybe not exactly like this, but we've seen good times and bad times, and this is just one more bump in the road. Nothing more. Before Mr. Pigg comes up here and says his bit, I just want to put that out there. Your homes are here. Your kids are here, their friends are here, your churches are here, the people who clean your clothes and give you your immunizations and your cheeseburgers — we're all in this together. Let's watch out for each other. Let's take care of each other. If we're not careful, we could let everything that's been happening lately convince us that this neighborhood is nothing but hard times and bad news. But we know that's not the truth. I look around this room and I see nothing but good people. Let's fight for those good people.

Now, join me in welcoming Mr. Clete Pigg."

He had on a different red shirt, but the same black belt and jeans, and he'd let his white hair blow a little looser than it had been when I bought my car.

He talked for a few minutes about the robberies and about what he felt was a "less-than-passionate effort on the part of the police to put an end to them."

"Now, I've raised five boys. You don't survive that without learning a few things. Like, making sure the seat is down before you sit, right?"

The crowd laughed.

"Seriously, though. I'll tell you a story. Back when the boys were between the ages of, oh, seventeen and ten or so, I bought my first junk lot." He took a deep breath and his chest expanded proudly. "Most of you know, I've made my living off junk. And I'd just bought my very first junk lot. Four acres of junk cars and parts. So I gave my boys a job. All that junk needed sorting and organizing. Some of it was good working parts that could be cleaned up and reused, but most of it was no good and needed to be scrapped. But there wasn't a good way of telling without looking at each piece. Now, one thing about my boys — they all know their cars. They might not *want* to know their cars. In fact, I would hazard to say they'd prefer to just drive the things and leave the "knowing" up to somebody else. You'll notice there's no "and Sons" on my building. That's not my choice. But that's a different discussion, right? The point is, I knew every one of my boys was qualified to sift through that junk and help me with this chore. So I gave it to them. It was a big job. I figured it would take them a good week or two to get through it all. So I took them out there and we talked about how we would organize everything, where the junk would go, where the good parts would go and all that, see. And I told them it would probably take all week. I told them I'd pay them $150 each to sift the lot.

"Then I left to go tend to my other business. When I got back, it looked like not one thing had been done. A few pieces were piled on the scrap pile, but not many. And of those pieces, two were still good! I don't mind telling you, I was hot. My boys — now that they're grown and out of the house — they like to make fun of ol' dad when he gets mad. They say my neck actually swells. Well, I'll bet that afternoon I looked like an old granddaddy bullfrog. I mean, I was blazing mad. Here they had a job to do, and they'd wasted a whole day. I stomped around and I lectured and I sermonized.

"I got them up the next morning and took 'em out there an hour earlier. I pulled up one of those scaffolds where I could get up nice and high and see everything. I took my lawn chair up there and my umbrella, and I just watched. And I told them I was only paying for five days' worth of work. They'd already spent one. At the rate they'd gone that day, it would take them six months! But I figured it was a five-day job, and I was paying for five days. But no matter what, we were coming back every day until the job was done.

"And you know what happened? Well, all *kinds* of efficiency and initiative! Four boys who are properly motivated and supervised can get an impressive amount of work done. That whole place was cleaned out within the next two and a half days. And they did a good job of it, too. If I remember correctly, we made a couple hundred off the refurbished parts, which I let them keep, and I paid them the full five days worth of work, although truth be told, they only worked about half that time.

"Listen, my boys weren't lazy, and they weren't uncaring about the job. But listen. We all work better when expectations are clear and when we know someone is watching us. Most of us don't *like* somebody standing over our shoulder, but when nobody's watching at all..." He shrugged and pulled a face. "We can all get a bit lackadaisical. Even good workers. Even conscientious people. We don't want to admit that about ourselves, but it's true. Our work ethic kicks into a higher gear when we're accountable to somebody."

He paced slowly behind the podium, rubbing his hands together. "So you understand that I'm not saying the LPD doesn't have some diligent officers. Now, I've known some of these officers all their lives. Some of them played t-ball with my sons when they were this big. I know their character. I know they're good people." He looked out at the audience. "I know they want to do right by you. But it doesn't hurt to let them know that we're watching them. We're watching them do their job. Because it's important. Their job is to protect us and we need them to be diligent — "

Viv went suddenly stiff beside me. She clutched my arm.

"What?" I whispered.

Her eyes darted back and forth. She leaned toward me and whispered out of the side of her mouth.

"Do you remember if I left my gun on the backseat?"

"What?!"

"Shh!" She glared at me. "Keep it down, for crying out loud. Just think. In the backseat of my car. Did you see a gun?"

I searched my mind frantically, but the only thought my mind could form was "What the actual freak, Viv?" I wasn't back there, you were, remember? We were both in the front seat."

"I know that. I just thought maybe you happened to look."

"What, just...*laying there*? Out in the open?"

"Yes. No, wait." She put her fingers to her lips and thought. "I remember I was looking at it while you got your G-Ma, and I put it down so she wouldn't have a hissy fit. I think I put my jacket over it. Maybe."

"Maybe you tossed a jacket on top of an actual handgun. So it's safe now?"

"Would you lower your voice!" She frowned and appeared to think for a minute. "It'll probably be okay," she said, leaning back toward me. "It's dark and nobody's going to be looking in the backseat of my car anyway."

I nodded. "Yes. Unless they are. What were you doing with your gun out, anyway?"

"I was just checking it."

Three people on the rows ahead of us turned and glared at us. We quietened down.

After a few moments, Viv leaned over and spoke low. "I was just checking to make sure it was loaded. In case anything went down tonight."

"Give me your keys," I said. "I'll go check." I could at least put it under the seat so if it went off, the worst we would have to deal with would be a shot ankle.

I bumped a few knees on the way out to the parking lot. My whispered, "Excuse me," were perhaps a bit louder than necessary. But neither my departure nor my minor disruption attracted Tony's attention.

I walked into the dark night and gathered my jacket around

me. It had cooled off some since the meeting started. Once I got away from the glow of the building's lights, the thought struck me that there were, after all, armed robbers in the area. And lots of armed and trigger-happy citizens. I made up my mind to check and make sure the gun wasn't in plain sight, and get my butt back into the safety of the crowd.

I peered into the backseat of Viv's Cadillac. There was a jacket there. But was there also...crud. Yes, there in the moonlight I could see the glow of a metal gun barrel just peeking out the edge of the jacket. It shone silver when I moved aside and the glow from the building touched it.

I clicked the button on the keyring. It chirped, and I thought I heard the door unlock. I reached for the handle, though, and it was still locked. I hit the button again. Another chirp. Another yank on the handle that yielded no results.

I frowned and decided to just use the key the old-fashioned way. There was no keyhole in the passenger door, though. I moved around to the driver's side.

"Aha," I said. I slid the key into the lock.

The horn honked and the lights flashed on. Then again. And again. HONK HONK FLASH FLASH.

"No," I said, jiggling on the key. It went in, but didn't turn. I fiddled with it, pulling it out a fraction in case that helped, then slid it all the way back in.

Then the horn stopped the intermittent alarm honking and went into one solid, incredibly loud blast that felt very much like the world coming to an end.

I danced around in a panic, then gave up and put my hands over my ears. "Stupid car!" I shouted.

"Hey, they're trying to steal that car!" someone shouted from out on the street. "Come on!"

I couldn't see anybody, but suddenly the memory of bullets flying and glass crashing flooded my mind, and I panicked. Leaving the key in the lock, I ran.

Upon reflection, it would have been smart to run back into the building. What I did, though, was sprint as fast as I could past the building and down a dark alley.

Dogs barked and I heard more shouts. I had no idea how close they were, but I was sure there was a bullet headed straight for my back. I wanted to scream but I was afraid of expending the energy.

I ran down the middle of the alley until something that passed for logic told me to move to the side, closer to the shadows so I wouldn't make such an easy target.

It was as if I had to order my feet to turn slightly to the right, they were so focused on forward motion. But I did — I moved to the right side of the alley and kept trucking. I risked a glance behind me to see if they were gaining on me. That's when I tripped over the water pipe.

I slammed into the ground so hard it knocked the breath out of me. I lay there, not even able to gasp, the pain in my ankle intense. Tears sprang to my eyes and I bent to grasp the ankle with both hands, sure it was broken.

I heard more voices, and looked around frantically. A green dumpster sat a few feet away. I slid toward it on my butt, desperate to get hidden. I crawled to the back of the dumpster and saw some space behind it, between the dumpster and the fence. I managed to crawl a little ways in, then flipped back over to sit on my butt, wedged between the chain link fence and the dumpster.

I held my breath as I heard the voices grow louder. Then I heard something nearer me. A snuffling sound.

I jerked my head around to see a black, wet nose sniffing me through the fence.

"Hey," I whispered. "Hey, there, nice doggie."

I just knew it was about to set up a baying howl, then lights would come on, guns would be cocked, and once again I'd be running for my life, this time on a bum ankle.

Instead, the dog set up an intense sniff session at my elbow. Apparently, whatever he smelled there held some interest for him, because he didn't appear to be interested in moving on.

I risked poking my finger through the fence and stroked his nose gently. The voices were getting louder, closer, and my heart hammered in my ears. It occurred to me that I could simply step out into the alley and explain that I hadn't been trying to steal the car, but the memory of all the "crotchfire" from the other night was too fresh in my mind. Better to let them pass and then come out later when things had calmed down.

As the voices got closer, I was able to make out some of the words.

"Crazy," "Idiot," "More to lose than we do," I thought, and, several times, *"cajones."*

It took me a moment to realize, given the last one, that they *might* not be talking about me.

My next thought was, if a group of men were walking down a dark alley in this neighborhood and they weren't talking about me, or looking for me, then they might be...

I sat up straight, my heart hammering once again, and tried to scoot toward the end of the dumpster so I could see around.

The sniffing at my elbow turned into a snuffle, and then into a soft whine.

I scooted back into place. The last thing I needed was to let them know I was back here. If they were the bad guys, their history of non-violence could go out the door.

They were right up on me now, and it took everything I had not to panic and flail around in an attempt to flee. I froze, straining to hear above the thundering of blood in my ears.

"He's gotta pitch in his share, regardless," said one voice very clearly. "He's not getting out of this without kicking in. One way or the other, they're gonna be contributors."

"Major contributors," said another voice.

"Yeah, he oughta give a little more, even, after all the fuss."

"No, now, we're gonna be fair. You know the ground rules."

They all laughed then, so I had to think ground rules to them meant something different than it meant to me.

They moved quickly down the alley, and I realized I hadn't even been paying enough attention to know how many there were. I felt like there were at least three distinct voices, but maybe more. And there could have been some there who just weren't talking. It was hard to tell without seeing them. The alley was soft dirt, no pavement to bounce footsteps off of. I could hear the whisk of pant legs brushing together as they walked, and occasionally the jangle of keys or change in pants pockets. But they moved so quickly that the alley was soon quiet once again.

I had to find Bobby and let him know what I'd heard. It could be a clue. It had to be the bandits, right? I mean, who else would have been running through the alley?

I moved to crawl out from behind the dumpster. Actually, I tried to move. I was wedged in pretty tight, though. I dug my heels into the ground and tried to scooch myself forward. If I could just slide along the ground, I could get past the edge of the dumpster and then get onto my knees.

Nothing. I felt the metal of the chain link fence biting into my hip and thigh.

Were my jeans caught? Or was I seriously so fat that I'd gotten stuck back there?

I rocked forward again, but rocked immediately back.

With my left hand, I reached up and wrapped my fingers through the chain about a foot above my head. I braced my right palm against the dumpster and pushed, pulling with the left.

I succeeded in making painful red marks against my fingers from the chain. My right hand lost traction and skidded across the metal of the dumpster with a soft shriek.

The dog snuffled at my elbow again.

"Stop!" I snapped at him, twisting at the waist to pull my elbow out of his reach. "Enough."

He stuck his nose through the fence and snorted.

"I mean it. Quit. No means no."

He whined.

"Respect my boundaries!" I almost shouted.

He plopped down on his butt and howled.

Immediately a light flashed on over the back porch, and light flooded the entire yard and half the alley. It was like a scene from a movie about a prison break.

"What's going on out here?" roared a not-at-all-friendly-sounding voice.

Light blinded me, and I held my hands up to block it.

Then I heard a gun cock.

I threw my hands above my head. "Don't shoot me don't shoot me don't shoot!"

"What are you doing back here?" the man yelled. Then he stuck his head back in the house. "Lucy! Get out here! There's some woman sitting at our back fence."

"What? Why?"

"Gus, come here, boy." The man patted his thigh as he crossed the yard toward me on giant tree trunk legs.

Gus lumbered up and trotted slowly to meet the man, then back toward me. I kept my hands up.

"Well," the man said. I couldn't decide if he had a grizzled-but-kindly expression, or if he was simply sizing me up to see if he wanted to keep me. "You're in a bit of a pickle, huh?"

"A bit," I said with a false grin, my teeth clenched. "I was just walking down the alley and I heard — "

"Why were you walking down the alley? You live around here?"

"She don't live around here," came a woman's voice at his elbow. I was so blinded by the floodlights that I hadn't even seen her come up. "I know everybody who lives around here, and she ain't one of 'em."

I nodded. "I don't live around here, that's right. I mean, I live in Lubbock, but across town. In Trailertopia."

"That's good to know, but doesn't tell us a thing about why you're walking through our alley."

"The thing is, I was walking and I heard these guys behind me. It sounded like they were running. And I thought — you know, I thought it was them. The robbers. And I panicked. I hid behind the dumpster until they passed, but then when the moved on, I was stuck and couldn't get out."

The man and woman looked at each other. They clearly did not believe me.

"I swear," I said, painfully aware of every lie I'd ever told and how I'd made just such passionate declarations every time the lie was not believed.

"No, the thing *is*," the man said flatly, "You keep *not telling* us what you were doing in the alley, and that *not telling* has me thinking that you have something to hide. Now, maybe you were running from those guys, and maybe you were running *with* those guys. Maybe you just couldn't keep up, and they left you here to fend for yourself and this is the best you can come up with."

I shook my head hard. "No, believe me. If I wanted to make up something I could do a lot better than that."

"Why were you in the alley? We've been listening to the scanner and there was a report of an attempted auto theft at the community center. You have anything to do with that?"

"Yes!" I said, not even caring that I looked like a car thief. I mean, they wouldn't shoot me if I was just a failed car thief. They'd call the police. And I wanted the police just then.

"I had something to do with that. I was the one who was trying to get into that car. I wasn't trying to steal it, though, I was just—"

"Call the cops," Giant Man said. Lucy hurried to obey.

"I wonder if maybe you could help me get out of here."

He nodded. "You're good right where you are."

"I won't try to run, I swear. I just..." I wriggled as much as I was able. "This is getting really uncomfortable. And that light. Could you put that light down? It's right in my eyes." Between trying to come unstuck from the fence and trying to keep from being blinded, I had my hands full.

"It won't be long."

"I swear, if you could just pull that fence back a little bit, I'll stay right here."

"Nope."

"I'll stay right by this dumpster. I just need —"

He turned and roared toward the house. "Tell 'em she's trying to flee!"

"I'm not trying to flee!" I leaned over and shouted toward the house. "Tell them I'm not trying to flee!" I turned back to him. "Not trying to flee," I said, sticking my lower lip out.

The cops came and shined their spotlight in my face. If you had asked me thirty seconds before what one more intense light would do, I would have sworn "not a thing." But it did. I had to put my head down in the crook of my elbow just to keep from crying.

After a bunch of questions that nobody was satisfied with the answers to — including me — the two cops and the two Henrys put their heads together to figure out how to get me out.

Mr. Henry and one cop pulled at the chain fence, and I scooted forward. An inch. And then I fell back.

"I must be caught on something," I said. I looked over my shoulder, but didn't exactly have the best vantage point. "Can you just — " I looked at the cop. "I mean, I have to be caught on one of the links, right?"

To his credit, he looked a bit embarrassed to have to get down low and check out the area of my behind. He stuck his fingers through the fence and prodded around at my thigh to locate the source of the trouble.

That was when Tony and Viv showed up.

Tony rushed across the yard. "Salem! What — " He took in the scene. "What happened?"

"I'm okay," I said, feeling equal parts guilty and idiotic. "I panicked when I set off the alarm and people started shouting. I thought I was going to get shot at like last time — "

"Last time?" the cop asked. "Last time you were breaking into a car?"

"I mean when — you know, with the shooting over behind the law office. People were shouting, "Somebody's trying to steal that car!" and I panicked and ran."

"Why didn't you run into the building?" Viv asked.

"Because I panicked!" I said, thinking that she could be a little more supportive and sympathetic. It was *her* weapon I'd been trying to conceal, after all. "I just ran. I hit my ankle on something and fell down." My ankle felt better now, which seemed oddly unfair. I could use a nice bruise or swelling or something that would back up my story. "Then I heard some guys, and I thought it was the Bandits, so I dove back here and hid. But when they left I couldn't get out. And the dog was sniffing my elbow and it was kind of weird and I made him stop, so he howled, and then the lights came on and this guy acted like I was a car thief and wouldn't let me go." Something suddenly occurred to me. "Hey! That's imprisonment! Officer!" I jabbed a finger toward Big Mr. Henry. "Arrest him! He was holding me captive!"

Big Mr. Henry laughed. "Good luck trying to make a case of that. You're the one who came on my property."

"That's right, it's your property and you are responsible for what happens here. You are liable. And believe me, our lawyer will be hearing about this. And for the love of Pete, turn that light out!" Bless Viv's heart. I think at least one of her rich late husbands made his fortune by suing other people.

Whatever, it got Lucy to march up to the back door and shut off the brightest light. The cops holstered their flashlights.

"Okay, well everybody just calm down," the cop said. "Nobody's suing anybody and we're gonna get you out. But first I want to hear about the bandits. Did you see them?"

"No, I was behind the dumpster and when I tried to lean out and get a look, that dog started whining and I was afraid they would hear him, so I stayed put. I heard what they said, though."

"My dog don't whine," Big Mr. Henry said.

I jutted my chin. "Like a little baby."

"What did you hear?"

I shook my head. "I'm afraid I can't remember a single word until I get out of here."

Tony set about trying to get me loose. He found a spot of the fence where the sharp chain tops were bent over, covered it with his hand and vaulted over. He crawled in behind me, his hands fumbling with the fence and my jeans, trying to find the catch. His shoulders were even broader than my hips, though (difficult to believe, but comfortingly true) so he couldn't get much traction.

I craned my neck around. "Thanks," I said. "And I'm sorry I'm such a walking freak show."

He laughed, but it didn't seem to me like he was feeling the humor so much.

"Can you see what's going on back there?"

"No. Can you feel it catch? Like, can you tell if it's really caught on something?"

"No, but the alternative is to think that my hips are actually so wide they're wedged tight, and I just can't make myself believe that."

He sat back on his haunches, turned halfway sideways between the fence and the dumpster. His knee pushed the fence away from us.

I hooked my heels in the ground again and tried to scoot. Nothing.

"Think we ought to call the city and see if they can get a dumpster truck out here to lift it out?"

"Good grief!" I said. "No." I pictured the dumpster rising and me with it, being squished against the fence like Play-Doh being rolled out.

"We could cut the fence," the other cop suggested.

"The hell you will," Big Mr. Henry said. The sweetheart.

"Why does everyone miss the most obvious step," Viv said.

Everybody looked at her, including me.

"Cut her jeans. That's the easiest and least expensive way."

The dumpster truck looked suddenly like a very appealing option. I wrapped my arms around my middle. "Nope."

"Do you want to just stay back here forever?" Viv asked.

"We can think of something else."

"What?"

"I don't know. Can't you guys get together and just — just *slide* the dumpster out a little? I mean, four strong men like you?"

They weren't buying it.

"But I don't want to walk around in my underwear," I said. But even I could see this was a sensible choice. "You know, if I just stayed here for a few days, I'll bet I would be skinnier and then I could get out. Two days, three tops. Don't even bring me any water. I'll get all dehydrated and..." They were all looking at me like I was both sad and crazy.

"Honey, you really don't want to be seen in your underwear," Viv said.

I turned back to Tony. "I don't want to do this," I said.

He cocked his head like he'd just remembered something. "Hang on," he said. "I'll be right back."

He vaulted back over the fence and trotted around to the front of the house. He was back within fifteen seconds, carrying some kind of black fabric.

"Sweats," he said. "Ma'am, do you have some scissors I could borrow?"

Nobody told Tony no, of course. He was just that kind of guy.

She came back in a few seconds and handed him the scissors. He passed them to me before he hopped back over the fence.

The ground rustled as he crawled back toward me once again. I could feel his hands on the waistband of my jeans. "Okay, now, Salem. You're going to want to be very still."

I laughed. "Don't worry. I won't move a muscle."

He made one cut at the side of my waist, then looked back up. "Um, would you gentlemen mind turning around? And turning that last light off?"

They did as they were asked, but stayed uncomfortably close.

"You know, I don't really see any reason for the Henrys to even still be here," Viv said.

"It's my back yard," Big Mr. Henry said. "I don't see no need for me to go anywhere."

One of the cops stepped close and said a few things, quietly. Big Mr. Henry took a deep breath and looked a little put out, but he and Lucy went into the house.

Viv, who apparently didn't have a decent bone in her body, had to be reminded that there was no real reason for her to be there, either.

"She's my friend. She needs my support right now."

"I'm okay, Viv," I said. "But thanks."

Viv lifted her chin. "Fine," she said. "I'll wait in Tony's truck." She stomped back to the front of the house.

As the scissors snipped gently down the side of my jeans and Tony's head was almost even with mine, I whispered. "Thanks."

"You're welcome," he whispered back.

"I have to tell you something."

"Something else?"

"It's just that — okay, I needed to do laundry today."

"Don't tell me you're wearing dirty underwear," he said, his tone mocking.

"I needed to do laundry but the washing machine broke. I'm not wearing *any* underwear."

He sucked in a breath. "Salem!"

"I know. Commando."

The cold metal of the scissors slide against my hip, against my thigh, pushing gently as the scissors worked again and again toward my knee.

"Don't tell me something like that now," he said. "I could stab you in the leg."

"I just thought I should warn you, so you wouldn't be completely shocked."

He cleared his throat. "Yes, well..."

"Unless you were going to be a gentleman and not look. In that case I've revealed my secret shame for nothing."

"Oh, I was *going* to look," he assured me.

"Tony!" I gasped his name just as he'd done mine a few seconds ago.

"I'm only human, Salem. There's just so much temptation a man can take. Here, I think you will have to get the rest of it."

I took the scissors but it was slow going using my left hand. "You're not going to look now, though, right?"

"Are you kidding? Of course, I am."

"Why, Tony Solis. I should tell your mother." For a second, I regretted the joke. A million years ago, when we were sneaking around behind his mother's back and meeting for secret trysts, I would make that empty threat. Neither of us wanted his mother to find out then, because we knew she would not hesitate to kill us both.

"She'd just tell me it's about time," he said. "You want me to come around the other side and do it from there?"

The scissors kept bending the fabric instead of cutting it, but I finally got it.

"Okay," I said. I took hold of the waistband of my jeans with one hand and the fence with the other. Tony got on his haunches again and put his hands under my armpits. He lifted me and moved up about a foot, then the edge of my jeans caught again.

"Ha!" I said, triumphant. I wasn't so fat I got stuck!

Except the tug almost made me fall again. I clutched the fence again. "Wait, wait." Tony held still, hoisting me in midair, and I quickly let go of the fence and ripped the bit of denim out of the fence.

I rose the rest of the way and stood, still clutching my jeans, trying to figure out the quickest logistical way to get from one pair of pants to the other without flashing my bare naked behind. I looked around the dumpster. There were a couple of alley lights but it didn't appear there was anywhere I could go that was completely dark.

I toed off my shoes and stood as close to the back of the dumpster as I could, while Tony stood behind me to block the way.

I took a deep breath and grasped the jeans with both hands. "Are you really going to look?" I whispered.

His face was dark, but I could still feel the intensity of his gaze. "Are you telling me you don't want me to?"

I thought for a second. "Nope." I slid out of the jeans as fast as I could, and he held the sweats for me. They were up and over my hips in record time.

I could see his teeth flash in the dark. He looked like a happy man.

"Okay, you two," one of the cops said. "All set?"

I took a deep breath, ridiculously happy. It was because I'd been rescued from my distress, I told myself. And a little bit because of Tony's smile.

Big Mr. Henry came out with a key and unlocked the back gate, and Tony and I followed the cops around the side of the house to the squad cars. I had to repeat my story to three more cops. It was kind of annoying and I should have been in a bad mood. But I wasn't.

CHAPTER TEN

Date Night

I was in such an obnoxiously good mood the next day, I started to annoy the other groomers at Flo's Bow Wow Barbers. I didn't care. Love was never failing. I finished my dogs, made polite conversation with Doreen and dredged up some actual admiration for the Snow Baby baby she'd received the day before. Back at Trailertopia I jumped into the shower, getting ready for Date Night.

I couldn't stop thinking about Tony's grin in the dark last night.

I was ready early, so I took Stump over to Frank's and went back into my prayer room for a quick thank-you prayer.

When Tony knocked, I opened the door and smiled at him.

"Surprise!" Tony's niece Isabella jumped out from behind him.

I jumped, only partly pretending shock. I put my hand over

my mouth to hide my dismay. "Oh my gosh! You scared me half to death!"

Isabella giggled. "You didn't know I was coming!"

"I did *not* know you were coming, that's right." I looked at Tony. "This is a surprise."

"I was at Margaret's house and said we were going to the movies. She begged me to take her." He shrugged. "She's been begging me to take her to see the new Scooby Doo movie for two weeks. Is it okay?"

What was I going to say, no? I did *like* Isabella. It just wasn't what I had in mind for the evening.

Isabella scooted happily into the middle of the bench seat and tugged at her seat belt. Tony reached over and helped her buckle it, tugging the belt to tighten it.

Immediately, she moved to slip the shoulder strap behind her.

"Nope, nope, nope," Tony said. He cocked his head at her. "Where is your memory, Bella? Are you a forgetful old lady? We just talked about this," he chided gently.

"But it's going to choke me," she said with a dramatic but clearly fake pout.

"No, I'm going to choke you if you don't wear your seat belt right, and then I'm going to take you home and no movie for you."

"You're so mean," she said, but with clearly no real heat in it.

"And don't you forget it."

We went to Joe's Crab Shack first, because it was near the movie theater and it had a playground for Isabella.

We got a table on the patio, and I tried to find something on the menu that looked both (a) not a thousand calories and (b) not so healthy that I would pout later. I gave up and ordered the chicken Caesar salad with the dressing on the side.

I couldn't help but pout a little, though, as we passed by the Julia Roberts romantic comedy poster and Tony bought three tickets for *Scooby Doo and the Creature From Inner Space.*

Isabella sat between us. There went the hand-holding. There went the possibility of Tony's arm around my shoulders. I mean, I liked Isabella, I really did. But less and less by the minute.

After the movie, she parked her butt once again between us, and I couldn't help but think that she would be just as safe by the door. But that would be silly and selfish, so I smiled and nodded and pretended to laugh as she told the same knock-knock joke ten times. Then she got quiet and fell asleep.

Tony's eyes met mine over her head and he smiled. For a second it was as if she was our child. It had almost happened. We'd had a child — well, we'd had a pregnancy. The promise of a child. But even if that pregnancy hadn't ended when a pickup t-boned me on the Idalou Highway, I couldn't imagine a moment when Tony and I looked at each other fondly over the head of our sleeping child. I could imagine, easily, lots of drama train-wreck moments. But a moment like this...no. Wouldn't have happened.

He pulled into Trailertopia and killed the motor, then reached up and flicked off the dome light before we opened the door softly, so as not to wake Bella. I pushed my door gently closed with a soft push, and he did the same, and silently walked beside me up the wooden steps of my front deck.

I turned to him, anticipating a good night kiss. But he was looking back toward the truck, as if he was distracted. A thought suddenly occurred to me.

The constant accompaniment of Tony's family members. It

wasn't just a coincidence. He was orchestrating things so we wouldn't be alone.

"Did she wake up?"

He kept looking toward the pickup. "No, I thought maybe...but no. She's still asleep. Well..." He turned toward me with that enigmatic smile. "I guess I'd better be going. Get her home." He leaned in to give me a quick peck.

I took hold of his shirt front and held on. Not roughly, but firmly. I stood on tiptoe and kissed him again.

"Tony," I said.

He raised his eyebrows.

"Are you keeping people around us so you can avoid being alone with me?"

As soon as the words were out of my mouth, I sank slowly back down and steeled myself. Tony would not lie to protect my feelings. Not when I'd asked him a direct question.

He didn't answer, though. He just looked at me with those deep brown eyes. I tried to read what was there. Sympathy? A touch of embarrassment, maybe?

"I don't know," he said finally. "Yeah, maybe. A little."

We stared at each other, neither of us sure what to do or say next.

I took half a step back. "You don't have to, you know. You can say you don't want to be around me. I can handle it."

"It's not that I don't want to be around you," he said. He reached out and ran a finger through my hair, from my forehead to my ear, his face serious. "It's not that. It's just..."

We stood in silence for so long that my heart became heavy with dread. If he couldn't say it, it must be bad. Very bad. Maybe he was ready to break things off for real.

At the thought, my throat got tight and my eyes burned. I blinked, panicked at the thought that this was the moment I'd been dreading, when I'd spent the entire day so convinced that he really wanted me.

"Salem, it's not — "

"Tony!" Isabella called from the pickup. She was crying.

He rushed down the deck steps to reassure her. I could hear him shushing her, telling her he'd take her home in just a minute. I walked to the edge of the deck, my arms wrapped around my waist, hugging myself against the mild chill of the night, and listened as he comforted Isabella softly.

He walked back to me with a lopsided grin. "I do come with a big family, you know."

"I know that. I also know it wouldn't *be* big if couples didn't manage some time alone every once in a while." I regretted that as soon as I said it. I didn't want to make him feel like he had to choose between his family and me. And I certainly didn't want to give the impression I was ready for us to have another baby. But the words were out there.

His smile faded and his jaw locked. He stuck his hands in his pockets. "Yes, well..." He looked at the ground. "I need some time, Salem. You have to give me some time."

I had a thousand questions, but I wasn't sure I was ready for the answers. So I leaned down, gave him a light kiss, and went inside.

CHAPTER ELEVEN

Escalation

All in all, I wasn't in the best frame of mind to be contemplating a weekend with my mother. Friday morning, I stumbled into my prayer room and lit my candles, but I was irritated before I even got started. If God brought me more confusing messages, I was not going to be happy.

Trust in the Lord with all your heart, and do not lean on your own understanding. **Proverbs 3:5 (ESV)**

I bowed my head and sat back. Actually, that felt like sound advice. It wasn't as if I had a better idea, at any rate. I said a prayer of gratitude, with a side plea to maybe remind me at regular intervals over the weekend that I was to remember that (a) Love never fails and (b) trust God over my own understanding, just in case it looked like (a) might be incorrect.

As Friday progressed, I felt myself reciting the two verses over and over. My stomach was in knots, anticipating the weekend ahead. By three in the afternoon, though, I decided I needed to call in reinforcements. I walked outside to the sidewalk in front of Flo's.

"Windy, call Les."

"Dialing right now, honey," Windy said.

Dakota pulled up in his pickup and saw me. He grinned and gave me a thumbs up. I returned the gesture, but inside I was kind of a wreck.

"My mom's going to be here in about three hours," I said. "I'm not sure I can handle it."

"Do you need to call her and cancel?"

"No, I — I can't do that. I have to go through with it. I just — will you pray for me? I mean, right now? And all weekend?"

"Of course I will."

He said a prayer, and I did feel better, if a little foolish. I was talking about a weekend with my mother, not combat.

"Bonnie and I will be thinking of you all weekend. Do you need a ride to church Sunday morning?"

"Actually, yes. I'm going to see if Mom will come with me, and if she does, we'll ride together." But who was I kidding? Mom wasn't going to go to church with me. "But I'll probably need a ride."

"Okay, then. I'll see you Sunday morning. Between now and then, call me if you need anything. Seriously, Salem. Day or night. Call me."

It was comforting to know that I could call, but I hoped it

wouldn't be necessary. I didn't like that what he said sounded uncomfortably close to what God was saying the other morning in my devotional time. I didn't understand it, but I didn't like it any more from Les than I had from God.

Trust in the Lord. Don't lean on your own understanding.

Love never fails.

I recited the words over and over as I finished my dogs, as Doreen drove me home yet again, as I watched the ticking clock creep closer to six, when she was supposed to be there.

The problem was, love kept getting pushed aside by a rotation of anxiety that I would set Mom off, then resentment that I should feel anxious at all, when I was the one trying to do the good thing here, then a long list of I-thought-I'd-gotten-over-that-a-long-time-ago memories.

A few weeks before, I had gone by the outlet store and picked up some cute place mats and napkins to decorate the table. I put them out now, thinking that I would have preferred to have an entirely different house to invite Mom to, but they did not sell those at the outlet store.

Frank came in and plopped down on the recliner. Stump climbed into his lap and was already getting droopy-eyed.

"Hi," I said. "Listen, I'm making a Fat Fighters recipe for dinner."

He froze, and his eyes got a little wide. "The celery thing again?"

"No, tonight it's spaghetti squash tacos."

He blinked. "Spaghetti and tacos don't go together."

"It's spaghetti squash. With black beans and taco seasoning."

He snorted. He was Hispanic, and his mother was an excellent — and authentic — cook. She would have fainted before she'd used pre-made taco seasoning.

But he wasn't at his mom's house. He was at mine, and the meal was free. "I just thought I should warn you. Also, my mom is coming over to stay for a couple of days."

Frank nodded. "Excellent."

"Yes, well...we don't see each other much, so if I start acting weird, it's because, well...I'm a little weirded out about the whole thing."

"No problem." He went back to watching some Spanish-speaking drama where a curvy long-haired rich woman and a maid seem to be having a disagreement about something.

I pulled up the Fat Fighters app and found the recipe I'd marked earlier. I read through it quickly, realized I had retained nothing, and read through it again. I read the first three steps and decided that was enough to be getting on with for now. I washed the squash, then cut it down the middle and cut out the seeds, tossing the soggy mess into the sink for the garbage dis-posal to deal with. I put the two halves on the cookie tray and slid it into the oven. Then I realized I hadn't preheated, and took it back out to preheat, going back over the recipe with the level of concentration of someone studying for the bar exam, then slid it back in when it seemed like enough time had passed for the oven to be at 375. Then I slid it back out when I realized I'd placed the squash with the cut sides up, when the recipe had clearly stated "cut sides down."

"Loser," I muttered under my breath. "Can't even cook a friggin' squash right."

I closed the oven. Frank was standing behind me.

"Aaagh!" I jumped back. "Jeez, Frank, what are you doing? You scared me."

"Who are you talking to?"

"I wasn't talking."

"I heard you say something."

I stopped for a moment, running the past fifteen seconds through my head. I realized with some embarrassment what I'd just said. Mom hadn't even gotten here yet, and already I was a mess.

"Nothing," I said. "I was just talking to myself and freaking out too much."

"Is this that weirdness you were talking about?"

"Yes," I said firmly. "Exactly. My mom makes me a little crazy."

Les had talked about this some in meetings, about how the addict and alcoholic tends to beat everyone to the punch, running themselves down before anyone else has a chance.

I tried to remember if my mother had ever come right out and called me a loser. She called herself that, then she'd wrap her arms around me and say, "We losers gotta stick together, right?" Others could be swept into this fun society, too — her friend Susan, mostly. They'd get drunk together and do something crazy or embarrassing, then giggle over what losers they were. It was a badge of honor.

Misery loves company. Those two loved each others' company, that was certain.

I hadn't thought about Susan in a long time, but the memory left a sour feeling in my stomach. Susan could be okay sometimes, but mostly I just wished she'd go away. Her son was a creep, and Mom never spent time around Susan without doing something that made me mad or ashamed.

Memories of Susan were not going to keep me focused on

loving my mom, so instead I recited the verse from that morning's devotional over and over. I chopped onions and cilantro and said, "trust the Lord" over and over under my breath until the words lost all meaning and started to sound like a made-up language.

Six o'clock came and went, and I checked my phone to see if maybe she'd texted me and I'd missed it. Nothing. I went outside and checked to make sure she wasn't driving around, lost, but the trailer was pretty easy to find. I walked out to the street and made sure you could see the number on the little white picket fence that covered the tongue of the trailer. Everything looked fine. I was glad I'd asked Frank to mow, though — the yard was no backyard paradise like the Bates place, but at least the grass wasn't overgrown.

I went back in and checked the beans. But they were beans — they were either hot or they were cold, that's pretty much all beans could do. It wasn't like I was making a souffle that might fall or something.

I stewed for a while, then decided to text her.

"Dinner's almost ready," I texted, because 'Dinner's already ready,' would sound too petulant and get us started off on a bad note. "Are you close?" I hit send, then stared at the phone.

Nothing, for ten more minutes.

"Frank, do you have your phone with you?"

He made a noise that sounded somewhat affirmative.

"Can you send me a test text? I'm not sure how reliable this thing is. She might have tried to call and I'm just not getting it."

He shifted in the chair and pulled his phone from his back pocket. He thumbed through a few things and then my phone buzzed. "Test Test" the screen said.

I frowned. "Would you mind calling? I'm not sure if she's into texting. You know that generation," I said, like I was all cutting-edge myself.

He pushed a couple more buttons. My phone buzzed.

I hit the green button.

"Hello?" Frank said. "You there?"

I was literally ten feet from him. But I put the phone to my ear anyway. "Yeah, I'm here. Thanks."

I hung up and checked the clock again. Six-thirty. Mom had never been the most punctual person. In fact, I thought as I rose and began pacing again, I shouldn't be surprised if she blew the whole thing off entirely. She wasn't exactly a person of her word.

I was getting mad again. I decided I needed to get up and think about something else. I took a fork and ran it through the squash, somewhat heartened when it came away looking like the spaghetti noodles it was supposed to. I turned the oven on as low as it would go, then scooped out the squash and plopped it into a casserole dish with a lid, and slid the whole thing into the oven, hoping it would just stay warm and not go to complete crap. I took the beans off the burner and did the same thing with them, and covered the chopped onions and cilantro with plastic wrap and stuck them in the fridge.

I moved to the sofa and stared at the television. It was now six-forty-five.

I got up, opened the oven and lifted the lid on the squash. It seemed fine. I thought about how gummy and gross real spaghetti got when it was overcooked, and hoped spaghetti squash wasn't subject to the same frailties. So far it looked okay.

I sat back down and tucked my legs under me. I stared at the

TV and thought about what excuses she would make. Car trouble was always a ready standby, as was getting lost. One time she'd tried to pull off getting stuck in traffic, but that wasn't something that happened often in Lubbock and never in Idalou.

"Tell me what's going on," I ordered Frank, gesturing toward the TV.

"You want to watch something else?" He held the remote out.

"No, I want to watch this. Tell me what's going on. Who's that lady? And why is she letting the maid lecture her like that?"

"That maid is her sister. Well, actually, she's her mother, but the rich lady thinks she's her sister."

I nodded. A family at least as screwed up as my own.

"What's she saying?"

Frank launched into a translation that left me completely behind. From what I gathered, the woman and the maid were pulling one over on the rich woman, and the rich woman was really in love with her husband's son, but they needed the old man to believe that she hated the son for some reason I didn't quite catch, but it had something to do with a milk allergy. Or maybe a large inheritance — Frank, whose accent was thick anyway, was talking pretty fast and the action was still going down on screen. There were lots of harsh words fired rapidly through clenched teeth from the maid and way too much wringing of hands from the rich woman.

Then a hot older guy walked in, wearing a silver suit that matched his hair. From the way the woman acted (reluctantly, stiffly affectionate) he was the husband, and from the music (ominous) he was not a nice guy.

The scene switched to two teenage beautiful people who were working a carnival booth. The girl was flirting with everything she had but she wasn't hooking the guy, and it reminded me uncomfortably of me and Tony. Then the show went to a commercial, which was in English and I could keep up with that just fine.

"You think she's going to show?" Frank asked.

"The show's back on," I said. "Who's that guy?"

Frank kept explaining and I kept listening with everything I was worth, trying to keep up. By the next commercial break, we had seemed to come to some tacit agreement that we wouldn't bring up the subject of my mother or how we were waiting for her. We just sat and watched, and sat and watched some more, until that show became another one and I thought I might be picking up some actual working Spanish.

Then I heard a low rumble.

"Is that thunder?" I asked, looking up.

"That was my stomach," Frank said, looking a little sheepish.

I checked my phone again. It was almost eight.

"Okay, that's enough. We're eating without her." I stood slowly, my legs sore and cramped from sitting so still for too long.

"We can wait, it's no big deal."

"No, we've waited long enough. I'm starving, you're starving." I picked up my phone and checked the messages again, just in case, but there was nothing.

"Windy, how long should we wait on a late guest before we go ahead and eat?"

Windy was silent for a minute. Then she said, "Honey, you've asked me a question I'm afraid I can't answer in a couple of seconds. The good news is, this goes straight to my personal email, and I'll be happy to do some research and get back to you as soon as I can. I hope that's okay."

Frank and I both looked at the phone, then at each other.

"That's cool," he said.

I nodded. "It is. I didn't know she did that."

We were finishing our second taco when I saw headlights in the driveway and Stump started to growl.

Mom rapped on the door a few seconds later.

I opened the door for her, plastering a smile on my face. "Mom," I said, giving her a hug, lifting my chin so as not to get a face full of the fake fur vest she wore.

I got Mom's bags settled in my room — I would give her my bed and take the sofa — and went to the living room to find Mom making polite conversation with Frank, her smile fixed on her face much like mine must have been a few minutes earlier. I picked up the plates and was carrying them to the kitchen when my phone dinged.

Windy, loudly enough for all to hear, said, "Honey, if someone is rude enough to keep you waiting after you've invited them to dinner, eat without them!"

Frank and I looked at each other.

"Good," Frank said, satisfied that we'd made the right call.

I turned back to the kitchen, avoiding looking at Mom.

After the dishes were done, I settled onto the sofa beside Mom. Stump backed up to me so I could pick her up. I lifted her and she got settled just as the news came on.

"Another robbery in the High Point area today, and this one is getting attention for the way it stands out from the others," Trisha said. "Good evening, and thank you for joining us." The opening music swelled, and the screen flashed to 'candid' shots of the Channel 11 news team — Trisha looking at some papers with intense focus, Rick the sportscaster running, in his shirt and tie, with his arms outstretched, the Red Raider football field in the background, like he was catching a football, and Carlos the baby-faced weather man talking to a group of kindergartners at their school.

"That girl looks familiar," Mom said.

"That's Trisha Thompson. We used to be best friends."

"Oh yeah," Mom said. "Are you sure that's her?"

"Positive, Mom."

"She certainly has put on the weight, hasn't she?" She looked at me with a grin. "I guess that must make you feel a little bit better."

I stared blankly, like I didn't catch on that she thought I should feel bad about my own weight gain. As if I hadn't been happy to see that Trisha had also gained weight when I first ran into her again, about a year ago.

The news was coming back on, so I turned back to the screen and tried to focus. There might be something that Viv and I could use.

"Police are investigating yet another robbery in the High Point area. That makes the third this month, and the twelfth in the last two and a half months. This one, however, is standing apart for the level of violence involved."

The screen switched to a bald guy with glasses wearing an LPD uniform. "Officers responded to a call at 6:38 p.m., and arrived on the scene to find one robbery victim on the ground, with an apparent blow to the head. Paramedics responded and the subject was taken to the hospital with serious injuries. The victim was an employee at the business. At this time we do not have any information on his condition. Evidence inside the business indicates that it was robbed. We are working with the owners now to determine what was taken."

The scene switched to a reporter who stood outside the Police Department. Patrice and Wayne, as you heard Officer Morris say, there is no information yet as to the condition of this robbery victim, but we do know that he is a male, around twenty-five to thirty years of age. Early reports indicate he was hit over the head with something like a baseball bat."

"Keelee, are we correct that this is the first time violence like this has been seen against the victims in these robberies?"

Keelee nodded enthusiastically. "That's right, Wayne. Up until now, the robberies have been fairly low-key affairs — the victims have all told of a gang of men clad in black, with black face masks, all converging on the place at once, with a lot of yelling and a show of force. In every case except this one, the perpetrators leave just as quickly with what money they're able to collect, without hurting anyone."

"Do police have any idea why this time was different?"

"No clue," Keelee said. Then blinked, apparently realizing how bad that sounded. "I mean, they haven't said — they might have a clue. I mean, I'm sure they *do* have clues, it's just — "

"I'm sure they have lots of clues, they just don't always share those with the news media, of course," Wayne said with a laugh. Wayne was a pro.

"Of course. That's what I meant." Keelee held her microphone with both hands and looked like she wanted to crawl into a hole.

"Thanks, Keelee," Trisha said.

Keelee nodded, blinking rapidly.

The little window with Keelee in it popped off and the scene shifted to just the two anchors. "We will continue to follow this story and bring you all the latest updates right here on KBST, and also on KBST.com as soon as we have them."

"Poor kid," Mom said. "She messed up."

My phone rang.

"Did you hear that?" Viv said, as soon as I picked up. "Things are heating up."

"I did hear that. That means something." I was beginning to think like a detective, I thought with a little thrill. Of course, Wayne, Keelee and Tri-Patrice had all just been making a big deal out of how unusual it was, so maybe I wasn't as quick on the draw as I would like to believe.

"It's significant," Viv agreed. "Let's meet tomorrow after work and go interview this guy."

"Yes, let's..." I looked over at Mom. We would probably need to do some mother-daughter bonding stuff tomorrow, like a chick flick and dinner at Applebee's or something. "Actually, tomorrow might not be good. Maybe Monday after work?"

"Monday? That's three days away. By Monday the whole thing could be over. Come on, now, let's don't let the police get all the glory."

But Mom. I kept thinking about what Les said. If this weekend was some kind of divine appointment for us to make peace with our past, I didn't want to be the one who messed it up.

"Sorry, I have plans already. We'll have to do it later."

"What plans? Tony? Bring him with us. It'll be good to have him around for muscle. Maybe he can get more information than we can."

"Not Tony. My mom is in town, remember? We have plans tomorrow." I covered the phone with my hand and turned to Mom. "We'll make plans, I mean."

"Oh, yeah, I forgot." Viv snorted. "How's that going?"

"Great," I said.

"She's right there, huh?"

"Yep, that's right."

Viv sighed. "Okay, well, I hope you don't mind if I do a little digging on my own and try to move the case forward."

"You do that." It was unlikely Viv would gather anything useful, but she enjoyed trying.

I hung up and smiled at Mom. "Maybe we could go see that new Julia Roberts movie tomorrow night. Get dinner somewhere?"

"Let's make it lunch and a matinee. I planned to meet Susan tomorrow night. She wants to hear all about Gerry."

"Oh, well...I work during the day on Saturday. It's all I can do to squeeze in a quick takeout lunch." My temper flared at the knowledge that she'd invited Susan into our mother-daughter-only weekend, but I tried to keep that out of my voice.

"But you came to my brunch last Saturday."

"I know, I arranged for the day off. The first Saturday off I've had in two years. It's kind of a big deal, actually, to get a Saturday off. I can't ask for another one a week later. With no notice."

Mom frowned. "Well. I guess it's all my fault then."

I took a deep breath and said "*love never fails*" three times fast in my head. "Nothing is anyone's fault, but maybe you and Susan could spend the day together tomorrow while I'm at work, then you and I could go out tomorrow night."

"I'll have to see if that works for her. She's pretty busy."

"Okay, well...we'll see how it goes." I faked a yawn and stretched. "But now, I need to hit the hay. Saturdays are busy and I have to be there early. I'll show you where everything is in the bathroom."

Mom was still asleep when Doreen picked me up for work the next morning. I wasn't sure if Frank would be over during the day, or how Stump would fare alone with Mom, so I carted her off with me.

I got a text from Mom around noon. "Spending the day with Susan, I'll see you at your place for our Girls Night Out!"

I rushed home after work so I could take a shower before the movie started. I was surprised to see Mom's car not in the driveway, and thought for a second that maybe I'd mixed up our plans and I was supposed to meet her at the restaurant. But no, I checked my phone and she'd said "at your place."

I let Stump run around the yard and sniff the grass for a minute. She'd come in when she got through.

Frank sat in the recliner.

"Did my mom say what time she'd be back?"

"Nope." Not taking his eyes off the TV.

With Frank, it paid to be specific, though. "Did she say anything?"

He appeared to be thinking. "Yeah, she asked where you keep the fabric softener. And she asked what I was doing here."

"What did you say?"

"I don't know and I'm watching TV."

I nodded. "I'm going to take a shower. Will you listen for Stump and let her in, please?"

I was halfway down the hallway when what he'd said about the fabric softener registered. "Was she doing laundry?"

"Nope."

"Why was she asking about fabric softener?"

He shrugged. "Maybe she *wanted* to do laundry? But the machine was broken. Remember?"

I remembered. I went back down the hall and opened the lid. Full of water.

"Did she happen to carry out a basket of wet clothes?" I called back to the living room.

"Maybe, yeah."

I nodded. "Okay, well." Immediately I became filled with dread. She would be mad because she'd tried to do laundry and I'd let her down with my broken machine. A mad Mom was a scary Mom. This night was going to be difficult.

I closed the lid on the washing machine. "I'm going to take a shower."

I sped through the shower, determined to do as the scripture had been instructing me. I trusted in the Lord. I did not lean on my own understanding. Every time I caught myself mentally rehearsing an evening full of conflict and drama, I reminded myself to cast my anxieties on God. I didn't lean on my own understanding of my relationship with my Mom, which was always full of conflict and drama.

I dried my hair and put on a little bit of makeup, then pulled on jeans and a black long-sleeved t-shirt with a ballerina neck. I stood too long in front of the mirror, wondering if Mom would think I looked alright. Her new life with her new high falutin' family came with a new wardrobe and a totally different sense of style. I rifled through my closet, looking for anything that could be considered the least bit trendy. I had three things pulled out on the bed and was buttoning up a white men's shirt when I realized how much time had passed.

I went into the hallway and looked toward the living room. She still wasn't here. We were going to have to hurry to get dinner before the movie.

"You're sure she said she would be back? I wasn't supposed to meet her there?" I asked Frank.

"You were?" He looked up from the movie.

"I was?"

He looked confused.

I took a deep breath. "I mean, I'm asking you. Did she say she would be back, or that I was supposed to meet her at the restaurant?"

"Oh, she said she was coming back. She said, "Tell Salem I'll be back for dinner.""

I checked my phone. No new texts from Mom.

With a groan of frustration, I texted her. "I'm home from work and ready to go." I waited a second. No response. "Are you meeting me back here, or should I just join you at the restaurant?"

Nothing.

I pulled on the ankle boots Viv had given me for my birthday. They were cute and dressed up my jeans enough that I felt a little bit better about how I looked. I went back to my bathroom and dug through the closet, finding a chunky necklace of turquoise that I'd had for a long time. I fastened it and fluffed my hair. At the risk of sounding like a lunatic, I didn't completely hate the way I looked.

I walked down the hallway, then back to my room. I checked

the mirror again. Nope, still didn't hate it.

I checked my phone. No new texts, and time was really running out to get dinner before the movie.

My phone dinged while it was in my hand, and I jumped, almost dropping it.

I checked the text. It wasn't from Mom, it was from Viv.

"You're not going to believe who that last robbery victim was. The one who got beat up with the baseball bat?"

I sighed. "Who?" I texted back.

"Your friend from the inspection sticker business. The one you tried to lead down the path to crime and punishment."

I hit the call button and dialed her number.

"Seriously?" I said. "That guy from Estacado Auto?"

"The one and only. They said on the news today. Apparently they did a number on him, too. He's still in the hospital."

"Wow. That's...weird."

"We need to interview him."

"Do we?"

"Absolutely. I'll come pick you up."

"Oh, I can't. I'm going to dinner and the movies with my mom."

"Oh yeah. I guess we could visit him tomorrow. He might be released, though, and I don't know where he lives."

The phone dinged again.

"Hang on, I just got a text."

I looked at the screen. "Running behind. I'll catch up with you at the movie."

Figures, I thought.

"Never mind," I told Viv. "Dinner plans just fell through. I could maybe do a quick interview before the movie, if you hurry."

"I'll be there in five," she said.

"What's the guy's name again?" I asked as I belted myself in. I should not have said "hurry" to Viv. She had her racing model Cadillac and she wasn't afraid to use it.

"Xavier Barnstable. He's at UMC. The little girl reporter from the news said he was in satisfactory condition and expected to make a full recovery. But still. Ouch. I wonder if he got a look at them and that's why they beat him up. Like, maybe he grabbed one of their masks and —" She made a ripping off motion. "So they had to rough him up a little."

"Something happened. Either that, or maybe they're just getting bolder with every robbery. You know, escalation. Pushing it further and further every time."

"Who knows?"

We stopped at the front desk to ask which room he was in, but the unhelpful woman there wouldn't tell us. "He's not receiving visitors."

"Are you sure?" Viv said. "I think he'll want to talk to us. You should call the room and ask him."

"I'm sure," the woman said. She flattened her lips in what was probably meant to look like a smile.

"You should just call up there and see. He knows us. We are helping the police investigate this crime and we can help him."

"Then you should share that information with the police. I'm sure they'll be happy to hear it."

I hooked Viv's elbow. "Give it up," I said. "She's not gonna budge."

We decided to wander around the building a little to see if we could spot anything that might look like a room under police custody, and it turned out not to be that hard. It was the only room with two cops posted outside it.

For a moment, I thought Viv was going to go for it and try to talk her way past them.

Then Marty came out of the room.

"Hey, Marty!" Viv said, like he was an old friend.

It took him a moment to place us, but when he did, he was friendly enough. "Hey, it's you two. Say, you didn't do this, did you? Retaliation for him not giving you the sticker?" He laughed.

My eyes went wide and I looked at the cops. I'm sure I looked guilty.

"Of course not, don't be ridiculous," I said, before realizing that I'd probably just made myself sound even guiltier. Quick, change the subject. "How is he?"

Marty shook his head slowly. "They banged him up good, that's for sure."

"Did he get a look at them?" Viv asked.

Marty glanced over his shoulder at the cop standing outside the door, and motioned for us to head back toward the elevator. "Not a thing," he said. "They had masks on, and he said only one of them talked." He pushed the elevator button.

Once inside with the doors closed, Marty shook his head again. "Poor kid is scared to death."

"Well, yeah," I said. "I'd be scared too if someone bashed me over the head with a baseball bat."

"He's not scared about that. I have a sneaking suspicion he knows more than he's saying."

"Why wouldn't he say?" Viv asked, then apparently remembered what Marty had said before. "Do you think it's someone he knows? From, you know, from *inside*?"

Marty was silent for a moment while the elevator stopped and the doors slid silently open. "I don't know. I'm not sure what to think. I don't want to believe he would be in on anything like this. He's a good kid. He made some bad mistakes and he paid for them. He's learned from it. I mean, you saw the way he was the other day. He's determined to stay on the straight and narrow. Just about militant about it. He drives the speed limit on the dot, and before he got a car he wouldn't even borrow mine because he didn't want to explain to the police about a borrowed car. I can't believe he would be involved in something like this."

"Maybe he's not involved. Maybe it's just someone he knows. Someone he could identify, but won't. To protect them."

Marty sighed. "Maybe."

The three of us strolled toward the front doors of the hospital.

"What makes you sure he's holding back?" I asked.

"Well, I'm the one who found him, so I heard everything first. He was in a lot of pain, of course, and not talking real good. But he said there were four guys. Then, when he was giving his statement to the police he said there were two."

"That seems like a fairly easy mistake to make."

"Yeah. It does." Marty nodded. "But when he was telling the police it was two guys instead of four, he looked at me like, "Are you gonna correct me." Kind of worried like." Marty frowned. "I don't know what difference it would make, but..."

"Have you heard how much longer he's going to be in there?"

"Not sure yet. At least a couple more days. Then he'll need some time to recuperate, of course. Might be a couple weeks or more before he makes it back to the shop."

"Does he have insurance?"

Marty gave a rueful laugh. "Yep, the kind we all have. The kind that costs an arm and a leg and doesn't pay for a pinky toe."

"Do you think he'd talk to us when he got out?"

Marty shrugged. "I couldn't say. I'll ask him, though."

I looked at my watch and gave a little gasp. I needed to be at the theater in about ten minutes.

"Viv, I have to go," I said. "I mean, we don't need to rush or anything," I said, remembering the scary trip to the hospital. "We just...need to leave now."

It was a scary trip to the movie theater, too. I clung to my seatbelt with one hand and the car door with the other, trying to remind myself to go limp at the moment of impact. "Slow down, would you?"

"You're the one with a movie to catch."

"And you're the one who just got a ticket and could be relying on me and Belle Court to get you around if you get another one."

I lurched against the seat belt as she threw on the brakes.

After I'd recovered, I said, "Why do you think he would lie about the number of guys there?"

"Who knows. Maybe he really did just get it wrong. He had been hit in the head. He might not have been fully conscious."

"Maybe. But I think we should assume everything means something, until we know for sure it doesn't."

Viv nodded. "Yep. That's what Matlock would do."

We were pulling into the movie theater parking lot. "What kind of car does your Mom drive?"

"Mercedes convertible," I said. "Silver."

"Ooooh, fancy." We drove through the parking lot, but didn't spot the car. "I guess just let me out here," I said as we pulled alongside the box office. "I'll find her inside."

"Do you have a way to get home if she doesn't show up?"

I opened my mouth to say, "She'll show up," then remembered who I was talking about. I did not want to spend money on a cab back to Trailertopia, and I didn't want to face the awkwardness of a rescue call to Tony.

"Maybe you could just circle the parking lot while I run inside and make sure she's here," I said. "I'll come out and give the thumbs up when I see her."

I dashed inside, but didn't see Mom. I checked the ladies room and the concession stand. Nothing.

Frowning, I pulled out my phone and checked messages. Nothing. I texted her: "Sorry, I'm just getting here. Are you inside already?"

No answer, but she might have heeded one of the seven hundred messages they give you to turn your phone off before every movie. I bought one ticket and headed toward the theater. If I saw her, I'd run back out and give Viv the okay to go.

My phone went off just as I was about to hand my ticket to the taker.

I sighed, turning the phone over.

"Sorry, can't make it after all. Enjoy the show, sweetie!"

I stared at the screen for a long few seconds while the ticket taker held his hand out.

"Ma'am?"

"I'm sorry," I said. "I've changed my mind."

I turned and dashed for the door.

Viv was still circling the lot. I ran onto the sidewalk and waved to her.

A group of five or six women were coming up the lot toward the box office. I held my ticket out to them.

"Y'all watching the new Julia Roberts movie? I have an extra ticket. Turns out I can't use it."

CHAPTER TWELVE

Too Far to the Other Side

Viv and I drove around for a couple of hours and talked to a few people, but turned up no more new information, just what we'd already heard. Xavier Barnstable had been beaten over the head. Most people thought it was the Bandits, but a couple of people thought it was related to his time in prison, rather than the other robberies.

As the time neared for the movie to let out, I asked Viv to take me home. "I need to be there so Frank won't be forced to make awkward conversation."

"Do you want me to pick you up for church tomorrow?"

"No, thanks. Les is picking me up."

I changed into pajamas and curled up on the sofa with Stump to wait for Mom. I fell asleep, waking slightly when Frank covered me with a blanket and left. The next thing I knew, sun was streaming in through the open curtain.

I checked the driveway. No Mercedes. I checked the bedroom. No Mom. I checked my phone. No more messages.

She stumbled in as I was finishing getting ready for church.

"Sorry I never made it back last night," she said. "Susan and I got to talking and I lost all track of time."

I made a noise that fell short of being an actual word.

"Let's you and me go out for breakfast. My treat."

"It'll have to be lunch," I said. "Les is about to pick me up for church. I had hoped we could go together, actually. You can meet some of my friends."

"Oh, no thanks. I'm not much of a church person."

"It's okay. My church is open to all kinds." I smiled.

"Thanks, but no. Who is Les, anyway? Another guy you've got hanging around here?" She looked pointedly at the recliner, now Frank-free. "You're stacking them up, aren't you? How does Tony feel about that?"

I didn't care for her tone or her insinuation, but as Les was on his way at that very moment, it wasn't hard to remember that I didn't want him showing up in the middle of a screaming match.

"Tony is very supportive of my having friends of all kinds. He knows that Frank and Les are both part of my support system. So he is fine with it."

"Your support system?" She laughed. "How is this Les guy part of your support system? Pay any bills for you?"

I looked around the trailer. If she thought I had only gotten this far, even with a sugar daddy...

"Les is my AA sponsor. You know, he counsels me, listens to me when I want to drink. Helps me navigate the pitfalls." *We've talked at great length about your visit,* I did not say.

She made a kind of *"hmph"* noise. "I never really saw much good in therapy. I mean, I haven't tried it, so I couldn't say for sure. But, it seems to me like, if talking really helped that much, we'd all be perfectly fine. Because nobody ever shuts up!" She cackled at her own joke. "Just get on with it, I say."

"Well, it is a lot of talking, but more than just random talk. This is more like, talking about the things you don't want to talk about. The things that all the other talking is meant to cover up. Those kind of middle-of-the-night voices that tell you you're not worth much."

"Oh, well, I never did that. I always knew I was a decent person. I had plenty of people who said it for me, but I never been the type to run myself down. I mean, what's the point in that? What good does it do? Who's to say one person is a good person and one is bad, right? It all comes down to what you do, and I've never done anything bad, so..." She cackled again. "I've done a lot of things that weren't good, but..." She waved a hand like she was shooing a fly. "But so what. All this self-talk stuff. It's just a bunch of self-involved nonsense. I mean, look at me? I had a hard life growing up. A really hard life. Do you see me moping around, spilling my guts to whoever will listen? Of course not. Like I said. Suck it up. Get up and move on."

I felt the familiar rise in temper whenever she referred to how "really hard" her life had been. Not that I thought it hadn't been. Her father had died when she was little, and I think G-Ma went through her own share of dud men and dud jobs before she bought the motel and finally found a bit of stability. Mom had at least a dozen failed happily-ever-afters under her own belt. Even if some of them were her fault, still...that was hard.

But I resented her woe-is-me because she refused to even consider that anyone else's life had been not that great, too. Even me. *Especially* me. The many times I had fought with her as a teenager and tried to get her to see that being uprooted every few months was getting old, she would belittle me.

You have no idea how easy you have it, she would sneer.

I kept my mouth shut, because I realized nothing good was going to come out if I opened it. It was silly. We would descend into an argument about whose life was harder. It was just silly.

Finally, I took a deep breath and said, "I think that's Les. I'll be back around noon, and we can get some lunch. If Stump starts to freak out after I'm gone, just tap on Frank's window across the yard, and he'll come take care of her."

Les and his wife, Bonnie, weren't there yet, but I stood out by the curb and waited anyway. Les took one look at me and knew things weren't going well.

"That bad, huh?" he said into the rear view mirror once I had climbed into the back seat.

I shook my head. "She stood me up yesterday. And this morning she thinks I'm a silly tramp who doesn't need things like support systems or therapy."

Les was silent as he drove us out of Trailertopia. Bonnie turned and patted my knee over the seat.

"I'm okay," I said with a smile. "Just a few more hours to get through."

Les didn't speak again until we got to the church. After he put the car into park and killed the engine, he said, "You know Salem, there's a good reason God gave us the commandment to honor our father and mother."

"And why is that?"

"Because we probably wouldn't, if he hadn't. Family is too hard sometimes. We need that commandment to hang in there. Keep hanging in there. Otherwise, our humanness would eventually cause us to break every tie."

After church, we walked back toward Les and Bonnie's car. Les had his head down, apparently lost in thought. As he unlocked the door, he turned to me.

"Salem, listen. Don't miss a chance to make peace with your mother. You might be tempted to just keep your head down and get through the next couple of hours. And that will be fine. But if God is orchestrating these events to put you two together for a purpose, he's going to keep at it until that purpose is done. He wants to heal you. He wants families to be whole. He wants *people* to be whole. That's love, even if it is scary and awkward sometimes. You might as well let it happen."

"Les, can I be honest with you?"

"Of course."

"I honestly don't know if I want to make peace with my mother." There. I'd said it. And when I said it, I knew I'd never said anything truer. I wasn't proud of myself. I wanted to believe I was one hundred percent the victim, and any relationship difficulties Mom and I had were entirely on her side: her failure to make us a stable home, her willingness to pawn me off on G-Ma at every opportunity, her penchant for taking off with one man after another, making no effort to keep in touch with me, her habit of putting everyone else before me.

But even if she was making an effort...I wasn't sure I wanted it. I wasn't sure I wanted to be around her. Which made me...what? Not a great daughter, that's for sure. I steeled myself to hear how Les would react to that.

"I know that, Salem." He said it like it was no big deal. "I mean, I can certainly understand it. She hurt you. Even when it's your mother, it's hard to want to be chummy with someone who's hurt you that deeply. But listen to me. You have to do it anyway. It affects every other relationship you have."

"I have a lot of relationships, Les, and not one of them is re-motely involved with my mother. There's you, there's Viv, there's Tony, people at work. Mom doesn't know any of you."

"But we do know you, Salem. And your relationship with your mother affects *you*. We're not all separate people, Salem. Think of it — " He stopped, and I heard him sigh, like he was grasping for a way to make me understand. "Think of it like streams."

"Strings?"

"No, streams. Like rivers. Your stream meets up with my stream, with Viv's stream, with Tony's stream. Our streams run together, separate, run together with someone else's. So every-thing that's in my stream mixes with yours, if only a little bit. But it's there. We think of our lives as these individual seg-ments, but it's all mixed in there, Salem. We can't just say, "I'm going to pick this and this to carry downstream with me." It's all mixed in together. Nothing is compartmentalized. We have to clean up our streams, if we want to bring anything good and clean to everyone else's. Don't miss the chance, if it presents itself. You said yourself, you only have a couple more hours to get through. If the opportunity presents itself to hash things out over the next few hours, even if it's awkward or painful, take advantage of it. Making peace isn't just about the absence of conflict, Salem. Sometimes peace is on the other side of conflict."

"Did you get all prayed up and sanctified?" Mom asked as soon as I came through the front door.

I sat my purse down and decided the best thing I could do was ignore her tone.

"I'm ready for lunch, how about you? Where would you like to go?"

"I thought you Christians didn't believe in working on the Sabbath."

I blinked.

Sometimes peace is on the other side of conflict.

In that moment, I *wanted* some conflict. I didn't even care about the peace. She had stood me up, blown me off, made fun of me, and now she was mocking my faith. At the moment, peace wasn't high on my list of priorities.

I sat calmly in Frank's recliner. My recliner, that I never sat in because Frank was always in it. I faced Mom straight on.

"You seem to have an issue with my faith."

She waved a hand and gave a light laugh. "I don't have any problem with it. It's silly, that's all. I can't believe you of all people are falling for it. But whatever. You're an adult. You can make your own decisions."

I bit my bottom lip and focused on remaining calm.

"I am an adult, and I deserve the common courtesy that every person deserves. You don't have to share my beliefs, but you don't have the right to mock them, either."

"Honey, I can't — "

"Don't call me honey." My voice was steely.

She drew her head back. "Can't a mother — "

"You never called me "honey" when I was a kid. You never treated me with any affection, any consideration. You weren't sweet to me then, when I needed you to be. Don't try it now, when I don't need it."

"See, I knew this was going to happen." She shook her head as if in disbelief. "That's what it always comes back to, doesn't it? I was a horrible mother. I screwed you up. You have no idea, Salem." She shook her head again, this time as if in sadness. "No idea."

"I *was* there, you know," I said. "It's not as if I'm getting my information second-hand."

"You didn't see all of it, though. You were just a kid. Life to you was just one big adventure after another, with the grownups handling all the problems. I shielded you from so much."

My mouth dropped open in disbelief. "Is that what you tell yourself? That I was *unaware*? That I didn't realize every time we moved — those adventures you speak of — that it was because you couldn't pay the bills? You think I didn't realize that every time you complained about the responsibility of raising a child, you were complaining about *me*? Every time you said a good man didn't want a ready-made family, you think I didn't realize you were blaming me for the fact that you ended up with one deadbeat after another? One *child-molesting* deadbeat after another?"

"Oh, please. Do not start in on this again."

The urge to scream at her was so strong, it was almost blinding. Her contempt for me and for what I'd been through made me so furious I was practically spitting with it.

I forced myself to stay calm. I faced her, determined now to see it through, all the way through. Because Les could very well be right. This could be the only chance. After this, I was quite sure I never wanted to see her again.

"All I'm trying to do is get you to see that things you did, things you said — they affected me. I have to deal with that, and I think a part of healing is to get everything out in the open."

Mom shook her head, her expression derisive. "Boy, that guy is doing a number on you, isn't he? Convinced you that we have to dig everything back up, rehash crap that happened a lifetime ago. What's the point? It doesn't change anything."

I took a deep breath and offered what I hoped was a conciliatory but firm smile.

"It does not change the past. But I've come to believe that what happens in the past continues to follow us around until we deal with it. And I don't want this to follow me around. I want to get well. I want to start living my life again, not just waiting for each day to be over so I can check another day sober off my books."

"Do you really think it's fair to lay all this at my door? I didn't make you drink. You made your choices, not me. Don't blame all your mistakes on me."

"I'm not blaming my mistakes on you."

"Of course you are," she said. "That's what alcoholism is. An excuse to blame someone and something else for your mistakes."

"I blame you for *your* mistakes!" I could feel the same pursed-lipped, flashing eyed anger mirrored in my own expression. "I blame you for me having to raise myself while you were out partying with Susan. I blame you for bringing home one child-molesting monster after another. I blame you for not paying the bills, for using me as your shield, for abandoning me to G-Ma's, for choosing everyone else over me!"

I no longer had any desire to "love" my way through this. I didn't want to think of Mom with love, or visualize healing light filling the room around us. I wanted to take this and bash her over the head with it; I wanted to make her experience deep, staggering pain — the same pain she'd given me.

"You chose every man who came across your path over me. You chose yourself over me. You chose Susan over me."

"See, I knew that's what this was about. As soon as I got here Friday night and talked about meeting up with Susan you started being difficult. You always hated Susan. You always resented the fact that I had a friend who was important to me."

"I did not," I said, remembering that there had been a time when I had really liked Susan, thought she was cool. And remembering the night that all changed. "Why did you not protect me from her?"

"Protect you from *her*? What are you talking about? Susan never touched you." Mom tilted her head, looking at me like I was crazy or silly.

"She didn't, but her son did. I'm sure you probably think I don't remember, that I was too young. But I do. Like it was yesterday. I was seven, we were at Susan's house,and her son was there for the weekend. Her teenage son. He was, what, 16? 15? You decided we should spend the night because you didn't want to drive home, and she said I could just sleep with her son, in his bed. I remember. I remember the look on your face when she said that. You knew it wasn't a good idea. You knew it wasn't right. I knew, too, but I wasn't sure why. I found out, though, didn't I? Later that night, I found out why it wasn't right.

"You didn't want to agree to that, but you were more worried about what Susan would think of you than you were about protecting me. So you just stood back and let it happen."

"I didn't know — "

"You knew! You knew the very next day! When I came out of that room a different person." I remembered that, too. The ride home the next morning, slumped against the passenger door, confused and scared. Sore. Trying to make sense of what had happened. I'd been flattered by his attention the day before when he wanted to play with me, when he was taking me to the store to get candy and when he let me play his video games. I thought I'd found a new friend.

The next day, and for weeks after, I had tried to tell myself it was okay. It was a good thing that had happened that night. It meant he liked me. He'd said it was a game we were playing. But I didn't like that game.

Seeing the whole thing from an adult perspective, of course, it was clear to me that this was what abusers did. They made you think it wasn't bad. And that's what victims of abuse did. They rationalized. They tried to find a way to make "okay" out of something that was not okay at all.

That morning after, Mom had tried to talk to me at first. She had stopped and bought donuts. I couldn't eat. She had talked about what we would do the next week. Maybe we'd go to a movie. She rattled on every once in a while, but I didn't respond.

We had pulled up at the house we were living in at the time, and she killed the motor, looked at me, and then said, "Well, if

you're going to pout, pout. But you're on your own with that."
Then she got out of the car and left me there.

I was seven years old.

"Why didn't you protect me?" I asked again, my voice soft.

"I always did the best I could with you."

"Did you? Was that the best you could do? Let Susan's son
molest me because you didn't want to rock the boat with her?
You didn't know how to tell her no?"

"You're such a victim, Salem. You think anyone gets through
life without getting knocked around a little?"

"I was seven! I was *raped*. I wasn't knocked around a little."

"You weren't raped. Stop being so dramatic!"

"It happened! It happened, and you let it. Why didn't you
protect me?" I asked again. "Why did you stand by and let that
happen?"

"Look, you have no idea what it's like to be a parent. You
can't see every little thing going on in your kid's life. You can't
protect them from every little thing."

"Stop saying 'little thing.' This wasn't a little thing. Why
didn't you speak up for me? Why did you never speak up for
me?" That last was a mistake, because it opened up the conversation from the one event and allowed her to latch onto her per-
secution complex about the whole of our lives together.

"Here we go again! I was the worst mother ever. I never did
anything right for you, did I? You never did appreciate anything, Salem. No matter how hard I tried, it was never enough
for you. I tried, Salem. Believe me, I tried. But it was never
enough. After a while, people just give up, you know?"

"I'm not saying it wasn't hard, being a single mom," I said.
"I'm sure it was."

"You have no idea."

"The point is, in that moment you had a choice to make. You had a choice between protecting me and risking looking like an alarmist fool — or even accusing your friend's child of being a pedophile and thereby losing your friend, or just letting the chips fall where they may and hoping for the best."

"I don't even remember what you're talking about. That never happened."

I went on, determined now to see this through. "What were you thinking, in that moment? I remember the look on your face, so I've imagined all these years what was going through your head. But I'd like to hear it from you. You knew it wasn't okay, didn't you?"

"That — what did you call him? Sponsor? That sponsor of yours has filled your head full of nonsense. There is such a thing as false memories, you know. People planting your head full of nonsense so completely that it feels like a real memory. You get so confused you can't even tell the difference."

"That could be the case, if this was something I just remembered recently. But I've always remembered this. I was aware of it then, I was aware of it later, when you brought men home. I knew what you were doing then. I knew what all the giggling and weird looks were for. I knew what was happening. And when one of those men tried to touch me, I knew I could not count on you to protect me. And when the next one touched me, I knew I could not count on you to protect me. And when the next one touched me, I knew I could not! Count! On! *You*!"

Mom grabbed her purse and stood. "I've had enough."

"Over the years, I feel like I've kind of come to understand what you were thinking. You were young and afraid and unsure of yourself. I didn't agree with it, and I wished a million times you had made a different choice. But I can kind of understand. I don't know what to think about Susan. I guess a mother doesn't ever expect her child will be a pedophile. But still — he was sixteen. He was almost a man. And you put a child into his bed with him? It seems so stupidly, stupidly inappropriate. Was she stupid? Or naive? Or was I some special perverted present for her son?"

"Okay, that's enough. I'm leaving." She stomped out the door.

I stomped after her. "Not without hearing one more thing. I am doing this because I believe it's necessary to get everything out in the open in order to heal. And I do want to heal. I want us to heal. And I won't do anything to mess up your wedding — "

"If you're even still invited," she shot hotly, yanking open her car door and throwing her handbag inside.

"If I'm even still invited," I allowed with a nod of my head. "If I *am* invited, I'll come, and I won't cause a scene. But I will not be friendly with Susan. If she's coming, you need to warn her to stay away from me, because if she starts a conversation, I will finish it by asking her what the hell she was thinking putting me into bed with her hormone-raging teenage son. And I don't think it'll get better from there."

"I should have known you would create some big unnecessary drama," she said as she jabbed the key into the ignition. "I should have known there was no way we could just enjoy our weekend together."

She shook her head as if it was just one big crying shame, the mess she'd spawned.

I watched her go, deadly calm, my arms wrapped tightly

around myself. After she'd gone, I walked slowly up the steps to my deck, went inside my trailer, closed the door, then leaned back against it and burst into tears.

CHAPTER THIRTEEN

Something Like a Prayer

I cried for a solid hour. I hated when I did that. It was so exhausting, and so weak. I hated feeling so weak. Worse, I knew I would feel better with one beer. One glass of wine. One drink would put everything back into perspective. I *knew* it would. It had worked hundreds of times before.

If I could have summoned the energy to peel myself off the sofa, I would have gone straight to the convenience store and bought a six pack; I would have told myself I could start the struggle over again tomorrow. Or not.

Les texted me. "You okay?"

I didn't reply.

Viv texted me.

"They're letting the Barnstable guy out of the hospital tomorrow. Let's interview him when you get off work."

I didn't reply.

I did not want to interview the Barnstable guy. I didn't want to think about Bandits or robberies or solving crimes. I didn't know what I wanted, but all I could summon the energy for was lying on the sofa with Stump, staring at the ceiling.

Stump seemed on board with this plan. She lay with her chest against mine, and I could feel her heartbeat through her chest. I considered praying, but I couldn't form coherent enough thoughts to even manage that.

Lying there with Stump, though, the world silent around us, felt something like a prayer.

Around six in the evening, I woke up from what must have been a two or three-hour nap. It seemed like a new day. I sat up and scrubbed my face. My tongue was stuck to the roof of my mouth. I stood and stumbled into the kitchen, ran a glass of water, and drank it down. I ran another one. Drank it.

I stood at the kitchen window and tried not to think too much. I just...took stock. I'd done it. I'd finally faced the most traumatic event in my life. I'd spoken it out loud. It was no longer a shameful secret.

And I finally felt something I had always known, logically. But now that the words were out there, I *knew* the truth of them. With all my heart. With all my soul. With all my strength. And with all my mind.

I had been a child.

It wasn't my fault.

The shame wasn't mine.

The adults in my life let me down.

It wasn't my fault.

I moved back to the sofa and scooped Stump up, nuzzling her fat neck until I got on her nerves. Then, in an uncharacteristically facing-things-head-on kind of way, I picked up my phone and said, "Windy, call Viv."

Viv picked up. "So you are alive."

"Very much so. I need to talk to Tony. Would you mind driving me over there? Were you busy?"

"So busy," Viv said. "Yoga class in fifteen minutes."

"Oh. Well, maybe after?"

"No, definitely now. Have you ever seen a 78-year-old man in yoga pants? It's not good."

Viv took one look at me and grasped the seriousness of the situation. "You look awful."

"I've been crying. Mom."

She nodded. "She's gone now?"

I nodded.

"You seeing her again?"

"To quote the Magic 8 Ball, the outlook is not so good."

She drove silently. When we pulled up at Tony's house, she said, "Do you want me to go in with you?"

I shook my head. "I will call you when I'm ready to go, if that's okay."

"Stump can come with me."

"Okay. No ice cream cones, though. She's watching her carbs." I closed the door behind me.

As she pulled out of the driveway, Viv rolled down her window and called out, "Not making any promises on the ice cream."

Tony was surprised to see me. "Salem? Is everything okay?"

"I'm sorry, I know it's not date night. I needed to talk to you, though. About...you know. The other night."

His face grew solemn. He nodded and stepped back for me to come inside.

He led me into the kitchen. "Cup of coffee?"

I shook my head. "I don't think I'm going to be able to sleep tonight as it is."

We sat at the table.

"I'm sorry I've been keeping other people around us so we couldn't be alone together."

"Are you?" I asked. "That doesn't sound like something to be sorry for, in the grand scheme of things."

He shook his head, smiling slightly.

He was so handsome. Tan skin, black hair, deep brown eyes, broad shoulders, full lips. I wanted to reach out and touch those lips. But I didn't have the right. Wife or not, I didn't have the right to make that move.

"I understand if you don't want to be alone with me, Tony. I do. This is silly, but I have to ask, just so I'll know for sure...is it the weight?"

He drew his head back, his brow furrowed a bit. "Salem," he said with a tender smile. I could see it really wasn't the weight, which was comforting and confusing in equal measure. I hated the extra weight so much. I couldn't see how anyone else could be okay with it.

"It's not the weight, and it's not that I don't want to be with you. It's that I do. I *do.*"

"You do? But..."

"I know you've changed. I can see that. You have changed. But this voice in the back of my head keeps wondering what I'm going to do if...you know."

I frowned. On the one hand, I knew. The voice wanted to know what he did if I went off the rails again — if I started drinking again — if I started screwing around with other men again. If I left him. Again.

But I needed, I found, to know what, exactly, Tony was afraid I would do. What his particular boogeyman was, where I was concerned.

"What?" I whispered, afraid but needing to know. "What you're going to do if what?"

"Last time I was naive." He leaned forward, his elbows on his knees. "I was scared, but for me it was about things like paying the bills, providing, you know, for you and the baby. But I thought, if I worked hard enough, I could make it work. I'm not so naive this time. I know now that I can't do it all by sheer force of will. I can't make everything work."

"I know that, too, Tony. I'm not expecting you to make it work all by yourself. I'm here. I'm — I'm — " I'm *what*? What had I done to further our relationship, aside from make myself willing to be adored by him? "I know we said we were going to play it by ear. And that sounded like a good idea at the time. But it seems like...well, we played things by ear until they felt a little too real. And then you got scared and pulled away."

He looked at the ground between his feet, then nodded slowly.

"I'm sorry I hurt you, Tony," I whispered around the sudden hot lump in my throat. "I'm sorry you feel like you need to protect yourself from me."

He raised his gaze to meet mine. "I know you are."

"Do you? Do you know that if I had it to do over again, I would do *everything* differently? That I can see so clearly now what I couldn't see before? And yet still, I can't promise you I won't hurt you again. Some days I feel like I can handle my life, like I can stay sober and stay in control. And *every* day I want to do that, I really do. But some days it feels like I'm doomed to failure, like it's just a matter of time."

I wanted to tell him how much it would mean to me to know for sure that we *would* be together, eventually, to know that he actually still loved me, that he wanted me beyond a sense of duty. It would mean the world to me to know that he stayed married to me for some other reason than, "because I said I would."

That was too much to ask of him, though. He didn't need the weight of my sobriety added to his own sense of duty.

I couldn't help but ask. "Why did you stay married to me, if, when the time came, you were just going to run from it?"

"I don't know!" The sudden outburst was so out-of-character that I think it even surprised him. He frowned, his lips flat, then rose from his chair and paced in front of me. "I don't know. It was the right thing to do. I still think it's the right thing to do. It's just that when it comes down to — to a real relationship with you, with real emotions and real risk, like you said..."

"It's a little too real?"

"Yeah. A little too real."

We were silent for a long time. I reached out and put a hand on his arm.

"Tony. I didn't give you any choice before. I put you through all that pain without giving you any say in the matter. And I don't have a right to even ask you to forgive me. That is your choice. But I do need to know. *Can* you forgive me?"

"There was nothing to forgive, Salem. You were hurting. You acted like a person who was hurting."

"You were hurting, too. You hurt more than I did, I think." I remembered the way he had sobbed, in the hospital, when he thought I was asleep. He was so young, and just as terrified as I was to be a parent at eighteen, but still...when our baby died, he had mourned as deeply as anyone ever had.

And instead of leaning on each other, helping each other through it as he wanted, I pushed him away. And when he refused to go away, I did.

"I appreciate the thought, Tony, but we both know that's only part of the picture. I was hurting and I lashed out at everyone and everything, but you were hurting too, and I hurt you *more*. I made it so much worse. Those are facts that need to be dealt with. I'm prepared to deal with them. I'm prepared to face it, Tony. In fact, I think maybe..."

I swallowed. I thought about everything thing I felt toward my mother now. Everything I didn't feel, actually. How I felt...dead, maybe? Numb?

"I think maybe some things are just too hurtful to get past, completely. As completely as two people who — well, who are married, who are in a committed, day-to-day relationship, would need them to be. Maybe some things are just too big for that. And the best we can hope for is more of a..." I shrugged. "More of a go-in-peace, no-hard-feelings kind of forgiveness."

He shook his head. "I don't believe that. Grace is bigger than that, Salem. God is bigger than that."

I had to swallow another lump then. I took a deep breath.

"Then here's what I think. I think you need to look me in the eye, and tell me everything. Everything I made you feel. Everything I did to hurt you. You need to say it out loud."

"There's no point in that. You were there. You know."

"I know. But I think you need to say it."

He shook his head and sat back down.

"Tony, you can't say anything about me that I haven't said about myself. Don't you think it will make you feel better, to get it out?"

"No, I think it will add pain to pain. It won't change anything. I don't see any point in bringing up old memories. I think we would be better off focusing on the future."

I nodded, tamping down my frustration. "Okay, that makes sense. But...see, it's like we're a stream."

"We're a string?"

"We're a *stream*. Like, you know, a river?"

He gave a slight nod. "Okay. We're a stream."

"And we can't just say, 'Okay, I'm starting from this point of the stream.' Like, draw a line and this is what we take with us downstream. It's all in there. Everything that has happened in our lives, and in our parents' lives, and their parent's lives — it's all in there. We didn't choose it to be that way, but that's the way it is. It's all part of us."

He didn't say anything, but he didn't look particularly agreeable, either.

"And our streams are flowing together now. So all the pollutants in my stream are mixed with your stream. I don't want it to be that way, but it is that way. Trying to ignore the lead in the water doesn't make the lead in the water go away."

"Streams don't have free will, Salem. You and I — okay,

maybe we're *affected* by our pasts, but we have free will to make choices not to repeat those pasts."

I was silent for a long time, but finally I said what was on my mind. "Tony, we're in limbo here. You're afraid I'm going to hurt you again. I'm afraid I'm going to hurt you again, too. I don't want to. I'm going to try very hard not to. But I can't..." I whispered. "I can't hope to be the wife you need if you *can't* forgive me. I feel defeated already. Like I've already screwed it up past the point of redemption, and there's no hope. I can't show up, every day, if I don't have some hope that at the end of it, we're going to be whole again." I shook my head. "What am I saying, *again?* There's no again here. If we could be whole, for the first time. You have to forgive me. And to do that, I think, you have to say it. You have to say the words, and I have to hear them. Because...sometimes peace is on the other side of conflict."

"Salem, I don't think — "

"Please, Tony, just say it."

"This isn't necessary."

"Just say it."

His mouth clamped. He glared at me. "You know, I gave you time when you asked for time."

"I know that."

"I gave you room when you wanted room."

"I know. And I appreciate it."

"So why can't you give *me* time? Why can't you give *me* room? Why do you have to give an ultimatum now?"

"I'm not giving an ultimatum."

"Of course you are!" he roared. "That's exactly what you're doing. Put up or shut up, that's what you're saying!"

"I just think — "

"How about you *stop thinking* for a little while? How about you just do what we agreed to do for once. We agreed we would take it slow, we'd just let things proceed at their own pace. You agreed to that, Salem."

"I know, but — "

"But it's not going how you want it to, so now you're changing rules in the middle of the game. Which is so! Freaking! Typical!"

He threw his coffee cup at the wall. He stood and paced in front of me, every line of his body rigid. He whirled on me.

"So typical! No matter what I did, it was wrong. You wanted my attention, I gave it. Then you wanted space. So I gave you space. But that meant I didn't care. So I came back, like a little trained dog. All I wanted, Salem, was to make you feel better, to give you some — some comfort, some stability, because I knew you needed it. But no matter what I did you pushed me away. Of course I'm afraid to get close to you again. How could I *not* be? I wanted you as much as I've ever wanted anything in my life, before or since. I wanted it to work. I wanted us to be together. And you!" He jabbed a finger at me. "You *left*!"

His face contorted with rage. With horror, I realized that I was *not* ready for this. I thought I was, but no - this was so much more intense than I was prepared to handle. I hadn't hurt him. I had *destroyed* him.

My throat burned so hot and all I wanted to do was put my hands to his face, to his mouth, to shush him, to soothe him.

But I was terrified and frozen.

"You left!" He jabbed his finger again. "You left me and went with —" He flung his arm wide. "How many men, Salem? How many men were you with after you left me?" He stopped and bent, thrusting his face into mine. "*How many?*" he roared.

"I don't know!" I said, scared into the truth. "I don't remember!"

"You left me and lived like a — like a — " He stopped, his throat working in fury, his mouth clamped tight.

"I didn't *know!*" I shouted. "I thought we were divorced!"

"You didn't know. Do you think that makes it any easier for me? That you didn't even bother to know I was waiting for you?"

"Why were you waiting? Why didn't you come after me?" I shouted back. "Why did you let me go?"

"Because you were awful! You made every moment more miserable than the last! And I knew the moment I *did* find you, you'd lash out at me again."

"Then why did you want to be with me in the first place? Why did you stay married to me?"

"Because I loved you!"

We both fell silent, the air heavy with tension and heavy breathing.

I burst into tears.

Noisy, messy tears.

Tony walked away, muttered something under his breath, but I think it was more to his detriment than mine. He returned with a box of tissues.

I'm not sure which it was — the fact that he loved me despite how awful I was, or the fact that he was a man who had a box of tissues in his house. I mean, *I* didn't have tissues. When I'd cried that afternoon at home, I had done what I always did — wiped my tears on toilet paper or gently used fast food napkins. But he had tissues. And something about that, or the way he'd shouted,

"Because I loved you!" made me love him so much I couldn't breathe.

I did everything I could to get it back together. I didn't want to manipulate him into backing off.

"Go on," I said. "Keep talking. Keep yelling. This is good. This is what I needed to hear."

He seemed to be spent, though. He sat beside me and rested his hand on my knee.

"Really, Tony. Go on."

"That's all, Salem. I didn't want you to leave. I didn't want you to — to be with those other guys. I wanted our marriage to work. It hurt when it didn't."

"It didn't hurt you. I hurt you." *Beyond repair? What if I had damaged him beyond repair? How could I live with that?*

So there were two big questions on the table, I realized.

One was, of course, could Tony forgive me? But the other was, could *I* handle seeing someone, day after day, who had something so big to forgive?

The painful truth of fighting for sobriety was that you came to know yourself well. Uncomfortably well. All the justifications and lies you tell yourself appeared as exactly what they were — lies and justifications, shabby pretenses at truth.

Some people, when they feel guilty about something, do whatever they can to make it right. Me, I get my defenses up. I get resentful of whatever is making me feel guilty. And I lash out at it.

I mean, I *used* to do that. I was trying very hard not to be that way anymore, but...what would it be like, living with that guilt all day every day? Would I be able to push down that tendency, again and again?

I wasn't sure he could handle me, and I wasn't sure I could handle him.

"Maybe this was a mistake," I said. "Or maybe, you know...this is just hastening the inevitable."

He didn't argue, which was kind of terrifying.

"But I'm glad you told me. I mean, if nothing else, I think you have the right to say to me whatever you need to say. You have the right to have your grievances heard, right?" I tried to smile but it felt wobbly.

"I'm so sorry, Tony. I can't even put into words how sorry. You didn't deserve what I did to you."

He turned and put his hands on either side of my face, searching.

I so wanted all he saw there to be love. Not damage, or pain, or fear. Just love.

Love never failed. And that was the only hope I had left.

I had been wrong when I told Tony I wouldn't sleep that night. I slept like the dead, like someone who was hiding from something. When I woke Monday morning, it was still there.

A yawning chasm of nothingness.

Out of habit, I stumbled to my prayer room.

I lit the candle, and knelt. Normally, I watched the flame for a couple of minutes, focused my thoughts. Then I read the scripture, and then I prayed.

But today, I just sat. I didn't open the book. I didn't pray. I didn't even think, aside from remembering scenes, words, from the day before.

I thought of God. I knew I should pray. But no words came. Not from me. Not from him.

Finally, I sighed, blew out the candle, and stood.

I wasn't sure how to proceed. I wasn't sure what to do. The only thing I knew was, I had to go to work. I had to take care of business. I had to get through this day.

Doreen was off on Mondays, so I had asked Viv to take me to work.

"Just one time," I said, when she complained about the early start. "I'll have the Monster Carlo back this afternoon, and it will be legal. You can drive it."

"I'll hold you to it. Do you want to go interview that Barnstable guy?"

"I don't know," I said. "I'm really tired. I might be coming down with something."

Maybe that wasn't just a line I was feeding her to get out of going anywhere. Maybe I really was coming down with something and that's why I felt so empty inside. Maybe it was the beginning of a virus or something.

I trudged through the day and asked Tammy, the other bather, to give me a ride over to Five Star to pick up my car. Mrs. Pigg had called me to let me know the part came in and it would be ready that afternoon. I thought about calling Viv, but I decided I wasn't quite up to Viv just yet. I felt a strong need to stay buried in the invisible cocoon I'd created since the day before.

When I got to Five Star Auto, Five was still working on the car.

"Almost done," he said with a crooked grin. Everything about him looked a little crooked, I realized. I hadn't noticed the week before, but I guess it had something to do with the eye twitch I thought was a wink. Something was not quite right about the way he moved. His motions were a little jerky; everything was just a bit lopsided.

"You better come in and have some ice tea while Five finishes up with your car," Mrs. Pigg said from the doorway of the office.

I joined her inside and we went into a little kitchen break room. She found two amber glasses that looked like they might be roughly the same age as my car.

We drank our tea and talked about the robberies, but she'd pretty much said her piece the other day and hadn't seemed particularly anxious to talk about it; I steered the conversation to family. I was not fishing for any information about the hot brothers.

"So, five boys. It must have been noisy around your house."

"Oh, lands. Don't even get me started. If it wasn't one thing it was another." She laughed. "The neighbors loved us, let me tell you. Always somebody fighting, somebody building something or trying to blow something up."

That actually sounded pretty nice. It had usually been deadly quiet at my house, unless Mom was in a yelling mood, or one of her boyfriends was.

"That sounds like my husband's family," I said. "Always something going on."

"I wouldn't have had it any other way. Even though I know they took years off my life, worrying about them. Between my five boys I've seen four broken arms, three broken legs, I lost count of the collarbones. One skull fracture."

"Jeez o Peet," I said, without thinking.

She nodded, taking a drink of her tea. We heard a motor start, and I realized Five had started my car. He must be ready to do the inspection now. "That one there. Walking across the

street one night and got hit by a car." Her voice trailed off softly.

"That must have been terrifying," I said.

She nodded. "Oh yes, it was. Touch and go for a while. First
they told us he wasn't going to make it. But all his brothers
gathered around him and told him they weren't going to allow
him to give up. At least one of them was by his side the entire
time, twenty-four hours a day, until he was able to come home."

I have to admit, that got me a little verklempt. I imagined
waking up in the hospital to four hot guys willing me to open my
eyes. Lordy mercy...I felt my heart stir for the first time in almost twenty-four hours.

Five bounded through the office and shouted down the hall at
us. "I have to grab a tool from the shop, be right back."

"Make it quick, the lady is waiting," Mrs. Pigg called after
him.

"He certainly seems to have recovered," I said.

"Right as rain most of the time," she said, staring out the
window.

"How long has it been?"

"Mmmm...I guess it's coming up on nine years now."

She seemed to be lost in her thoughts, so I said, "I'm just going to hit the bathroom if that's okay."

"Sure, sure, just across the hall and down two doors."

When I came out I went back to the break room, I could hear
Mrs. Pigg arguing with Reverend Pigg.

"It wasn't right. They're friends. They've had it rough."

"They had the same opportunity as everyone else. They got
the same deal."

"We could have done better by them."

"They could have done better by us!"

I stopped in the hallway and cringed. I did not want to walk in on anyone else's drama. I had all I could deal with on my own.

That was it, though, and I heard Five jog back up the steps to the office. I moved back to the front room and joined him there.

"Okay, you're all set and legal. Everything works again." He wiped his hands on a dirty red rag and handed me the key.

"And I am mobile once again," I said.

Where was I going to go?

CHAPTER FOURTEEN

A Serious Design Flaw

I headed to the one person I knew who had walked the walk I was facing. I went to Tri-Patrice.

The first time I'd come to the television station to see Trisha, I'd been there to fight, and getting in had taken a bit of stealth and subterfuge. We were friends now, though, and the people there were used to me, so I walked right in.

"Hi Salem. I have another list of nutcases, I mean concerned citizens, for you if you want them."

"Sure," I said. "Do you have time to talk?"

She checked a clock on the wall. "Actually, yes. I've got about an hour before I need to start getting ready for the ten o'clock.

Come on back to my office."

She closed the door behind us and sat at her desk, immediately kicking off her shoes. She gave a groan of ecstasy. "Oh, praise all that is good and holy. There is nothing like the joy of getting out of uncomfortable shoes or bras. Okay, the witch hunt that is the Knife Point — I mean *High Point* Bandits. You would not believe the calls the police are getting. Anyone who appears to have more than two dimes to rub together is suddenly a suspect."

"I guess I can rest easy then," I said with an attempt at a smile.

"Me, too. Let me pull up that list — "

"I'm actually not here to talk about the Bandits," I said.

Trisha looked up from her computer. "No?"

"No. I..." Now that I was there, I was so nervous about bringing up the subject that I wasn't sure I could go through with it. Trisha and I had had one very brief conversation about the issue and then had both pretended like it never happened.

And as it turned out, nothing had happened. About eight years earlier, when Trisha and Scott Watson were engaged to be married and I was engaged in full-time alcoholism, his friends had brought me to his bachelor party and put us into bed together. Scott was drunk, too, and his feeble protests weren't enough to overcome the nasty goal of his friends, who didn't think highly of Trisha and were happy to play this "joke." Trisha found us like that early the next morning. I'd forgotten the event until Trisha and I met up again years later, but she reminded me of it — in a confrontational, screamy kind of way — and bits of it came back. Trisha, crying, heartbroken and betrayed by the man she loved and the girl she'd once considered her best friend. Scott, beside himself with remorse and heart-break. Me, still too drunk the next morning to do more than feebly protest and try to play it off as a joke.

Over the next few weeks after Trisha confronted me with this betrayal, we learned that nothing *had* actually happened. Scott's friends had put us into the bed together, but we'd both passed out. All we had actually done was *sleep* together.

But during the time Trisha thought I *had* had sex with Scott, she had come to hate me and when the time came to get revenge on me, she took full advantage of it. But she had forgiven Scott. She loved him, he loved her, and whatever they had together was worth it to her to forgive him. I needed to know what that took.

"Look," I finally said. "I hate to bring this up, because things between us have been going so well. But I need to talk about — you know, about that time. With Scott. And me."

Trisha's face went carefully blank. "What about it?"

I took a deep breath. "The thing is, I need to forgive some-one. Well, my mom. I guess it's okay to tell you. I need to forgive my mom. And I thought I had. Months ago. But then I saw her again, and it all got dredged back up again, and..." I raised my hands, palms up. "It all just rises back up again. The resent-ment. The anger. The unfairness of it all. And I know it must have taken you a lot of — of *something*, to forgive Scott when you thought, you know, that he'd..." I gave a lame tilt of my head.

"Yes, I know." She, too, took a deep breath, and sat back in her fancy executive chair. "And yes, it took a lot of something."

"I'm sorry to bring it back up. I just feel like I need some guidance beyond what Les is telling me."

"Les does seem to have some superhuman grace thing going on," Trisha agreed with a wry smile.

"He always tells me it's the Holy Spirit and I have it, too. But I have to admit, either I don't have as much as he does, or I'm not using it right. Because it does *not* seem to be working."

"And you need to hear from a mere mortal?" She smiled to let me know she wasn't really insulted, or trying to insult Les either.

"Yes, something like that. I mean, you married Scott. Even after you thought he'd had sex with your best friend, the night before your wedding."

She nodded. "Yes, I did."

"How?"

"Well, it wasn't easy. And if you'll remember, it wasn't quick. We got married two years after we'd originally planned to. For the first six months, I wouldn't even talk to him. I moved away and didn't tell him where I was. He finally heard through the grapevine where I was living and he started calling and writing me letters. He wore me down so that I finally agreed to meet with him. But I was so hurt and it was just...it was hard. Every time I thought about it, about you two..." She shrugged, looking very sad. "It just hurt."

"Trisha, I am still so sorry..." We both knew that, although it *didn't* happen, it very well could have. I wasn't above it.

"I know, Salem. And he was, too. At the end of the day, I guess that's how I was able to forgive him. He was sorry. He was very, very sorry. Heartbroken. As broken as I felt over the whole situation, he was more so. I loved him, and he was sorry. I actually felt bad *for* him, he was so broken by it. I mean, imagine being responsible for that kind of hurt."

I nodded, but I didn't have to imagine it. I knew very well what it felt like to be responsible. All I had to do was look at Tony.

"All I can tell you is, forgiveness isn't an event. It's a choice, and it's one you have to make over and over again. For years, it kept popping up. Years. Every time we'd argue about something else, it would be there, between us. And I had to make the choice every time to brush it aside. Choose forgiveness again. After a while it just became a little more automatic. Sometimes it was still so hard, even after a few years. But I had to make the choice, over and over."

I shook my head. "That's what I was afraid of. That's a messed up system."

She laughed, and I could hear tears in the edge of her voice. "Tell me about it."

We were silent for a moment, and then Trisha said softly, "Do you mind if I ask what, exactly, you need to forgive your mother for?"

I opened my mouth to answer, but then closed it again and gave her a shrug and a crooked smile. "So much stuff. Basically, just not loving me enough."

Trisha made a sympathetic "go on" kind of noise.

"I mean, I'm pretty sure she loves me. Sometimes she could be really cool, you know. Fun. We had a good time together, sometimes. But so much of the time I was just a pain in her neck. I cost too much. I was too much trouble. I was a hassle. I ruined her life."

"So, just a bad relationship in general?"

"Yeah. Well, no. Not really. There are specific things. The way she never prepared me. Like, the first day of school, when all the other kids had new school supplies, new backpacks, new school clothes. I had last year's clothes that were too small and *maybe* a pencil if I could find one. The way we moved around all the time. I mean, you remember how many times we moved?"

She nodded. "Yes. You'd show up halfway through the year, be there a few weeks, then you'd be off again."

"Somehow we always ended up back at Idalou. Because Susan was there," I said with a sneer. "Susan. That's another thing. That's the main thing, actually." I took a deep breath, then spit it out. "She let her friend's son rape me because she didn't have the nerve to stand up to her."

Trisha gave a little gasp. "Salem! I'm so sorry!"

I wanted to shrug it off, act tough, as if it didn't matter. That's how I would have acted, a few years ago. But I didn't see any point of coming this far if I wasn't going to go all the way.

"Thanks," I said. "It was pretty awful. But it turned out to be only the first time. You might remember my mom had a nice string of boyfriends and fiances and husbands. Not all of them were interested only in my mom. After what happened with Susan's son, I knew she wouldn't protect me."

"Salem, that is so sad."

I nodded. "Yeah. It is. The thing is, I am so...I'm just resentful, you know? She didn't protect me. She chose her friends and her boyfriends and her husbands over me, every single time."

Trisha leaned back and ran a hand through her hair, looking stunned.

"I'm sorry," I said. "I shouldn't have put this on you. It's too much."

"No, no, I'm glad you did. I mean, I'm not glad — " She gave a weak smile. "I'm glad you can talk to me. I just...don't know what to say. And I'm seriously wondering if this is something you *should* forgive."

I gave a short humorless laugh. "Yeah, me too. I keep checking the Bible, though, and it seems fairly clear. Forgiveness is kind of a requirement."

We sat in silence for a long moment.

"Well, I suppose if we only had to forgive the little things, it wouldn't be worth much."

I leaned forward. "Can I tell you something weird? I feel like, if I can forgive my mom for what she did to me, then Tony can forgive me for what I did to him. Is that crazy?"

"Not crazy, exactly, just..."

"One thing doesn't necessarily cause the other, though, right? But I keep thinking of this reaping and sowing thing. If I sow forgiveness, I'll reap forgiveness."

She shrugged again. "I guess that makes sense."

I leaned back. Then forward again. "Plus, I just don't want to carry around all this resentment, you know. I want to keep my river clean."

She gave a distracted nod, and I started to explain it, but then went back to the resentment thing.

"So for me, I feel like forgiving her would be a good thing. But then I feel like, she doesn't deserve it. And she really doesn't. You said forgiving Scott was possible because he was really sorry. She's *not* sorry. Not at *all*. I tried to talk to her about the thing with Susan's son, and she just got defensive and blew it off. Acted like I was making the whole thing up again. That's what she always did — acted like I was just telling a whopper lie because I wanted attention." I leaned my head back and stared at the ceiling. "She never believed me."

"I believe you," Trisha said softly.

I raised my head. "Thanks."

She was staring at me. Her expression had changed.

"What?" I said.

"I believe you." She took another deep breath and leaned forward to put her elbows on her desk. "Okay, since we're spilling our guts here. One reason I felt like I *should* forgive you for the thing with Scott — I didn't, of course, but I — I *did* feel guilty about it — was that part of me felt like it was my own fault, in part."

"Your fault? You weren't even there."

"No, but..." She put her hands over her eyes, and I realized she was as afraid to talk about this as I had been. "Remember that guy your mom was living with, the one with the handlebar mustache?"

"Ummm, yeah," I said dryly. "He was kind of hard to forget."

"Okay, so one time when I was over there, he — he made a move on me."

It was my turn to gasp. "No! Really? I mean — " I shook my head. "I'm sorry I said 'really.' I believe you. He was a piece of crap. I just — I didn't know."

"I know. I never told you. I never told anyone. But I'll never forget it. You and I were lying on your bedroom floor looking at *Teen Magazine*. Then your mom had called you out to the yard to help carry groceries in from the car. He came in and sat down on the floor beside me, which I thought was weird. But I didn't want to be rude, so I just lay there and let him talk. But then he scooted closer. And he put his hand on the back of my thigh. I mean, I just froze. I didn't know what to do. He hadn't done anything yet, just put his hand on my thigh, but it felt so wrong. I could hear you and your mom bringing in the groceries and arguing, and I hoped you would come in there. But you didn't. And I guess when I didn't move, he took that as his cue to go higher. So he slid his hand up higher. I was paralyzed. I just laid there like a slug, my heart pounding. He moved it up higher. Finally he got all the way to the top of my legs, and he cupped my bottom, and he squeezed so tight that his fingers went into my crotch. When I felt his fingers against me, I just — " She shuddered. "I jumped up and ran out of the room. I could hear him laughing this evil laugh."

I shook my head in disgust. "I remember that laugh."

"I gave some excuse to you and went home. I locked my bedroom door. I'd never done that before — locked my door. But I had never been so terrified. I didn't know what to do. I felt like I should tell someone, but I was so afraid for anyone else to know."

"I know." I understood perfectly. The thing to do in that situation is to tell, of course. But I knew the full weight of shame and fear that came along with being violated in that way. So did the perverts. They knew the likelihood of a kid telling anyone that someone had touched them were slim. Because when that happens to you, you don't want anyone to know. You want, desperately, for it not to be true. It takes time to work through that feeling, and by then it really feels like there's no point. By then, you knew, people would start asking questions like, "Why didn't you say something?" and other hard-to-answer questions, which, inherently contained the assumption that you, somehow, held responsibility for the question.

"I thought a thousand times about telling my mom, but I couldn't do it. It took me a few days to realize that if he'd done that to me, he would probably do it to you, too. I thought I should warn you. But I just...couldn't. I couldn't get myself to say the words." Her eyes had filled with tears. "I'm so sorry, Salem. I should have talked to you about it, I should have told my parents."

"Trisha, you were a kid. You were traumatized."

She gave a snuffly laugh. "Traumatized. He touched me through my clothes. Compared to what he could have done, it was nothing."

"It was *not* nothing!" I shot back. "Look, there's not some kind of bar to reach for things to qualify as real trauma. What he did was wrong, it was a violation of his position, of your trust, and it caused real harm."

"If I'd said something..."

"It wouldn't have made any difference. Memory is a weird thing, but if I remember correctly, that was the third man who couldn't keep his hands to himself. By that time, I'd decided that if anything was going to be done about all the men, I would have to do it myself. So I just told G-Ma I was moving to the motel until he was gone. And that's what I did. It didn't take long. I think I was back in Idalou before summer came."

"Yeah, I remember when you moved, and when you came back. I was so relieved and thought that everything had worked itself out, and there was no need for me to talk. But Salem, if I had, maybe your mom would have believed you. That would have helped, wouldn't it?"

I shrugged. "Maybe. But Trisha, let's remember — there's one bad guy in this situation. One. He's to blame. You and I were kids and bear no responsibility."

Even all these years later, on some level I had to remind myself of that. The truth was, as a kid I had a bad attitude and a smart mouth. The handlebar mustache guy — whose name was Keith — liked to tell me how he was going to make sure I got an attitude adjustment. He'd said someone needed to teach me respect, that someone needed to teach me to either shut my mouth or put it to good use. Rebellion got me into trouble every time. Well, not every time. Rebellion also got me to G-Ma's and out of that house. After that, every time Mom brought a new guy home, I found a way to be out of the house and never alone with any of them. Best to not give them the chance.

"If you'd said something, it might have turned out differently, but probably not. I learned how to protect myself, and that was what I needed to do. She kept up the cycle of man after man, and the best thing for me was to learn to keep myself out of harm's way." I leaned back and groaned. "I can't believe she's getting married again. At least I don't have to worry about what *he'll* try to do to me. He'll be hers to deal with."

Trisha broke the following silence with another sigh. "Anyway, back during that time with Scott...part of me thought that it was my punishment for not protecting you. That you'd been traumatized and — and *damaged* — by that man, and the way you acted was the result of that. And it came home to roost with me because I hadn't protected you when I had the chance."

I had to reflect on that a bit. *The way you acted.* I knew what she meant. In high school I became a rebellious, promiscuous punk, drunk as often as not. I had a need to push things as far as I could push them. I had a need to shock. And Trisha hit the nail on the head. I did it because I was damaged.

So what did a damaged person do to become undamaged? I felt such a need to knock the dents out of myself, to sweep eve-

rything clean and pour boiling hot water to kill germs and scrub
out all the nooks and crannies. I didn't want to carry this damage around with me for the rest of my life.

That was what forgiveness was supposed to do, I thought. It
was supposed to lighten the load. But it certainly didn't feel like
that to me. Instead, the process of forgiveness felt like switching
one load — the burden of resentment, anger, the desire for revenge — for another. Forgiveness felt like the burden of willing
yourself to l iayt aside, again and again, every time it came up.

That wasn't the way it was supposed to work, I was almost
certain. But it was working that way, at least for me.

Walking out of the Channel 11 office, I checked my phone. It
was almost eight o'clock. I thought of Stump and felt guilty. I'd
left her with Frank all day, which was not a big deal except she
would be expecting me home long before now. To ease my guilt,
I drove through and got a family order of chicken strips, fries
and gravy.

We sat in the living room and ate while Frank watched TV. I
checked my phone seventeen times to see if Tony had called.
Nothing.

Viv had called, but I was too exhausted to talk to her.

"I'm really exhausted," I texted her.

"I'll drive."

Of course you will. That's a given.

"I still think I might be coming down with something. I'm
going to do some Facebook research on Xavier. We can get back
to interviewing people tomorrow."

Tomorrow I'll get my groove back, I promised myself. *I will.*

First I went to the Channel 11 page to read about the story.

There were many postings of "Praying for healing" and "God be with you during this difficult time." Interspersed were comments of "save your sympathy" and "do you people really think it's a coincidence that the first time things get violent, it's when an ex-con is involved? There's a story here they're not telling us."

That one got a response from JimBarbBennet. "If you can't keep your judgmental comments to yourself, just stay away. This is my nephew, and I know for a fact that he's a good man and an honest man. The only way he was involved in this burglary is as a victim! You can take your negativity and shove it."

I clicked on JimBarbBennet's profile, which seemed to be mostly pictures of grandkids and recipes for brisket and pineapple upside down cake. I clicked through Jim and Barb's friends (Jim was largely absent from any communication) but did find a link to Xavier's mom, who appeared to be Jim's younger sister.

Xavier's mother Priscilla Barnstable had a large contingent of support, which was nice to see. "You hold your head high, girl," encouraged one poster. "You and sweet Xavier are in our prayers, sister."

Priscilla was apparently active on a couple of Facebook groups that were for families with incarcerated loved ones. I kept scrolling until I found a picture of Xavier with Priscilla on the day of his release, and scrolled again to find a picture of them smiling broadly for the camera, Xavier holding a framed high school diploma.

I scrolled back up and found another post from Priscilla, with a link to her blog.

I clicked the link. Priscilla's blog was devoted to news on prisoner and family rights, news of overturned convictions, prison abuse and police corruption. I had to allow for the possibility that whatever "research" I gained from Priscilla might be a bit skewed.

She hadn't posted in a few weeks, since before Xavier was attacked. I figured she'd been busy. I clicked through to updates on Xavier's progress, introductions from other moms and dads she'd met and built friendships with over her experience of having a child in prison.

It was so sad. Whatever these kids had done, they were loved. Their parents had had hopes for them, expectations for them. They had to go to sleep every night knowing their child was lying down amid possibly violent other prisoners. That they could very well come out changed, hardened, different children from the ones who went in. And that's if they came out at all.

I wondered for a moment how my mom would have reacted if I had ended up in prison. It was more than just an academic question — I *had* gotten three DUIs. That was more do-overs than a lot of people got. Added to that, I doubted life *after* a stint in prison would be easier for me to manage than life before prison had been. So the prison revolving-door syndrome could very well have been my life.

And that's assuming I hadn't killed or injured someone on one of my drunken rides through town. Even now, with almost two years working on sobriety, the realization that I could have killed someone, could have taken someone's life and broken countless hearts, made my breath catch and an icy ball form in the pit of my stomach. I could have. It was only — what? The grace of God? Shear blind luck? — that I was sitting with my new Smart Enuff phone on my saggy sofa in Trailertopia instead of in prison learning how to cope with the fact that *I* was the bad guy this time. I was the bad guy.

I didn't like to think about that, of course. During the day, I could usually turn my thoughts to something — anything — else. But at night, sometimes, I woke with a strangled cry, heart thudding, sometimes with the remnants of a barely-remembered dream, of violent impact, of terror, of soul-destroying regret. On those nights I lay awake for hours, the reality of what I *could* have done real and horrible and inescapable, seemingly the only important fact in the world. I could have killed someone. I could have.

One night I was so overcome that I actually called Les and woke him up. He came over to Trailertopia and sat with me until I finally fell asleep on the sofa to the steady sound of his reassurances that everyone was okay, that I was okay.

The next morning, I felt so foolish. I'd woken him up and hauled him out of bed by freaking out about something that *already hadn't happened.* And when I feel foolish, I tend to get defensive.

"You didn't have to do that," I grumbled the next morning. "You didn't have to come over here and sit with me. I would have been okay."

"Probably," Les had said evenly, unperturbed at my gritchy attitude. "But I didn't want to take a chance on probably. Things look a lot worse in the middle of the night, Salem. Sometimes obstacles that are perfectly manageable in the daylight are too much to deal with at night. I don't know why that is, but it is. Just remember that, next time you wake up scared. Everything looks better in the morning. And if you get scared again, call me. Promise me. I'd rather come over here and sleep in your recliner than know you spent a night in anguish."

I promised him that I would, but the next time I woke up in a panic, I did not call him. I thought about it, and I knew he wouldn't be mad if I did, but I couldn't bring myself to do it. Instead, I thought about him and everything he'd said, all the promises he'd already made to me that had proved true, and I repeated over and over again, "Everything will look better in the morning."

It always did.

That was mostly, of course, because I only had near-misses to deal with. Now, in the safety of the evening light, I allowed myself to dwell on the what-ifs. What if I was in prison right now? I wouldn't know Viv. I wouldn't have Tony. G-Ma might come visit me, maybe, but I was fairly sure Mom would not. For sure not after this past weekend.

My mom would not create a blog and a Facebook page devoted to creating a safe place for families to support each other and their incarcerated loved ones. I was quite sure of that. Would she join such a group?

Probably not.

Stump grumbled, then stood slowly and raised her paws to brace against my chest. She gave me a solemn look, then sniffed at my face. She leaned back with a quizzical look like, "What's the problem?"

"Stump, if I went to prison would you make a Facebook page for me?" I scratched the fat around the base of her tail, where she liked it best. If I had gone to jail, I never would have found Stump that day by the side of the road. She likely would have died from exposure, been hit by a car, or been taken to the shelter and put to sleep. The thought once again had the ice ball forming in my stomach. My sweet baby. If she was in prison, I would absolutely make a Facebook page for her, no question.

I eased her back onto the seat beside me. I picked up my phone again and scrolled back to the Facebook page. I posted on the page:

Priscilla, you don't know me, but I met your son a few days ago, just before he was attacked. I was a customer at the garage. You should know that he acted in a very admirable, honorable way. He was very professional. You would be proud of him. In the short time I talked to him, he conducted himself in a way that makes it very hard for me to believe he is anything but in-nocent in the robbery on the automotive. Please know that not everyone thinks he's guilty until proven innocent.

I sat back and read it. A little smarmy, but I felt like one mom talking to another one. Silly as that seemed.

My phone dinged. I stared at it. I was sure there was some way to make it not ding for every little thing, but I had no idea how. I tapped randomly at the screen and a Facebook notification popped up: *Isabella Barnstable has replied to your comment on her page.*

Well. That was quick.

"Thank you so much for your note. These last few days have been very difficult, and the way the police are acting doesn't ease my mind one bit!"

I stared at the message. Should I ask? Start a conversation with her? Marty had said in the hospital that he thought Xavier knew more than he was saying. Maybe he had been more open with his mother than he had with the police. It was certainly worth a shot.

I texted Viv: "Remember a little while ago when I said I was tired and not up to interviewing anyone? I think I'm about to meet Xavier's mom. Are you in?"

CHAPTER FIFTEEN

Recon

At first, I didn't think we were going to get anywhere with Isabella Barnstable. She met us at an all-night Waffle Factory and seemed to be more interested in interviewing us than being interviewed *by* us. She was way more organized than we were. She took names, dates, phone numbers, backup phone numbers, work numbers, references.

Plus, physically, she was kind of intimidating. She had a barbed-wire tattoo circling a well-developed bicep. This was a mom who appeared to be quite prepared to defend her son.

Viv reached into her bag. She was going for the business cards.

I put my hand on her arm. "I am begging you. No."

Viv frowned at me. I ignored it and turned to Mrs. Barnstable. "Can we just let our record speak for itself? Do you remember the C.J. Hardin case?"

She gasped. "I *knew* I knew you from somewhere."

"That was us alright," Viv said.

It was mostly me, but whatever.

"We are looking for these High Point Bandits," I assured her. "We intend to find them. We are confident than when we do, we'll be able to make it very clear that your son is not involved in any way." I *didn't* actually know that, but I figured if it turned out I was wrong, she would have bigger things to worry about than us.

"We just want to talk to him. I heard he came home today."

She made a face. "He went back to his apartment. I begged him to come to the house, let me keep an eye on him for a few days. But he fought for too long to get his independence and he doesn't want to give it up now." She looked at us, still frowning, as if she couldn't quite make up her mind if she was going to allow us access or not.

"I'm sure he's already said everything he knows to the police. But we've found that sometimes people are more open with us. More relaxed. Maybe not him, necessarily. But some people are. We've talked to a lot of the people in this neighborhood over the last week. And maybe something he says will click with something someone else told us, something they haven't told the police."

She continued to frown at us, then sighed. "I'll ask Xavier if you can come visit him. It'll be up to him. But I think it's good idea. I think the more eyes we have on this business, the better."

"That's what Clete Pigg says," I said.

She made another face, this one even more severe than the frown she'd had pinned on us. I supposed not everyone fell for his Redneck Santa charm. "Yes, well...as I said, I'll ask Xavier how he feels about speaking to you. If he's okay with it, I'll let you know."

Viv and I walked out into the night, silent. It was not as late as I thought, but I was still tired.

"Maybe we can talk to Xavier tomorrow," I said.

Viv was quiet. Which was weird. She started the car and drove back toward Trailertopia.

"You look tired," she finally said.

"I'm going to bed as soon as I get home. A good night's sleep will do me good."

She pulled to the curb beside my trailer. "That's all it is? You just need a good night's sleep?"

I did a gut check. "I don't know what's happening with Tony," I said. "I'm scared he can't really forgive me."

"You weren't sure if you wanted to be married to him or not, remember? Not sure how you felt about him."

"I remember. And I'm still not entirely sure. But..." I looked out the window. "It's going to kill me to know he can't forgive me."

"You have to do what you can to make amends and move on."

"I know." I heard the same things in AA she did.

"Have you talked to Les about this?"

"Sure." Les and I talked about Tony a lot, the same way we talked about Mom a lot. Les wasn't supportive of me getting back into a relationship with Tony, because he figured I had my hands full with taking care of myself for a while longer, and he was right.

But this wasn't some former roommate I'd left hanging with a huge phone bill. This wasn't a send-a-check-and-a-prayer-and-move-on kind of amends.

This was Tony.

"I'm really confused by him. He stayed married to me. But he can't trust me."

"He needs time."

"I know."

"We don't get to set the timetable for anyone else."

"I know."

Viv was silent.

I was silent.

Finally, I sighed. "If he doesn't forgive me, I really don't know if I can forgive myself."

"It can't work that way."

"I know. But...there it is anyway."

Cast your burden on the Lord and he will sustain you. Psalm 55:22 (ESV)

I sat for a long time the next morning, running the words over and over in my head. What I had said to Trisha the day before was true. It was unfair. It was unfair that I had to choose forgiveness over and over, when I'd been completely blameless in what happened to me. It was unfair that Tony should have to do the same thing. It *wasn't fair.* I didn't understand how this could possibly be God's method.

So I cast that on him.

"I don't get it, God," I prayed. "I don't get it, I don't think this is right, I think there's a serious design flaw here. So consider this me, casting it on you. I expect you to sustain me, through whatever today brings."

Wednesday. The next day was Thursday, date-night-with-Tony day. Now that I'd thrown down the gauntlet, so to speak, it could be the first Thursday in months without a date night.

"Put up or shut up, that's what you're saying."

He might choose to shut up.

"I'm trusting you to sustain me," I said again. And I got up to go to work.

Isabella Barnstable called me around lunch.

"Xavier said he would talk to you for a little while, but he's sure he doesn't have anything worth sharing. He remembers very little."

"I understand."

"I would prefer to be there with you, but I'm not going to be able. I'm trusting you to be respectful, and to know when to clear out if he looks too tired or asks you to leave."

"I understand," I said again. The last thing I wanted to do was get on Priscilla Barnstable's bad side. She was kind of scary.

Viv might be another matter, but I decided I would just have to drag her out if it became necessary. She was old and thin. I was young and thick. Surely I could overtake her.

That evening after I settled Stump in with Frank, and Viv picked me up in the Cadillac, I lectured her.

"He's been through a traumatic and painful experience. Plus, his mother is fierce and it looked like she worked out."

"She had some guns alright," Viv acknowledged.

"So we're going to be respectful. We're going to be gentle with our questions. And we're going to leave if he acts like he wants us to leave."

"Sure, sure, no problem," she said, with a wave like this was all understood.

I leaned toward her. "Viv. Seriously. I'll carry you out if I have to."

She snorted. "Give me some credit. I know how to manage people. I know how to be subtle."

Xavier opened the apartment door wearing flannel pajama pants, a t-shirt and a ball cap. I could see the white edge of a bandage under the cap.

He looked tired already. "Mom said you'd be coming by." He motioned for us to come inside, then moved to a sofa where he'd obviously spent the day. A blanket was wadded up at the end, and the coffee table was covered with debris from the day — a magazine, two water bottles, an empty bowl. "Sorry the place is such a mess."

"Don't worry about that," I said. "I hope you're feeling up to talking to us. If not, we can come back another time."

"But of course, time is of the essence," Viv said. She pulled her notepad and gold pen from her handbag. "We don't want these Bandits to hurt anyone else."

"It wasn't the Bandits," Xavier said. He met both of our gazes straight on. "I told the police that. It wasn't the bandits."

"How can you be sure, though?" Viv asked. "My notes say that you didn't see their faces." She looked at what I could see was a blank page.

"The Bandits always work in a group of four. There were only two when I was attacked. And the Bandits never hurt anybody. These guys..." He pointed to his head. "Obviously, different M.O. Maybe somebody wanted police to think it was the Bandits."

"But that doesn't mean — "

I put a hand out to stop her. "He said it's not the Bandits. He was there. He would know."

She narrowed her eyes at me and clicked her pen a couple of times, but let it drop. "Do you remember us?" she asked. "We were at the automotive a day or so before you were attacked."

He nodded. "Yeah, kind of. Things are a little fuzzy."

I didn't really want to remind him, but at the same time, it seemed appropriate to bring it up, given what we wanted to talk to him about.

"We came to see you about an inspection sticker on my car. I had heard a rumor that if I just asked for a sticker, and not an inspection, I would get it. And I wasn't very confident that my car would pass inspection, so..."

He gave one slight nod. "I heard that rumor, too."

"If you remember, when we made the suggestion, you weren't exactly receptive to the idea," Viv said.

Xavier gave a slight grin. "Yeah, I kind of remember that. Sorry if I overreacted."

I looked over at Viv, who was drawing a smiley face on her notepad.

"Don't worry about that," I said. "You were right. We shouldn't have asked. But that's why I contacted your mother. I wanted her to know that my experience with you was you were *very* opposed to doing something illegal and unethical. Some people were posting — " I stopped, suddenly hesitant and unsure how to say it.

"I heard about that, too. Because of my *history*." Again with the crooked smile.

"That's part of what we'd like to ask you about," Viv said. "If you don't mind, of course. Can you tell us what happened back then, when you went to prison?"

"That doesn't have anything to do with this," he said, his

mouth grim.

"I'm sure it doesn't. But we've found that it helps to have the whole picture."

"It's two different pictures. Two different events. Not connected."

"You don't have to talk about it if you don't want to," I assured him. "Your mother told us that you robbed a store and were caught. Someone was injured."

He nodded. "Yes. I robbed a store."

"Why?" Viv asked.

I gave her a look. I would have put that one solidly under the "don't ask" heading.

Xavier's mouth thinned, but he answered. "There was a girl I wanted to impress. So I let myself be...I robbed a store, to get money to buy a car, to impress her. But instead I got caught. I didn't get the car or the girl. End of story."

Viv wrote, *End of story, huh?*

I made a conscious decision to quit looking at what Viv wrote. "Do you mind if we ask — because of the recent robbery, that's all — did the injury happen the way *your* injury did? Was someone hit over the head in that robbery?"

"No." He looked out the window, and I thought that was going to be it. Then he said, "That happened later. When I was driving away. The police were chasing me and I panicked and...this guy ran out in front of my car and I hit him. That part was an accident."

"That part," I repeated. "But the robbery — you pleaded guilty to the robbery, is that right?"

"That's right. I made the decision to do that, and I owned up to it." He shifted on the bed and met my gaze squarely. "I did the time, and I don't plan to go back. That's why I reacted the way I did when you came in for your sticker. I'm doing all I can to build my life back up and keep my nose clean. I don't plan on ever going back there."

"I understand," I said. "I've had a few run-ins with the law myself. I've never been to prison, but that's due more to luck than to good choices. I feel like I've been given a second chance to get things right, and I don't intend to do anything to jeopardize it, either."

The front door opened and Five Pigg stuck his head in. He took us all in and grinned. "Hey, buddy! Got some company?"

He bounded into the room with that off-kilter way he had, his movements a bit jerky. He went to Xavier first, reaching out and grabbing Xavier's hand to shake it.

Xavier moved slowly, allowing his hand to be shaken and then letting it drop back into his lap.

"Five." His voice was stiff.

"You guys?" Five said, recognizing us. He put his hand to his head. "Wow! What are you two doing here? I didn't know you knew Xavier."

He turned back to Xavier with a questioning glance. "Xavier? You know these ladies?"

Xavier gave a slight nod. "We've met a couple of times. What's up, Five?"

Five shook his head. "Just checking on my buddy. I heard you were home and wanted to see what I could do."

Xavier shook his head. "I'm good, thanks."

"Bring you anything? Couple of meals? Run some errands for you?"

"No, Mom's taking good care of me."

"We want to help. Mom and Dad, all of us." He laughed, and when he did, his right eye twitched and squinted. "All of us. You know how my family is. When you get one of us, you get all of us."

"Yeah, I know," Xavier said. He did not laugh.

Five winced then, doing the squint-eye twitch thing again. He put his hand to his head again, pressing the tips of all five fingers into a half-circle over his eye, down to his cheekbone. "Sorry, I had a head injury a few years ago and every once in a while I get these killer headaches still. You know about that, Xavier?"

He turned to Xavier, who nodded once. "Yeah, I know about that."

Five laughed. "Jeez, listen to me. Of course you do. One thing about that injury, it messed with my memory, too. I mean, I remember everything, it just takes me a while sometimes to access it, you know? Like, I remember that Xavier and I have been friends for, like, our whole lives." He laughed and made a big sweeping motion. "Our whole lives. Like, I played t-ball with this guy!" He swung his arms as he talked, causing his whole body to rotate toward Xavier, then toward us.

I'd spent enough time around drunks that I could recognize the behavior — the exaggerated gestures, the rambling conversation. I slid my gaze over to Viv. She met my gaze and we silently agreed that we would hit the road as soon as we could manage it.

"That's good," I said. "It's good to have lifelong friends like that." I leaned forward in my seat, ready to rise and make our goodbyes.

"Exactly!" Five said, with a huge bow toward me that had me

sliding back into my seat.

There was something in his eyes that didn't look drunk. Some intensity that alcohol would have dulled, not intensified. Drugs, maybe?

"Life long friends are a *gift*!" He jabbed a finger toward Xavier. "A gift. That's why I'm here for my friend, me and my whole family, really. Because we've been through this, and we know the kind of help he's going to need. Know it from *experience*." He leaned over and clapped a hand on Xavier's shoulder. He jostled the injured man a little and leaned down. "Not, of course, that you're going to have to deal with anything like what I did. Your injury is not nearly as bad as mine was. Not *nearly* as bad. Yours was just your head. My whole frigging *body* was wrecked." He laughed again. He had a creepy laugh.

Viv stood. "Well, we'll let you two catch up. Xavier, we appreciate your time and help. We want to help you find whoever did this to you. Please call us if you think of anything else that might be helpful. Anything at all."

With a defiant look at me, she dropped one of our "business cards" on the coffee table.

"Y'all don't rush off on my account," Five said. "I just came by to check on Xavier, but I'm leaving and I'll let you get back to your visit."

Viv looked at me and sat back down.

Five leaned over again and pounded Xavier on the back a couple of times in lieu of a hug, then met his gaze again. "Remember what I said, bro, okay? I meant it. We all meant it. Anything you need, we've got your back."

After he left, the room was silent for an uncomfortable moment. Xavier stared at the door, appearing to have forgotten we were even there.

"Well, like I said, we need to get going, but please let us know if you think of anything else."

"I won't," Xavier said, still staring at the door. "I mean, I would, but I won't think of anything."

Viv and I, having no response to that, left.

We wasted no time getting out of there. "What a weirdo," Viv said once we were back in the car.

"Xavier, or Five?"

"Five. Xavier's not weird, he's just hurt. And scared, I think. Five is a little weirdo, though. I can't believe he's got the same DNA as that hot fireman."

"I think the head injury probably has a lot to do with his weirdness. Do you think he was on something?"

"I wondered the same thing. Maybe. Was he that weird when you bought the car?"

"No, I don't think so. I mean, he was *kind of* weird. He kept doing that eye twitch thing. But he seemed a little...manic tonight."

"Weird," Viv said again.

I was so focused on analyzing Five Pigg's behavior that it took me a while to put a couple of things together.

"What did Xavier say? He was driving away from the robbery and hit someone with his car?"

Viv thought. "Yeah, I think so."

"You were taking notes."

"I didn't take a note of that, just that he didn't like to talk about the other robbery."

I pulled my phone out of my pocket. "Windy, can you search the Lubbock AJ?"

Windy's wavy lines waved and she said, "I'm searching right now, sweetie."

Viv pulled into a darkened parking lot and we waited for Windy to get back with us.

"Okay, honey," she said. "I'm ready. What are you huntin' for?"

"I need a search on the words "robbery" and "head injury.""

"And Lubbock," Viv said.

"Got it."

We waited in silence as Windy hunted for us.

"Here are the top three results," she finally said. Then she rattled off the headlines:

"Robbery at Estacado Automotive Leaves One Injured"

"Armed Robbery at Dairy Queen Leaves Man with Head Injury"

"Robbery, Assault at 7-11 Leaves One Injured"

"Good grief, there are a lot of armed robberies and injuries in this town."

I sat back and frowned. "These are all pretty recent — within the past year or so." I hit Windy's icon again. "Windy, do another search, this time for "Robbery, head injury, and Pigg.""

"Please," Viv said, leaning toward the phone. She gave me a look. "Your manners sometimes, Salem."

We waited in silence again. Windy's lines waved.

The phone lit up, and Windy said, "Here are the top three results."

"Teenager Injured as Robber Flees"

"That's it!" I said. I tapped the link.

"That's it!" Viv echoed. Then she slapped my arm, knocking the phone from my hand. "Look at that!"

A car had just driven past us.

"What?" I asked, searching for my phone in the dark seat.

"That was him! Xavier!"

I looked toward the red taillights growing distant down the highway. "Are you sure?"

"Positive."

"We should call Bobby," I said.

"And tell him what? What have we figured out?"

I thought. I wasn't sure, actually. Except Five Pigg was weird, and Xavier was scared but he was heading toward Five Pigg's car lot at this very moment.

"This has got to be related," I said. I tapped the link for the last article Windy had found. "Yep, this is it. Xavier Barnstable was arrested for robbery and for hitting a pedestrian as he fled the scene." I sat back, trying to put the pieces together.

"Xavier insists his robbery wasn't related to the Bandits. He said whoever did it might be trying to make it look like the Bandits. Maybe he's telling the truth. Maybe Five Pigg hit him over the head for revenge, and did the robbery to pin it on the Bandits."

Viv frowned. "Well, I guess that's something."

I echoed Viv's frown. "It's something." It wasn't solving the big case, though.

Viv sighed, then started the Caddy and pulled onto the highway. "Let's head down there and see what's going on. Maybe we can at least overhear enough to pin this one robbery on that little weirdo."

Viv killed the lights and pulled into the motel parking lot.

"Watch the pothole in front of — *ummph*!"

She hit the pothole in front of room three.

"Do you think we ought to tell your grandma what we're doing? She might decide to shoot my car and say she thought it was the robbers."

I peered down at the office window. The cardboard sign was up. "Looks like she's gone to bed already," I said. I didn't want to add "interrupted sleep" to my long list of offenses.

We closed the car doors softly and moved quietly around the corner to the car lot, stepping over the pipe rail and crouching between cars. The office lights were on, and the car we'd seen driving down the highway minutes before was parked where Viv's Caddy had been parked just a week and a half before.

We squatted beside a white four-door Camry and watched for a few minutes.

I heard voices, but couldn't make out words.

"Can you tell what they're saying?" I whispered to Viv.

She shook her head.

I frowned, wondering if maybe we should go back and call Bobby, just to be on the safe side. But I hadn't actually learned anything he didn't already know. Xavier Barnstable had injured Five Pigg in a robbery gone wrong almost ten years before, and he'd been injured in an eerily similar incident just last week. It proved exactly nothing related to the other robberies.

And anyway, Viv was at that very moment crab-walking away from me toward the building.

"Wait!" I hissed. I leaned over and scurried after her.

She plastered herself against the side of the building and looked up at the lighted window. The voices were louder here, but still not very clear.

I put the building at my back and looked up. Nothing to see. I leaned around Viv.

"There's a little break room at the other end of the building. I was in there when I came to pick up my car. I think they're —"

Viv turned and started climbing the wooden steps toward the office door.

"Viv!" I screeched as softly as I could. "What are you doing?!"

She made a shushing movement with her hand, then patted her handbag, reminding me that she was carrying. That gun gave her all kinds of stupid courage.

I hesitated a moment, my heart hammering, but I decided I'd rather be with Viv and her gun than out here in the dark by myself.

We stepped quietly into the office and I drew the door shut. I could hear the two men now, plainly, because their voices were raised.

Viv crab walked over to the counter where Five and I had made our car deal last week, and ducked behind it. In a panic, I joined her, dropping to the floor with a thunk that seemed to ring through the whole small building.

Viv gave me a look. We both waited, with our breath held, for some sign that I'd been heard.

A few mumbled words, and then Five spoke.

"I guess we're even now."

"Even?! Last time I checked, I'm the one who did time."

"I'm the one who ended up with thirty-seven stitches and had to relearn how to walk!"

"That was your own fault! You ran! You ran and left me there to deal with the mess you created!"

"Hey! We both were in on it. It wasn't as if I had to twist your arm to pull that job. You were all about the free money."

Xavier was silent for a long time. Then he said, "That right there is the *only* reason I kept my mouth shut. I made that choice. I could have said no. I could have pulled the plug on the whole thing. But I wanted money for a car to impress Allison, so I went along with it. I regretted it the moment we ran out that door. I've regretted it every minute since then."

Footsteps, coming down the hallway toward us. I ducked lower and scrambled to get myself under the counter. When I did, I saw a crack where the front and sides of the counter didn't quite meet. I saw legs moving down the hallway. I leaned closer, so I could make out both men, now in the hallway.

Xavier stopped, then whirled on Five and stuck a hard finger in his face. "But I've done the time and I've paid the price. I can walk around now holding my head high because I know I learned the lesson and I'm not the same person I was then. You..." He sneered at Five. "You never learn. That hit you took, it didn't do anything for you but make you more of a *loser*. More of the baby who needs everyone else to take care of him."

Five thrust his chest out and rushed at Xavier.

Xavier, despite his injury, stood his ground. He faced Five squarely, his own shoulders pulled back. Instantly, he seemed about half again as big as he'd been before. I figured maybe that was something he'd learned in prison — how to face down a threat using body language.

It worked on Five. He stopped and rocked back on his heels.

"Do they even know what you did that night? Or do they still think you just *happened* to be crossing the street when I came along?" Xavier said.

Five didn't answer.

Xavier studied him for a minute. "I wonder what they'd say if I told them. If I told them you were with me that night, that the whole thing was your idea in the first place? If I told them that you were driving the car and freaked out when you realized the police were chasing us? You know what I think? I think they know what kind of chicken son they raised and wouldn't doubt me for one second."

Xavier shook his head. "It wouldn't matter, though, would it? They're doing this for you? This whole robbery thing? All of it to help out poor, poor Five. Five who wasn't blessed with the same opportunities as everyone else."

Five's face darkened, and I thought he would rush the other man again. Then, with what looked like a visible effort, he relaxed. "You know I wasn't trying to run and leave you that night, Xavier. You know I wouldn't do that. We were brothers, you and me. I had your back. I was trying to deflect attention, that's all. You know, divide and conquer. I was gonna distract them so you could get away." Then he got a weird look on his face, like someone dropping a bomb he'd been planning for a while. "And I'm sure you didn't really mean to hit me. I was afraid you'd be mad, once I realized how it must have looked. But I never really thought you'd be mad enough to hit me."

Xavier apparently wasn't buying it for one second. "You bailed out and left me in the passenger seat of a car cruising down the street, Five! It was all I could do to scramble over the console and take off. I had *no* idea where we even *were*! Of course I didn't mean to hit you! I was just trying to get away from those flashing lights!"

His tone was anguished. The tone of someone who carried guilt and remorse.

I knew that tone.

Maybe I moved. Maybe that's what they heard. Maybe my sympathy for Xavier took on actual physical weight and alerted them to our presence.

Whatever it was, both men froze, and turned to look in our direction.

I heard Viv gasp softly, and we both stopped breathing.

Then Five took a step toward the counter.

Viv's eyes went wide, and she fumbled for the handbag. Lifting her left hand, she held up three fingers while the right fished for the gun.

Five took another step.

She thrust the three fingers at me several times, until I realized she was indicating a "count to three" move. I nodded. What were we going to do on the count of three? Shoot them? I didn't know. But I nodded anyway.

She finally got the gun loose from her bag and it waved wildly around our cramped little space. My own blood froze at the idea of being shot in the head at close range. I grabbed the muzzle and pointed it towards the men.

Viv appeared to get her nerves under control and nodded at me. Then she held her three fingers up again and nodded — one...two...three!

She screamed and leapt to her feet.

Belatedly, I screamed too, but with much less conviction. I tried a leaping move but it was more of a flailing scramble into an eventual standing position. Somewhere in all the commotion I bonked my knee and it hurt pretty bad.

It didn't matter, though. All anyone saw was a crazy white-haired lady with a gun.

"Back up!" Viv screamed. She stepped out of from behind the counter with every inch of power she had at her command, her chin high and her mouth set.

Both men backed up, their hands inching slowly into the air.

"All right now, let's just see what we have here." She pointed the gun at Five. "You're the robber." Then she turned to Xavier. "And you're covering for him."

"And you're a crazy old bat with a gun!" Five said. "Now we're all caught up."

Viv took an angry step toward him. "I'm a crazy old bat with a very big gun," she said. "And I'm not afraid to use it."

The look of defiance on Five's face quickly gave way to submission. He stepped back again. He finally slide his gaze over to me. "I knew you two were going to be trouble."

"You're smarter than you look, then," I said, with much more derision and confidence than I felt. I had to recover from the indignity of my own clumsiness, though. "The jig is up, Five. You're caught dead to rights. Viv and I will both testify, and so will Xavier. Right, Xavier?"

Xavier was looking less convinced, though. I supposed a previous stint in prison followed by a traumatic head injury would make a person hesitant to get involved.

Viv, luckily, had no such hesitation. She switched the gun to the left hand and dug in her pocket. "Doesn't matter, we'll call the police and they'll be happy to take — "

Five took a quick step toward her.

Viv jumped back and raised the gun in both hands. "Back up! I will shoot you, you fat little toad!"

"You're not going to shoot me, grandma. You're all bluff." He took another step.

"Oh yeah?" She lowered the gun toward his knee, then squinched her eyes tight and squeezed the trigger.

The gun clicked. It did not go boom.

We all looked at Viv. She looked stunned, then questioningly at the gun in her hand. She squeezed again. Nothing.

It dawned on all of us at once that what Viv held was, for whatever reason, not going to resolve this situation.

Viv threw the gun at Five, turned around, and sprinted out the door.

"Run, Salem!" I heard her shout from what already sounded like thirty yards away.

I ran.

We circled the building and ran toward the street. Where were the cops that were supposed to be patrolling the streets? Where was the traffic? Where was anybody?

I ran for all I was worth. Viv was way ahead of me. I thought about getting my phone out, about shouting for help, about doing anything, but my body was in essential-personnel-only mode, and had deemed feet and legs the only essential personnel at that moment.

We ran toward the motel. Viv had already rounded the corner.

"Open up!" she was shouting. "Let us in!"

I came around the corner to see her pounding on G-Ma's door. I drew up beside her, resisting the urge to push her aside so I could knock the door down, looking frantically back and forth between the door and the corner where Five would surely appear at any second.

I pounded on the door beside Viv and shouted. "G-Ma! Call the police! Let us in!"

I saw a shadow move behind the curtain and pounded some more, frantic now that help seemed so close. "G-Ma! Let us in!"

I checked the corner of the building again. Nothing yet, but he couldn't be far.

Then, from behind the door, came G-Ma's angry voice. "You hoodlums aren't coming in to my place and stealing my money. I've got a Colt 45 aimed at your head right now. I'm gonna count to three and them I'm gonna start shooting!"

"G-Ma, no! It's me! It's Salem!"

"One!"

"G-Ma, no! It's — "

"Two!"

As one, Viv and I said very ugly words and turned around to start running again. We hit the Cadillac. The doors were locked.

Viv scrambled for the key fob and jabbed the button.

Nothing. Not a freaking thing.

"I hate this damned car!" Viv growled.

We gave up and headed for Mario's.

We made it to there just as Five rounded the corner of the motel.

He ran up and pounded on G-Ma's door. I used half a second to worry about what he might to do G-Ma, then decided she had seemed like she was prepared to protect herself.

BOOM!

Okay, that answered that question.

Hiding behind the corner of the restaurant, I risked a look back. G-Ma's shot had gone wide, but it had been enough to scare Five off and he was headed straight toward us.

I grabbed Viv's hand and led her into the back entry way of Mario's.

"Mario showed me where he keeps the spare key," I whispered. With shaking hands, I scraped the side of the box and tore the paper away. It took three attempts to get the key into the key hole, but finally it turned. I jerked the door open and we ran inside.

We kept running until we were well away from the door. We huddled in the back beside the storage room, clinging to each other while we both pulled out our phones.

"Are you calling the police?"

"I'm trying!" Viv said. "My hands keep shaking. Your crazy grandmother almost shot us!"

I had hit the wrong icon three times myself. Finally I hit the home button twice and shouted, "Windy! Call the police!"

"Well bless your heart," Windy said. "I'm calling right now."

Viv and I took a collective sigh of relief.

Then we heard a scuffle of feet in the next room.

"Did you close the back door?" I whispered frantically.

"No, did you?"

"You were the last one in!" I fairly shrieked, but it didn't matter anymore because he was there.

"Looky here! My lucky day!" Five approached us with arms wide open, a gun in one hand.

"You can't do anything to us!" Viv shouted the words, but they were too full of trembling to carry much weight. "We already called the police -"

"Honey, I'm going to need your address so I can tell the police where to go," Windy said just then.

We all stared at the phone. Then Five shouted, "Fourteen thirty-seven Avenue G!"

"Okay, sweetie, help is on the way."

Five grinned at me. "There now. Help is on the way. To somewhere on the other side of town."

"Xavier knows who we are. He knows you're chasing us. He will make sure you don't get away with this."

Five scoffed. "That chicken? He's already proved all he cares about is saving his own neck. He hasn't said anything about the robbery, and that makes him an accessory already."

"You forget, my grandma is right next door and she has a gun." I admit this was nothing but pure last-ditch effort, but it was something.

"Yeah, I'm scared of her," he said. "If she gets out of that recliner she'll be a real threat to mankind. Now come over hear and let's talk about what we're going to do to make sure you keep your mouth shut."

I did not want to talk about that. For a second, I considered making idle promises. I opened my mouth and said, "Wait, we don't need to do this. We can — "

Viv screamed like a banshee, ran into the storeroom, and threw the bolt.

Five and I looked at each other.

I turned to the door. "Are you freaking kidding me?" I shouted.

No response.

Five grinned, looking easier now. "Don't worry, she's not going anywhere. This way I'll have time to deal with you one on one. In a more personal way." He stepped closer, leering.

Well now, that was creepy as all heck. I had to believe that, despite what he said, help was on the way from somewhere. My phone was supposed to have GPS — maybe Windy was programmed somehow to access that information and send the cops to the right place. Maybe Xavier really would stop thinking only of his own neck and send the cops after Five. Or maybe G-Ma would get up from the recliner...nope. That one wasn't going to happen. But maybe one of the other possibilities, if I kept him talking...

"Why are you doing this, Five?" I asked. "Just tell me that."

"Because if I don't, you'll tell the police and I'll go to prison." He gave me a look like I must be stupid or something.

"No, not this. The robberies. Why all the robberies? Your family is successful."

"Yeah, see, see there," he jabbed a finger and said with a sneer. "My *family*. My family is successful. Everybody else is doing good, Five, what's the matter with you?" He lowered the gun and leaned in to scream at me. "I don't even have my own name! I'm just the last of the Pigg brothers. We already have four, why did we even need another one? He's just like the rest. Except he's not. He's not handsome, he's not brave, he's not a good salesman, he's not a great athlete. He's just the last one off the assembly line and got stuck with the leftover genes that nobody else wanted!"

He slammed his hand against the wall.

I stammered to find my voice. "That does sound pretty overwhelming," I said. "I was an only child and always wished I had siblings to hang out with. But it sounds like that could have its drawbacks."

"Sister, you don't even know. It didn't have to be that way, of course. Those guys were all just complete jerks who loved torturing me. I was everybody's favorite punching bag since I was born."

I *tssk*ed and tried to arrange my face into something that

would look like compassion.

"You can't even imagine how mean four older brothers can be. Each one trying to outdo the other."

"So this has been to make them pay. But..." But that didn't make sense. All of the brothers had been robbed, but lots of other businesses had, too.

"Oh, they're paying, all right. But even those big shots don't have enough for what I need." He looked happy, then. "All together, they could only kick in about forty percent."

"Needed for what?"

He looked proud. "I finally figured it out. The business I could run that would be more successful than all of theirs. All of theirs *combined*."

"How exciting!" I said. "What is it?"

He clamped his lips shut and said, "Uh-uh. I'm not telling."

"Oh, come on! What business could be more profitable than insurance?"

"Believe me, this one is. This one will have people coming from all over the county. Hell, all over this part of the state. We'll probably end up being one of the biggest employers in town. Well, not bigger than Walmart, but..."

"But one of the biggest," I said, to keep him on his positive track. He was less scary on his positive track.

"Exactly. One of the biggest. Bigger than car sales and insurance and football — I mean, come on. Randy wins all the games, but it's not like he owns a frigging NFL team or anything. He's a high school coach. He works for the boss. In my business, I'll be the boss. I'll be too hot to drop!" He gave a whoop.

A thought occurred to me and I spoke before I had a chance to think.

"Oh my gosh. You're going to buy a Krunchy Kreem franchise!?"

He froze and narrowed his eyes at me.

My blood turned cold. "I mean, that's a fantastic idea! A Krunchy Kreem franchise! Jeez! You'll be printing your own money."

He gave a grudging nod.

"And you're right. You'll need lots of employees. You'll be giving people jobs."

"Good jobs."

"Right. Good jobs. With good benefits."

"I'll be sponsoring Little League teams and charity runs. It'll be my business on the side of Randy's football bus."

"Exactly. I mean, this is the kind of thing that can really boost the whole neighborhood." Another thought struck me. "Oh my gosh. Is that why you're robbing all these local businesses?"

"Do you have any idea how much it costs to open a Krunchy Kreem?"

I searched my mind frantically for a plausible figure. "Too darned much!" I said at last.

"Exactly. Too darned much. But it's a good thing for the community, so in the end it'll be worth it. Believe me, those jackasses wouldn't pitch in when they had a chance, but they'll be glad enough to take the boost in their income when the place gets set up and going strong."

I nodded. "You know, that's actually very smart."

"I know, right? I mean, yeah, people didn't want to invest, but they'll be getting the rewards of my own hard work, so it's only fair. I tried to do it in a way that would give them a portion of the profits. But no. Nobody wanted to risk their nest egg on a loser like me. But whatever. I'm the type of person who knows how to adjust their sails and find another way around the horn, if you know what I mean."

I wasn't completely convinced he knew what he meant, but I nodded anyway. "They had their chance."

"Exactly. They had their chance." He stopped and looked around, frowning like he'd just remembered what he was supposed to be doing. "Anyway..."

"Well, I just really think you're very smart and you're going to make a great business owner," I babbled. "Personally, I can't wait to get a donut and a cup of that awesome coffee — "

"Shut up." He frowned and put his hands on his waist. "I have to think a minute."

He shifted, then paced a few steps before me.

From the corner of my eye, I saw something shift behind him. I darted a glance. Viv was tiptoeing slowly toward us, her arms upraised, holding something white and rectangular.

I quickly looked way, terrified of giving her away.

I took a breath and said in what I hoped was a soothing voice. "Look, I know things look kind of bleak right now, but there's no reason this has to change anything."

"Oh, I'm not planning to change a thing," he assured me. "I'm just trying to figure out what to do with you."

"Me?" I squeaked. "You don't have to do anything with me." I risked a glance toward Viv. She was a little closer now. What was that thing in her hands? And how could that possibly stand up to the big gun in Five's hand? "You don't have to do anything with me. I'm on your side. I think you have a fantastic idea. I'm all for it. Count me in. Heck, I'll even chip in for the franchise fee. And look at me. You know I'll be your best customer."

"Shut up!" He shouted. He rubbed his head. "I would like to trust you, but I know I can't. This has to stay in the family. I tried to trust Xavier and look what happened. He was about to rat us out and we had to lean too hard on him. No, Daddy's right. When it comes to the important stuff, you can only trust family."

"Umm, well," I said. "You're lucky there. My family is small, but to the last person, they're the ones I trust least."

He spared me a sympathetic glance. "That sucks."

"Tell me about it. I mean, I wasn't anybody's punching bag, so I didn't have it as bad as you did. But my family is no bunch of saints, believe me."

"Tell me about it. Your friggin' grandma is a little too trigger happy if you ask me."

"Yeah, umm, sorry about that. She's a little on edge with all these...you know."

He paced and rubbed the back of his head.

Viv ducked behind the big silver cooker.

"Well, it's almost over," he said. "We're down to the last few thousand now. So once we get Mario's share and a couple others, we'll have what we need to proceed."

He turned and looked at me, and I saw that once again, he realized that I was one of the things standing between him and his goal. I darted quick glances around the room, looking for a big knife or a stick or something, anything to knock him back a little. I couldn't believe this odd little guy was that much of a threat, and yet the gun in his hand and the gash across Xavier's head said otherwise.

He caught me throwing glances around and started to follow

my gaze, at the same time Viv had begun to rise from her hiding place. She realized he was turning toward her. Her eyes got big and she dropped like a stone.

I don't know what it was — the pent-up nerves, the way your senses are heightened in times of stress, and for me that happens to include the sense of humor, or something about the way Viv's eyes had bugged out — or maybe it was just my own innate freak-show-ishness. But the whole thing suddenly struck me as hilarious.

I barked out a loud braying laugh. I clamped my hands over my mouth, but it was too late.

Five cocked his head and lowered his brow, confused.

Which made it so much worse. Have you ever tried not to laugh while people looked at you like, "Why are you laughing?" And it's the funniest thing ever?

Probably that's just me.

I couldn't breathe! I doubled over and told myself to get it together, but that has never been particularly effective for me.

I looked up to see Five looking frantically around the place, trying to figure out just what the heck was so funny.

In a panic, I whirled around and pounded on the metal door. "Viv! Viv, let me in! He's going to kill me!"

"Shut up!" Five stepped close and roared at me. "Just shut up and let me think!"

I threw a glance over my shoulder. Beyond Five, Viv edged quietly up, the white rectangle lifted over her head.

I whipped back around, afraid I would give her away.

"Viv! Hurry! Let me in!" I pounded on the door.

"Aaaiiiiieeeee!" With a war cry, Viv screamed and brought the white thing crashing down on Five's head.

Five froze. We all froze. Waiting for what, I didn't know.

Then his brow furrowed, and he slowly turned toward Viv.

Then he collapsed.

"Is he out?" I whispered, frantic.

"I don't know." Viv bent a little but we were both afraid to get very close. He still held the gun. Pulling a face, she nudged at him with what I could see now was the heavy porcelain lid to the toilet tank from the women's bathroom.

Five made a snorting noise and sat up.

Viv screeched and bashed him in the head again. He stayed down this time.

CHAPTER SIXTEEN

Peace on the Other Side

The police showed up almost immediately. Two squad cars, then two more, then Bobby.

He looked from Viv and me to Five, who was by this time sitting up again, albeit in handcuffs.

"Okay, you two. Give me the story."

I told him, the words spilling out so fast that they made no sense. He finally put his hand on my arm and said, "Let's go down to the station so we can get some quiet."

We followed him outside. G-Ma was talking to another cop, gesturing at the hole in her door furiously.

"If you people would do your job and get those Bandits off

the streets — "

Bobby stepped close to her. "I have it on good authority that arrests are imminent, ma'am."

G-Ma frowned, but that appeared to take some of the steam out of her. "Yes, well...not before my building is damaged and my peace of mind shattered. But...good."

"And how *is* your business?"

G-Ma lifted her chin. "Never better."

"Is that right?" Bobby crossed his arms and looked around the empty motel. "All legal, I assume."

"Of course," G-Ma said with a snort. "I'm converting the motel into a shopping center." Her eyes met mine.

I smiled. "What a fantastic idea," I said.

"Yes, well, I hear it's worked very well for some places in Amarillo, so it should work even better here."

At the station, Viv and I explained to Bobby everything we'd learned, but it turned out we really hadn't needed to. Xavier had gone straight from Five Star Auto to the cops and told them everything. They were in the process of getting arrest warrants and rounding up the Pigg men as we sat in Bobby's office.

Viv and I eventually staggered out of Bobby's office. Down the hallway, I could see that Charlotte Clancy-Pigg, Emily Pigg, Desiree Pigg, and Mama Pigg were all in the front reception area, with various expressions from fear, anger, to contempt on their faces.

Charlotte's was definitely of the angry variety. She recognized me, giving me a curt nod as we walked down the hall toward them. As we approached, Mama Pigg was giving them all a lecture on the importance of standing by your family.

One of them must have said something she didn't care for, because Mama Pigg got indignant and said, "Then I feel sorry for you, and for your family. Because family doesn't turn its back on family."

"Oh. My. *God!*" Charlotte stood with her arms folded tightly across her chest, vibrating with anger. "Would you shut up! This isn't about family. It's never been about family. It's about Five! That loser!"

The loud crack of Mama Pigg slapping Charlotte came so quick that I wasn't sure I'd even seen it. But she did it, alright. Charlotte gasped and put her hand to her cheek, and Mama Pigg drew her shoulders back in defiance.

The cop behind the desk slapped handcuffs on her, of course, and she had to sit on the bench all uncomfortable.

I went over to Charlotte. I didn't want to say something obnoxious, like, "Gosh, did your husband and his brothers really rob a bunch of businesses so your brother-in-law could have his own Krunchy Kreem franchise? Seriously?" But I had to say *something*.

"Man," I finally settled on. "This is some crazy stuff, huh?"

She rolled her eyes, but I think it was more at the situation than it was at me.

"Not for this bunch. Well, actually, yes, even for this bunch, this is crazy." She glared at the other two sisters there. One was sitting on the bench with her legs crossed, trying to look like she did this every day of the week, but her foot was doing ninety-to-nothing. The third one was talking quietly to another cop.

"You didn't know?" I asked Charlotte.

"Are you kidding me? Of course not. Apparently they had a whole system worked out. Five would provide the cars from his lot, and then four of the five would take their turns pulling the robberies. The fifth one was in charge of monitoring the police traffic and getting the hideaway spot for the car ready. Then after everything settled down again, they would take that car back to the lot and find another one to use the next time." She shook her head again. "I thought he was working overtime at the station." She looked at the other wives. "I'm not sure how much they knew, but Randy knew better than to tell me something like this."

"Because he knew he wouldn't have your support," Mama Pigg said. "He knows what kind of wife you are. He knows he can't count on you."

"Damn right he can't count on me to support him in felony crime! I'm not one of the standard Pigg robot wives."

The sitting blonde glared at her. The taller one blinked coolly and went back to her hushed conversation.

"And he knows I certainly wouldn't have been in favor of doing it for Five."

"You've always resented Five. You never had a kind word to say about him."

"He's a lazy loser who pulls everyone else down with him and expects Mommy to come clean up after him."

Mama Pigg stared straight ahead, her mouth tight. "You have no idea what it's like, living with a head injury like that."

"I know what it's like being in a family with someone living with a head injury like that. It's disaster, followed by lame excuse, followed by disaster, followed by lame excuse. It's having to make allowances and excuses for someone who isn't mature enough to take care of himself."

"It's not a question of maturity. He was fine until that accident."

"Then why was he in the accident in the first place? If he was so mature, what was he doing robbing that store?"

"That wasn't him, that was Xavier and you know it." Mama Pigg blinked and shifted in her chair, her mouth drawing up tighter and tighter. "And besides. They were both punished for that."

"At least one of them learned his lesson."

Mama Pigg frowned and looked at the floor. "You're so self-centered, you can't even see it. Family is there for each other, always. You fight and make up and hurt each other and forgive each other. The whole reason for family is that there are people there who are guaranteed to have your back. No matter what."

Charlotte snorted. "Whatever you say. I'll stick with my canine kids, thank you very much."

"Well, they are very cute," I assured her. Then Viv and I left.

I woke up Thursday morning feeling like I'd been hit by a truck. I was exhausted and it took all the energy I had to roll over and rub Stump's belly. I felt guilty about leaving her alone with Frank for the past several nights. In true Pigg family fashion, I knew Stump had my back, no matter what, but she was going to destroy something of mine if I didn't spend some cuddle time with her.

I called Flo and asked if it would be okay if I took the day off.

"I'm not sick or anything, I'm just really tired and could use a break. If we're not too busy, I mean."

"No problem, honey," Flo said. "You caught the Knife Point Bandits. You've earned a break. We can cover for you today."

So Stump and I lay on the sofa for half the day, while I took turns wondering if Tony was going to call and cancel our date, and trying not to think about it.

Les showed up with tacos at lunchtime.

"I went by Flo's and they said you had taken the day off. You okay?"

"Sure," I said, unwrapping a taco and edging away from Stump's sniffing snout. "I'm just tired."

"Late night?"

I nodded as I crunched. "We solved the High Point Bandit case," I said, trying to sound modest.

Les laughed. "Is that right?"

"Yeah," I said. "No big deal."

"You know it's all over the news, right?"

"Oh. No, I didn't know that." I really should watch the news. "Crazy, huh? That family was robbing everyone so Five Pigg could open a Krunchy Kreem franchise."

"That's what I heard. Clete Pigg justified it because it would benefit the entire neighborhood. Like a forced investment opportunity." He shook his head. "Craziness."

I remembered something that I'd put at the back of my mind. "Jeez-O-Peet. One day last week, Viv and I were interviewing some of the robbery victims, and there was this guy who owned a dry cleaners and a donut shop. The cleaners was robbed, but not the donut shop. Because they knew it would go out of business, once a Krunchy Kreem moved in."

Les laughed and shook his head again. "I guess they were going by a moral code of some kind, even if it was a messed up one."

I ate my tacos and thought about moral codes;: how we did what we thought was the right thing to do, even if our justifications or reasons didn't make sense to anyone else. I thought about what Mama Pigg had said the night before. The whole point of family was to have people who had your back, no matter what. *You fight and make up and hurt each other and forgive each other.* I supposed that could translate to any group, though. We form groups because we feel a need to be a part of something bigger. Even though, sadly, it often didn't work out the way it was supposed to.

I thought of Mom.

I thought of Tony.

I sighed and looked at Les. "I have a feeling I know what you're going to say, but...I have to ask anyway. How do you forgive a person who isn't sorry?"

"Holy spirit," Les said.

Of course. I knew better than to give voice to the groan of frustration in my head. But I needed to get some real answers.

"The thing is, I know I need to forgive my mom. I can feel it. I know it's the right thing to do. I know it's the good thing to do — it will help me. And I *want* to. You know that. We've talked about this before. But Les, every time I think I've forgiven her, it just pops right back up. Over and over."

He nodded. "Forgiveness is rarely an event, Salem. It's a process. It's an over and over kind of thing."

"That's what Trisha said, too. I have to tell you, I hate that."

He nodded again, unperturbed.

"I mean, seriously. That is *majorly* unfair. If I can work up enough — enough *whatever* — to make that decision the first time, that should be enough. If I can say, okay, you damaged me, and you caused all this crap in my life that wouldn't be there if you had been doing your job, but I'm going to forgive you — I should *get the grand prize*. I should get the peace. It should be mine. For *keeps*."

Les just smiled.

"Seriously, Les. Why would God make it this way? I'm not the one who did anything wrong. I was the innocent bystander who got sucked into the tornado of dysfunction."

"I agree."

"So why should I be the one to have to do all the work?"

"You're not doing the work, Salem. The Holy Spirit is. You're making the choice, over and over."

"It feels like work to me." I sighed. There was no point pouring energy into trying to get Les on my side here. It wasn't going to happen. "When I get to heaven, I'm going to take this one up with God. I told him in my prayer time yesterday that I thought there was a serious design flaw somewhere along the line."

He laughed and kissed the top of my head. "So, I take it the weekend didn't go very well?"

"Not at all. I did what you said. I didn't miss the chance to make peace. I was even prepared to get to the peace on the other side of the conflict. But she wasn't having any of it. She was defensive and blew it all off. I was making a big deal out of nothing. I was blaming her for all my bad choices. She did the best she could in an impossible situation, and I'm an ungrateful snot for not seeing that."

"And you'd hoped for...?"

"I want her to be sorry! Les, she let — " I stopped and swallowed. "She stood by and let me be raped when I was just a kid. And she won't even acknowledge it. I want her to recognize that she had the power and the responsibility to protect me, to take care of me, and she didn't do it. She failed. And I want her to recognize that, yes, I've made some bad decisions myself, but I made them based on the information that she gave me. That I wasn't worth protecting. That I wasn't worth taking care of." I wadded up my taco wrappers and tossed them into the bag.

"You know that everything you just said is true, right? It's not dependent on her recognizing it. She had the responsibility, and she failed. It affected you. Those are facts. Whether she ever says it or not, it's still all true. Her acknowledging it doesn't *make* it true. It just is. You get that, right?"

I opened my mouth to answer, but then closed it again. *Did* I know that? "I guess I need to ponder that," I finally said.

He nodded. "Absolutely. Think on it, Salem. Truth is truth, whether she recognizes it or not."

I looked at him, feeling a faint flutter of something. Hope? Clarity?

"She didn't give you what you needed, and that's a tragedy. But she's not the only source, Salem. Your heavenly father wants to give you everything you missed out on. He wants to restore you to what you had before, what you should have. Every time that resentments pops back up, it's nothing more than a block that needs to be dealt with. It's real, and it's justified, and you can acknowledge it for what it is. You have a right to feel what you feel, and I don't recommending you pretend like that resentment isn't there. But don't camp out on it. Because it's blocking the complete healing and restoration that God has for you. It's not easy, Salem, but it is simple. You just make the choice, over and over."

I nodded, my throat tight and my heart full.

He stood, then put a hand on my shoulder and leaned over so

he could meet my eyes. "And Salem? I know she's not sorry, but does it help to know that I am? I'm sorry that happened to you. So sorry. It shouldn't have. It was wrong. It wasn't your fault. And it was wrong."

Well, what else could I do but burst into tears? I nodded, sobbing, and then he folded me into his arms, and I sobbed some more. I finally pulled away, wiping my face with my hands.

"That actually does help," I said. I sniffed and rubbed at the damp tear marks on his shoulder. "Thank you."

"You deserve to have someone affirm you, Salem, and I'm glad to do it."

"I feel a lot better, Les. Thank you."

"Anytime."

"I'm probably going to need to hear it again," I warned.

He gave a simple nod. "Probably. Like I said, it's an over and over kind of thing, but the load gets lighter and you get stronger every time you pick it up. And I'll be here."

After Les left, Stump and I fell asleep on the sofa. I woke up about an hour later, still preoccupied by my conversation with Les. I decided that I'd spent enough time recuperating, and I wanted to get out and get some air. I patted my leg, and Stump and I headed out to the Monster Carlo.

G-Ma's door was already replaced. A man with a tool belt was carrying the old door with the hole away when I pulled up.

G-Ma stood on the sidewalk talking to a woman, both of them gesturing energetically so that at first I assumed they were arguing. But no. G-Ma put her hand on the other woman's arm, and the woman bobbed her head in a nod, and they both laughed.

"Holy cow, Stump," I said as I put the Monster Carlo in park. "That's Felicia!"

I got out of the car, already preparing the lecture I was going to give G-Ma once I got Felicia out of there.

"There she is. My granddaughter."

Felicia looked at me and her face went from friendly to stony instantly. "We've met."

"It was Salem's idea that I do this," G-Ma said. "Fantastic idea. Very exciting." She turned to me and put her arm around my waist. I almost fainted. G-Ma wasn't the demonstrative type. "And Felicia is going to rent one of the new shops." G-Ma beamed between us.

I sighed. G-Ma had completely missed the point of what I'd been trying to get her to do.

"I'm going to open a nail salon," Felicia said, rolling her eyes at me.

"You do nails?" Then why were you a hooker, I didn't say.

"Not yet, but she's going to stay here and go to school, and we've already talked to the people at the small business development thingamajig, and she probably qualifies!"

"Probably!" Felicia squealed back, apparently unable to contain herself even with me standing right there.

"And Bonnie likes to bake, so she's going to get some ovens put in Mario's restaurant. So she'll bake cakes and cookies and stuff, and rent one of the shops for her business."

"And Georgina and Vanessa make jewelry, so they're going in together to open one."

They kept talking, all excited about their plans. I couldn't help but get caught up in all the excitement. I hadn't seen G-Ma this excited in...well, ever.

Something occurred to me and I blurted it out before I thought. "Wait. Are all these girls..." I looked at Felicia and froze.

"Working girls?" She raised her chin. "Yep. Anything wrong with that?"

I shook my head quickly. "Nope. Not a thing."

"I hated so much thinking that these girls had no safe place to go. And now they do!"

I swallowed and hugged G-Ma again. "I'm really proud of you, G-Ma. This is a very good thing you're doing."

"I know. Oh! And you know Mario's nephew Billy? He's got a landscaping business. He's going to fill in that pool area with a little bridge and pond and stuff."

"A water feature," Felicia said.

"Right! Water feature! And we can probably put some tables out there, with umbrellas. Like a sidewalk cafe kind of thing. I wonder if we can find someone to run a coffee bar."

"Ooh, that would be perfect!" They took off down the sidewalk, jabbering about their plans.

"You should see about renting one out to a Krunchy Kreem franchise," I called after them.

They stopped, both drop-jawed, then squealed and gripped each other's arms.

"Or, you know, just a regular donut shop."

But they moved on down the sidewalk, the jabber escalated in pitch and enthusiasm.

"Just kidding," I called, louder. "No Krunchy Kreems. You want to stay away from the franchises. Concentrate locally. No Krunchy Kreems!"

G-Ma was so happy she'd forgotten to complain about

Stump. I picked her up and we got back into the car. I looked at Stump.

"Well," I said. "Looks like everything is under control here."

Stump and I drove around for a while, and I became a little more used to the mammoth machine. Not entirely comfortable, but better. We drove out to Prairie Dog Town, and I let Stump run around and sniff stuff while I watched the little guys run around. I kind of wanted to stay late enough to watch their sunset ritual of rising on their back legs and lifting their front legs as if in prayer. I checked my phone for the tenth time. Nothing from Tony. No reason to assume he wouldn't be at the trailer at the usual time.

I drove back to Trailertopia to shower and get ready.

Mom's car was in the driveway. I pulled the Monster Carlo to the shallow curb and opened the door. Stump clambered over my lap, digging her heavy little paws into my legs as she pushed off and tumbled onto the grass.

I put my feet on the ground but stayed in the seat for a moment. I wasn't sure I was up for this. After an afternoon with a happy G-Ma and prairie dogs, I wasn't prepared to harsh my mellow just yet. But it was my house, and it's not as if I had anywhere else to go.

I closed my eyes and said a quick prayer. "If you set this up, God," I said, "You're going to need to walk me through it."

I climbed the deck steps with great trepidation, which rankled. This *was* my house. I didn't need to dread coming into my own house. I yanked the door open and stomped inside.

Nothing. No Mom.

Stump and I looked at each other. No Frank, either. That in

itself wasn't too strange. He did, on occasion, have other places to be besides my recliner. But not very often.

Jeez-O-Peet, I thought. I hope she hasn't killed him. Or he killed her. Or they killed each other.

I set my purse on the bar and headed toward the bedroom to get the stuff for my shower. As I passed the "laundry room," Mom said, "Hey."

I screamed and threw myself against the hallway wall.

"Ow!" I rubbed my elbow. "What are you doing? You scared the crud out of me."

"I'm sorry," she said, but she didn't look sorry. She looked like she was trying to hold back a giggle. "I thought you'd see the car out front."

"I did, but..." I guess I should have known she was somewhere on the place, but I hadn't considered finding her in the laundry room. "Hey, what are those?"

"Those" were not my washer and dryer. My washer and dryer were ancient and rusted, with a bungee cord wrapped around the dryer door to keep it closed, and a pair of vice grips in place of a knob on the washer. These things were...well, they were shiny and new. They had all their original parts. When they worked, they probably would not make my trailer sound like it was being dragged down the road at seventy miles per hour.

She shrugged. "I knew your washer broke down and I thought...you know. You could use these."

"Well, yeah, but..."

"It's not a big deal. You needed it, and there have been lots of times when you needed something and I wasn't in a position to give it to you. Now I am. So...here."

I wasn't sure what to say, and I couldn't speak anyway. My

throat had closed up and my eyes and nose were burning.

"That's really thoughtful, Mom," I finally managed. "Seriously. Yes. I can really use these."

"Okay, well come here and let me show you how they work."

She pointed out different settings and gave instructions for all kinds of options that I would never, ever use. We both knew I would throw everything into one load and use one setting to the exclusion of all others, but it seemed to make her feel better to go through the motions.

"Now, don't forget, you have to clean the lint filter every single time."

"Good grief, Mom, I know. I've been doing my own laundry since I was eight years old."

"Yes, well..."

I had inadvertently ventured into awkward territory, so I leaned over and pulled out the lint filter. "Look at this. It feels very sturdy." I looked closer. "Look, there's already some lint in it. It must have been returned. Which is fine, of course, I have no problem with that at all."

"No, I used it. I did your laundry."

For the first time I realized there was *different* laundry hanging on the bar above the machines. Stuff I'd been letting pile up for weeks, even before the machine broke.

"Holy moly," I said, heading around the corner to see the empty basket in the closet. "You did all my laundry? The entire Mount Washmore?"

She laughed. "Every bit. It didn't take long, either. That thing is fast."

She headed back into the kitchen. "I need to get back to Amarillo now. I told Gerry I'd be home before dark and I'm just going to make it now."

"How long have you been here?"

"A couple of hours, I guess. Your...friend...let me in."

"Frank. Good. I'm sorry I wasn't around. You should have called me."

"Oh, well, I wanted to surprise you."

"You did that." I was still kind of wondering if those shiny new machines were really mine.

She hoisted her purse onto her shoulder and picked up her keys. My heart started to pound again.

We stood there in awkward silence for a moment, and I said, "Listen, Mom..."

She held up a hand. "No, Salem. Seriously, it's not that big a deal. Like I said, there were lots of times I wanted to be able to help you and I couldn't. Now I can, and I'm glad to do it. It's not a big deal." She jangled her keys. "I do need to be going, though."

I stepped up and gave her a hug, thinking, *Love never fails.* "Be careful driving home."

"I will." She gave me a flat smile. "So, I'm going for my fitting next Saturday. For my wedding dress. I was supposed to do it in the afternoon, but I could see if we could move it to the evening. Give you time to drive up. If you want to be there."

"That sounds great, actually. I'm happy for you, Mom," I said, surprising us both — her, because I said it, and me, because I meant it.

I showered and toweled off, standing in front of a newly washed rack of clothes. It had been so long since all my clothes were clean, I found some I hadn't seen in months. It was almost like getting new clothes. When I pulled on a pair of jeans that had been snug last time I wore then and found them to be a trifle loose, I decided that miracles, indeed, were possible.

I got ready in time to have some prayer time before Tony would, I still assumed, be by to pick me up.

I lit my candle and bowed my head. Thoughts swirled through my mind, but I found I didn't have words to corral them all.

I did have feelings, though. Senses.

I had peace.

I had hope.

I didn't have a guarantee that things would work out the way I wanted them to, specifically. Not with me and my mother, not with me and Tony, not with anything else in my life, come to think of it.

But I had peace. I knew God would sustain me, and whatever I had to face next, I could. I would be okay.

For someone who constantly pinballed from one neurosis to the next, it was a pretty great feeling.

So when Tony came, he was the one who seemed nervous, and I felt remarkably composed.

"I'm glad you're here," I said, stepping aside to let him in.

The first thing he did was look at the recliner, where Frank was not sitting.

"Are we going out?" he asked.

I smiled. "Yes, if you want to. I asked Frank to keep Stump at his place tonight."

He nodded, looking around the room and taking a deep breath. "Okay, yeah."

"Look," I said. "The other day...I wanted to give you an opportunity to say whatever you needed to say to me. That's all. I didn't mean to give you an ultimatum, or set the time table, or anything, but I did both of those things. And I'm sorry. I thought it would help you, to face me and say it out loud."

"It did," he said.

Instantly my nose started to burn and I felt like there was a horse standing on my chest. "Did it?"

He nodded.

"Well, good. So." I faced him and took a deep breath of my own. "So I know I kind of sprung that on you without any warning, and you might not have had the chance to get your thoughts together and say everything you really wanted to say. Is there anything else you would like to say to me? Anything that occurred to you after I left?"

He nodded again.

I steeled myself. "Okay, good. Go ahead. I know I cried and everything the other day, but it's okay. I really want you to say it. Everything."

"Just that I have regrets, too. I wish I'd done things differently. So many times I wanted to come after you and I just...didn't."

I stopped in my tracks. "You – you thought about that? About coming after me?"

"Yes. All the time. I thought I should find you. Do something. But I didn't."

My throat closed tight. "I wanted to find you and throw you over my shoulder and carry you back home. But I knew you would just run away again."

"I wish you had."

"And I wish, if I had, you would have stayed."

Hot tears were running down my cheeks now, and I dashed them away.

"I might have. I told myself for a long time that if you would just show up, prove to me that you really loved me and wanted me to be your wife, I would stay with you." I remembered too well what a miserable, unhappy wreck I was, though. Addicted to alcohol, addicted to drama, furious with the world and willing to take it out on whoever was closest. Tony was closest and would have borne the brunt of that fury. "I probably wouldn't have, though."

"I know. We were kids, Salem. We acted liked kids."

"I know. But I'm sorry I hurt you, and I'm sorry I lost the baby, and I'm sorry it took me so long to grow up."

"Salem." He drew me to him and held me. He felt so good – warm and solid, and I decided in that instant that I was tired of second-guessing him, waiting for him to lead.

"I want to be married to you," I said, shocking myself as well as him. I stepped back and looked up at him. "I feel like you're the one who's constantly gone out on a limb for us, always taking the chances. So I'm putting myself out there this time. I want to be married to you. Like a real marriage. You might not want that, and that's okay. I mean..." What did I mean? "You still get to make the choice and you get to keep your time line, and...I wanted to tell you how I feel. I love you. I know you might still have some thinking to do and need time, but just so you know – I'm in. I don't know if you're up to another try with me. I don't know if you believe that I've really changed or you want more time for me to – I don't know – prove it? And if you do, that's fine. I can wait. I just think...if you're willing to give me another chance, a real chance, and put up with all my weirdness and annoying stuff, then I'm certainly willing to put up with yours."

Tony remained frozen.

"Am I terrifying you right now?"

"No, no, it's just – *my* weirdness?""

"Oh, you're not weird. It's just...everyone has quirks. If we were to give it a real go, you know, you'll have to put up with Stump. We're a package deal, of course. And Viv, too, probably. And my constant neurotic freak-outs about my weight. And I'll be happy to put up with your stuff. I mean, so you're not the kind of guy to pin me up against the wall and kiss me breathless anymore. Big deal. I can handle that. It's worth it, right? We're not in our teens now. We don't need that. We could have something deeper, you know. A connection."

He nodded silently, looking at his hands.

Silence roared into the room. I had to clear my throat just to make sure I hadn't suffered a case of spontaneous deafness.

"I am terrifying you right now. I knew it." I stood and paced. "Look, it's okay. Don't feel like what I just said was any kind of – I mean, I just wanted you to know. I've been wondering how you felt, and I thought maybe you were wondering how I felt, so I thought I'd just put it out there." I spread my arms out wide. "Just...lay it all out. That certainly doesn't mean you're under any, you know, obligation – "

"Salem," he said again.

"Mmm-hmmm?" I said brightly, hoping to make it clear that he could stomp all over my heart just then and it was really no big deal.

He opened his mouth but then closed it again.

"You don't know what to say?" I offered.

"I don't know what to say."

"Should I offer you a multiple choice? Like, (a) I want to be married to you, too, (b) I never thought we'd be at this point and now I'm considering faking my own death to get out of it, or (c) — "

"I don't know what to say. And when I don't know what to say, I just don't say anything."

"Well, that's...very sensible. I ought to try that some time."

"Could we just...could we go to dinner? And maybe a movie?"

I nodded quickly. "Sure, of course." I stood and waved a hand. "You're hungry, obviously. And once again, I'm springing huge decisions on you at a moment when you're not prepared. Let's get some dinner."

He remained frozen.

"Not that I'm actually asking you to make a decision," I clarified. "I'm just telling you how I feel. So you can make a — a what do they call it? I fully informed decision. When the time comes. For you to make a decision. Not that you need to make one. Now. Or ever."

"Salem."

"I'm shutting up now."

He stood and walked to the door of the trailer.

Okay. So, we were going to go to dinner, and a movie. And it was okay, because I wasn't dictating the time line. I was giving him space. I was giving him time. I was stating my truth and letting God sustain me through whatever happened next.

Tony stopped, one hand on the doorknob. He looked at me, his face solemn.

I knew in that moment he was going to tell me no. No, he didn't want to be married to me. No, he couldn't forgive me. No, grace was not big enough to cover this.

I lifted my chin, unsure if I really would be able take it like an adult but determined to give it my best effort.

He cupped my chin, his eyes darting between mine, to my lips, back up. Then he stepped in, backed me against the wall. And he kissed me breathless.

Want more of Salem and the gang? Sign up for my newsletter and get free short stories, excerpts from upcoming books, and publishing news. Go to www.KimHuntHarris.com.

Other Titles in the Trailer Park Princess Series
The Middle Finger of Fate (Book One)
Unsightly Bulges (Book Two)
Caught in the Crotchfire (Book Three)
'Tis the Friggin' Season (Short Story)
The Power of Bacon (Short Story)
Mud, Sweat, and Tears (Short Story)

Coming in 2017
Knickers in a Twist

ABOUT THE AUTHOR

*This is me. I bought this outfit
and got my roots done for this picture. You can't tell, but I also got
a pedicure. It was a big day for me, let me tell you. My hands are
curled up because I didn't want to spring for the mani.*

The award-winning author of the Trailer Park Princess comic mystery series. Kim Hunt Harris knew she wanted to be a writer before she even knew how to write. When her parents read bedtime stories to her, she knew she wanted to be a part of the story world. She started out writing children's stories, and her stories grew as she did. She discovered a gift for humor and a love for making people laugh with her tales, and the Trailer Park Princess series was born.

Kim loves to not only make her readers laugh and entertain them with a good mystery, but also to examine the issues the everyday people face...well, every day. Issues like faith and forgiveness, perseverance, and tolerance. Set in Lubbock, Texas, the fun books feature a cast of quirky characters, outrageous situations, a drama queen of a dog, and from time to time, a tear or two.

Kim lives with her husband of more than thirty years and two kids in West Texas.

Made in the USA
Columbia, SC
11 July 2017